'There's true passion in every written word . . . With a storyline that promises more, *Gleam* is definitely not one to discard'

SCIFINOW

'Hugely entertaining'

SFX

'Partly inspired by Mervyn Peake's *Gormenghast* . . . Fletcher manages to do justice to this fantasy legend'

AVID FANTASY REVIEWS

'Alan's sidekicks are beautifully grotesque and Fletcher isn't too precious about keeping all of them alive, which I find quite refreshing in this sort of book'

THE HORROR HOUTHOUSE

'*Gleam* is a strong start to a very interesting world. Anyone looking for a science fiction tale of grim darkness should definitely pick this one up'

STARBURST

'A very accomplished novel. It'll be a long wait for the sequel!'

UPCOMING4.ME

'Beyond fascinating . . . I quickly fell in love with this book'

BIBLIOSANCTUM

'Absolutely one of my favourite books of the year'

LIZ LOVES B

'I, for one, look forward

TOR.C

Also by
Tom Fletcher

The Leaping
The Thing on the Shore
The Ravenglass Eye

GLEAM

TOM FLETCHER

Jo Fletcher
BOOKS

First published in Great Britain in 2014 by Jo Fletcher Books
This edition published in 2015 by

Jo Fletcher Books
an imprint of Quercus
55 Baker Street
7th Floor, South Block
London
W1U 8EW

A CIP catalogue record for this book is available
from the British Library

ISBN 978 1 84866 255 1 (PB)
ISBN 978 1 84866 254 4 (EBOOK)

10 9 8 7 6 5 4 3 2 1

Typeset by Jouve (UK), Milton Keynes

Printed and bound in Great Britain by
Clays Ltd, St Ives plc

To and for
Beth and Jake

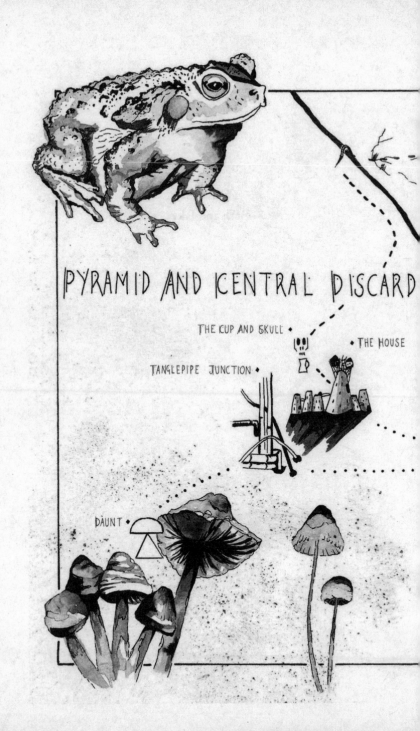

PYRAMID AND CENTRAL DISCARD

THE CUP AND SKULL •

• THE HOUSE

TANGLEPIPE JUNCTION •

DAUNT •

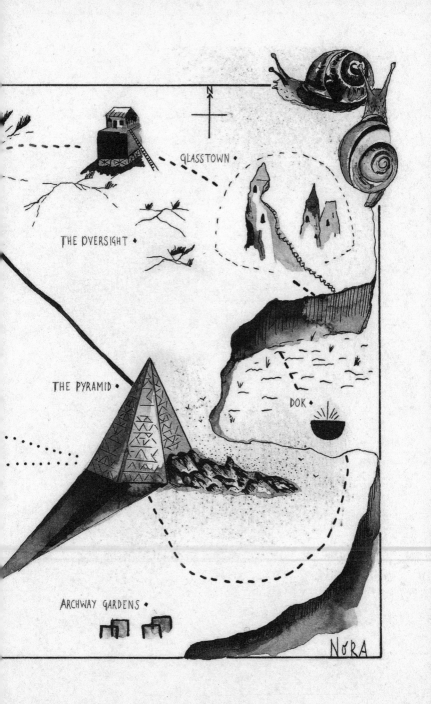

Prologue

Nobody in living memory ever saw it from outside – that was part of its strangeness – but if you were to see it from outside, you'd see what looked like a great curved circular wall, like a great skull emerging from the verdant, swampy landscape: a skull with its crown knocked in. On closer inspection the wall would reveal itself not to be a wall but instead a mass of architecture, a confusion of stone buildings all pressed up against each other, so squashed and interconnected as to be all one structure. Close up they are a riot of different colours, but there are so many of them that from a distance their colours run to a muddy grey. They all prop each other up like drunks. They have arms around each other: gantries and bridges. Closer still, and you can see that some appear to have given birth to others: what at first looked like a chimney is in fact a fat tower; what looked like an ornate balcony is some kind of mansion house that's erupted like a boil. The structures branch and intertwine. Now you can see that they are thick with old rusted pipes and scattered irregularly with odd-shaped windows, some with glass and some without. As intimated, there is something organic about the architecture, but at this near distance now you can see that there is plenty of real, actual flora involved too, spreading across the various surfaces. Moss and lichens on a gigantic scale. Forests of trees growing on the vertical plane, all bending upwards. Flocks of white birds twist and wheel in the air around it. The skull, that is: the edifice. They nest in its sheer sides. They call to each other with cold voices.

Inside that exterior ring, the buildings are not so tall, which is why the place looks like a bashed-in skull, or like it's got a wall. But they are just as densely packed, and just as disparate and strange. The scale is beginning to disorientate you. You feel as if you have a handle on it, but then details betray just how wrong you are. That's not a shrub: it's a vast and ancient oak tree. That's not an old bowl left out after some rooftop picnic, but some kind of swimming pool or water tank. And swimming in it . . . that's not a beetle. What is it? You're not sure. What looks like a row of terraces is actually a towering red-brick mill of some sort, and even that is nothing to the building on top of which it has been constructed. It is a bright, clear day, and the sunlight is bringing out the blue of the slates, and setting the red bricks on fire. There is an abundance of both.

Shacks and shanties of wood and metal encrust

stretches of the roofscape like colonies of small molluscs. Herds of sheep and goats graze on the side of a tower that's leaning crazily. These living things seem impossibly small. Despite the bright colours and the signs of life, there is something nightmarish about this, about the size of it. A fast-flowing river springs from the gigantic, jagged mouth of a marble pipe, and then, later, somewhere else, plunges as a waterfall over the edge of the roof of a huge and ruined castle. A human and a donkey both stand on that rooftop, further back, and drink from the river. There are lakes with a rainbow sheen that no living creatures touch. There are complex metal things that look like they used to move once upon a time, but are now rusted fast. Machines. Old, broken machines, some as big as the buildings. Like the buildings, their functions are unclear.

Your eye is drawn now, as all eyes here are, to the centre. From the centre rises the one structure that is not tarnished with extraneous growth, or overwhelmed with moss, or just rounded and worn by erosion. It's a vast, black, six-sided pyramid, separated from the rest of the chaos by a ring of ashen wasteland. The wasteland is the top of a hill, which slopes down into a darkness from which all the rest of the chaos emerges. This is the only visible ground in the whole place, and it's grey and dusty and somehow creepy. The pyramid itself, though, looks clean and new, and its edges are all sharp. Its stone has depth and shine. Every block of it has been carved into a relief of intricate symbols. The slopes of the pyramid are full of openings – windows, balconies, galleries – that are all difficult to see, because the interiors of these surface details are also black. Around the top of the pyramid – a thin and vicious point – hangs an elaborate metal framework, which supports a whole battery of objects made out of glass and bronze. Telescopes and mirrors, magnifying lenses and orreries, measuring devices. Like an explosion of glass and bronze just frozen in that instant, and all glinting in the bright sunlight. The sun is going down now and the glints are reddish. It is from this range of artefacts, possibly, that the name of this whole hulking edifice derives its name: Gleam. That's what most of its inhabitants think, and as we don't know any better we will proceed under the same assumption. The truth is that nobody living knows for sure. Nobody living knows much of anything about Gleam; they're all kept busy just trying to get by.

For now.

PART ONE

I

Getting It Wrong

The Pyramid was full of light. The huge and complex array of crystals, mirrors and lenses at the structure's tip harvested the shine from the sun, moons, stars and planets, and focused it inwards, where it was reflected and bounced from one storey to another, refracted though great glass panes and stored up in frosted globes that would release it slowly throughout the night.

Alan lay on his back in the pool, gazing up at the enormous white globe that hung above him. The water was treated with minerals that made it dense, enabling Pyramid workers to float in it without having to swim or kick. As a consequence – Alan had always assumed unintended, but perhaps not – the water was milky-blue and opaque.

The globe was beginning to glow a soft yellow colour, which meant that outside the sun was setting, which meant that it was nearly time.

Alan rolled over in the water, swam towards the side of

the pool, and, once he was in shallower waters, stood up. The pool-room occupied one entire high-level Pyramid storey. Like the Pyramid, it was hexagonal, as was the pool itself. Alan was one of perhaps two hundred bathers, yet the pool was not crowded. Nobody spoke. Speaking in here was forbidden. The only sound was that of the milky-blue water cascading into the pool from channels carved into the marble floor at each of the six corners. Each of the six walls had a long window that ran the length of it. The sunset was livid over Gleam: a liquid sky full of thin pink and orange streaks, the ancient ruins that surrounded the Pyramid stark and black against it. A Third-Tier Assistant Alchemical Co-ordinator stood by one of the windows, waiting for him. He didn't know her, but she was recognisable by the combination of a perfectly shaved head, red drawstrings on the hood of her thick brown cloak and the eyebrow notches.

Bloodletting appointments were assigned to Pyramid workers according to the day, hour and minute of their birth, but as Alan hadn't been born in the Pyramid, he had been allocated the nightfall slot, along with all those other bastards and freaks who'd come in from outside – from those black, stark ruins known collectively as the Discard.

Alan walked naked from the pool. The Co-ordinator handed him a towel. He felt eyes on him as he dressed; his heritage as a Discard baby was obvious in the red-brown tone of his skin, and Pyramid natives were not ashamed to stare. They were all painfully pale; so pale as to be luminescent. Almost translucent. Because he was from the Discard, they called him Wild. Wild Alan.

Stupid fucking Pyramidders. Except he was one himself now. There could be no us-and-them, not any more. That was what Marion kept telling him. 'For Billy's sake,' she'd said, now that they had a son, 'drop the aggro. Let the chip heal from your shoulder.'

He'd agreed.

The Co-ordinator turned back to the window as Alan stepped into his trousers, shrugged on his shift, and fastened his own cloak around his waist. The cloaks were far too thick, given the perpetual heat, but like everything else their purpose was symbolic, their cuts and colours and details laden with so many various meanings that Alan hadn't bothered to try to decode his own, let alone anybody else's. Once he was dressed, she led him to the Bleeding Atriums.

The stairwells and corridors of the Pyramid were wide and clean and airy. They passed terraces with intricate topiary and off-shift Pyramidders sipping cool drinks from long glasses, courtyards full of glass statues and tinkling fountains, vast spaces occupied by polished brass machine sculptures that spun noiselessly in mid-air. All of the walls were white marble, veined pale blue, whereas the exterior of the Pyramid was black. Alan remembered it from his childhood: a shining black monolith, looming over all.

The Bleeding Atriums were small hexagonal chambers with six black leather chairs, equally spaced, each facing one of the six walls. Orange light came in through small, high windows. The chairs were elaborate constructions – large brass cogs and wheels allowed them to recline, and from their metal armrests extended tubes and wires that intertwined and spun off into spidery machines that sat over each chair like the spun-sugar domes that desserts came served with in the Refectory.

The Co-ordinator gestured to one of the chairs. Alan sat down, despite the bile rising in him. He rolled up his sleeves. The Co-ordinator moved to stand behind the chair and turned the machine on. It came to life with a hum and a buzz. Alan could feel it vibrating around him. The chair slowly tipped him back. Alan watched the Co-ordinator as she screwed two new needles into the apparatus. Once she was done, she looked at him. He leaned back and closed his eyes.

He felt the needles slide beneath the skin on the under-sides of his forearms. A moment later came the pain. He gritted his teeth. He felt as if two small ugly creatures were crouched at either side, sucking him dry via proboscises. He could almost hear them slurping and gulping. The pain increased as the letting went on; the needles were thick, their appetites large.

But this was just the price to pay, not merely for their safety and security, but for Billy's. For their homes within the Pyramid. Two pints a week: not a lot to give. Not really.

Enough to leave you weak, though. Enough to leave you tired. Enough to leave even Alan pale and eye-bagged and capable of nothing but sleep.

He could do it. He could give it, for Marion and for Billy. To keep the peace. Everybody else did it; why shouldn't he?

He gritted his teeth and screwed up his eyes. He wanted to squirm in the seat, but couldn't risk dislodging the needles and the inevitable re-insertion.

As the volume taken increased, the buzzing of the machine grew louder, and the chair began to vibrate. Alan's skull felt as if it were coming apart. This was when the headache began. This was when the headache always began, and it would last until almost the following week's letting.

Then, abruptly, the vibrating stopped and the sound ceased completely. Alan gingerly opened his eyes, wincing as they let the little light in. The Co-ordinator was smiling as she withdrew the needles, unscrewed them, and posted them into a small hole in the marble wall. 'There we go,' she said. 'That wasn't too bad, was it?'

Alan stared at her, squeezing his head between his palms. 'You get let too, right?' he asked.

'Of course.'

'Then you know exactly how bad it is.'

The Co-ordinator's smile vanished. 'Blaspheme again and—'

'All right, all right.' Alan stood up, still massaging his temples. 'So I suppose you're as unlikely as the rest to tell me what the blood's used for?'

'What do you mean?'

'By Green's teeth.' Alan laughed to himself. 'Hey. It's like trying to get blood from – from a—'

'Stop it.' The Assistant Alchemical Co-ordinator's tone was sharp. 'It's a ritual.'

'Aye, right.' Everything in Alan's field of vision was white-edged and pulsing. He closed his eyes again and sat back down.

'I'm going to need you to leave right now,' the Co-ordinator said, 'or I'll summon the Arbitrators.'

'Okay,' Alan said, rising slowly to his feet once more. 'Okay. I'm going, see? I'm going.'

He walked unsteadily from the room.

The bloodletting was the hardest aspect of Pyramid life to swallow. And how long had he been a Pyramidder now? Since he was eight. Twelve years . . . Though *fuck*, no. He'd never been a Pyramidder and he never would be. He still dreamed about Modest Mills; being able to run around outside. And not in some courtyard or *garden*, but the *real* outside – the Discard. The ruins and the rivers and the great, knotted trees. He missed the birds. Sometimes you could see birds from Pyramid windows, but there were special squadrons of Arbitrators assigned the sole task of shooting them down. And he remembered people making things and selling things and saying what they wanted and sleeping where they wanted and being in control of their own lives and not having to endure that awful, Green-damned *bloodletting*. He remembered bright colours and market stalls. He remembered animals. Not the horrible things they had in glass boxes in the Pyramid classrooms, but sheep, cats, rats.

He remembered the fire and the screaming and the blood on his parents' faces as . . .

Of course, Marion's life had been different. She didn't know what it was really like outside. She'd been raised on fear and lies. And she hadn't witnessed what he'd witnessed: the Arbitrators marching in, their knives flashing in the firelight, the . . .

It wasn't that he simply didn't want to endure the bloodletting, or the Daily Stationing. It wasn't that he was so selfish he couldn't tolerate it for her sake, for Billy's sake. It wasn't selfishness. It wasn't pigheadedness. It was just that he wanted to know what it was all *for*. And, given his experience, he couldn't imagine that it was all for anything good. Marion put that down to paranoia.

Their quarters were on the South-East Straits. He realised that he was on their corridor, not having taken in any of his surroundings, when he heard Billy screaming. This wasn't the usual hungry-or-tired tantrum-style crying, though; it was louder, more desperate. It plucked at something inside Alan's throat and made him cold. He started to run.

The entrances to Fifth-Tier Workers' apartments were smooth archways with polished bronze doors that were weighted to slide inside the walls once unlocked. The door to their apartment was locked, but scratched and dented. Alan quickly unlocked it; it rolled sideways.

Marion stood in the middle of the room, holding Billy to her. He was rigid and screaming, his little head bright red beneath his blond curls. Marion was red-eyed and wet-faced, tears still coming. Her blonde hair was plastered across her face. Blood ran from her nose and a burst lip, shockingly bright against her alabaster skin. All of their furniture had been overturned, their clothes ripped, Billy's toys smashed. Food was splattered across the marble walls and smeared over the Tracker Tablet, on which Alan and Marion had to keep track of all of their Utmost Vitals – hours Stationed, productivity, hours slept, food consumed, days chaste, dates of attempts at conception, and more, and yet more – the list was endless. Even Billy had Utmost Vitals, though Pyramidders under sixteen had a slightly shorter list than the adults. Alan rushed in and went to put his arms around Marion and Billy.

Marion pushed him away. 'What did you *do*?' she yelled. 'What the fuck did you *do*? What the *fuck* is wrong with you?'

Alan shook his head. 'What? Marion, what's happened

here? I didn't do anything. What . . . Tell me what happened.' He stepped forward again.

Marion backhanded him across the face, hard. 'Of *course* you did something! You're always doing something!' Her voice was raw. 'The fucking Arbitrators, Alan! They did this! They came here, they did this, they' – she pointed to her face – 'they did this. They made Billy watch. And they did it because of you. Because of something you'd done.' She sat down on the floor and laid Billy down across her lap. Alan wanted to lift him up, enfold him. He kicked and shrieked. The noise was deafening. Marion pointed at him, at Alan. 'You told me – you *told* me – that you'd stopped.'

Alan's face burned. He didn't say anything.

'You *told* me.' She crumpled as fresh sobs rose up.

'Marion, I'm sorry. I have stopped. I've stopped now. But—'

She glanced up.

Seeing the look in her eyes, Alan's words momentarily failed him. 'Marion, it's important,' he said. He'd believed the words true until he spoke them.

'What's important?' Her words were lizard bones.

'That people know.' Why did he continue trying to justify himself? His reasoning was hollow in the face of the hurt wrought on Marion.

'So you have done something.'

'Should I just have let this go?' Alan pointed to his

nose, all bent out of shape. 'The imprisonment?' He didn't want to argue with her, but she had to know that he'd had reasons for doing what he'd done, and that he hadn't anticipated this.

'You provoke them! Alan, you fucking idiot, you've got a son now! Stop kicking the dog!'

'My mum and dad?' Alan realised that he too was shouting, and his own cheeks were wet. 'My mum and dad? All those people? I provoked that, did I?'

'Of course you didn't. But you told me you'd stopped. You *promised*.'

Alan stepped over shards of glass and bent down to pick Billy up. 'Hey, son,' he said quietly. 'Hey.' But Billy kept on crying, and tried to wriggle free. 'Talk to me,' Alan said. 'You're a big boy now. You can use words.' But Billy didn't.

'He's upset,' Marion said, taking the boy back.

'I can see that.'

'Alan, I'm sorry. You have to leave. You've put Billy and me at risk, and you living here is a danger to us both.'

Alan stared. But as sick as the notion made him, he knew she was right. 'No,' he said. 'I mean, I understand. I don't want to, though. I love you. I love him. I love you both. I've stopped, I've stopped. I won't do it any more.'

'You've promised that before,' Marion said. 'Can't you see? Billy comes first, Alan! Not you! Not your principles, not what you saw, not your grievances! Billy! Our son!'

'It's for him I do it all.'

'So you *do*. You're still at it.'

'All I've done is meet with Eyes a couple of times on the terraces and—'

'*Stop*.' Marion rose up. 'Alan, you lied to me. I know you have your reasons. I understand your reasons, too. But look at me. Look at us. Look what they've done to us, because of you.'

Alan took in the bruises on Marion's face, Billy's hysteria, the destruction that had been visited upon their home: the enormity of his mistakes made explicit for him. True guilt blossomed within him and it was a physical sickness. His head was pounding. He felt as if his flesh were fizzing. 'Yes,' he said, quietly. 'To go is the last thing I want, but I know I must.'

'It will be past curfew now, so you'll have to head straight for the Discard. You can pack a bag.'

'The Discard.'

'Yes.'

'Marion . . .' Alan's heart had wrenched itself free inside him and was sinking. He hurt all over. 'I love you. I love Billy. I can't lose you. I can't.'

'We love you too. But you staying here will hurt us. Even if you never put a foot wrong again, you are marked. We will be held in suspicion.'

Alan didn't say anything.

'For Billy,' Marion said.

Alan knelt down and took his son in his arms again.

His little body was hot. The boy's crying had subsided, and he looked up at his father with big blue eyes. His flushed cheeks were covered with snot. His small mouth was closed and serious. 'You're thinking hard, hey?' Alan said. He didn't know why he said that. He brought Billy up to his chest and squeezed him. Billy put his arms around Alan's neck and his chin on Alan's shoulder.

'Let me put him to bed,' Alan said.

Marion nodded. 'Okay.'

But Billy wouldn't settle. He kept standing up in his cot. He thought everything was okay again, and wanted to play. 'Good morn-ning!' he kept saying, with a big grin. Alan sat on top of his Billy's wooden toy-box and tried to conquer the trembling of his lips in order to smile back. When he was able, he'd whisper, 'Lie down, son,' or 'Close your eyes.' And he'd pick the child up and lay him back down. Billy would pretend to sleep for a moment – loud, whistling snores – and then 'wake up' once more, standing up with another grin and 'Good morn-ning!'

Marion pushed aside the drapes that hung from the archway into Billy's room, and came in holding a soft leather satchel. 'Here,' she said.

'Where Daddy going?' Billy asked.

'Daddy's got to go out,' Marion replied.

'Daddy going to tation,' Billy said, which was what he said on those mornings when Alan had the Daily Stationing day shift.

'Not this time,' Alan said. He stroked Billy's hair.

Billy looked up at Alan and Marion for a little while. 'I'm tired now,' he said. 'I want a bobble, plee.'

'I'll get you a bottle,' Marion said, leaving. 'Say night-night to Daddy.'

'Night-night, Daddy.'

'Night, Billy,' Alan said. He picked up his bag, took hold of Billy's hand, smiled briefly, then pushed through the drapes.

Marion was standing by the shining bronze door. Alan walked over and she opened her arms to him. 'Don't let him forget that I love him,' Alan said. 'And don't forget that I love you, too.'

'I won't,' Marion said. She kissed him deeply. 'I love you, Alan. Take care of yourself.'

'I will see you again,' Alan said. 'I'll find a way back.'

Marion gazed into his eyes. 'But not if it hurts him. Not if it hurts him. Not at that cost.'

'Not at that cost,' Alan repeated.

'Now go.'

Alan went to the door, then stopped. He moved over to the corner of the room and picked up his guitar: something Eyes had chanced upon out there in the Discard, and brought to Alan years ago, when he was still a child. A ten-bug piece of shit, but even so, these things were difficult to come by. Its name was Snapper. The meetings with Eyes had grown infrequent over the years; Eyes was less and less able, and the Arbitrators were less and less willing to turn their backs on such behaviour. So was Marion.

He put the guitar on his back and left, head down, not entirely friendless.

Curfew meant that if anybody saw him out, he'd be frog-marched to one of the Chutes and dumped. *Discarded*. But that didn't matter; he had nowhere else to go anyway. In fact it would be best if the Arbitrators knew that he'd gone. He was stumbling, numb. The sense Marion had made was still percolating through him, frequently igniting into white-hot self-loathing. *Look what I did*.

He considered trying to ascend to the Upper Executive Offices and – what? Kill somebody? He'd fantasised about such a thing time and time again, but the truth was that he'd never even heard the names of any of the Executains, let alone worked out who was responsible for what. Maybe he could just kill them all.

But murder wasn't in him, unfortunately.

And it would probably mean they'd slit his throat before Discarding him, and then he'd definitely never see Marion or Billy again.

He thought about going to Tromo, the Arb who'd saved him back in Modest Mills, but Tromo didn't do anything unless there was something in it for him, and right now Alan didn't have anything to offer. As it had many times before, his mind skittered around the deal made with Tromo on his behalf back when Modest Mills was sacked, and its potential consequences. Besides, if Alan remembered correctly, Tromo was up patrolling the Astronomy and Engineering Compliance Executive Offices, and so not at all easy to reach.

He came to a window. The slope of the Pyramid meant that he could look straight up. By now the sun was down, but Satis was full, its ochre disc pocked and shadowed. Corval was half shadowed, but what could be seen of the smaller orb was more colourful – blue and green bands were still catching the sun's light. And then there were the stars: scattered all over, but to the south was a bright, roundish cloud of them – stars gathered so thickly they looked as if they were swarming. Pyramidders referred to the star cloud as the Battle, but Alan remembered his mother calling it Green's Eye, and it still looked like an eye to him. Various stars moved slowly around, blinking. His mother always told him they were dragons, great winged lizards that lived in space and spoke with light and flame, not words. He'd told Billy the same thing.

Billy. He had to go. If he was going to help Billy in any way, he had to escape straight away. He tore his gaze from the sky and looked out over the Discard, the expanse of mountainous ruins, the weird, twisted towers, the vast metal archways, monolithic and rusted. Huge square buildings buried beneath foliage and even forests. It was all indistinct in the dark, but here and there turrets and broken domes were silhouetted against the sky, and in places fires burned. When Alan stood alone on a balcony or a terrace, he could hear noises: the wind through leaves, metal grinding against metal. Very occasionally he'd heard what sounded like human voices raised in anger or fear. And sometimes sounds that could have been human, but could equally have been animal: strange barks and whistles. Once there'd been a long, cold howl.

He was *from* the Discard, almost. He shouldn't be afraid of it. Though, really, Modest Mills had been something of a halfway house; even there he'd been warned not to venture off into the wilds. To watch for snakes, crocodiles, bandits and cannibals.

His head was splitting, and sickness had settled in his gut. His feet dragged. The bag felt very heavy. He came to the nearest Chute. An innocuous branch from the main corridor led him to a round chamber lit by one of the white globes. The walls were intricately decorated with rows of overlapping symbols in inlaid brass and bronze: triangles, eyes, discs, stick figures, fish, hands. The symbols repeated in various patterns, spiralling up around the chamber until they met with the ornate globe casing.

In the centre of the floor was a round hole. Alan looked down it. It was like one of the helter-skelter-style slides at the children's pool he'd taken Billy to the previous weekend. Damn it. Sorry, Billy. The guilt he felt was poison.

He sat on the lip of the Chute and then waited for a patrol to happen across him.

2

Discard Nights

Twelve years after ingesting him, the Pyramid spat Alan
back out, and Alan found that twelve years was long
enough to have softened him. The Discard was not kind
to newcomers, and nor did it recognise him as one of its
own. And Alan did not recognise the Discard, either; he
remembered only a tiny part of it – Modest Mills – which
was gone. It had been a small town, the town of his birth,
where he'd had parents and a home. But it had been
reduced to the ash and dust that whispered softly around
the base of the Pyramid and settled into deep drifts
against its side. After crawling out of the Discard Chute
and digging his way through these drifts, Alan was dizzy
and parched. He lay amongst the ruins for a while, looking up at the sky, and the Pyramid that occupied so much
of it.

Eventually he stumbled off in the direction that he'd
seen Eyes go after their few clandestine meet-ups. He still
felt weak after the Bleeding, and grew hungry as well as

thirsty. He was torn between wanting to meet somebody in order to ask for help, and hoping against hope that he encountered nobody. He followed a wide path that descended between abandoned buildings. He started to worry that he was too exposed, but none of the alleyway mouths or the holes in the sides of the buildings looked particularly inviting. All around were night-sounds: small movements, doors banging in the slight breeze, architecture settling. The occasional call of a nocturnal bird. There were no birds in the Pyramid, but Alan had heard their voices from the terraces on occasion. Now they sounded far too close.

That night he passed out in a great hall that housed a vast machine comprised mostly of copper tubing which had long since turned green. He was awakened by a pair of emaciated hands pawing at his legs and kicked out. His foot connected with a face and something squealed.

'I'm sorry,' said his new friend. 'I'm sorry. I'm sorry. I'm sorry. I thought you was dead. Just a little hungry is all. Just a little hungry. But seeing as you're not dead I won't bother you no more. A bit of meat's such a rare thing! The rats and lizards are too fast for a skinny wretch such as myself. So sorry.'

By the light of the bright moons Alan could see the man scuffling backwards, away from him. He was almost skeletal. His bald head was grey and spotty. Alan's skin crawled. Why would he be carrying meat? Then he woke up properly and jumped to his feet. He couldn't see a weapon on the man's person, but that didn't mean he didn't have one, or couldn't find one. But then why hadn't he just tried to bludgeon Alan while he slept?

Perhaps he *was* just hungry; perhaps he genuinely didn't want to kill anybody.

But Alan did not hang around to find out. He ran beneath the strange machine's appendages and out of that ruined building, and he kept running.

The unpleasant night became an unpleasant day, and the unpleasant days and nights became hard, painful weeks. The Discard was teeming with animal and insect life, but all the creatures Alan encountered were faster than him and he had no aptitude for tracking, trapping or hunting. There was an abundance of greenery, but he did not know which plants were edible and which were poisonous. He frequently discovered colonies of mushrooms, but he was wary of consuming them for fear of making himself ill, however badly his hunger hurt him. It was an effort to resist, but resist he did, all the while fantasising about fat brown mushrooms sizzling on a metal plate over a campfire. Building campfires was something else that he was bad at. But he survived, thanks to the Discard's apparently infinite population of snails. They couldn't outrun him, and he was reasonably sure they weren't poisonous: he remembered people in Modest Mills frying them with garlic and selling them at market stalls to passers-by. Alan ate them raw – shuddering at their gritty, rubbery flesh – until he got better at building fires. After that, he toasted them on sticks. They were still gritty and rubbery, but they were not as slimy.

Without intending to, he found himself in a network of buildings and couldn't work out where the exit was. The ground he'd stood on upon first leaving the Pyramid was now lost to him. He wandered through vast, abandoned mills, clambered down rusty metal ladders, used thick twisted vines to climb up sloping chimneys, stalked quiet, dusty corridors of pale stone, crept up on nesting pigeons and sent them cooing and squawking up into the air. He stood at windows, looking for landmarks that would help him travel with more direction, but as soon as he left any particular window he became disorientated again. It felt like whichever window he stood at – however many storeys he ascended or descended – he gazed down at yet more red-tile rooftops, either blazing in the sunlight or gleaming coldly by the light of the moons. And he gazed up at yet more buildings soaring upwards, away from him, culminating in spires and spindles or messy knots of metal pipework. The architecture looked impossible.

In another attempt to take stock of his location he tried to get to the bottom of the building he was in, but the deeper he went, the darker the interiors grew, and he became unnerved. The less light made it through the windows, the more moss and mould dampened the floors, ceilings and walls. Large, dull beetles scuttled from his footsteps. But he kept on going until, at the top of one stairwell, he heard a strange noise echoing up from the green, dripping depths; metal scraping metal, and something like laughter. He turned and fled.

He had expected to meet more people. Once he saw somebody several rooftops away, sitting on top of a chimney pot, wearing a large, outlandish hat, smoking, and sipping from a shiny hip-flask, as if there was nothing to be afraid of. Alan almost dived from the windowsill he was leaning over, shouting 'Hello! Hello!' but by the time he'd lowered himself down into a small paved courtyard and then climbed up a drainpipe onto the top of the building that the stranger had been sitting on, the stranger had disappeared.

As he continued on his aimless journey, though, he saw more and more people. Just never close up. The ones he wanted to speak to all avoided him, and he ran or hid from the ones who tried to approach him. They were all grimy and skinny and desperate. Who knew what they wanted, or what weapons they carried?

Alan's diet of snails grew tedious and, despite his best efforts, he fell sick. He put it down to drinking bad water. The little food he managed to eat went right through him, and whenever he did manage to fall sleep he was woken in short order by the urge to vomit. He considered returning to the Pyramid – but no. He wasn't going back until he could do something good for his family. Returning now would be bad for them. He wouldn't fuck things up for them any more.

A week or two later, he was still unable to hold any food in his belly. He was dehydrated and his head felt like it was on fire. His skin was dry in some places, greasy in others, and he stank. He was encountering many more people now, but they kept well away. Traders selling dried meat and vegetables and whisky from backpacks went past but he didn't have the bugs. He remembered bugs — a species of iridescent beetle, their bodies varnished — from Modest Mills, but he had no idea how to lay his hands on any now.

Had he been wrong about the Discard all this time? Maybe the Pyramidders were right. Maybe it was just a hellish labyrinth, offering nothing but a variety of ways to die. If you were *born* out here, well, then maybe you had a chance, but if you were a Pyramidder . . .

But he *had* been born out here. He was *not* a Pyramidder. He kept going.

He almost forgot that Snapper was a musical instrument until one night he heard somebody else singing. The man was drunken and not very good, but he followed the sound of it. The air was warm. He crawled, exhausted and emaciated, to an ancient-looking archway wreathed in soft, shaggy moss. Beyond it, occupying one corner of some kind of ruined plaza, there was a large wooden shack. Golden light spilled from its windows. A gigantic hairy bull of a man stood in front of it, arms folded. A sign hung above its door, and the sign read 'THE WAXY NUT'. The song ended, and there was a moment's silence before a cacophony of voices suddenly erupted – loud shouting, laughing and cheering.

Then somebody else sang a different song.

Alan approached the shack. The bouncer glanced over him. He did not look impressed, but his eyes were not cruel.

'I was hoping to sing,' Alan said. He spoke slowly, because he was out of practice, and he did not want to fuck this up. 'Do you think that is a possibility?'

'You any good?'

'I'm usually very good. But I'm hungry and thirsty, so my voice will likely be a little rough.'

'As rough as them dog's arses inside?' The bouncer laughed. 'They'd take some beating as far as rough voices go.'

'So I can enter?'

''course you can,' the bouncer said. 'This is a friendly pub. But they likely won't give you nothing to eat until after you sing. It's a contest, see. Nice big juicy snake steak for the best singer.'

Alan bowed his head. 'Thank you,' he said.

The bouncer stepped aside, and gestured to the door.

So Alan fell into a different kind of Discard life. He met other Pyramid exiles – The Waxy Nut catered primarily to men and women kicked out of the Pyramid for loving members of their own sex – and began drinking heavily. He drank with sad, stubbly apes in ragged dresses, old prostitutes with rosy cheeks painted onto cracked white greasepaint, disgraced holy men, and orphans whose parents had been killed by cut-throats, fever or venom. The Nut boasted a staggeringly poor selection of whiskies, one home-brewed beer that tasted like old dishwater, and a bewildering variety of mushroom teas, with which Alan experimented liberally, despite the ugly consequences of addiction being painfully evident all around him. Intoxication provided a respite from the remorse. He and Snapper regaled the regulars almost every night – sometimes with folk songs, sometimes with his own compositions, and sometimes with long, experimental pieces brought on by the mushrooms. And almost every night he drank himself to sleep in the bar. He found that if he did not drink, he could not sleep. When he did sleep, his sleep was full of nightmares. The nightmares were many, and he would awake with the sense that his rest had been distorted and broken by their volume and their jagged shapes. If he was not drunk, or performing, he was chewing his lip to pulp and remembering the marks on Marion's face in almost perfect detail. Sometimes he woke to find himself naked and entangled within the limbs of others; sometimes male, sometimes female, sometimes groups. On these occasions he'd find a quiet place outside, alone, and whisper words of love, shame and contrition to Marion, though he knew she couldn't hear him. It was like praying. It *was* praying. But then he'd start drinking again, straight away, in an attempt to shut his brain down. The Nut's cheapest whisky was called Dog Moon, and drinking it was like standing over a bucket fire and inhaling the hot smoke, and Alan had discovered a taste for it.

He found out where Eyes lived from a transient who stopped by one night. He'd made a habit of asking about his old friend. There was no other way of contacting people; in the Pyramid, they'd had a network of message chutes, but there was no such thing out in the Discard. So he left The Nut behind, promising that he'd not be long, and set out on another journey.

He played Snapper and sang songs at campfires for bugs. He bought Dog Moon, food – roasted pigeon, frog's legs, dried apple, cured goat meat – and a couple of long knives from itinerant traders. He saw strange and terrifying things from great distances: beetles the size of dogs; a woman pushing a cart full of writhing snakes along the top of a huge metal pipe; green glowing eyes staring at him across the canyon between two rusting complexes at night; bandits stabbing a man in the stomach, and leaving him twitching beneath a ruined archway. For a long time Alan couldn't work out how to get to that archway in order to help; by the time he did get to the man, who'd been wearing a gigantic and magnificent snail shell on his back, he was dead.

By the time he found Eyes, he had grown harder and leaner, and built something of a reputation as a singer. Eyes knew a place – a safe place – where Alan might be able to entertain the residents in return for a roof over his head and daily hot meals.

Alan was glad of that; the nights were full of eerie voices and the days were full of colourful spiders. But even in a safe place, even with good food in his belly, even in a room with a lockable door, he found sleeping difficult, and his dreams were haunted by Marion and Billy, their bloodied bodies bearing wounds that he himself had inflicted; his waking hours, too, were twisted up by love for them, love that had nowhere to go, it seemed, somehow, and deep inside him there was a rage, the flames of which were fanned by the memories of his family's faces, and the whisky did not dampen it at all, however much he drank. It only grew.

3

In the Halls of the Mushroom Queen

There was no legal power in the Discard, but there was the Mushroom Queen. Of all the Discard lords and ladies, she had the greatest power and reach, and her halls were the grandest, and her whims were the cruellest. If there was one person in the whole of Gleam that it was absolutely imperative not to piss off, it was the Mushroom Queen: Daunt the Undaunted, Lady Redcapper, the Pale Sadist. But here he was. *Here he was.*

Four years after his exit from the Pyramid, Alan stood beside Daunt's throne, trying not to let his nerves betray him. More than anything else he just wanted to be back in the House of a Thousand Hollows; it was the closest thing he had to a home these days, and the only really safe place available to him.

Daunt had had her throne made of *bone*, for Green's sake. Its arms were large crocodile skulls, jaws wide open, human skulls nestled within. The throne shone by the light of the roaring fires, both of which occupied fireplaces that stretched the entire length of the hall. Two hunched little men carrying huge baskets of wood on their backs hurried up and down the room keeping the fires alive. Their bodies had been twisted over time by the weight of their burdens, and due to the constant heat their skin was red and dry. They wore nothing but loose pantaloons, into which they tucked their greying beards. Onto their foreheads, Daunt's sigil had been tattooed: a black triangle pointing upwards, crowned by a half-circle. A symbolic representation of the mushroom, the squat fruit on which she had built her empire. Many of the people gathered in the halls for the evening's entertainment wore this sigil on their foreheads, as did Daunt herself. Those who did not wear the symbol were paying customers, or entertainers, or clients. Or a mix of all three, like Alan. But Daunt's feasts were as much for her people as for anybody else; she had many ways of keeping them fiercely loyal, and these lavish events were one of them.

Like much of the Discard, Daunt's halls were not readily visible from the outside. They were reached through a labyrinth of empty rooms and overshadowed rooftops. Through tunnels carved out of heaps of waste, and between the rusting metal hulks of dead machines. There was perhaps some vantage point from which to view the halls, but if it did exist, Alan hadn't found it. Whenever he was here, he felt as if he were at some deep level; deeper than he'd normally venture. He suspected that the halls were themselves all located inside a different, larger structure, itself perhaps buried beneath the piles of broken things from which the Discard took its name. Whatever their origins, though, whatever their first purpose, the halls now were a series of large open spaces interconnected via high archways, the largest chamber presided over by Daunt's throne, which was raised on a semicircular dais. The floors were paved with black stone and the walls were of some kind of smooth grey brick, covered with the mounted skulls of prey that Daunt's mushroom gatherers had hunted and killed in the depths of the Discard. Gigantic reptilian jaws grinned down, alongside others that were disconcertingly difficult to identify.

The queen herself sat on the throne, legs crossed, arms resting on the crocodile skulls. She wore a wooden circlet decorated with tiny wooden mushrooms. Her long blonde hair was loose tonight, her green eyes bright, the pupils small. She wore a flowing green skirt, but her arms, torso and feet were bare. Two naked, musclebound skinheads massaged her hands, their thumbs circling her palms, the scents of mint and lemon rising from the oil. Her lips were slightly parted in a half-smile. She caught Alan looking and he averted his eyes, cursing himself. If Daunt wanted him, she could have him. He would go willingly. He was as much her slave as those beardy shufflers down by the fires. But better she didn't know that.

There was no way she didn't know.

'Are you going to play for us, my sweet?' she called.

Alan spun back to face her again, hoping that his cheeks

were not too red still, and bowed low. 'I will,' he said. 'I mean, I am. I am going to play for you. Now?' He cleared his throat. 'Would you like me to start now?'

Daunt's smile widened. 'Is there anybody else playing?'

Alan looked around. 'No.'

'Then you're on, Hollowboy. Silence isn't . . . good for me.'

Alan nodded. The halls were hardly silent, and he didn't really like being called 'Hollowboy', but he didn't say anything. He fumbled taking Snapper from his back and the guitar slipped through his sweaty fingers. He caught it again before it hit the ground and stared for a moment. 'Sorry, Snapper,' he whispered.

He was usually more together than this. In the past he'd only met Daunt out in the wilds, and their encounters had been purely business: she sold him mushrooms. Her power and allure were diluted away from her own halls, and he'd always had an escape route planned if things went south. And more recently he'd only dealt with various knuckleheaded subordinates, who – though large and lumpen – were hardly threatening. Here, things were different. Here, he was in her claws.

'A slow one,' he said. 'A slow one, to start with.'

'If you insist.' Daunt withdrew her hands from the masseurs and clapped once, twice, three times. Though the halls were full of voices and laughter, and the clapping sounded small, it had the desired effect. Everybody fell silent and turned to look up at the dais. Daunt stood up and, wordlessly, presented Alan.

Alan looked down at the crowd. The crowd looked up at him. There were bikers in their leather waistcoats and extravagant headdresses, transients dangling assorted junk from their many belts, white-robed Glasstowners, warty green-skinned Toadies, hermits bearing highly polished shells proudly on their backs and, of course, fungus fiends, already slightly foamy around the mouth. No Mapmakers, which was something of a relief. Alan had heard that Daunt had a relationship with the Mapmakers, and he believed it – it was surely the only way she could have established a supply chain from the lower levels, which was where the mushrooms were strong and plentiful. Where the effects of the ascending Swamp could be felt. Alan had been apprehensive at the thought of potentially meeting one of their number, but it had always been unlikely – the Mapmakers generally did not attend social gatherings outside of their own tribes.

All these people, with their whiskies and beers and berry wines, and their salted garlic snails and their stuffed vine leaves and their roasted sunbladder-heads and their trays of sausages, splitting and blackened almost to perfection – *sausages*! A true delicacy in the Discard, and vastly expensive – and their pipes and, of course, their fried mushrooms, mushroom soup, and pots of mushroom tea – all these people, they'd all been having a perfectly nice time, and he, Alan, Wild Alan, Hollow-boy, was about to ruin it.

He licked his lips. He took off his long coat – torture up in the hot Gleam sun, but a necessity down here – and rolled up his shirt sleeves. He deliberately slowed his movements so as not to appear nervous, and in doing so regained a modicum of control over his shaking hands. He looped Snapper's strap over his neck and adjusted it. The hall was still silent and all eyes were on him. He hadn't expected this, in truth. He'd expected to be stashed away in some dingy corner, playing to and being ignored by a roomful of determinedly intoxicated liber-tines. And right now, that was what he wanted. This was a hard crowd to read. He'd better steer clear of anything too factional, too partisan to this settlement or that com-munity. Which was tough, because so many of the classics had their roots in turf.

Of course, there was one song whose sentiment would raise no Discard hackles. 'The Black Pyramid' always went down well. Some Discarders were indifferent to the Pyramid, but most feared or hated it, and the song was a song of defiance against it. And it was slow and simple – at least to begin with – and he should just about be able to pull it off, even in this state.

There was no generator down here – it was all open fires and flickering candles wedged inside skulls and gut-tering paraffin torches – so he didn't have a microphone.

The rooms looked good, acoustically, so he was all set to do without, but then from nowhere some skinny, symbolled lackey wheeled out a contraption consisting of a frame bearing a large, twisted brass megaphone decorated with small, horned figures dancing around – inevitably – mushrooms. The lackey made a respectable attempt at nodding and bowing and pointing and backing away all at the same time, and slipped on the lip of the dais, cracking his knee. Alan nodded his thanks as the emaciated man hobbled into the shadows, and started to play. The amplifying device actually had two megaphones, he saw, twisted around each other. One for his mouth, and one with a lower, wider aperture for – he guessed – whatever instrument the singer happened to be using. He found a pedal at the bottom of the frame that swung a beater at a skin, and kicked it. The sound was pleasingly solid. When he started to sing the volume surprised him, and he sounded different – slightly distant, slightly warped – but he liked it. He relaxed. He loosened his fingers and raised his voice, and started stamping on the pedal, and a couple of hermits started to dance, their glossy shells bobbing up and down as if they were floating on top of the crowd. Others were smiling, nodding. A few started murmuring to each other again, but not too loudly, so that was okay. It was all okay. As long as they were happy, it was okay.

He could ignore them now.

Alan closed his eyes, and threw himself into it. His mind and body dissolved into the air and he lost himself.

When he found himself again, later, he was painfully thirsty, drenched in sweat and almost slipping from the edge of the stage. No, he corrected himself: not stage; dais. He was on a *dais*. He giggled. What had he drunk? He glanced backwards at the empty glass bottles littered about where he'd been standing. Some beer, some whisky. Some other stuff. And still so *thirsty*. He laughed again. Already there was other music playing, and he wanted to dance, but it was not easy to dance to. It was just drumming; one loud, rhythmic beat. He felt a cool hand on his wrist, and turned to see that it belonged to the Mushroom Queen. She handed him a tall clay cup, but was studying his arm.

'New tattoo?' she enquired, pointing at an ornate black beetle with a human skull visible in its carapace markings. 'Very nice, Hollowboy.'

Alan stopped gulping down the water she'd given him in order to answer her question. 'Yes,' he said, 'yes, new. How did you know? How did you notice?'

Daunt smirked. 'I see a lot, Hollowboy. I see an awful lot. I open my third eye, my fourth, my fifth, and I observe. I am observant. Some use my fruits to dull their vision, or confuse it; I use them to sharpen it.' She grinned. 'Come. It is time for the next entertainment.'

Daunt swept past him. She had her naked attendants

on fine chain leads, Alan saw now. They followed her, their hard, lean bodies glistening, and Alan rushed after, then past them so he was walking at Daunt's side.

'Your first audience in my halls,' she said. 'They enjoyed you. I enjoyed you. You did well. I will have you back.'

'Thank you.'

'Your reputation is not entirely undeserved.' She looked sideways at him. 'Your reputation as a singer, that is.'

Alan took a deep breath. 'What other reputation do I have?'

Daunt smirked again. 'You know fine well. Do not play the fool with me. I intend for you to be one of my men tonight. There is no need to fence.' She pressed herself against him and kissed him full on the lips. He could feel her breasts through his cold damp shirt. She broke free and undid his uppermost done button. 'You may as well just take that off,' she said. 'It is foul. Your body is much more pleasing without.' And around them, people were indeed removing their clothes, some as they danced, some as they kissed. The beating of the drum was louder and faster now. Alan's skin felt hypersensitive; every brief contact sent waves tingling across his whole body. Something he'd drunk, perhaps. Some fungal liquor he'd downed unknowingly in the mindless space between songs. Or spores in the air. Daunt's parties were legendarily debauched, and the provenance of her power probably had something to do with it.

What was the next entertainment?

Alan followed Daunt through one of the archways into a long rectangular space. People were squeezed onto the little floor space that bounded a pit in the middle of the room. In the pit were two small silver bowls, their surfaces pitted, each full of fragments of something that looked like dried orange peel. The bowls rested on a surface of some fine grey dust, possibly ash.

The crowd parted for Daunt. Alan remained at her side, and she did not motion for him to be removed. He had expected greater security than this. Though presumably the masseurs were also bodyguards. He certainly didn't want to provoke them. He had no doubt that the chains were decorative, and as insubstantial as cobwebs against the slabbed muscle beneath.

He watched as two similarly built – and equally naked – men jumped down into the pit. Daunt clapped delightedly, and the drumbeat accelerated to an aural blur. A woman dressed in rags and covered with mushroom tattoos held out a platter of small red things that smelled deliciously of spices. He took a handful and thanked the woman, but she was gone, offering food to the next spectator. The morsels were meaty at first, but melted into nothing. Some kind of offal, fried in something bright. Luxury food. He watched as the men in the pit bowed to their queen, sat cross-legged opposite each other and tipped the silver bowls to their mouths. They inhaled the orange fragments and chewed furiously. Alan looked across at Daunt, who was rapt. Her empty throne was bobbing its way into the room, carried by enthusiastic members of her following, and when she noticed it behind her, she quickly climbed backwards into it, trying not to take her eyes off the men in the pit. They were getting to their feet. One made claws of his hands and snarled at the other. The men collided, one lowering his head and smashing his skull into the other's, and the room erupted into a roar that nearly knocked Alan from his feet. He could tell from the men's expressions that they were howling and screaming, but he couldn't hear a sound from them. It was disconcerting. Their nails drew ribbons of blood across each other's taut flesh. They grappled and punched and kicked and bit. Yellow drool ran from their mouths. Alan watched, his jaw dropping, as one headlocked the other and thumped him repeatedly in the face. The one in the headlock grabbed his opponent's penis and squeezed, hard. Alan flinched, looked away, looked up at Daunt. She could barely contain herself. She was pointing and laughing hysterically. There were whoops from the crowd. He looked back into the pit, and one was on the floor, being kicked in the ribs. He couldn't tell them apart. They were both covered with streaks of blood now, and blood poured from their noses and ears, and spattered across the floor of the pit as they moved. The one on the floor somehow wriggled into a position where he could reach the other's shin with his mouth. He sank his teeth into it. Now they were both on the floor, writing around after each other. The ash coated their skin, sticking to the blood and the sweat and rising in clouds around them.

Alan felt hot breath on his neck. Daunt was leaning down to speak to him. 'They can't feel pain,' she said, her lips brushing his ear. 'Isn't it wonderful?'

Alan just nodded.

'They can't really feel anything.'

One bone-cracking blow after another. The muscle-bound bodies were hard and heavy. Faces were pushed into the ground. Everything was grey. Fingers were forced through skin. Extremities were pulled and stretched. Details blurred. The fight became impressionistic: impossible bodies in torturous configurations appearing in glimpses through the fog of ash. Sometimes dark fluid sprayed out. The crowd seethed and swayed. Fists pummelled the air and mouths opened to cheer and did not close again. Everything was slow. People were touching each other. Alan's skin tingled and his cock grew. There was some kind of music but he could not work out what it was. He looked up at Daunt and saw that she had a hand beneath her skirt and her eyes were half closed. Her other hand found the top of his head and she ran it through his hair. One of the men in the pit suddenly hauled himself up over the side and stood before the throne. He could only open one eye, both ears had gone, and blood bubbled from between his lips and ran in black tracks through the grey filth coating his chest. The crowd quietened. He raised one hand and in it was something soft and fleshy, no doubt torn from his opponent's body, but due to the state of it, and the ash, Alan could not tell what it was. Daunt wound Alan's hair around her fingers as she clenched her hand into a fist, and the whole room heard her gasp.

Later, she took him to her private chambers and bade him play for her, then pleasure her. 'You are the appetiser,' she explained to Alan, as the pit-winner, still bleeding, watched from the corner of the deep red room. The room was a nest of furs and silks and skins and dark wooden chests. A censer burned. Cabinets lined the walls, full of glass bottles, the contents of which were difficult to determine. As the pit-winner watched Alan and Daunt, he drank some kind of concoction that, Daunt explained, would keep him going for as long as she needed. His presence would normally have put Alan off his stride – not because he was a man, but because he looked near dead – but something in the air or the food or the drink enabled Alan to shrug off his reservations and devote himself. He didn't want Snapper seeing, though; he turned the guitar over before he began to perform his ministrations.

Later still, when Daunt was preoccupied with the bloody, hulking beast, Alan scanned the shelves for what he wanted. The sex coupled with the increasingly strong smoke from the censer made it difficult to concentrate. He got dizzy looking at all of the glass and all of the reflections in the glass. Green glass, red glass, yellow glass, brown glass; fat jars, delicate vials, tall bottles, twisted baubles.

There. He thought he'd spotted it.

His mouth was dry. He hadn't expected to get this far. He hadn't expected to be presented with this opportunity. Except maybe it wasn't an opportunity; maybe the hulking beast-man currently grunting away beside him was Daunt's security. How would Alan have fared in that pit? He didn't want to think about it. And that wasn't to mention Daunt herself – she was notorious for the punishments that she delighted in meting out personally.

He looked at the mushrooms that his contact had demanded – the distinctive pale green cap, thin white stems – in their uncoloured glass vials. He looked at Daunt and her lover. They seemed to be occupying each other completely.

He looked back at the mushrooms.

4

Tanglepipe Junction

Wild Alan hauled himself up a shaky ladder onto the broken gantry of a circular metal tower, Snapper strapped to his back, and turned to look down at the vast tangle of silver pipework that he'd climbed through. Large cylinders, like the one behind him, reached upwards from the maze like big stubby fingers, and attendant ladders and gantries hung from their sides. His audience sat on these walkways, or stood on ramshackle wooden bridges that had been thrown up between the fingers, or looked up from the pipes below, or peered from holes in the sides of the cylinders that had been created by rust, but now functioned as windows.

Coloured glass lanterns swayed gently in the warm breeze, and clouds moved slowly across the night sky. The moons hung low and full and purple. Alan swung the guitar round and ran his fingertips across the steel strings. He winced. Snapper was already badly out of tune. He could hear the audience murmuring. There were more of them down amongst the pipes, he saw, down amongst that nightmarishly convoluted network. Some pipes were wide enough for rows of people to stand on them and look up, others just right for strad-dling. Some were smaller still, and served as hand- and foot-holds, but little else. More and more people were appearing from the labyrinth. *It's a whole village*, he real-ised. *Maybe there'll be a bed for me tonight*.

He left the House of a Thousand Hollows so rarely that he didn't really know the places he was likely to get a good reception, or where the people were hospitable. In his limited experience, small communities like this were usually on the defensive side – they'd accept trade and entertainment from travellers, but wouldn't wel-come them into their homes. When the show was over they'd hurry back into their dwellings with fixed grins and hands on knife handles, then slam their doors and double lock them. He understood that. He was always relieved to arrive back at the House, find his own room and bolt the door.

He was pretty high up here, and could see a long way out. It was the first time he'd been above the skyline in days. He took in the view as he tuned his guitar.

Pipes ran out from the metal tangle in all directions in long, straight clusters that kept on going until they were so distant, so fine, that they looked like strands of hair. They shone in the moonlight. Although they were beneath Alan's vantage point, they were still far above the swamp and many of the buildings, which lay in darkness. Close to the tangle, large pale boxy structures rose from that darkness, their sides thick with creeping plants that looked black now, but would be revealed as dark green by the daylight. The tops of other, smaller buildings were just visible around them: a variety of peaked roofs and flat, tiered roofs, a jostle of eaves and tiles, everything pressed up against everything else. All of the buildings in Gleam were connected to their neighbours at some level by the old architecture or new – apart from the Black Pyramid, which stood alone.

The largest pipe cluster led directly to the Pyramid, which hulked on the eastern horizon like a monster, like a god. The Pyramid was the tallest thing in Gleam. It rose from a shadowed wasteland of discarded products; a scrapyard of faulty rejects: broken things that were not pleasant to think on, the intended purposes of which were never obvious.

He strummed the guitar again. *As in tune as it'll ever be.* One day he'd buy, beg or steal a nice new one; an instrument that wasn't all battered to hell, that hadn't lost strips of plywood, that didn't have gouges in the mahogany-stained finish. One with level frets from the get-go. But he wouldn't. Not really. He was Snapper's and Snapper was his and that was the way it would always be. He held the neck to his eyes. He'd levelled Snapper's frets himself with some sandpaper from a dented old toolbox he'd found in a dusty, abandoned attic, and then varnished the whole thing back at the Thousand Hollows. He put the guitar down and took off his fingerless black leather gloves. Then he shrugged off his long brown wool-tweed jacket. Beneath it he wore a white shirt, black trousers and black braces. He rolled his shirt sleeves up, revealing brightly coloured tattoos of birds with women's faces, devils swinging their legs from sad crescent moons, and toads wearing top hats. He took a cigarette from the packet in his shirt pocket and lit it with a match, then blew the match out and flicked it over the railing. He inhaled deeply and held the breath. Something stronger would be better. Cigarette between his lips, he crouched down and took a wineskin from the inner pocket of his coat. It didn't have wine in it, but beer from an inn called The Toad Inside that he'd passed through a couple of days back.

He could hear his audience talking, their voices growing louder. They were not restless, not yet, but he'd have to start soon. He took the cigarette in his fingers, which were shaking, and tested the railing. It wobbled slightly. He stepped back from it and took a good long swig from the skin. Should've saved some whisky. He always sang better with some whisky in him. 'Right then,' he whispered. He picked Snapper back up and slipped the strap over his shoulder.

He slammed the side of his fist into the huge metal canister behind him and the *boom* exploded outwards, far louder than he'd ever expected. But it stopped the talking. 'Right then!' he shouted. 'I'm Wild Alan, and I'm here to sing you some songs.'

A cheer came back, also louder than he'd expected, and he grinned. He was fully functional tonight. This time he'd begin with something fast. 'Ruth of the Rooftops' was always a good starter. His fingers danced over the fretboard almost of their own accord, bypassing his brain completely. The strings sang out loud and clear, the sound travelling well through the damp night air. He played for a while before singing, warming up, settling on a pace and then falling in with it. When he did sing, his voice was low and resonant. Years of practice meant that he could project well enough, so even outside he could make the lyrics clear to the audience.

When he came to the chorus, he pressed the head of the guitar into the side of the cylinder the gantry was attached to and used it as an amplifier. He kicked it too; a steel-toecap boot was the perfect beater for such a drum. His black hair fell in front of his face as he played and he rose and fell on the sound, taking the crowd with him – up for songs of love and lust and justice done, and down again with songs of Modest Mills, songs of exiles and massacres. He sang songs about how Gleam would end, and songs of how Gleam had come to be. He sang songs about loners and misfits and freaks and wandering demons and gang warfare and Bed Men and Bright Women and the Honeyed and the Forests of Dok, legends of the Discard and the Warehouse Wastes, and – vitally, finally, once they were rapt – horror stories about the Black Pyramid, and the monsters who ruled—

An arrow appeared, quivering, in the metal just to the left of his head. He fell to the floor, song truncated, and another whistled above him and pierced the cylinder, right where his throat had been not a moment before. Shit. The sudden silence was total.

'Shut yer fuckhole, scumbag!' somebody shouted. A harsh voice. But he couldn't see who or exactly where from without raising his face, which he was not about to do. He swung Snapper round onto his back and scrambled forward, beneath the railing. He turned round and slid off the gantry, not looking down, absolutely refusing to look down. The ladder was to his right; he hooked his foot around it and pulled himself over. An arrow could get him in the back at any moment.

And he'd been singing so well, too.

Who wants to hurt me? But the list was long, and he knew it.

He reached up, grabbed his coat and threw it behind him. It billowed down through the night air to land – hopefully – somewhere on the knot of pipework beneath. He descended the ladder at speed, dropping a few rungs at a time and braking with his hands. People were shouting now, and the whole Junction was reverberating with the sound of heavy footsteps.

Another arrow hit Snapper, severing at least a couple of strings. The guitar rocked, the strings lashed back like whips, and Alan lost his footing. He cursed as his knees bounced off rung after rung. More arrows glanced off the cylinder and clattered down around him. *Fuckers.* Snapper ricocheted off pipes to his back as the tangle swallowed him down. At least he had some cover now.

He finally caught a rung with his foot. It snapped, weak with rust, but the next one held. He looked down. His coat had landed on a lower gantry, not far beneath him. He quickly climbed down to it and stepped off the ladder.

He was deep in the metal forest. Fat segmented ducts wormed through the tangle, as did rows of thin copper tubes. Ranks of thigh-wide silver conduits wove in and out of each other, vertically and horizontally and diagonally. Some pipes had been painted green once, some yellow, but they were all streaked orange with rust now. Metal walkways led from the gantry and disappeared into the morass, forming passages with walls and ceilings of dense pipework. The tangle flickered with yellow light; sconces had been hammered into the metal and torches burned at various intersections within. The ladder extended further beyond the gantry on which Alan stood, down into darkness.

This was Tanglepipe Junction: a small settlement that had grown up around the congruence of some of the trunk pipes that Alan and other travellers used to make their way around the Factory. But the trunk with the cart was . . . which way from here? It was over the other side of the tangle, beneath the largest of the cylinders.

People were running and screaming. Alan could see figures climbing ladders, descending ladders, could hear gantries shaking as people rushed back to the relative safety of their homes inside the structures. Maybe this wasn't about him; maybe the attackers were here to settle business with somebody else. Or maybe they were just raiders passing through.

Maybe he could just slip away.

He quickly took Snapper from his shoulder and donned his coat. He took his gloves from the pockets and put them back on. Before strapping Snapper back onto his back, he examined the damage. It was painful to see. The arrow had hit the guitar dead in the neck, leaving a pale wound that nearly split the wood in two. The broken strings lolled around like horrible, ungainly living things. But Alan had no time to remove them completely.

He could climb down yet further, or disappear into the tangle. Neither option was appealing. The tangle was more likely to house the shooters, and the ladder . . . well, all Gleamers knew to stay as high as possible at all times. *Down is out* was the mantra.

Decision made, Alan darted into the nearest passageway. With a little luck, he could even find his way through this maze and catch the big trunk cart without anybody even seeing him.

But the luck was not with him.

A woman emerged from a shadowed alcove, a long curved knife in her hand. She wore pale breeches and a brown leather waistcoat and her long blonde hair was tied up into a topknot. She grinned as she passed into the dancing light of a torch.

'What a voice,' she hissed through her teeth. 'I'd recognise it anywhere.'

'Daunt?' Alan said, stepping backwards. 'What a relief! I was worried it would be somebody unfriendly.'

Something hard and cold pressed into the back of his neck.

'I'm unfriendly, warbler,' said a soft voice from behind, the kind of voice that suggested very bad teeth. It was accompanied by a cloud of stinking breath and flecks of warm spittle. 'I'm a right nasty fucker.'

'I don't think you've met Bittewood, Alan,' Daunt said.

'No, I don't think I have. Is he the bad shot?'

'He is more of a close-quarters kind of man, it's true.'

'I'm a knife man,' said Bittewood, and the hard cold something pressed into the back of Alan's neck was pressed a little harder.

'Daunt, I thought we got on,' Alan said. He swallowed. 'What's all this about?'

'We did get on. We did.' Daunt moved closer, her own knife up. The green eyes that had been so bright and lively in the bedchamber were now hard. Her cheekbones were high and sharp. She looked thinner than she had the other night, too thin, and by the light of the torch she had a cadaverous aspect. 'But you ruined it, Alan, didn't you?'

'I don't know what you mean.'

'Don't lie.'

'Please just tell me.'

'You owe me a lot of money, Alan. A good old mountain of bugs.'

'I pay when I pick up, Daunt. You know I do.'

Daunt bared her teeth. 'I'm giving you an out here, rat. I'm not talking about what you buy. I'm talking about what you *stole*.'

Alan shook his head. His mouth was dry. Daunt was one of the more vengeful and vicious Discard authorities, and that was saying something.

'Queen of Mushrooms don't stay queen by giving shit away, warbler,' Bittewood breathed into Alan's ear. Alan shuddered. He could sense his captor's size.

'Bittewood here is right,' Daunt said, 'and you know it. I don't give my wares away for nothing, not even to friends, let alone chancers like you. And I don't tolerate theft.'

'But they weren't for nothing. I paid in kind.'

'With your cock?' Daunt laughed, a short sharp sound. 'No! More like I should have charged you for the fucking and all. It was a disappointment. And I'd heard that was one thing you were good at.'

'I am good at it.'

'You were shite.'

'I'm not just going to stand here and be insulted.'

Bittewood snarled, 'Let me cut him, Daunt. Just a little bit.'

'Not yet.' Daunt grabbed Alan's face, her long nails digging into his cheeks. 'What did you do with what you took? Did you sell them? There were too many for just you. Have you still got them?'

She was hurting him. And that 'Not yet' had sounded stone-cold serious. It was time to get to the point. 'I don't know what you're talking about, Daunt. I played your hall. I watched your meatheads brawl. We ate some soup together, drank some tea. I bought some mushrooms. We fucked. I left. I didn't take anything. I didn't steal from you.'

'You took the vials?'

'I don't know anything about the vials.' He resisted the urge to swallow. 'I didn't take any vials.'

Daunt put her knife to Alan's throat. 'Take your coat off,' she said to him and then, to Bittewood, 'Search him.' Bittewood removed his knife from the back of Alan's neck, allowing him to unstrap the guitar and shrug his coat to the ground.

Bittewood stepped around to stand in front of Alan.

Alan hoped his face did not betray the fear he felt in that moment. By the Builders! Bittewood was big, he'd already known that, but he hadn't realised how . . . ugly he was. He had long black hair, but it was thin, greasy and straggly, and he was bald on top. His bloodshot eyes were large and icy blue, and they bulged out of the mess of scars and full, yellow spots that was his face. His mouth was wide, his lips wet, his neck long and his torso bare and hairless. His skin was pale and greyish. He was not particularly musclebound, but he was very tall and wiry, and his long, dirty fingers felt as strong as iron as they prodded and poked all over Alan's body. He had a crossbow on his back and a rusty – maybe bloody – short-sword at his waist. He stank of old sweat gone acrid.

'Aren't you cold?' Alan asked, as Bittewood picked up the discarded coat and started going through the pockets. 'It's not as—'

Bittewood shoved two fingers into Alan's open mouth and felt around. 'Be quiet,' he grunted. Alan gagged, tried to turn his head away, but Bittewood grabbed him by the hair and held him. Daunt laughed, mirthlessly. When Bittewood was done he withdrew his fingers and wiped them on his brown plus-fours, a look on his face that might have been a smile. Alan spat. 'What swamp-hole did you pull this fucker out of, Daunt?' he asked. 'What possessed you? He's a creep. He's a monster. You're better than this.'

'Well, Alan, there are some folks out there who don't take me seriously.' Daunt put her mouth to Alan's ear. 'It's hard to believe, I know.'

'There are heavies, and then there's that.'

'Lots of us have heavies. I'm the only one with a Bittewood, though.'

'Thank the Builders.' Alan watched as Bittewood shook Snapper around, listening for anything hidden within. 'As if I'd keep glass vials in my mouth, anyway. He just did that for fun.'

'Probably.'

'He makes me uncomfortable. Are you done with me yet? I want to go. I want to get far away. I want to have a wash.'

Daunt lowered her knife. 'You understand that I can't just let people steal from me,' she said. 'I have to uphold my reputation. I have to send messages.'

'You have to keep people scared.'

'Yes.'

'Of course I understand. I didn't take your bloody mushrooms, Daunt. I love 'em, but I like you, and I don't steal from people I like.' He lowered his voice. 'Though the Daunt I know and like wouldn't be associating with that lanky pus-bag.'

'Desperate times, Alan.'

'Well, rest assured, I'll be telling everybody just how bloody terrifying your new pet is.'

Daunt nodded. She looked into Alan's eyes for a moment, then nodded again. 'Right then. Bittewood, we're done here. He's telling the truth.'

'Don't trust him,' Bittewood said. 'Could've taken them. Could've hid them. Could've sold them.'

'I know that. I didn't think he'd have them on him. He's not an idiot. Just wanted him to get to know you, really.' She grinned at Alan. 'You're not an idiot, are you, love?'

'I'm a lot of things,' Alan said, 'but I'm not an idiot.'

'Glad we understand each other.'

And with that, Daunt and Bittewood disappeared back into Tanglepipe Junction.

Alan waited until the echoes of their footsteps had died away, and then exhaled. His feelings were mixed. He picked up his coat and ransacked the pockets himself. Then he went through them again.

The vials had gone.

'Shit,' he said. 'Shit, shit, shit.' He scanned the gantry, and found some shards of broken glass balanced just on the edge. The vials must have fallen from his pocket when he'd dropped the coat. Beneath the gantry was only darkness.

Alan kicked the railings, and a couple of them broke off, spinning into the void below. 'Fucking *hell*,' he said.

5

Pyramid Slope

In a shadowed alcove on the sloped southern side of the
Black Pyramid, Wild Alan looked at the palm of his
young son's hand and saw the brand there, red and still
weeping.

'Who did this?' he asked.

'Nobody.'

'Who?'

'I get picked on.'

'But who by?'

'They tell me my father is a stupid wild animal who
lives with all the other stupid wild animals.'

Alan let go of Billy's wrist, put a roll-up in his mouth,
lit it and inhaled deeply. The moons looked down, full
and rusty. Alan held the smoke in his lungs while he
thought, and then exhaled. 'I'm not an animal,' he said.
'And who is it, telling you this? Doing this?'

'Everybody.' Billy was wearing one of those stupid
grey robes they dressed the kids up in, and it was far too

long, pooling around his feet. Bit tight around the middle, though. Pyramidders didn't want for food. Billy was six years old but he looked older to Alan. Not that Alan knew any other six-year-olds. There were families living in the House of a Thousand Hollows, but Alan tried his hardest to avoid them. He didn't even know Billy that well, truth be told. Still, to Alan's mind, children were brought up too quickly in the Pyramid.

Billy's eyes were big and round inside his big round face, and big round tears hung trembling from his long eyelashes. 'Everybody tells me, Dad. They tell me you're no good at all.'

'Son,' Alan said, 'I don't know if I'm any good or not.' He sat down, back to the wall, and took Billy's hands again. 'Don't stick up for me if it means getting hurt.'

Billy scowled. 'I don't,' he said. He yanked his hands away from Alan and walked over to the low wall that guarded against the drop. Beyond the wall, the smooth black stone of the Pyramid sloped steeply down into the blasted wasteland that surrounded it. Alan joined Billy at the wall and looked out. On the other side of the wasteland, the buildings of the Discard were black silhouettes against the stars: a skyline of mills and chimneys, ruins and scaffolding, domes and turrets. Columns of smoke rose from it, clear in the bright moons, and the flames of torches and campfires could be seen nestled amongst the architecture.

'How can you live out there, Dad?' Billy asked.

Far down inside Alan's chest the familiar pain was back. 'I'm sorry, son,' he said. 'I wouldn't have chosen this.' He took a hip-flask from the inside pocket of his suit jacket and drank deeply from it. 'I'm sorry they pick on you.'

'Probably they would pick on me anyway.' Billy's voice was resigned. 'I'm fat.'

'You're not fat.' Alan put his hand on Billy's shoulder. 'Don't say that, son.'

'Eating is my favourite thing.'

'Billy, I need to know about your hand.'

'Vurnit got chosen for the Alchemists. I wanted to get chosen for the Alchemists but I didn't, Vurnit did. We're in the same batch but he still got chosen.'

'You could get chosen when you're older. But maybe you'll change your mind about what you want to be.' *Please, please let him change his mind.* 'What if you got chosen for the Alchemists and then decided you wanted to be a cook, or a gardener? You'd be stuck then, wouldn't you?'

Billy wrinkled his nose. 'Those are jobs for stupid people,' he said. 'I want to be an Alchemist.'

Alan wanted to scream.

'So they gave Vurnit his pendant,' Billy resumed. 'I asked him to see it – you know how they make them all different – and he said no.' He paused. 'Vurnit is very thin and clever. His robe fits him just right. Everybody likes him because he's funny but he's not funny in front of the teachers.'

Though Alan's childhood had been vastly different from Billy's, he reckoned it was probably a universal amongst six-year-olds that 'funny' was a euphemism for 'naughty'.

'Is he a friend?'

'Kind of.' Billy nodded vigorously. 'But he wouldn't let me see it. He was showing it to the others but he put it in his pocket whenever I went over to him. I didn't even want to see it that much, I was angry with him, but Mum had told me I should try and make friends.'

Alan took another swig from the flask. 'You should listen to your mother,' he said.

'I do. Anyway, I asked him if I could see it and he was just ignoring me.' The tears were welling up again. 'Everybody was nice to him all day and nobody was talking to me. And I'd be a better Alchemist anyway. And I couldn't do my work because I was all hot and sweaty. And after classes I was crying in the corridor on the way home and Vurnit came up to me and asked me if I was all right. I said I was. He asked if I wanted to see the pendant and I said yes. I think I said yes too quickly. He held it up for me to take and I thought we were going to be friends properly. I took it in my hand and – it made a sound like bacon – like, hot, sizzling. It didn't hurt at first. Then it did, and I couldn't let go. I started shouting and Vurnit was laughing. The others were laughing too. I cried in front of them.'

Alan tried to control his voice. 'Where were the teachers?'

'They don't watch us outside of school.'

'Where were the Arbitrators? The Administrators?' Alan spat. 'Were there no fucking Alchemists prancing about? Where was your mother? Give me that hand.'

Billy backed away from him.

'Billy, I—'

'Don't swear, and don't blame her.'

'I'm not. It's just—'

'It's not like you were there either.'

Alan gritted his teeth. The side of the Pyramid sloped down away from them, as high and steep as the sharp white mountains that could sometimes be seen catching the sunlight to the west. Black stone carved with elaborate designs gave way to alcoves like the one in which they stood, gave way to windows with balconies, gave way to columned galleries that spanned the whole side. The Pyramid was not as solid as it looked from a distance. It was a honeycomb: a hive of monks and drudges. It was intricately hollow and the closer you got to the shining, haloed point of it, the more ornate the detail and architecture became. Alan put the hip-flask to his lips once more and held it there, drained it, grimaced and put the flask away again.

'I want to be here for you, Billy. I would be if they let me.'

'Why didn't you just stay?'

'They exiled me.'

'But only because you kept breaking the rules.'

'Billy . . .' The Dog Moon was hot in Alan's stomach, but did nothing to burn out his fury. Vurnit and his friends, the Teachers, the Alchemists, the Administrators, the Astronomers – the whole damn lot of them, they could all go to hell. Billy was old enough to know what they were now. Old enough to hear the truth.

'Billy, I wasn't born in the Pyramid. Did you know that?'

Billy shook his head inside his oversized cowl.

'There was a small town at the base of the Pyramid called Modest Mills. You can just about still see the ruins of it now: fallen-down walls and the outlines of buildings, all half buried by the dustdrifts. It wasn't all dust then, though; it wasn't a wasteland. Modest Mills was white stone and brick and wood, proper human-sized houses, not like the cells up here in the Pyramid, and not the giant ancient buildings of the Discard either. Modest Mills was where I was born. We weren't Pyramidders, nor were we proper Discarders; we were in-between. We traded with both. The Alchemists and Astronomers sent their lackeys down for supplies from the Discard Wilds, the Forests of Dok, the Warehouse Wastes – animals' parts, y'know, certain fungi, swamp plants, metal bits and pieces from the old machines. And Discarders came to sell. They did buy, too, but mostly just from each other. The Pyramidders didn't have much that the Discarders wanted, from what I recall.'

'I'm getting cold. I want to go inside.'

'Billy, please don't go. Don't leave me, Billy. I'm sorry for losing my temper. It's just the thought of somebody hurting you. You don't know – you *can't* know.'

'I know what it's like to be the one getting hurt, though.'

Alan laughed. 'Aye,' he said. 'There's that. How does it make you feel?'

'Sad.' Billy sat down next to his father and then looked up at him. 'Angry, too.'

'I'm angry, Billy. That's why they kicked me out. I was angry then and I'm still angry now.'

'They should call you Angry Alan, not Wild Alan.'

'Where did you hear they call me that?'

'Mum. And school. I said it before.'

Alan laughed again. 'Well,' he said. He put an arm round Billy. The whisky was making him feel loose-limbed. 'Modest Mills was a hot little town – all the Discard is hot, there isn't the breeze you lot have up here – made out of white stone and brick and wood, and there were bright little birds flitting around everywhere. The market never closed, rows and rows of stalls with canopies all the colours you can imagine, all the traders shouting all day and the singers singing all night. I wanted to be a Modest Mills singer. Even then I knew that girls liked singers. I don't know why that mattered to me back then – I was only your age – but it did. I wanted the attention, the costumes, the power – I didn't know what the power was but I could *feel* it. Some singers could just stop everybody dead. It was a kind of magic. It was a magic that was real, that I could learn.'

'You're a singer now.'

'Yeah, but not a very good one.'

'What happened to it? To the town? Did Discarders come and kill everyone? Did they burn it down? Weren't you scared of the Discarders, anyway? And weren't there any swamp monsters? Teacher Grumblepip says that most Discarders die before they're forty because of swamp monsters, but here in the Pyramid we all live to be a hundred. Was it the monsters that got the town?'

'No, Billy. If it was Discarders, or swamp monsters, then likely they'd have made it a big part of your lessons. It was Pyramidders who destroyed Modest Mills. And they didn't just destroy the buildings. They destroyed the people. A load of Arbitrators swept out of some low gate, all armoured up like nothing I'd ever seen, all shining darkly like bronze statues, and they tore through the streets with knives and with fire and with chaos and they killed every last citizen.' He lit another roll-up. 'Well. Almost. All but one.'

Billy didn't say anything.

'Maybe you don't believe me. I know what they tell you in this place. I know what they tell you about the Discard. I know how wise and magnificent they appear. I know that what I'm telling you sounds impossible. But it's true. I watched Pyramidders slaughter my friends and family, Billy. I saw them kill little children. I saw . . .' He stopped. 'I won't tell you everything I saw, but it made me very sad, and very angry too, and even though one of the Arbitrators scooped me up and carried me back inside, and even though the Pyramidders fed me and watered me and taught me and bathed me and sheltered me, I stayed angry, and I have been angry ever since, Billy. Even though I met your mother and fell in love I stayed angry. And we had you, and you were such a joy, such a tonic, but I was still angry. And it was being angry that got me exiled. I shouted at people and asked questions and I mistrusted the Teachers, and the work that the Administrators and Alchemists and Astronomers made us all do drove me mad. I told others how Modest Mills had been razed to the ground. I wrote it down. I sang songs about it in the plazas, and when the Arbitrators came and locked me up for singing, I wrote songs about that. And then I sang those songs. The next time they didn't just lock me up, they broke my nose.'

'The Arbitrators don't hurt people, though.' Billy's voice was quiet. 'They're there to help citizens and resolve disputes.'

'When I sang songs about them beating me up, the Arbitrators visited our home. I wasn't in. They scared your mother, they scared you.'

'They're not scary.'

'They can be. They scared your mother enough for her not to let me back in.'

'She said you chose to leave.'

'She was right, in a way. I couldn't see it then but I can now. I should have stopped before it got to that point. Before they threatened her. Before they threatened you. But I kept on causing trouble, breaking rules. That was my choice. And your mother did the right thing.' Alan hugged Billy to him. 'I'm sorry, son. I'm so sorry. I miss you. And I should be here for you.'

'I miss you too, Dad.'

'I'm drunk.'

'You smell.'

'Stupid wild animals do smell.'

'You're not stupid.'

'Billy, I shouldn't have told you all this.' Alan had drunk too much. His judgement had been bad. His judgement had always been bad. And who was he kidding? He spent more or less the whole time having drunk too much. 'You can't repeat it. You can't repeat a word of it. Don't tell anybody what I've said.'

'I won't.'

'Why don't you and your mum come out to the Discard with me?'

'I've already told you, Dad, we're not doing that. It's dangerous out there. There are monsters. I've seen them in the tanks . . . scary men with those horrible bloody horns.'

'I've never seen them out here, Billy. It's not like that.'

Billy spoke carefully. 'I think you must have got some details wrong. You're very drunk, Dad. The Arbitrators aren't like that. It was probably Discarders who burned your town down, everybody knows they're mad.'

'No. Billy, no—'

'Dad, I've got to go. The Arbitrator's back, look.'

Alan realised he'd had his eyes closed. He opened them and saw a tall, masked figure standing in the shadows of the alcove. Billy had got up. Alan stood too, and embraced his son. He took a small parcel wrapped in hessian from his jacket pocket and gave it to Billy. 'It's not an Alchemist's pendant,' Alan said, 'but it's something. Happy birthday, Billy. And tell your mother I love her.'

Billy nodded, blinked rapidly a couple of times, then scurried away past the Arbitrator. He vanished into a shadowed hallway and was once more lost to the Pyramid.

'You'll be wanting your Benedictions, I suppose,' Alan said.

The Arbitrator nodded. He was a good head taller than Alan and dressed in loose, red-brown cloth, with a highly polished bronze breastplate strapped to his chest. He wore a crested bronze helmet with a smooth, convex mask, completely devoid of features but for a horizontal slit across the eyes. Inside the Pyramid, Arbitrators did not carry weapons.

'I don't have them,' Alan said. 'I had them. I acquired them at great personal risk. I went far above and beyond this time, Tromo. But I don't have them any more.'

The Arbitrator neither spoke nor moved.

'But it's the thought that counts, right?'

'Alan. Tell me that this is a lie, or the beginning of some joke.'

'Nope. The Mushroom Queen herself, she tracked me down and set her crazed thugs on me. They were undisciplined fighters and I defeated them, as you can see.' Alan turned his face one way and then the other. 'Not a mark on me. But alas, the vials slipped from my pocket during the tussle and fell into the deeper darkness. And to be frank, your wrath is less frightening than those depths and what may dwell within them. So here I am.' Alan put a cigarette in his mouth. 'With nothing to give you.'

'I will need the Benedictions,' Tromo said. 'Monthly.'

'Ha! Not likely, Tromo. Even Daunt doesn't just have them all in monthly. That's why she's so mad about it. These were rare, difficult to come by, extremely high-value.'

'I know. I know that. How dense are you? That's why I want them, Alan. That's why my associates want them.'

'Can't be done.'

'You don't have a choice.'

'What? Don't yank me about, Tromo. And take off that damn mask.'

The Arbitrator lifted the mask, revealing a lined, elderly face. Chinless. He sniffed. 'It's Troemius-Wylun,' he said, 'and you well know it. Given everything, you should pay me more respect.'

'Refusing to use the stupid names you all have up here is paying you respect,' Alan said. 'It's saving you the embarrassment of having to respond to "Troemius-Wylun".'

'Ever just,' Troemius murmured. 'Ever righteous. Ever ignorant.'

'I do have choices,' Alan said. 'That's what's different about the Discard.'

'Your choice, then, is this. Bring me what I ask for and see your son once a month. Or do not bring me what I ask for and let your son face the consequences of your actions. Again.'

Alan stared at the Arbitrator. 'Blackmail?' he said. 'I don't believe you.'

'You can choose not to believe me, if you want.'

'I thought you wanted to help me see Billy – to help Billy see me. I thought there was an element of compassion in this arrangement.'

The Arbitrator smiled thinly. 'A naïve thing to think. I don't have a particular interest in your relationship. It's a means to an end.'

'So you're just squeezing me for all you can get.'

'The risks I'm taking here are extraordinary and I owe you nothing. If anything, you—'

'Spare me this sanctimonious horseshit, Tromo,' Alan hissed. 'You've made it clear that any risks you take, you take for yourself. And you didn't just save my life back then out of some sense of virtue. It was a transaction, not generosity, and it was a vicious transaction at that. I owe you fuck all. And besides, I thought we'd agreed a price for these visits. I thought this arrangement was fixed and I thought we were being decent about this.'

'We did, and it was, and we were. But you haven't met the terms, have you? And besides, a brothel is not a fitting environment in which to raise a child. You parents *did* run a brothel, did they not? So I didn't just spare you: I gave you the chance of a much better life by bringing you back into the Pyramid. So you *do* owe me for that opportunity, even if you went on to squander it. In fact, in rearranging our deal, I'm being quite generous.'

Alan bit his tongue. He had a knife at his waist and could almost feel it drawing his hand. He turned away from Troemius. As much as the man repelled him, he was the only weak link in the Pyramid's defences, and so the only means by which Alan could see Billy at all. He couldn't risk refusing him, or killing him, or he might never see his son again. He turned back. 'Enough of this reminiscing,' he said, his voice restrained. 'We need to settle on new terms.'

'Agreed. I'll need what you were supposed to give me tonight, monthly.'

'That's impossible.'

'The Discard is very large, Alan, and mushrooms are plentiful.'

'Not those ones.'

Troemius shrugged.

'You're a fucking monster.'

'No. All the monsters live in the Discard.'

'So if I deliver, I get to see Billy monthly.'

'Yes. Or less frequently, should you or he prefer.'

'And if I don't?'

'Then I'll think up something suitably swift and painless.'

'I won't be able to do this, Tromo. I can't – it's just not possible.'

'Yes,' Troemius said, starting to lose interest. 'You are in a bit of a situation. But as they say, desperation is the mother of invention.'

'Do they?'

Troemius shrugged again, smiled his thin smile once more and replaced the mask. He walked backwards away from Alan and disappeared into the Pyramid.

Alan swore. Tromo was a pig. They were all pigs, here. Cold-blooded and dead-eyed pigs. He hopped up onto the wall and looked down. The descent would take time – he would be reaching the bottom in daylight. Most of the way he could scramble and slide, but there were points where he'd have to climb and drop. It wasn't too arduous though, and he knew it well. The alcove where he met Billy was on one of the lowest inhabited floors of the Pyramid, so he was unlikely to meet any Pyramidders on the way. He put his hip-flask to his lips and was disgusted to find that it was empty. He needed to dull the pain of his thoughts.

He coated his hands in chalk from a small pouch at his belt, and began his journey downwards. Hand under hand, foot beneath foot, down the cool black marble.

6

Big Old Lash

Alan took his boots off and splashed cold water from a bucket across his face, hoping to dispel the glue stink from his nostrils. He picked Snapper up off his bed and ran a finger over the fixed neck; he'd done the job himself at Loon's workshop, where there were clamps and glues he could use. Loon herself had been busy at one of the cauldrons, intent upon her own work. She had grunted acquiescence when Alan asked to borrow a bench and buy some glue, but hadn't spoken another word to him. She got like that when she was busy, and she was always busy.

The join in Snapper's neck was ugly, but the glue was dry and it would hold. He'd replaced those strings he had spares for, but that still left him down two. No mind. It would have to do.

He went to the window of his room in the House of a Thousand Hollows. A gang of transients had accumulated around a bucket-fire on a flat rooftop down and across from him. He put his boots back on and went over there with a bottle of Dog Moon in each of his deep coat pockets and Snapper once again on his back. Maybe some of them recognised him, maybe not. Their reactions to his arrival were all shanked by the half-cut toad sweat they were passing around, but they were welcoming enough, especially when they saw the whisky he was carrying. Mostly they just carried on their conversations with each other, a low murmur of voices interrupted occasionally by laughter. One man, all beard, offered Alan a fat snail on a stick to toast, which he accepted. There were snails in every crevice: between the flagstones, in cracks in the walls, creeping over the remaining tiles on the nearby rooftops. Not just on this rooftop: the whole of Gleam was crawling with snails and they were a staple foodstuff for the transients.

Most of them there were topless in the Gleam heat, displaying scrawny and wasted bodies. They smeared the toad sweat into red gums with dirty, calloused fingers. Their skin was red-brown from the sun, and black in the creases. All but one were right gone on the sweat, but then, Alan judged, anyone living their lives under full Discard exposure should be forgiven for wanting to escape them, temporarily, now and again. He twisted the lids from the Moons and passed one off to the left, swigging from the other. The object was to get pissed, steaming, messed up. This wasn't just drinking. This was drinking with intent, and it wasn't as easy as he always made it look.

Above them all, the deep blue sky was made distant by small, pink-limned clouds that floated against it. Striped Satis looked just like a child's ball that had been booted up there and caught fast by the blue; it appeared closer than the white sliver of moon, though this was an illusion. The rooftop on which they all stood was surrounded by other rooftops, most peaked and tiled, but with tiles missing and ivy weaving in and out of the resultant holes. From one ancient window stuck a silver birch, which Alan had often looked at from his own window but still didn't understand the provenance of. Like the clouds the tree too shone pink.

This rooftop was one of several transient crossroads to be found in the environs of the House of a Thousand Hollows. Travellers met around the ever-burning bucket fires to find journey companions, exchange news, trade a little, imbibe a lot and hook up. They were welcome to use the facilities of the House itself if they could pay, but many couldn't, living more of a hand-to-mouth life than House residents, and most of those who *could* pay wouldn't, out of principle. 'Might as well be the Pyramid,' they said.

The bottle of Dog Moon was passed to the one soberish member of the group, a woman with short dark hair and black diamonds tattooed around her nipples, and she addressed Alan as she took it.

'You can use that thing?'

'What thing?'

'On your back.'

'Oh!' Alan lifted the guitar over his shoulder. 'Well, yes. Playing the guitar is almost the only thing I can do. One other thing I can do is sing.' He took another slug from his own bottle and passed it on. 'On a good day I can do both at the same time.'

'Is today a good day?'

'By no means whatsoever.'

The woman smiled. 'What songs have you got?'

'"Black Sheep Shepherd".' Alan tuned the guitar as he spoke. '"The Ladies of Liss". "The Ballad of Modest Mills". "The Pit and the Pyramid". Do you know these ones? "Old Green". Just say if any of these would fill the hole. Are those tattoos from Spider Kurt? I wrote a song about Spider Kurt, called "The Poker". I have some very similar diamonds from him on my inner thighs. "Frogs and Toads". "Rooftop Ruth", also known as "Ruth of the Rooftops". "Dog Moon Thinking". That's another of mine. "Mushroom Queen". Any requests?'

'"The Pit and the Pyramid", then,' said the woman.

'A good slow one for the sunset.'

'Aye,' the large-bearded man chimed in, his voice slurred. '"Pit and Pyramid".'

'You've really been at the sweat, hey? It'll be even slower for you, friend.' Alan ran his fingers over the strings and then put the instrument down. He took his jacket off and rolled his shirt sleeves up. He should have changed his shirt before coming back out. His boots and trousers were still covered in the thick sticky-soft dust from the expanse around the Pyramid. He picked Snapper back up. 'Okay. I'm called Alan, and this is "The Pit and the Pyramid".'

Alan watched the transients as he played. They were watching him back. Most of them swayed in time. He knew what toad sweat was like: the sense of interconnectedness, the feeling that they *had* to move. Everything would seem slower to them than it did to him, as well. It was not an unpleasant intoxicant, and it conferred a peacefulness, mindfulness and warmth that he felt many people could benefit from sometimes. But it was not really a social drug. These travellers were more or less rooted for the night, and there would be no real party on this rooftop.

After the song was done, the group applauded and he drank some more whisky, spilling it down his chin. He started playing another song, feeling like maybe he'd do three before moving on, when he realised that everybody was shouting and pointing to the low wall running around the edge of the rooftop. He looked over and there was something strange poking up beyond it: some kind of long tendril, like the shoot of a new plant. Except it was much larger, the size of a human arm, and it was moving from side to side. Then another appeared, grey-green and shining in the last of the daylight. They looked wet. It took him a moment to recognise them. They kept growing or, rather, more and more of them became visible as their owner neared the lip of the rooftop. This was some specimen.

Soon the horns were towering over them all, bending and swaying as they looked around. They were joined by two more shorter, fatter ones, and then, suddenly, the bulky mass of the snail's body. As it slimed up from the wall, its mouth was briefly visible: a downturned crescent lined with tiny sharp denticles, the only feature on the otherwise blank, smooth underside. Alan had seen some giants, but never one this big. He ran to the wall and looked over.

'Fuck me,' he said.

'Must have come up from the real depths,' the woman said. She was at the wall too. 'It's got a saddle hanging off it. Swampies use them to get around. Some of the traders down there have whole caravans of the things.'

'What's your name?' Alan asked.

'Churr. Look at its shell.'

The snail, now crawling over the wall and onto the roof, had a long shell coiled unevenly to a tip that pointed backwards. It was covered with moss and lichen, and colonies of smaller, ordinary snails were nestled into the dips between coils. Discernible beneath all of the growth and the grime was an intricate pattern in white and red-brown. Beyond the snail, the side of building they all stood on stretched away, a pale yellow expanse vanishing into shadow. The snail's mucoid path glistened: a trail coming up from out of the darkness.

'It picked the wrong rooftop,' Churr observed. 'This'll feed us for weeks.' The group had been swollen by newcomers carrying weapons.

'It's drawing quite a crowd,' Alan said.

'What's it got that you haven't, eh?' Churr said.

'It's that lovely shell. I should acquire one.'

'It's true. You're just a grey old slug. Give me that whisky.'

Alan passed her the bottle. 'I don't want them to kill it,' he said.

'You don't strike me as the squeamish type.'

'It's not that. It's just . . . I bet it's old. It must be so old.'

The snail was crawling along the edge of the rooftop. A long-haired woman with a cruel-looking hooked spear was shadowing it, as was a man with a long, curved knife. The sky was darker now and the snail lit mostly by fire. Its flesh was translucent, glowing orange with refracted firelight. Tubes could be seen within. There were shouts and sounds from nearby rooftops and windows as onlookers gathered. Parents were waking their children and bringing them out, wrapped in woollen blankets.

'You transients must see all sorts,' Alan said. 'You must go down deep sometimes.'

'Not swamp-deep. Really, we stick to established

routes. We go where the trade is, or where we know the pickings to be rich. We survive by foraging, borrowing, buying and selling. I do a good business collecting and selling toad sweat. Easier to do all that by staying up here where the people are.'

'You don't explore?'

'We might be tough, but we're not suicidal. This is the Discard. I mean, do you?'

Alan considered. 'I take your point,' he said. 'So this kind of creature is unusual?'

'Yes, but not unknown.' Churr turned to face him. 'I don't believe you haven't had this kind of conversation with a transient before. About where we go, what we do.'

'I'm just trying to get to know you.'

'Aye, right. And I suppose your motives are entirely honourable.'

'I'm not honourable,' Alan said. 'This is the Discard. I mean, are you?'

Churr didn't say anything. She smiled, folded her arms over her chest and looked away.

The squelches and shrieks of the snail being killed echoed around while Alan and Churr were fucking hard in a room full of small cracked jars that had once contained a kind of ink, judging by the shiny black patina on the floor. Churr had black diamonds all over her and he traced them with his fingertips as she rode him. Whoops and cheers from the roof of the building reached them through the open window, as did the flickering light of campfires and the Gleam torches. The floor was smooth and cool against his back. Churr leaned down to kiss him and he put his arms around her. They moved their hips in circles. Sweat pooled on his belly. She stiffened and shook as she came, and he let himself come too then, his stomach tightening, his hips jerking and his mind filling with white light for all too brief a moment. Afterwards he felt lost again. Churr got up and went to the window. The dried ink on the floor was alive with reflected light. He walked over to her and stood next to her. 'That was good,' he said.

'I thought so too.'

'What now?'

'I need a drink – more drink. Not whisky, though; something long and cold.'

'I know a place.'

'I'm sure you do. But we're not going there, we're going to a place I know.'

'Some dirty, dangerous transient dive?'

'Exactly.'

'Perfect.'

In The Cup and Skull, Alan sank pint after pint, talking little. Churr knew the barman – a big bald man with a long grey goatee and leather jacket – and spoke mostly with him. The light in there was electric and green, and strong-smelling smoke hung thickly in the air. Alan realised after his third drink that he should be spending the evening alone. He thought about the wound on Billy's hand and ordered another.

'What's wrong with you?' Churr asked him.

'Nothing.'

'You've lost interest now we've fucked.'

'No,' Alan said, but as soon as she said it he knew she was right. 'I'm sorry. I shouldn't have got you involved in this.'

'I'm not involved in anything.'

'I mean *me*. This. You should be with some better people.'

'I'm quite capable of choosing my company.'

'I'm not much company, though.'

'No. So. I'll ask again: what's wrong?'

'It's a long story.'

'Summarise.'

'I used to live in the Pyramid. My wife and son still live in the Pyramid. My son is being bullied by his classmates. In a few years the Alchemists will start Bleeding him. I have – *had* – an arrangement with one of the Arbitrators that meant I could visit him, but things have changed.'

'What do you mean, bleeding?'

'In the Pyramid the Alchemists use blood for their magic. They take it from the workers. It's the price the citizens pay for their nice thick walls, I guess.'

'Fucking Pyramidders.'

'Billy won't leave. Marion won't leave. They're safe there, in a way. I can't promise them a life out here. I can't promise that they'll be safe.'

'They prefer the Pyramid, even with the bullying, the Bleeding . . .'

'Yes. So if I were to save them—'

'Who would you be doing it for?'

'Exactly.'

'You can't tell them that they don't know what they want.'

'No. It's insane that they would choose that over the Discard, but the lies they learn in there ensure it.'

'The answer is obvious, Alan.'

'Is it?'

'Let them live the way they want.'

'But he's my *son*. Marion is an adult – she can deal with the consequences of her decisions. But Billy . . .'

'So find a way to stay in touch. Find another way to visit him. Talk to him. Tell him your truths. When he's old enough he can choose for himself.'

'You know what I need?'

'What?'

'Mushrooms.'

'I haven't got any on me, but Pighead probably does.'

'No, I don't mean—? Pighead? Who's Pighead?'

'Barman.'

'Oh. No, I don't mean right now. Actually I could use some right now. But what I mean is, to get to see Billy I need mushrooms. That's the cost of getting in. I used to get mushrooms for an Arbitrator, but now he wants more – more than I can get from my usual supplier. And not just some little efforts from some damp room in the House or something, but the strong ones. And a lot of them.'

'You know, if you're talking about a way into the Pyramid – there are a lot of folks out here who might be interested in helping you out. The Arbitrators are getting a little too bold with their raids, taking people's bugs, taking their livestock . . .' She paused. 'I was talking to a woman at a bucket-fire over near the Hinning House a few months ago. She said they took her brother's neighbour.'

Alan felt the anger stir. He remained silent for a moment. Then he replied, 'No, I'm not getting into the politics of it. This is about my son and only my son. I'm not waging war. I'm not dragging any innocents into my mess and I'm not going to provoke any backlash. I don't need a gang, I don't need an army, I just need some rare and powerful mushrooms.'

'Oi!' Churr shouted. 'Pighead! Got any mushrooms in?'

'Naturally,' Pighead growled. 'Wait a sec.' He ducked behind the counter for a moment and then reappeared. 'I got long-leg bonnets, toadthrone, rustcaps, dream-meat and tunnellers. I'd have more but those damned bandits are getting braver.'

'Dream-meat, I think. Alan? Dream-meat? I know this isn't what you were talking about, but they'll take the edge off another long, hot Discard night.'

'Go on then. And hey, Pighead, you got any teeth? Old Green's Teeth?'

Pighead frowned. 'A couple. Didn't think you were the sort. What, you want 'em?'

'Yeah.'

'You know teeth?'

'Yeah, I know teeth.'

'Why do you want teeth, Alan?' Churr asked.

'Because they're strong. I want out of my skull, Churr.'

'But it's such a pretty skull.'

'The outside of it is okay, I grant you. But inside it's a right mess.'

'Well, you want to get fucked up tonight, that's up to you. But in the longer term – what you're saying is, we need to get our own supply.'

'I hadn't thought that far ahead. But yes, I suppose that is the logical conclusion. And what's this *we*? *Our*? I don't know about that. We've only just met.'

'Maybe Daunt and I have our own history.'

Alan squinted at Churr through the haze. 'Wait. You want to go up against Daunt?'

'That's what it would take, right? That's what we're talking about?'

Alan shifted uneasily in his seat. 'That's what *you're* talking about,' he said. 'This conversation's kind of getting ahead of me.'

'But Daunt *was* your usual supplier.'

'Kind of. I couldn't afford to buy what I needed, so . . .' Alan trailed off.

'You *stole*? From *Daunt*?' Churr tipped her head back

and laughed, more loudly than she had all night. 'Oh, Alan. You poor little thing.'

The night was reshaping itself around him and he hadn't even taken anything yet. 'Daunt and me go way back. We're good friends.'

'Let me clarify things for you.' Churr took Alan's chin in her hand and looked into his eyes. 'You're not Daunt's good friend. You're wrong. You don't know her at all. You're an idiot. You don't mess with Daunt. You're fucked. Okay?'

'Okay,' Alan mumbled.

'You need lots of potent mushrooms for your friend at the Pyramid. You've burned your bridges with the only real supplier in town. Are you rich?'

Alan shook his head.

'You're not rich. So you can't just hoover them up from all the Discard's Pigheads. The only option is to set up our own supply.'

'This *our* again . . .'

'I've got a good eye for an opportunity.'

'I've got my own friends, Churr.'

'Have you got a Mapmaker? I can get you a Mapmaker.'

'A what? No, of course not. We don't need a Mapmaker. Do we?' Alan wrenched his face free of Churr's grip. 'What do we need a Mapmaker for?'

'Getting safely to Dok.'

'What?' Now Alan laughed. 'Firstly, no way am I

tangling with those psycho Mapmakers. Secondly, no way am I going anywhere near Dok. I'm happy in most stinking hellholes, but even I draw the line at Dok. Thirdly – yeah, I stole from Daunt, and maybe that was foolish, but surely setting myself up as her rival would be drawing her attention in a much more obvious and confrontational manner. And you – I like you a lot, and I know you can handle yourself out here in the Discard, but I don't want you putting yourself in all of this danger for my sake.'

'It would be for my own sake.'

Alan stood up. 'Maybe so. But . . .' He trailed off.

'But what?'

'I'd feel bad.'

'I could make you feel good again.'

Alan sat back down. 'It's like you know me really well,' he said.

'You're quite a simple character.'

'Is that so?'

Pighead interrupted, bearing a tray laden with teapots and small cups. 'Mushroom teas,' he said, putting the tray down. 'Dream-meat in this 'un, and Old Green's Teeth in that 'un.' He eyed Alan warily. 'Good luck,' he said, and then returned to the bar.

'The point is,' Churr said, 'you may have your own friends, you may not want me to get hurt, etc., but this is my plan. My idea. My potential profit.'

'Then why aren't you doing it anyway?'

'Maybe I will.' Churr smiled as she poured herself a cup of tea. 'The question is, are we colleagues, or rivals?'

'All I am is drunk,' Alan said. 'You're taking advantage of me. Listen, I'm not committing to anything – not tonight.'

'At the very least acknowledge that if you want to see your son again, you have to somehow secure a supply of mushrooms from Dok.'

Alan nodded. 'I suppose that is the awful boiled-down truth that I was dimly aware of but was hoping to run away from for the night. Yes.'

'The other awful truth you need to confront is that you've pissed Daunt off.'

'She doesn't know it was me who stole from her, though.'

'Doesn't she?' Churr raised an eyebrow. 'Well, that's interesting. I guess I have some leverage.'

Alan paused for a moment. 'I guess you do,' he said, feeling miserable.

'Good. Well done. Now then. Let's drink our tea and have fun.'

'This night isn't going the way I planned it.'

'Maybe you chose the wrong woman to sleep with.'

Alan poured his own tea. It was green with pale flecks floating in it. 'I'm looking forward to this,' he said.

'You're mad, then.'

Alan didn't say anything.

Churr lifted up her cup. 'To Billy,' she said.

'To Billy.'

A writhing mass of pale, arm-thick worms spilled out of the snail when it was cut open. They slithered towards Alan and wrapped themselves around his arms and legs, lifted him up, up, up into the sky. They were utterly smooth and featureless. The shell had been smashed into millions of uniform triangular pieces that formed a pattern when he looked down upon them: an intricate mosaic depicting Marion's face. He laughed to see her again. She was smiling at him in a way that she hadn't since before Billy was born. The mosaic covered the flat, stone rooftop, beyond which was only darkness. When Alan inhaled, the darkness rose up into the sky like black mountains; when he exhaled, the mountains receded once more, as if he were blowing them flat. The remains of the snail crawled across the mosaic, pulled by more worms, like a slug with tentacles, disrupting the pattern of Marion's face.

'Get away!' Alan shouted. 'Get away, slug!' But it either didn't hear him, didn't understand him, or didn't obey him. It left a thick trail of pink slime behind it. The black mountains rose and fell all around. Slowly the worms turned him around so that he was facing upwards. He could hear Marion's voice from below: 'Get the fuck out, swine!' It was a scream, but it sounded distant. A black diamond hovered in the sky like a hole. All around it stars were pinpricks in a purple sheet. The diamond descended towards Alan's face and he saw that it was the entrance to a tunnel. Marion's voice came again: 'I hate you, I hate you, I hate you.' The tunnel was made out of black and white diamonds, receding. It was like looking into a mirror reflecting another mirror. He strained and twisted as much as the worms permitted, but the tunnel curved just enough to prevent him seeing the end of it. The purple of the sky darkened as he inhaled, lightened as he exhaled. The sound of his breath was almost deafening; he could hear it rushing into and out of his lungs, whistling through the narrow passages of his nose and throat, first one way and then the other. He could feel the oxygen filtering through into his blood and the blood moving through his veins. He felt like it was beating against the inside of his skin.

Something was falling down the tunnel; something wet and bright. It sped towards him and he saw that it was a person. She fell out of the tunnel and landed on top of him; she was naked and covered with ink. He was naked too now, somehow. Churr. It was Churr. She slapped him once across the face, and then again. She leaned forward and opened her mouth and cold black ink gushed out of it, all over his face. The ink was ice cold. He pulled her down against him, so that her breasts pressed into his face. He grabbed hold of her buttocks, slid one hand down and around her upper thigh. His fingers, hand and then arm disappeared inside her. She started kissing him but her tongue was a pair of long, rough fingers: Bittewood's fingers. They probed around behind his teeth and in the back of his throat and made him gag. He tried to fight her off but her skin was now fused to his; there was no space between them, and their bodies were gradually melting together. She was sinking through him. He kicked and thrashed but his limbs were bound by the soft elastic of her flesh. He couldn't see or even breathe. All was dark and he was suffocating. Then, in the distance, there was something gleaming: a point of light. It was a torch being carried towards him. The boy carrying the torch drew back his hood.

'Billy,' Alan tried to say, but his voice was muffled and quiet.

'Dad,' said Billy.

'I'm sorry, son.'

'What?'

'I said I'm sorry.'

Alan tried to move towards his son but couldn't. Billy's face was older than Alan remembered it. He walked towards Alan and reached out and gently placed his fingertips on Alan's eyelids and closed them. 'Goodbye, Dad,' he said. 'Maybe we'll all get some peace now.'

Alan leaped forward, got tangled in the bedclothes, and fell sprawling onto the floor. He lay there for a moment, still. He didn't recognise the room. It felt real, though. It had the anonymous air of one of the House of a

Thousand Hollows' rooms for hire. Alan's mouth was dry and his skin was wet. 'Churr?' he croaked. 'Hello?'

Churr was lying face down in the bed. He watched her until he was sure she was breathing. He crept to the sink, but when he tried to turn the tap it just swivelled in its socket and nothing came out. His brain felt like a sick toad. He was hot and couldn't stop shivering. He went to the window and looked out. It was still dark. He had not slept; his experiences had not been dreams but hallucinations. Chimneys opposite the window were expressing long jets of steam in a seemingly random sequence. The steam was bright blue in the moonlight. Sometimes pipes thought long-dead came back to life, suddenly spouting water or vapours. There were some Mapmakers who devoted their lives to tracing working pipes – or even dormant ones – back to their sources to find out what their original purposes were, and who, or what, was keeping them operational. That usually meant going deep down, though, and as far as Alan knew, not many of those fools came back.

His clothes were a sad pile on the floor by the bed. He put them back on, slowly.

On his way out of the room he noticed a half-empty bottle of Dog Moon on top of a low bookcase. The bookcase was full of ornamental crystals, covered with a thick coat of dust. He took the Moon, and then closed the door softly after himself.

7

Eyes Disappointed

'This isn't a good way of dealing with anything,' Eyes said, standing over Alan.

'It's my way.'

'Yeah, I know. That's why you're such a Green-awful mess.'

'Well thank you, Eyes. Now please fuck off. Let's have this conversation when I'm sober.'

'You're never sober, though. That's the point. And show some respect to your elders if you would, you little pisspot.' Eyes rubbed his head and tutted. 'This can't go on. Trust me. I know it well, and you know that I know.'

Alan glanced up at Eyes. The man looked older than he was. His ruined eyes were two red-raw holes in between . . . not crow's feet: turkey's feet. His head was hairless and spotted. His skin was grey and his once-red beard white and untidy. And right now his frown was severe.

'See this face?' Eyes said, pointing at himself with his

thumbs. 'This is how you'll end up. You don't want that now, do you?'

'Don't worry, Eyes,' Alan said, 'I'll kill myself before I ever get as old as you.'

Eyes hit him, hard, across the back of the head. He wore thick rings on his big, gnarled fingers and the *crack* they made against the younger man's skull was followed by silence as Alan folded up. Eyes watched, mouth twisting. He had various tics and his mouth twisting uncontrollably was one of them. 'Sorry,' he said. 'You deserved it, but I *am* sorry.' He fiddled with the buttons of his waistcoat and then put his hands behind his back. Eyes would be visited by trembling fits at times of distress – periods of severe shaking that lasted indefinitely – and he'd always try to hide it from Alan by putting his hands behind his back. The gesture was tantamount to announcing it.

Eyes did not live in the House of a Thousand Hollows but in a rambling wooden shack built on soil rich with humus that, according to Eyes, had once itself been wooden buildings. The shack was one of several nestled against a long, high wall enclosing a flat square space – probably the top floor of a huge building that had somehow lost its roof. The space was vibrant with plant life and smelled of earth and wild garlic. The soil at the far side of the expanse was always damp; rainwater drained towards it, then stayed there. Alan had told Eyes that this place wouldn't last forever, that it would eventually collapse, but Eyes would have none of it.

The place was maybe an hour's travel from the House. The kitchen table was piled high with rhubarb. Alan had come over for some of Eyes' peppermint tea, but so far Eyes was withholding.

'I didn't raise you for this,' Eyes said.

Alan didn't say anything.

'What is it, then? What's the excuse this time? What grand and terrible pain are you trying to kill?'

'It's about Billy.'

Now Eyes stayed his tongue. For a moment. Then he flung his shaking hands into the air. 'Billy,' he said. 'Well, there's not much to say to that. I know it's hard, Alan, but—'

'Actually I don't need your advice, Eyes,' Alan said. 'No "Everybody's got it hard in the Discard" crap. No homilies. No platitudes. I'm only here for some tea, something to clean me out, and then I'll be on my way.'

'And then what? You'll do it all again tonight?'

'No. I've got a plan. Things are going to change.'

Eyes sat down. 'Tell me about Billy. What happened?'

'He's being bullied – but then, that's what happens in there, isn't it? That's how it operates. It's so normal that nobody sees it, but the place runs on bullying and fear. In no time at all they'll be Bleeding him, and then he'll be manning his Station until he's an old husk, and then they'll put him in the gardens to die.'

'But you knew that already.'

'Yes, Eyes, I knew that already. Thank you for your

sensitivity; it is much appreciated.' Alan started chewing at a fingernail and then he said, 'Also, fucking Tromo's wanting more and more before he'll let me see him. He wants these new mushrooms – a kind Daunt had little of, and what she did have, I . . . I lost.'

'Nothing else he wants?'

'Nothing that he's told me about.'

'Why not just kill him?'

'You really are old-guard, Eyes, you know that?'

'I'm not. You're just soft.'

'If I kill him there'll just be another Arbitrator takes his place, and this one'll be a paragon of virtue who I won't be able to bribe at all.'

'Then why not *threaten* to kill him? Blackmail, like?'

'Maybe. Maybe.' Alan thought about it. 'But the whole reason they exiled me in the first place was for my activities and the reason the little wretches pick on Billy is that I got kicked out for making trouble. If Tromo were to talk . . . if I were to make more trouble . . . No, I don't want to risk the Management hurting Billy. Or Marion.'

'So what, then?'

'I'm not going to need your help, Eyes.'

'You don't know how much of my help you need, Alan. That's always been the case. Now talk.'

'Don't try to talk me out of anything.'

'Talk. And I'll brew up.'

'I need to go to Dok.'

Eyes laughed as he hung the kettle over the fire, but Alan just shrugged.

'You mean it,' Eyes said.

'Yeah, I mean it.'

'And you think you don't need my help.'

'You're not coming with me.'

'I'll decide for my own damn self if I'm coming or not.'

'Eyes . . .'

'I know, I know.' Eyes held up his shaking hands. 'I know. But I can still hold a knife. I can still fight. And I can still move sharp enough. It's just the shaking now and again.'

'What about your ointment, though?' Ever since Eyes had had his eyelids ripped off in the dungeons below the Pyramid, he'd had to treat the wounds with a special cream that both prevented infection and solidified into a mask that kept his eyes moist while sleeping. Before the torture, his name had been Guy.

'If I were to come – and it's a big *if*, still – I'd just ask Loon to make up a big batch for me. No problem. The woman's a genius.'

'Will it keep?'

'She'll find a way. But so: if not me, then who're you planning on taking with you?'

'I do have other friends, y'know.'

'Yeah, yeah. You've always got friends, Alan – it's just that none of them last very long. So who?'

'Spider Kurt, if he'll come.'

'What? You, me and Spider? The band? Are we just going on tour?'

'He's tough, though. You know he's tough.'

'Yeah, he's tough. Who else?'

'A transient called Churr. It was her idea. I think she's tough too.'

'All transients are tough.'

'And Churr knows a Mapmaker.'

'Hell.' Eyes found two mismatched glasses, both chipped, and spooned a tiny bit of sugar into each. Alan noticed, and suddenly felt so grateful to the old man that he nearly welled up. But that was probably just the hangover. 'A Mapmaker, eh?' Eyes continued. 'That's probably *too* tough.'

'You ever met one?'

'Not close up, no, and I've never really planned on it.' He ran a hand over his head. 'Probably not a bad idea though, all things considered. Dok, eh?'

'Dok. Yeah.' Dangling from a hook in the ceiling was a net full of small muslin bundles. Alan watched Eyes root through it, bringing each bundle to his nose and sniffing it until he eventually found two that smelled right. These he dumped into a small brown teapot. The kettle started to whistle.

'And what then?'

'What do you mean?'

'You get the mushrooms, you deliver them – all easier

said than done, naturally – and then they don't kill Billy. Then what?'

'Then nothing. That's it.'

Eyes frowned. 'No,' he said, 'that can't be it. You've got an in, and you've got an . . . an *opportunity*. We're talking about the bloody Pyramid here: the monsters who killed your good old mother and father, and they *were* good, too, your mam and da. They'd see this for the gift it is.'

'Don't.'

'And the taxes! The raids! The *kidnappings*, lad!'

Alan shook his head. 'Rumours,' he said.

'You know it's not damned rumours.'

'I lived inside that thing for years,' Alan said. 'I would know if they were spiriting folks away up into it.'

'It's big enough for all sorts to be going on in there without you knowing.'

Alan shook his head, but Eyes was right. 'Look,' he said, 'look, I'm not interested in any of that. Maybe it happens, maybe it doesn't. You and me, we're angry with them for different reasons. I'm angry at what they did to Marion, what they might still be doing for all I know, and what they're doing to Billy. This isn't your fight.' He reached for his glass of steaming tea. 'This isn't political,' he said.

'You know the taxes are real. *Taxes!* That's too grand a word for it. It's just theft. You know the raids are real.'

Alan closed his eyes and drew the fragrant steam up

through his nose. 'That used to be my fight,' he said, 'when I was in there. That was my fight, and Marion and Billy paid the consequences. I'm not going to keep kicking that dog, Eyes. I just want my family to be safe.'

'As long as that Pyramid gets away with doing what it does, no family is safe.' Eyes was gripping the back of a spindly wooden chair, his knuckles turning white.

'Maybe I have to make it explicit,' Alan said, his voice hardening. 'If I have to choose between trying and failing to take down the Pyramid for the sake of the whole damned Discard, thereby putting my family at greater risk, or trying and possibly succeeding to keep just Billy and Marion safe, then I will choose the latter. Do you understand?'

'I understand that you're abandoning your principles,' Eyes said, turning away.

'I'm abandoning *your* principles,' Alan said, 'and it's a decision that I'm comfortable with.' He finished his tea. Usually they shared a whole pot, but not today. 'This hasn't been the pleasant, amiable chat I was hoping for. I apologise.' He stood up.

'No,' Eyes said after a moment. 'I'm sorry, lad.' He let go of the chair. His hands shook wildly. 'I'm just – when it comes to that bloody thing, that bloody Pyramid, I can't think straight. It's just – it's like I hear the word and a door opens inside me and all these monsters come out and they take me over.'

'It's because of what they did to you,' Alan said.

'It's part of what they did to me,' Eyes said, and fell into silence. Alan couldn't remember the older man ever looking so sad and wretched. He went over and embraced him.

'I will help you if I can,' Eyes said, just before Alan left.

'I'm arranging a meeting at the Cavern Tavern,' Alan said. 'Seven o'clock tonight. You don't have to come, but if you do, you'll be welcome. Thank you for the tea.'

8

Spider Kurt

Spider Kurt was bent over the soft, shining flesh of an ageing woman, bamboo in hand. From the end of the bamboo protruded a long, red-tipped needle of bone. The woman shuddered as Spider pressed it into her naked back. He'd split his greying beard into two and then tied the two ends into his long hair so that it didn't tickle her. Through the open window came the distant sound of a deep, insistent drum beat and an accompanying chant.

The wooden floorboards of the long room were almost red beneath layers and layers of varnish. The white walls were just about covered with a mosaic of framed tattoo designs – skulls, flowers, devils, sirens, the planets, snakes, pyramids, crystals. The designs had a certain geometric aspect in common and were mostly made in red and black, but the frames were all different colours and shapes and sizes, some flamboyant and some basic. Various tattooists were at work, the studio quiet but for the music coming in from outside. Each had a workstation with a bed, a stool, their tools and inks, and a display of their own artwork. On each of the beds a customer sat or lay, flesh exposed to the needles. Some of them appeared to be asleep. The room was warm.

The tattooists did not look up as Alan entered, or as he walked past them. There were six: four men and two women, and their concentration was total. The room was hot and three of the men were stripped to the waist, their bodies bright with intricate ink: flowers blooming, hot-air balloons crashing, mare-toads wearing crowns. The room smelled of antiseptic ointment and all of the surfaces were scrupulously clean. Spider always said that it was the cleanest place in the House. Jones wore a tight black blouse and short black trousers. Her hair was jet-black and cut severely straight across her forehead. She had black triangles tattooed on each cheek and a small silver stud in her nose. She primarily did planets and toads – she'd given Alan his last-but-one piece, a frowning yellow moon, top hat askew, on the back of his left hand.

He thought about stopping to speak with her as he passed her station, but she didn't look up and so he hurried on.

Spider's customer was getting a large beetle and mandala across her upper back. The beetle was splayed out as if pinned – Spider had rendered it in almost scientific detail. He was beginning work on the mandala now, a symmetrical pattern that echoed shapes from the beetle. The woman was grimacing, Alan saw, fingers clutching at the soft leather of the bed. She was more elderly than he'd realised. She had long white hair and not many teeth.

'Very nice,' Alan said.

'Thank you,' Spider said. His voice was quiet and deep. 'Take me the rest of the day, though. Come back tomorrow.'

'I don't want a tattoo. Not today, anyway.'

'This'll still take me all day.'

'I only want five minutes, Spider.'

'Well then. We're due a break once I've finished these lines.'

'Well then. I'll wait.'

'That okay, Lucy?' Spider asked the customer.

'Sure, okay by me,' she said. 'Getting tough down here.'

'You're a dream sitter,' Spider said. 'The spine hurts like hell.'

Spider Kurt, tattooist, used combinations of bamboo sticks and bone needle combs to make his art. The combs were complex, delicate arrangements used for long straight lines and shading; the bamboo sticks were handles for the combs. People who paid could commission designs, specifying figures and styles, but he would also tattoo people who couldn't pay, on the condition that the design was entirely of his creation. These were swirling, abstract affairs that could take days to complete, often inked under the influence of vast quantities of strong

mushroom tea; the whole experience was more like some
kind of meditative episode for both Kurt and the tattooee
than a standard sitting. Alan watched him finish the lines
of one half of the beetle mandala. His deep red shirt was
unbuttoned to the sternum, revealing a thick mass of
black chest hair that his beard usually merged with. Visible today were a couple of thick gold chains. Above his
big hooked nose, his brown eyes narrowed as he focused.
The top of his head was bald, but the hair he did have was
long. His fingers were hard and heavy with gold rings.
What was it with older men and gold rings? Kurt was
seated, but when he stood he was tall and almost spookily
thin.

At a signal from Spider, Lucy sat up. She swung her
legs so that her back remained to the two men and walked
over to the window, where she stretched.

'What do you want?' Spider asked.

'I'm going to Dok and I need a fighter.'

'None too shabby with a chair leg yourself, if I remember correctly.'

'You're too kind. But I'm no Spider Kurt.'

'You've got a Mapmaker, I take it.'

'Yes.'

'Payment, then.'

'A share in any profits from the New Dok Trading
Company.'

Spider smiled behind his beard. His eyes shone. 'What
about the Mushroom Queen? What about old Daunt?'

'We'll be rivals. Nothing to worry about. A bit of healthy competition is good for business.'

'They shouldn't call you Wild Alan. They should call you Mad Alan. Snakeshit Crazy Alan.' He coughed. 'Stupid Alan.'

'Are you in or not?'

'Of course I'm in. When do we leave?'

'Can you meet us tonight in the Cavern Tavern? Seven o'clock?'

'I'll be there.'

9

The House of a Thousand Hollows

The House of a Thousand Hollows was a labyrinth, an old beehive, a crumbling ants' nest. It was a warren of overflowing closets and empty attics, busy landings and dusty ballrooms, cobwebbed stairwells and torchlit chambers, forgotten hideaways and lively drinking halls. Corridors made their way through acres of abandoned rooms; they felt like tunnels winding through the earth itself. The House of a Thousand Hollows was a fat, round, stone tower that rose up out of the shadows and murk and kept growing; precarious extensions sprouted from its top, some of brick, the later ones of wood. They hung out over the dizzying drop below, threatening to fall. The House was already big enough to accommodate all those who wished to live there but, Alan reflected, people liked to have their space. Anybody moving into the House from outside might find the idea of sharing a corridor almost oppressive, and so they'd throw a quick shack up on the top. If there was one thing the Discard had plenty of, it was space. Everything else was a struggle. Unless you'd hitched yourself to the right caravan.

There were two other Safe Houses in the Discard – Wha House, and the Hinning House– and all three were topside: big, strong, easily defended buildings. Officially at least, they were in alliance, sharing knowledge and the obligation to support each other in the case of attack from bandits or gangs. Alan didn't know if there had ever been such an attack; generally, Discarders did not have the commitment or discipline for such a thing. It would mean great risk for relatively little reward. It was far easier to obtain bugs or food or liquor just jumping down from some shadowed scaffold and slitting a throat.

Anybody new to the House would get lost, and quickly, but Alan had lived there for four years now and he knew his way around most of it – the parts that mattered anyway: the pockets of inhabitation, the kitchens, the taverns. There were still floors where he'd never set foot, and passages he'd never taken. Nobody used the lower storeys for anything: across much of Gleam, the lower storeys had been given over to the swamp and the things that came up out of the swamp.

As Alan continued down the corridor, the route lit by small, clean torches, his footsteps were muffled by the faded red carpet. He wasn't far from the Cavern Tavern here, which in turn wasn't far from the Sleepless Pavilion or Maggie's own quarters, so the ways were kept in good repair and the torches were replaced regularly. The rooms he walked past were not all occupied, but those that were not were cleaned and left open to air, ready for the next transient, of whom there were many. As well as being a home to many, the House of a Thousand Hollows was a popular sanctuary for travellers: it was a safe haven in a dangerous place. It was food and drink. It was company and, thanks to Alan, it was music, at least for as long as he made Maggie her money.

You couldn't just live in the House. You had to offer something; you had to have something Maggie the Red could use. Bugs were good, of course, but Maggie's web was large and complex, and even Alan didn't know what she got from most of her subjects. Sometimes he worried that his role and his skills were too obvious to everybody else; the House's previous singer, Kate of the Corner, had won her place by knocking her predecessor's teeth out. She was a good performer – certainly the best around, by that point – so Maggie had been happy to have her, whatever her methods for dealing with the competition. But Kate of the Corner had had her belly sliced open by a desperate transient in a rooftop dive-bar after she'd won the last of his bugs in a game of cards. Alan had been at the table that night; he'd wiped the blood from his eyes in time to see the other players turn on the transient and then vacated the scene in a hurry, taking the news of Kate's demise straight to Maggie.

The Cavern Tavern was a great hollow in the western side of the House. A section of the exterior wall had at some point been knocked through, or blown away – as to what by, and when, accounts varied – and part of the floors of four storeys had been destroyed, presumably by the same event. A crater was left in the vertical surface of the House. But for as long as anybody living could remember, this crater had served as a meeting place. A bar had been put in, with barrels of beer and bottles of wine stored in the room below. The rough-edged overhangs that looked down on the space had been turned into balconies. The gaping hole in the wall had been made safer – if not completely safe – by an ornate, cast-iron railing. It now provided a view over south-eastern Gleam, with the Black Pyramid dead centre of the panorama. An ancient honeysuckle curled around the metal. There was a low stage. The huge floorspace was filled with tables and chairs.

The Cavern Tavern wasn't quite busy yet. There were customers, huddled around tables or sitting alone up on the balconies, but the space swallowed their voices. The bar was being tended by one of the Pennydown twins – Quiet Diaz, Alan thought, though he still was never sure, even now. His brother would join him later, when it got busy.

'Evening,' Alan said, putting his elbows on the bar. 'Diaz, is it?'

'It is,' Quiet Diaz replied. He betrayed no intention to move. His small eyes were steady and his little mouth flat. His features were all clustered in the middle of his gigantic, pasty, hairless head, and they were not amused. He wore a long, loose black shirt that hung almost to his knees and stood with his arms folded, his hands hidden in the voluminous sleeves. He looked like the Black Pyramid itself, but with a big pale melon stuck up on the point of it.

'What do you want?' Diaz said.

'As if you have to ask.'

'Dog Moon.'

'See? You already know.'

'Stuff's disgusting.'

'It's cheap.'

'It's whisky for tramps and idiots.'

'The name's Wild Alan.' Alan held out his hand. 'Pleased to meet you.'

Quiet Diaz's mouth curved into a small, derisive smile, as if of its own accord. 'You're joking,' he said, 'but you're bang on.'

'Look,' Alan said, leaning in and lowering his voice, 'I like Dog Moon actually, and what I like about Dog Moon is that, although it tastes like shit, it burns like hell. The burn is what I want. I *want* the burn, Diaz. I am all about the burn. And, anyway, I don't give a fuck what your opinion is on anything. Now serve me, quickly, and then we can stop talking to each other.'

The little smile on that giant face turned into a deep frown and Diaz turned away, his movements languid. Alan was sure that he was moving slowly just to irritate him. Diaz took a glass from a shelf and reached for an open bottle of Dog Moon.

'No,' Alan said, 'not a glass. A bottle. A bottle, man. What do you take me for?'

Diaz looked at him for a moment. 'You don't want to know,' he said, before reaching under the counter for a full bottle of Dog Moon and plonking it on the counter. 'How many glasses?'

'Five. And make it two bottles, actually.'

Alan took the bottles and the glasses and deposited a handful of bugs on the bar, their shells iridescent in the light of the sunset. 'Thank you,' he said, and turned away.

He sat by the railing for the view, and for what little breeze there was. Gleam was either warm or it was hot, and tonight it was hot. Hot and humid. Steam rose up from the swamp, as did fireflies, small, skittish lizards and the smell of green.

Beyond the window, the air was alive with the buzzing of insects and the cries of birds. No human voices, though. The House was unusual in that it had space around it; most buildings in Gleam were at least squashed up against each other, if not actually conjoined. But the House rose alone. It was connected lower down, but only by bridges. There was some distance between the House and the closest structures, which were nameless, as far as Alan knew. They were round towers, like the House, but smaller, and they were swaddled in rusted pipes. The setting sun turned them pink. Flocks of white birds flew around them, tiny in the distance.

Spider arrived first, as silent as ever, carrying his battered old violin case. He folded himself into the chair opposite Alan and nodded before taking a glass and filling it. He knocked the drink back, repeated the process, wiped droplets of whisky from his tangled black-and-white beard and spoke.

'All right?' he said.

'Yes, thank you. And you?'

'I'm all right.' Spider entwined his fingers together. 'Thought we could put on a show afterwards.'

'Well, we've got to earn our keep.'

Spider raised his eyebrows. He was wearing a severe black suit that made his skin paler and the bags under his eyes darker. It was something that Alan, Spider and Eyes had settled on way back: formal wear at all times, but wear it how you will. He lit a roll-up and put it in his mouth.

Eyes arrived soon afterwards, preceded by the scent of his strong-smelling ointment. He clapped Alan on the back and threw himself into a chair. 'Lads,' he said. 'Lads, lads, lads.' He reached for the Dog Moon with a shaking hand and poured himself a glass, which he sipped. He wore a visor to keep the sweat from his eyes. 'Is this Churr meeting us?'

'Yeah,' Alan said. 'And the Mapmaker.'

Spider and Eyes looked at each other. Spider laughed. 'A Mapmaker? Coming into the *House*?'

'Yeah.' Alan felt like he was shaking as much as Eyes was.

'You ever met a Mapmaker, Spider?' Eyes asked.

'Not really.'

'Maybe they're not that scary,' Alan said.

'Aye, right.' Eyes laughed.

'What's the plan, then?' Spider asked.

'Really we need to wait for Churr. It was her idea originally. We were talking about my visit to the Pyramid, and how Tromo wants more mushrooms than I can buy or steal. Churr has some kind of history with Daunt that I don't know about, and she saw that we have a mutual interest in getting to Dok and stocking up, even setting up our own trade route.'

'If it was that simple then everybody'd be at it,' Eyes said. 'Daunt has serious muscle.'

'We're going to start off small, though. Firstly, we need to just get to Dok and back, with enough mushrooms for me to see Billy and for Churr to make some bugs. Daunt won't even know about it. Then I guess Churr will start ramping things up. Our involvement at that point is moot. I don't know what she's thinking, or what you're thinking, or even what I'm thinking.'

'What's in it for the Mapmaker?' Spider asked, making roll-up after roll-up and lining them up on the table.

'I don't know.'

'That's probably something we should establish.'

'It's a friend of Churr's.'

'Mapmakers don't have friends. It would be interesting to know how they know each other.'

'We'll ask her,' Alan said. 'So, Eyes, are you in?'

'Yeah, I'm in. Dok might be hell, but it's a hell I haven't been to yet.' He stole one of Spider's smokes and lit it with one of the small candles from the middle of the table. 'Besides, who knows what havoc we could wreak inside the Pyramid?'

'What do you mean?' Alan asked.

'We could give them any old shite, Alan! They won't know the difference. They say there're rivers of poison in Dok. There'll be all kinds of toxic mushrooms down there. Stuff that could cause them real damage.'

'No, I told you, we're giving them what they want. I'm not risking trouble with the Arbitrators. I'm not risking the safety of my family, Eyes. No. No. *No.*'

Eyes smashed his fist into the table. 'Then fuck you, Alan!' He hit the table again and glasses fell over, rolled, hit the floor and smashed. 'This is *the Pyramid* we're talking about! The fucking Pyramid! You getting to see Billy, yeah, well that's fucking great, but what about everything they've done to us?' He was standing up now. 'We're not aiming high enough, laddie! In fact, fuck Dok. Let's aim for the Pyramid direct. Get Billy and Marion out. Get all the good ones out, if there *are* any other good ones. Kill the rest. But is Marion even good, now? Can you say that? Isn't she one of *them* now?'

Alan stood up too, and back-handed Eyes across the face.

'Oh, that's rich,' Eyes said, smiling through the nose-bleed, 'coming from you. Don't tell me you still love her – not you, with a different squeeze every night, you. Who was it last night? You still into women, or are you back on to lads again? Might as well move right into the Sleepless Pavilion, earn your keep that way. You must be pretty good in the sack by now, whoever knocks on the door. What would Marion say if she knew? You think me questioning her allegiance is worse than what you do again and again and again? Aye, right.'

Every muscle in Alan's body was tense; his hands were fists and his knuckles were white. Eyes was grinning at him, blood all over his wrinkly face. He looked completely mad, especially with those red eyes and the thick ointment around them. He *was* mad. He'd been mad ever since he came back from the Pyramid dungeons.

Spider carefully finished off another roll-up and refilled his glass. 'Sit down, Alan,' he said.

Alan sat back down. 'I shouldn't have hit you,' he said. 'I'm sorry.'

Eyes had the trembles badly now. Alan felt sick. What the Pyramidders had done to Eyes in the dungeons beneath didn't bear thinking about. His eyelids had been only the beginning. It was no wonder the old man harboured such anger. He did well not to surrender to it wholly. And Alan owed him so much – his life and more.

But still. Times like this, Eyes' words cut him right down to the bone. It was because there was truth in them.

'I miss Marion,' Alan said, 'and yes, I still love her. I haven't seen her in four years, but I love her, I love the Marion I knew. Maybe she's changed, but there's no reason to believe that she's changed so much.'

'Funny way you've got of loving a soul, is all.' Eyes wasn't appeased, not yet.

Alan looked at him levelly. 'Eyes, Marion kicked me out. You know that. She doesn't want me. Let me find what echoes of the love we had where I can.'

Spider had drifted off to the railing after sitting Alan back down. Now he turned around. 'Are they going to show?' he asked.

Alan didn't know. 'Yes,' he said.

'You should get 'em out of there,' Eyes said, pinching his nose. 'Billy and Marion. I'm not talking about causing trouble. I'm talking about finding another way. Dok . . . I've been thinking. Dok is bad, Alan. Dok is the worst. No fucker goes there for a reason. Every fucker's scared of it.'

'That's how Pyramidders see the Discard, though. Billy and Marion – they wouldn't come with me. Nobody leaves the Pyramid of their own accord. You don't know what it's like in there, Eyes – the things kids are told about the Discard. The horrors they're warned of as they grow up. The beasts they believe are lurking just outside the Pyramid. Imagine: you are kept warm and safe, you are fed and watered, you have gardens and fountains in which to wile away your spare time, and you know that when you are old you will be looked after. You are blessed. You are lucky. To leave the Pyramid for the Discard is to throw all that security away for a life of desperation and uncertainty: a life of raw snails, undercooked toad-meat and venomous snakes; a life spent hiding from bandits and cannibals – and worse things, inhuman things. They have creatures from the swamp kept alive in great glass chambers up there, exhibited for all the Pyramidders to see, to show them what they'd be up against. Weird things, the like of which I've never actually seen since I was kicked out.' Alan shook his head. 'People with ten legs. Men and women with twisted horns and dead eyes. Heads on a torso like garlic on a rope.'

'The Horned,' Spider said. 'I've heard of the Horned. I didn't think any had been seen in decades, though. There used to be reports – I remember my uncles telling me – reports of the Horned from deep down. I had one uncle – he had his teeth filed into fangs and played the hurdy-gurdy. I thought he painted his face white but apparently he had some kind of condition. He spent a lot of time on the lower levels . . . What was his name? He told me about the Horned. Told me he hunted them in return for spirit salves, potions he said sent him a long way from his own body. Uncle Staniforth! That was it.' Spider took a long drink. 'He was a funny one.'

Alan waited to make sure Spider had finished before saying, 'Well, exactly. So I rock up at the meeting place, Billy's lanky old dad, with his shitty guitar and dirty hair, and say . . . what? Come with me, son! It's a better life out here in the Discard, out here in the Factory wilds, with our Horned and our Uncle Staniforths – who sounds delightful, by the way. Yes, it's dangerous, and yes, it's dirty, and yes, you will have to eat toads, and sometimes there won't even be toad, and no, you won't always have a roof over your head, and it does rain, yes, it rains hard, and yes, there are cannibals, and thieves, and gangs, thugs, killers – worse, dangerous snakes, yes, horrible insects, crocodiles and worse, still worse . . .'

'Wouldn't you have left?' Spider asked. 'Of your own accord?'

'Probably.' Alan put a cigarette in his mouth and lit it. 'But I knew things.'

'Why don't you tell Billy those same things? Why don't you explain the cost of Pyramid living? What it really is. Tell him what happened to you, to your parents. Tell him what they did to Eyes.'

Alan exhaled thick white smoke and narrowed his eyes against it. 'He's only six. Too young. And besides, we never have much time.'

A boy carrying a tray laden with empty glasses hurried past the table, but Eyes stopped him with a hand to his arm. ''nother Dog Moon, boy, if yer please,' he said. The boy nodded wordlessly and rushed off, sweat running down his face. The Cavern Tavern was full now, and really hot. Alan was glad of the window seat.

'When they exiled me I thought that was it,' he said. 'I thought I'd be dead within the week. Something else I owe you two for.' He looked up from his tumbler and smiled, then raised the glass. 'To you two,' he said. 'To my friends. To the band.'

Spider and Eyes echoed his words and downed the spirit. Spider winced. 'Rough stuff for necking,' he said. He refilled his glass once more.

Eyes fished a small clay pot of ointment from his trouser pocket and smeared some of the oily grey substance into his dry red eyes. 'Going to have to pick up my job lot,' he said.

'Go soon,' Spider said. 'The swamp's squeezing the bandits, so banditry's on the up. Traders say there's disruption on the way. They reckon the House won't be much better-provisioned than the rest of the Discard before long.'

'Well.' Eyes screwed the lid back onto the pot. 'Nothing keeping us here then. When are we heading for Dok?'

'Depends on our erstwhile conspirators,' Alan said. 'But let's prepare to go soon. The day after tomorrow.'

'Then I'll pay Loon a visit in the morning,' Eyes said decisively. 'Alan, we know more about Dok than Pyramidders know about the Discard. You know that. Come on – this Churr, she's got into your head. I'm not wagging my finger here. Who and how you love, that's up to you. But if you think we can really do this . . . I want to. I do. But I don't know. I don't know if even with a Mapmaker it's a good idea. I think it's not a good idea, Alan.'

'I'm inclined to agree,' Alan said. 'But I've run out of good ideas. As for Churr, things are complicated. I'm not infatuated. But she has . . .' He looked down into his drink. 'She has leverage.'

Neither Eyes nor Spider said anything. When Alan raised his head, he saw them looking at each other, eyebrows raised. 'Shut up,' he said.

'Nobody's saying anything,' Spider said.

'Kid,' Eyes said, 'we don't want to know.'

'What it boils down to is this: you don't have to come. But I'm going.'

'I am thinking of accompanying you,' Spider said, 'because I have an academic interest in certain plants and substances, thought lost to the swamp, which may yet exist in Dok, it being so proximate to the swamp itself. I am still in two minds, however, so don't bank upon my company just yet. I have appointments that I would need to cancel – appointments I am loath to cancel.'

Alan nodded. He tried not to let on how desperate he was for Spider's assistance: the man's reputation as a fighter was fearsome, but unlike most other famous fighters in the House or its vicinity, he had an aura of calm that almost negated Eyes' nerves.

'Something else I wanted to ask you,' Alan said.

'Unrelated. Daunt's got a new pet. Some beast called Bittewood. Have you heard of him? More of an *it*, really, but let's be kind.'

'Never,' Spider said.

'Same,' Eyes said.

'Not a known thug, then. He doesn't seem sharp or . . . *spiritual* enough to have come from the tribes. Maybe a transient, but again, probably not sharp enough. Maybe a bandit.'

'The swamp's throwing all kinds up these days,' Spider said.

Alan felt again those fingers in his mouth and shuddered. *The swamp*. His mind wouldn't linger too long on the swamp; it always skittered away from it like a startled lizard. But soon enough that wouldn't be an option. He watched small lights moving out over the Discard – lanterns and torches. The sides of the Black Pyramid were now peppered with glowing apertures. Somewhere in there were his son and his wife. He hoped they'd be happy to see him, when the time came. 'Never mind, then,' he said. 'Let's wait for Churr and this Mapmaker and drink.'

Spider lifted his scuffed violin case up onto the table. 'Let's play,' he said, 'and wait, *and* drink.'

10

Arbitration

The audience was drunk and raucous. There was clapping and cheering, condensation dripping down the whitewashed walls, the smell of liquor thin in the air. Alan looked out over them as Eyes got comfortable at the drum-kit behind him. A crowd of outlaws, misfits, loners and freaks. There were faces he recognised, people who made the House of a Thousand Hollows their home, their community, and then there were transients, drawn to the House looking for hot food and a roof over their heads, for once. The amps clicked and buzzed as Spider plugged in two mics, one for Alan and one for Snapper – a rare treat, thanks to Maggie letting them use the House's generator. Spider swayed back and forth over by the amps, generating feedback, and as it merged with the sound of the crowd, Alan felt his breastbone begin to resonate, and grinned. Eyes was adjusting the drums, bringing the hi-hat in a little bit, lowering the stool, absentmindedly running his sticks over the skins. Spider handed Alan his guitar and he took it in both hands, then lifted the strap over his shoulder. He waited until he could hear Spider's violin and plucked a string. It sang out clear, falling into Spider's swirling notes in just the right place. There was a structure to the music, a pattern; they just had to find it – and then it happened: they were there. It felt like magic as his fingers danced up and down the neck. His playing was clean, even if the amps were fuzzy.

He moved back to the microphone and looked out across the bar. The whisky was hot in his belly. People were gorging themselves on Maggie's chilli now, great red bowls of the stuff, cooling their throats with copious quantities of beer, but a few of the regulars had started stamping their feet in time to the beat that had emerged from the tumbling notes. It was fast and low, a version of Black Pyramid that always went down well.

They were three songs in when the first scream rang out. The music faltered and Alan opened his eyes. He gazed around the newly silent room. The oblivion he'd been working towards vanished. There were strange new people in the room. They looked familiar, but they were in utterly the wrong context and so he couldn't put a name to them. Not at first. Then – *Arbitrators*. Fucking Arbitrators. And that one there, behind the bar, standing where Quiet Diaz had been, all red with fresh blood, was lifting its arm at him, Alan, and putting a megaphone to its lips.

'If your players surrender themselves,' it said, its magnified voice raspy, 'we'll leave you in peace.'

The crowd were all staring at him again, but now with very different expressions on their faces. Arbitrators stood all around the room, bows pointing at particular members of the audience, holding them hostage.

'What have we done?' Alan said into the mic, but not confidently enough. He sounded weak. He cleared his throat and spoke again. 'Why do you want us?'

An arrow flew into and through a fat man's neck. He gurgled, flailing about, splattered chilli everywhere, then and fell off his stool and out of sight. A moment later blood fountained up, followed by more screams, and the room erupted. Tables overturned as half of the room rushed towards the stage and half ran roaring at the Arbitrators.

Alan gripped the mic's wire in his fist and swung the mic around. It looked like a vertical black disc, just hovering there, but when the first stage invader – a gaunt, long-haired man with silver hoops in his ears – scrambled up onto the low wooden platform, Alan let the mic fly and it crunched into Long-hair's mouth. He fell backwards, spitting teeth. Alan didn't have time to gather it back up all the way – more audience members had turned Arbitrator and were clambering over Long-hair to get at him. They'd probably never liked him anyway. He wanted to look up and see how the rest of the crowd – the good ones – were faring in their fight against the Pyramid scum, but he couldn't.

He cracked another bastard in the temple with his makeshift mace and wrapped its cable around the neck of another, then he realised that Eyes and Spider were at his side and Spider was thrusting something into his hand. The knife was long and curved and vicious and *perfect* – perfect for fighting the enemy, at least. Not fellow Discarders.

'I don't want to use this!' he shouted, brandishing it in front of him. 'Not on you. Fuckers, *listen* to me! We're the Discard! We don't—'

He was interrupted by the whistle of an Arbitrator arrow, and then a beefy woman with sunburned arms smashed a pint glass over his head. '*No!*' he wailed. He tried to smack the side of her head with the flat of the knife but it twisted in his hand and cut her deeply across the face. He felt it stick on her cheekbone and the sensation ran through his hand and his arm all the way down to his stomach, where it felt like nausea. She went down and he stepped backwards, using the knife as a threat, as a shield.

Eyes appeared to be suffering similar reservations, but not Spider. He was stabbing and slashing and running people through without even blinking, without even breaking a sweat. He had a knife in each hand: not curved, like the one he'd given Alan, but straight and razor-sharp. Eyes was armed with a small wood-axe, but he was using the back of the head like a club.

Who were these arseholes coming for them? Did

they not see that if they worked together, they could easily overpower the Arbitrators? Were they so craven? So traitorous?

A man came at him with a chair leg; Alan ducked, cracked his attacker's knuckles with the knife and then, once the man had dropped the chair leg and was grasping his broken hand with his good one, Alan stood up and kicked him hard in the bollocks. The man doubled over and Alan got him on the back of the head with the knife hilt. With each blow he landed he felt less guilty – the adrenalin, maybe. Ultimately he had to defend himself, whether he was being attacked by Discarders or not. Spider was moving methodically, gracefully, ruthlessly, and then suddenly nobody was attacking Spider any more. They'd got the message. That was the way to do it: scare the bastards away.

But, in truth, the crowd was in chaos. Now that the band members were defending themselves properly, the rush to get them had slowed. And the Arbitrators were beating their way in from the back; those who'd been eager to capture the performers were being crushed by others who were just trying to get away from the merciless, well-trained attentions of the Arbitrators. Those Arbitrators without bows had an array of other weapons attached to their belts – cudgels, knives, and short-swords – and they were employing all of them enthusiastically; those with bows were no more restrained.

Had the Discarders been single-minded, they could have given the Arbitrators a good run for their money. Had they been prepared, and sober, and single-minded, the Arbitrators wouldn't have stood a chance. You didn't get by in the Discard without learning how to fight. But they'd been taken by surprise in a safe place; they were drunk, confused and divided – it was a rout, and a bloody one. Dead House inhabitants lay everywhere, slain by arrows, by blades and by trampling feet. It wasn't impossible that some of the more experienced and less particular Discarders – and Green knew there were a few of those – had taken the opportunity to settle old scores.

Alan surveyed the damage from the rear of the stage, where he had his back to the wall. Spider, next to him, gave him the side-eye. 'Don't think because they're Discarders that they're your friends. We're not all on the same side.'

'Should be, though,' Alan said.

'Why? Most Discarders couldn't care less about the Pyramid. Many would like to live in it. They don't feel like you do. Remember that.'

The tall helmets of the Arbitrators were getting nearer, closing in on them. 'I don't know why they want us,' Alan said. 'If it's because of me, I'm sorry.'

'The way Spider fights, it ain't no problem,' Eyes said. 'Just let him kill 'em all.'

Spider shook his head. 'We can't win this one,' he said.

'Close combat I can do. Close combat with an arrow in my leg – no.'

'You reckon they want us alive, then?' Eyes asked.

'If they wanted us dead, they could have done it more easily than this.'

'They're not having me alive again,' Eyes said. He was as white as his shirt and shaking like a leaf. 'Not this time. Not this time. Give me a knife, boys, to turn on mesel'.' His knees went. 'Fuck,' he said. 'These fucking bastards. Look what they've done to me already.' Alan tried to help him up, but his legs wouldn't take his weight. 'Let me just sit here. Leave me be here on the floor. If I didn't have such a tremble I'd play dead, that's what I'd do. Here – give me a knife so I don't have to play at it.'

The Arbitrators beat down the remnants of the audience and finally emerged into full view of Alan, Spider and Eyes. They stood in a solid semicircle just before the stage, their armour spattered with blood. Their tall helmets gave them the air of strange, long-necked creatures. Moans and coughs filled the air. The room stank of blood and vomit.

The Arb with the megaphone stalked through to the front. The plumage of his helmet was silver; all the others wore blue feathers in theirs. He had somebody with him, held in a headlock: the serving boy, just a kid.

The Arbitrator pointed at Alan again, but with a sword this time. 'Alan. You and your companions are to come with us back to the Pyramid.'

'For what? Is this an arrest? What have I done?'

'An arrest? No.' A raspy laugh. Alan thought the voice was male – more likely male than female, anyway – but he couldn't be entirely sure. 'Use your brain, worm. We cannot arrest anybody in the filthy Discard, because in the filthy Discard there are no laws and we have no jurisdiction. This is not a legal operation, worm. This is a strike. A seizure. A kidnapping.'

'Somebody must want me for a reason, though.'

The Arbitrator didn't speak. Its face was invisible behind its mask, and so its expression could not be read.

'You don't know, do you?'

Raspy spoke again. 'Take them,' it said. 'Alive.'

The Arbitrators moved slowly forward, swords drawn. Their lack of speed wasn't down to caution, or fear: it was entirely deliberate. Their steps were perfectly synchronised. Down where he was on the floor, Eyes wrapped his arms around his head and moaned.

The way they'd handled this did not bode well for their expedition, should they ever get to go.

One of the Arbitrators reached over its shoulder and drew forth what looked like a bag of some sort, but then it passed it to its colleague on the right and when it took hold of it, Alan saw that it was in fact a very finely webbed net. They spread the net out amongst themselves, each holding it with their left hand whilst keeping their blades in their right. Once the net was distributed, they stood still. They were about six feet away.

'Throw down your weapons, Discard scum,' Raspy said into the megaphone. He had the point of his sword pressed against the boy's stomach. The boy's shirt was soaking wet with either sweat or spilled drink. A pale pink blossom marked where the sword's tip had already broken his skin. 'You've got enough blood on your hands already, don't you think?'

Alan felt as shaky as Eyes looked. He glanced around the room, his gaze settling on nothing. He didn't know what he was searching for. A way out of this? But there wasn't one. And Raspy was right: there was blood everywhere.

'You did this,' Alan said quietly, 'not us.'

'You tell yourself that if you must. Soon you won't be able to deny the consequences of your actions, or of your words. Now. Put your knives down.'

Alan knelt down and put his knife on the floor. Spider followed suit. Eyes had already dropped his axe.

'Hands on the back of your head.'

They complied.

The Arbitrators resumed their approach. Alan found himself watching their feet as they got closer. In the Pyramid the Arbitrators went barefoot or wore light strappy leather footwear, but they'd donned boots for their sojourn into the wild. They were less of an advantage than they'd thought, most likely; they were obviously more worried about getting moss or insects on their skin than they were about speed or balance.

Not that their lack of speed or balance had thwarted them in any way.

By the Builders, they were fucked. What a mess. And still Alan didn't know for what. He was staring at the Arbitrator's boots in front of him, right in front of him, racking his brains, when he suddenly felt something brush past his head and his view of the boots was obscured by a tattered grey cloak.

Between him and the Arbitrator stood a short cloaked figure with its hood up. The Mapmaker? The newcomer's arms hung at its sides, but its hands were empty of weapons, though the nails were long and curved and wickedly sharp. They were painted pale green: the green of lichen, of verdigris. Chunky, skull-shaped rings of the same colour and others – pastel pink, silver – decorated the fingers.

The blocked Arbitrator laughed. 'What is this? A child?' The laughter was picked up by the others.

Alan's heart sank. Not salvation, then. He tensed his legs to jump up and swing the child – a girl, judging by the hands – behind him. If she wasn't in the way, then perhaps they wouldn't hurt her. Perhaps.

Then the first Arbitrator to laugh started screaming. Something wet and warm drenched Alan's head and face: a shower of blood. The girl was gone, and so was the Arbitrator's face. He staggered around, his skull in full view, clutching at his ripped throat. Alan stood up. The girl was leaping from one Arbitrator to the next, landing on each like a cat might before swiping at their throats with her now gory hands. She wasn't blocking any blows directed at her, merely sliding out of the way like something inhuman, like oil. The blows landed instead on the Arbitrator she'd just leaped from. She was standing on shoulders, hopping from the tops of helmets, somersaulting in mid-air, surrounded at all times by a fine mist of Pyramidder blood.

Her hood was down. Her pale blonde hair was cut into a severe fringe across her forehead and the sides of her skull were shorn to the same line. A heavy plait whipped around her head. She'd smeared pink dye into the skin surrounding her large eyes and was shining red up to the elbows. A high-pitched humming sound vibrated through the air. Alan thought maybe it was coming from the girl, but he couldn't be sure. She was moving too fast for him to make out her facial expression with any certainty, but he thought she was smiling.

Raspy was bellowing at his subservients, but they weren't listening. Two archers shot at the girl but their arrows sank into the flesh of her target instead. Then she was on one of the archers, sitting on its shoulders. She ripped its helmet off, revealing a woman's face, and stuck her thumbs deep into the woman's eyes. She roared and staggered backwards, slipped on something and fell. The attacker placed her hands on the top of her victim's head as she went over, rose into a handstand and cartwheeled forwards.

Alan shook himself and grabbed his knife. Eyes and Spider had already rejoined the fray and those Arbitrators left standing were looking decidedly shaky. Alan clambered on top of a table to see where Raspy had got to; he was at the side of the room, holding the megaphone to his face as if he were about to speak but saying nothing. The boy was gone. Alan jumped onto the next table and booted an empty pint pot in Raspy's direction. It was an unexpectedly accurate shot, but Raspy ducked and the glass shattered harmlessly against the wall behind his head. But Alan came up fast behind it and pounced on Raspy as he stood back up. He grunted through the mask as they both went down. He had his sword in his right hand but his right arm was pinned beneath him. Behind them Alan could hear more movement, and shouts, crunches, gurgling, screams, and then more screams. Alan straddled Raspy, hilted him in the wrist and took the sword away as Raspy's fingers spasmed open. He slid it under Raspy's breastplate, increased the pressure, felt something give and heard Raspy groan. But he couldn't do it. Not now, not like this. This wasn't self-defence.

'You're a worm,' Alan breathed into Raspy's ear. 'You're a Green-damned maggot.' He withdrew the sword and placed it against the prone man's neck. The sounds of combat had stopped, but Alan could hear dripping. Lots of dripping. He took Raspy's mask off. Beneath the mask was a middle-aged man, pale, sweaty. He was looking at something behind Alan. His eyes were wide and his lips were wobbling, as if he was about to cry.

'What just happened?' he whispered. 'What the fuck just happened?'

Alan made sure not to turn around. He leaned in and forced a big, merciless grin. 'This is the Discard, son,' he said.

II

Blood Drunk

It was as if all of the alcohol that had been in the blood that ended up flooding the Cavern Tavern had somehow got into *him*, Alan thought. He was staggering and reeling; he did not know where he was. He hadn't wanted anybody to die – but then, nobody did, did they? Nobody really wanted that, did they? All of the death had intoxicated him in a thoroughly unpleasant fashion. It was like the *end* of drunkenness: the fuzziness of sounds, the swirling rooms, the desperate trying and failing to make sense of things.

He was sick, and sick again. Vomit splattered down a stairwell and sprayed against a wall. He was *not* drunk; this was the bodily aftermath of being exposed to so much sudden and gory death. He was trying to get away from it. Not to escape justice – just the scene of a kind of violence he'd never dreamed of before. Though that wasn't strictly true. He *had* dreamed of it, of course. His dreams were full of such horrors. And the real horror of his dreams was that he was the *cause* of it. And here he was, in reality now, the cause. His body was moving but his mind was not controlling it because his mind was paralysed with remorse. It was like a toad, frozen prior to being cooked.

He was talking. 'We can't do it,' he was saying. 'We can't go on. We're not doing it. No death. No killing. No death. I am not a killer! We're just . . . It's over. It's over.'

Cool hands rested on his face. Large green eyes were burning out from a blaze of pink, staring into his own. 'You did not do this,' said a voice. 'The Pyramid did this. This is what the Pyramid does. It did it to your parents when you were a child, and it will do it to your child now you are a parent. This will keep happening, Wild Alan, until somebody stops them.'

Alan could not remember what he said in return, though he was sure that he said something.

The other voice continued, 'Your family, then. Your family only. Not the Pyramid. Your family. Do not run. You cannot just keep running. You must do what you promised to do. And if there is any more death, it will not be your doing.'

He spoke again. Words that were straight away lost to him.

'If you do not do this, there will be death. That is the alternative. And not just any death, but your son's. That is the balance you must weigh.'

Alan shook his head. 'A drink,' he said. 'Get me a drink.'

'Is that what you need?' the voice asked. 'To cope with the consequences?'

Alan nodded.

'Then that's what we'll get you.' The cool hands stroked his hair. 'When you feel as if the remorse will slow you down, you need to stamp on that remorse. Use your willpower. Use the whisky. However you do it, you must do it. Come, now. We all have our own ways of coping. There is no shame in trying to dull the pain sometimes.'

Somebody put a bottle in his hand.

'Especially if the pain is slowing us down.'

He took a drink.

'There is no shame in it at all.'

12

Exile

Maggie had no grand chamber, no throne-room, nothing like that. Instead she invited Alan, Eyes, Spider, Churr and the newcomer to attend her on the Old Roof: that is, the stone roof of the original building, which these days had several stilted storeys, wooden platforms and scrappy dwellings teetering above it.

They exited the elevator tower and crossed the roof-top garden to the boundary wall, where Maggie stood with her bodyguard. Though the air was cool and fresh compared to the sweltering heat of the Cavern Tavern, it had not been a cold night and already insects were buzzing and chirruping in anticipation of the day. The mossy grass carpeting the roof was soft and springy beneath their feet and dewdrops glistened in it, diamonds in the receding dark. Here and there metal pipes ran beneath the moss or emerged from the towers or protruded up into the air from rusted brackets screwed into the boundary wall. Steam rose from some of them, dispersing in the night. Some of them shook periodically. Some were cold to the touch and full of holes. Tall flowers clustered thickly beneath the small, wiry trees at the far end and in the shadows beneath the walls. Though their colours were unclear by the light of Satis and Corval, Alan knew them to be shades of yellow and purple. Large bushes with glossy dark green leaves and pale blue flowers also grew alongside the walls, and it was from these that most of the chirruping emanated. Great square wooden stilts supported further additions to the House above, but the Old Roof had no walls to obscure the view over Gleam, and the various higher levels had a smaller surface area than the roof on which they stood, meaning the skies were visible, too. In the middle of the large space, fireflies danced above a long, oval pond that had nearly dried up. Usually couples sat at the edge of the pond, holding hands and talking quietly, and people stood at the wall or lay down in the wet grass.

There was nobody else here now, though. Nobody but Maggie and Birdface.

When he reached the wall, Alan rested his elbows on the top of it and looked out over Gleam. It was nearly dawn, and the sky over the eastern horizon was growing pale, gradually swallowing up the stars. Beneath him, a broken gutter hung away from the wall, attached only by a shaky-looking drainpipe. It gently swayed above the dizzying drop to the next level down, which was currently shrouded in darkness.

The House of a Thousand Hollows was the tallest structure in this vicinity, but not by much. Alan looked across the wide empty space that surrounded it at the ridge of a long, low, tiled rooftop, which ran for two or three hundred yards before switching sharply to the right and then curving away until it eventually disappeared behind the cracked, dirty-white Dome of the Toad. The tiles were red, but looked almost black by the light of stars and moons, and many of them were missing; the roof was full of holes. The ridge was thick with round white chimney pots of varying heights protruding from beneath the tiles like mushrooms. The moons were bright enough for Alan to see more rooftops between the chimney pots, and more rooftops, and more chimney pots, and more white domes, and white archways, white towers, and then, further away, clusters of great chimneys reaching up into the sky. And every building, every structure, was connected. Often, the connections were later additions – bridges thrown up between windows, or buildings joined when other, smaller buildings were constructed in the space between them. It was a labyrinthine chaos of tile and stone. And when the moons sank and the sun rose, the stained white of the architecture would burn as red as the tiles, he knew. Gleam was black and white by night and red by day. Apart from the Pyramid, of course. The Pyramid was always black.

Maggie turned to him, and he to her.

Maggie was the power behind the House. Her face was

small and lined – wizened, almost – and her eyes were bright. A mass of curly red hair tumbled from her head, vivid and vibrant despite her advancing years. She wore a red cotton dress, cinched at the waist with a yellow cord. She wore silver bracelets on both wrists. She held a glass of red wine in one hand. A bottle was balanced on the wall.

Alan had never seen her unsmiling before.

Birdface, on the other hand, he'd never seen smiling *or* unsmiling. In fact he'd never seen Birdface's face at all. Nobody had. Birdface wore a thick, floor-length cloak – always, despite the frequently intense Gleam heat – of large black feathers. Nobody knew Birdface's gender, due to Birdface's face being a child's beaked mask that appeared to be grafted onto Birdface's actual skin. It was an elaborate child's mask of hard textured leather, decorated with glass beads embedded in the surface around the eyes. The largest beads marked the apex of each eyebrow; to either side of them, the size decreased. The beads shone different colours in different lights. The eye-holes were blacked out with some kind of mesh, through which Birdface could see, presumably, but which meant that nobody could see their eyes. The leather of the mask was pale cream. The beak was large and long and black; Alan thought it was a real bird's beak, but from what species, he had no idea. The lower half was missing, leaving a small hole though which Birdface's own dry lips could be glimpsed. The mask was surrounded by wild black hair shot through with streaks of grey. There was a small ribbon of pale skin visible between the mask and the hair, and the skin was puckered and shiny. The cloak came up to the bottom of the mask, hiding Birdface's chin and neck.

Birdface smelled musty and bad, and left feathers behind wherever it went.

People said that once, one of Maggie's gang leaders had threatened to withdraw protection from the House unless she doubled his wage. She'd refused, so he'd drawn a saw and threatened to withdraw protection *and* cut off her wine-drinking hand unless she doubled his wage. He hadn't known Birdface was there; Birdface had swooped out of the shadows and enfolded the man inside the cloak. Moments later Birdface opened up the cloak and the man fell out in pieces. Well . . . most of him. His eyeballs, testicles and right hand were never found, they said.

'Alan,' Maggie said. 'Spider. I have to think about the House.'

'Maggie. Don't do this.'

'I like you, Alan. You know I do. And I like what you bring to the place. Or, rather, I did.' She let a frown briefly cross her face. 'What you brought to the House this past night, I like not so much. Not at all.'

'The Cavern Tavern . . . that carnage . . . that was not my doing, Maggie.'

'Have some humility, Alan, for fuck's sake. Take responsibility for your actions and their consequences.'

'They didn't make an accusation against me. I don't know what they want me for — truly I don't know what action prompted those particular consequences.'

'Am I really to believe that?'

'Yes!' Alan was surprised. 'You mean you don't?'

'No, I don't. This is not the first time you've stirred up the ants' nest. You like to prod and needle. The songs, the visits, the — whatever you did that got you kicked out in the first place. A response was always going to be inevitable.'

'Everybody likes the songs.'

'That doesn't mean they want to follow you to certain death at the hands of the Arbitrators.'

Eyes cleared his throat. 'Ma'am,' he said. He cleared his throat again. 'Excuse me, ma'am. But—'

Maggie held up her hand. 'Do not think, please, that I am not sympathetic to your perspectives. I know what they did to you, Eyes, or at least I know some of it. I know, Alan, that they are manipulative and violent and that you are scared for your loved ones. But I cannot and will not have you here within the House of a Thousand Hollows if your actions — or even your intentions — jeopardise the safety of other House residents. It's not that I think you are wrong. Do you understand?'

'Ma'am,' Eyes said.

'Does this go for Spider too?' Alan asked.

'I'm afraid it does. My judgement is this: that Alan and Spider be exiled from the House forthwith, and that

Eyes, and that you two' – she gestured to Churr and the girl in the tattered grey cloak – 'be barred fully from all House venues and environs as of your immediate exit. This condition to be relieved after six Corval cycles, which should be sufficient time for all your various issues with the Pyramid and the Arbitrators to be resolved one way or another. Birdface, do you have their faces?'

Birdface gave a single brief nod.

'Six months?' Alan said. 'That's a long time to last out there when the Arbitrators are after you.'

'Those Arbitrators lying in pieces on the floor of my establishment suggest that perhaps you have no need to be afraid. You stay on the right side of your new friends here and I think you'll be just fine.' Maggie then turned to Churr and the girl. 'Please,' she said, 'what are your names? The names by which you are most frequently known.'

'Juke Churr,' said Churr.

'Bloody Nora,' said the girl.

Maggie frowned. 'I'm not in the mood for jokes, girl.'

'It is not a joke.' Her voice was soft and quiet, slightly melodic.

Alan glanced at her, at Bloody Nora, if that *could* be her real name. Her face betrayed no attempt at humour and no disrespect. There were no smiles or smirks. Her small mouth was turned ever so slightly down and the look in her eyes was deadly serious. And given the blood that had been crusting all over her arms and face before she'd washed herself, the name was entirely fitting.

'Birdface,' Maggie said, 'do you have their names?'

Birdface nodded once again.

'Bloody Nora is a Mapmaker,' Churr said. 'Mapmakers can go wherever they want.'

Maggie glared at Churr. 'Quiet yourself right now,' she said. 'The reports I received make it patently obvious that Nora is a Mapmaker. Do not think that I have not taken this into consideration. Do not patronise me so.'

'But—'

Birdface swept towards Churr, coming to a halt in between Churr and Maggie. Churr's voice dried up.

'To answer the unvoiced question,' Maggie said, 'I have an arrangement with the Mapmakers. If Nora is caught within the House ever again, then it will be her own Council she has to answer to, not me – a much more intimidating prospect, I think you'll agree.'

Alan was starting to feel as if every prospect was more intimidating than every other prospect.

'Now,' Maggie said, 'if you'll excuse me. I have a very large clean-up effort to co-ordinate. Diaz the Rowdy will see you to the Favoured Bridge.'

'Wait,' Alan said. The word had escaped of its own accord. Everything was happening too quickly. 'Wait,' he repeated, 'no. Maggie – please, no.' This couldn't be happening again. First Marion, now Maggie.

'I'm sorry, Alan,' Maggie said. 'I am.' She walked over to him and put her hands on his shoulders. 'A word of advice. Forget about the Pyramid. Stop playing with fire.

Let your family live their lives, let them make their own choices, and you embrace your life here, in the Discard. The House of a Thousand Hollows is not the only Safe House.'

'No. But it is the best.'

Maggie smiled. 'Yes. It is the best.' She kissed Alan on the forehead and moved past him, ignoring the others. Birdface followed.

When Alan turned, he found himself face-to-bulging-stomach with Diaz the Rowdy. He looked identical to his late twin brother, Quiet Diaz, except his eyes were red-raw from crying, and burning with pure hatred. Behind Diaz was a hand-picked company of heavies and thugs.

'I'm sorry,' Alan said.

Diaz the Rowdy said nothing; he just turned and walked towards the door in the corner turret.

'I could take them all,' Nora whispered, next to Alan. He hadn't realised she was there. 'But I won't.'

'No,' Alan said. 'No.'

The Favoured Bridge was a wide thoroughfare that connected the House to the rest of the Discard, one of many such thoroughfares, but as the name suggested, the Favoured Bridge was the busiest. It was the highest, for a start, so it was furthest from the swamp, and it was the widest, and it had railings on either side, so it was the safest. It was the sturdiest too – many of the bridges were hair-raisingly narrow, the ancient-looking stone crumbling away in places. Others were gerrymandered, ramshackle things that people had built from their windows. And they all had a wide gap to cross.

The House end of the Favoured Bridge was connected to the Sleepless Pavilion, the men and women of which were famous throughout the Discard for their beauty, their skills and their stamina. Alan estimated that the Sleepless Pavilion provided most of Maggie's income and enabled her to afford so much in the way of protection. The other end of the Favoured Bridge opened onto Market Top, which was as close as the transients got to their own town. The conglomeration of tents and stalls and caravans was where House residents went for their supplies too, including, for example, mushrooms.

So Alan knew the Favoured Bridge and Market Top well – but it felt different this time. This could be the last time he would cross the bridge. *The last time*. He looked over the railings while he was being shepherded along by Diaz the Rowdy, balking at the green dark of the depths. It was *so* dark, even now, after sunrise. He'd always considered himself quite comfortable outside of the House – some residents never left – but as he crossed the Favoured Bridge for potentially the last time he realised that he'd only felt that way since he'd had the House to return to. Before Kate of the Corner's demise, life in the Discard had been frighteningly precarious.

There would be no quick scurry back to the House if he got into trouble now.

Once Diaz had escorted Alan, Eyes, Spider, Churr and Nora beyond the other end of the Favoured Bridge the giant man turned around and went back the way he'd come. He had not spoken a single word. Alan watched Diaz's back as he went. He'd never got on with the brothers, not since the day after the twins' twenty-first birthdays, when they'd failed to open up the Cavern Tavern because they were sleeping off monstrous birthday hangovers. So Alan had done it for them – a favour, really. And maybe he hadn't been very diligent in collecting payment from the patrons – well, okay, maybe he hadn't made any effort at all – but he'd done a damn good job of getting people in through the door. And maybe he hadn't done enough to prevent or discourage the impromptu boxing tournament, but it had been a lot of fun, and he'd made a lot of bugs out of it. And maybe he hadn't stuck around to clean up all the vomit and blood and piss but . . . well, it wasn't his job, was it?

The House had snared a few new rent-paying residents that day – transients and miscreants signing tenancy contracts under the misapprehension that that kind of chaos was typical – so Maggie hadn't minded too much. The Diaz brothers had minded, though. They had minded a lot.

Alan watched as Diaz the Rowdy walked back across the bridge, wanting to say something to him, something better and more powerful than merely *Sorry*. Something that might really change things for Diaz. But he couldn't think of what that something might be.

There wasn't anything.

He sighed and looked down at his feet. 'Let's go and get a drink,' he said. 'I really want a drink. And a smoke.' He patted his pockets. 'Green *damn* it,' he said. 'I left my coat. My smokes. My guitar. My money.'

'How many bugs are we talking?' Churr asked.

'Never you mind,' Alan said. 'Enough. Loads. Bloody loads.'

'Your guitar is out, and safe,' Nora said.

'What?'

'Your guitar is out, and safe,' she repeated.

'I – thank you.' Alan stared at her. She looked young; eighteen, perhaps. 'How?'

'I removed your instruments,' she said, 'while you were failing to cope. I also removed a certain something else.'

'What was that something else?' Alan thought back to when Nora had disappeared after all the fighting. Well, she hadn't really disappeared; he and the others had fled the abattoir environment of the Cavern Tavern and only realised later that Nora wasn't with them. By the time Alan had finally steeled himself to open the door and poke his head back into the gory murk, Nora was gone.

'Come and let me show you,' Nora said. 'Then a drink, maybe.'

13

Bloody Nora

Nora had Raspy tied to a fat rusty pipe. He had his back against the pipe and his hands tied to his feet around the other side of it so that his spine was uncomfortably curved. He was also suspended above a large rectangular pool of something that looked like oil and facing straight down into it.

'Here it is,' she announced. 'It's a he.'

There were countless such pools set into the stone floor of this gigantic cube of a building. They were regularly spaced, and stretched off towards each of the four walls. The ceiling was far away, lost in shadow. The large pipe, part of a grid system, looked busy with valves and stopcocks and, above the pools, some very complex nozzles, which looked like they had delivered something into the pools once upon a time. They were long and tapered, becoming thin copper pipes themselves, and knotted and contorted into bewildering, labyrinthine tangles. Some of these thin pipes still retained their sheen; others were dull and oxidised.

There was a machine in each pool, too: long cylindrical things like rollers of some sort, connected at each end to poolside runners via a sequence of gears and wheels. They reminded Alan of mangles. Piled up against one end of their pool's machine were their instruments, cases and coats.

'What are we here for?' Alan asked. 'What is *he* here for?' His voice echoed around the massive interior.

'Don't you want to know what they wanted?' Nora asked.

'Oh! Oh, yes. Of course.' *Wake up*, he thought. 'Thank you, Nora.'

'That's quite all right.'

'I thought you'd done that . . . thing. That thing you did to the others.'

'No,' Nora said, smiling up at him. 'The face thing? No. You and I, Alan; we need to have a talk.'

Alan nodded. 'Yes,' he said warily. 'Maybe after we've learned a few things from our friend here, Churr could introduce us properly.' He looked pointedly at Churr as he said this.

'Stop being so useless,' Churr said.

Alan looked back up at Raspy. He really could have done with a drink, or something to sharpen him up a bit. He *was* being useless. He opened his mouth to ask Raspy a question.

an arrow through a neck

He couldn't think of anything.

fountain of blood

He imagined his own blood spraying out in front of him, all thin and warm.

long-hair spitting teeth

a knife to the face

He felt dizzy and sick.

a sword, in under the ribs

He looked down into the pool but the thick, dusty liquid looked red to him. He saw Raspy's sneering face reflected in it. He remembered how close he'd come to killing the man. The nausea rose up his throat with a vengeance. He backed away, turned around, crouched down. 'I'm not really a fighter,' he said, to nobody in particular.

'That's not true,' Spider said. 'You can fight when your blood's up.'

'We are in the Discard proper now,' Nora said. 'You will have to fight.'

'He's prob'ly just hungover,' Eyes said. 'Silly bugger. Ignore him.'

'I can't believe,' said Raspy, from up above, 'that we were sent into the filthy Discard for the sole purpose of capturing *you*. And my men all died for it. For *you*.' He spat down into the pool. His saliva just rested on the top of whatever was in it. 'What a waste.'

'You didn't have to do it,' Alan said, standing back up. He swayed slightly. 'That's the point, isn't it? That's the difference between you and me. I lived in the Pyramid too, once, but I didn't just do what I was told.'

'And now look at you.'

'Yeah, well.' Alan met Raspy's contemptuous gaze. 'I've got my dignity.'

There was a moment's silence, and then Alan darted to the edge of the pool to throw up, noisily. He could feel everybody watching him. When he was done, he cleared his throat and wiped his mouth with the back of his hand. 'I haven't had any sleep,' he said. 'That's the problem. That's all the problem is. Does anybody have a hip-flask?'

'I got mine but no way in hell are you puttin' your lips round it now,' Eyes said.

'Okay. Thanks, Eyes. Okay. Next steps, people. What's the plan?'

'We extract information from our prisoner,' Churr said. 'Well, if you want to. Which I presume you do. They came for you, after all. You must want to know why.'

'Yes,' Alan said. 'Yes, I do.' He addressed Raspy. 'Arbitrator. Do you know why you were sent to detain me?'

'Contrary to your assertions last night,' Raspy replied, 'I do. Yes. But never in Green's whole hell will I reveal our reasons to you.'

'Surely if you had captured me, I would have been told why.' Alan folded his arms and strode along the side of the pool, away from the site of his regurgitations.

'Yes.'

'So why not tell me now?'

'Two very different sets of circumstances.'

'You mean, had I been captured I would not be free, whereas here and now I *am* free, so I am able to act upon the information, whereas if I was captive then I would not.'

'. . . yes.'

'So it's information that I could, if I were in possession of it, act upon?'

'. . . yes,' Raspy said again. He sounded unsure. 'But doesn't all information fall into that category?'

'No. You have revealed something. Now.' Alan made eye contact with Raspy and grinned.

'This is pathetic,' Raspy said. 'I've never been interrogated before and I doubt I ever will be again, so I have very little in the way of reference points, but this must be up there as one of the worst interrogations ever.'

'*Down* there, more likely,' Alan said. 'Not *up* there. Down there. At the bottom of the league table, see, rather than at the top. High is good, low is bad. Generally. But don't worry. I'm just getting started.'

'You're loving this, aren't you?' Raspy said. 'An Arbitrator all trussed up for you to do whatever you want to.'

'That's interesting,' Alan said. 'Why would I love such a thing? Either you think that I'm the kind of person who would leap at the chance to torture and debase a fellow human being, given the opportunity, which in fact says far more about you than it does about me, or you know something about how I feel about Arbitrators.

Which you couldn't possibly know, unless we've met before.'

Raspy didn't say anything.

'It's not as if we've ever met, is it?' Alan made a show of standing on tiptoe and peering hard at the captive. 'Have we? We haven't, have we?'

Raspy still didn't say anything. He looked angry.

'So how do you know how I feel about Arbitrators?'

'Because of your history with us. We were briefed.'

'I don't see how my history with the Arbitrators is relevant to your successful apprehension of me.' Alan's voice rose and his smile had disappeared. 'And, let's face it, you folks are pretty stingy with the details of past atrocities committed by yourselves, because in the Pyramid you've got an entirely undeserved reputation that requires a hell of a lot of maintenance. Haven't you? For instance, a zero-tolerance approach to the dissemination of unhelpful or negative stories about the Arbitrators. Including within the Arbitration Service.'

Raspy didn't say anything.

'So don't expect me to believe that they *briefed* you on the Modest Mills massacre, on my incarceration – which was for the aforementioned dissemination of blah blah, etc., by the way – or on the near-fatal beating you lot gave me, or on the vile threats you made to my wife and child.'

Raspy looked even angrier than he had before.

'So I'll ask you again: how do you know how I feel about you slimy, foul Arbitrator shites?'

Nothing.

'Is this – the fact of you even knowing about all that, which I notice you're not attempting to deny, or even pretending to be surprised by – perhaps connected somehow to why you were sent out here to get me?'

'Congratulations,' Raspy said. 'A round of applause for the self-righteous cunt with vomit down his shirt. You've worked it out. Whatever, I don't care. You're going to kill me anyway.'

'You mean that you were sent out here to capture me because I've somehow told people how awful you all are? Except I haven't. I haven't told anybody.' He thought for a moment. 'Except . . .' His eyes widened.

Now Raspy was grinning down at him. He looked like a gargoyle up there, tied to the pipe, his head at an unnatural angle, his features twisted into an expression loaded with self-satisfaction and menace. 'Has it clicked?' he rasped.

Alan didn't say anything.

'Your precious little boy has been asking all kinds of difficult questions,' Raspy said. 'Telling all kinds of stories. What did you call it? Dissemination of . . . of . . .'

'Fuck you,' Alan breathed. 'He's a *child*.'

'Yeah,' Raspy said. 'But he's *your* child. So we were going to bring you back in and use you to give him a little demonstration about the price you pay for not adhering to the letter of Pyramid law. We could have just killed him, of course, or thrown him out, but getting rid of children tends to fuel more rumours than it stops. Scaring children shitless, on the other hand . . . That works very well.' He mused for a moment. 'Little shits'll believe *anything*, as long as they respect the liar.'

Alan felt disembodied. When he spoke it happened automatically, as if his mouth was working all on its own while his mind and soul floated off to one side, observing. 'So what's happening to Billy now?'

'He's alive,' Raspy said. 'He's in isolation, but he's alive. As you say – he's a child.'

'But doesn't even that mean the kind of awkward disappearance you were hoping to avoid?'

Raspy spat again. 'Nobody was expecting us to fail.' He tossed his head towards Nora; it was the only way he had of gesturing. 'Nobody was expecting us to fall foul of a Mapmaker. Mapmakers don't get involved, do they?' He laughed, slightly nervously. His tone was now the least confrontational it had been; he sounded almost afraid. 'Everybody knows that.'

Nora was smiling serenely up at the incapacitated Arbitrator. From beneath her cloak she withdrew a leather roll. 'Alan,' she said, 'I will find out more about the Pyramid – where your son is being held, its defences.' She turned to face him. 'You probably don't want to stick around for the extraction, though. Given how you feel about violence.'

'I don't want to stick around anyway.' And Alan found he was walking away, past pools of multicoloured sludge and weird, forgotten machinery, and he didn't know where he was going, and his head was full of blood and full of noise.

When Nora came to him afterwards she came alone. Once again she was living up to her moniker. Her cloak and arms were covered; in fact, now Alan could see the cloak was a palimpsest of stains, old and new, and not just dark reds and browns, but dark greens and blues and purples. But her arms and hands were bright red and still wet.

She found him perched on the minute hand of a gigantic stopped clock that adorned one of the interior walls of the pool building. The clock was visible from the floor – it was large enough to be visible from wherever in the building you were. It was accessible via a staircase inside the wall that, on Alan's ascent, had been thick with cobwebs. At the top of the staircase there was a chamber that was almost fully occupied by the clock's mechanism, all gears and wheels, and all rusted fast. And there was a tiny door which provided access to the clock face. When Alan first opened it he recoiled from what appeared to be an immediate sheer drop, then, approaching more cautiously, he spotted a little ledge which was actually wide enough for him to feel comfortable on. From there he was able to step out onto the minute hand – it was a good two feet wide – and walk along it. It didn't shift or creak or move in the slightest. He didn't really think about the potential consequences of the hand moving, or failing to take his weight, or his blasé dismissal of those consequences, until later.

He sat right on the very tip, his legs dangling over the end, and looked down through his feet. Screams and grunts echoed around the space as Nora did her thing. The pools beneath him were luridly bright; each one was a slightly different colour and all of them had a multicoloured, oily sheen. His view was slightly spoiled by the grid of large pipes, one of which Raspy had been tied to, but even so it was remarkable. It was a bit like the colourful geometries he experienced when he drank some of Spider's mushroom tea: Spider's own special blend of dream-meat and long-legs. What he'd give for some of that right now.

He tried to wrest his thoughts away from mushroom tea, from drugs, from alcohol. He found himself fantasising about sex with Churr and put a stop to that, too. There was something he had to think about: something huge, something awful, something more important than anything else. He knew what it was, he just couldn't articulate it to himself. He couldn't put it into words.

Billy was in trouble, and it was his fault.

How had he got to this point? He wasn't aware he'd ever stopped being a child himself. He'd always thought that at some point he'd realise how to be an adult, how to be a parent. As if he'd reach a certain age and then the next day wake up a different, more capable human being who knew what was what and how the world worked and how to navigate it. How to be responsible for another human being. But no. He'd become a parent and suddenly he'd had to pretend to be an adult, for Billy's sake. He'd known he was a fraud, though: he was playing at it, like he played at everything else. And in addition, once he'd become a parent, he'd realised that his own parents had only been pretending all that time, too. They hadn't been adults any more than he was. Becoming a parent meant realising that there was no such thing as an adult, not really. Everybody was a fraud. Everybody was just pretending. Adults were just children with scary responsibilities, and parents were just children with children of their own.

Billy, I'm sorry.

'Hello!' said a little voice from behind him.

He turned and saw Bloody Nora sitting on the minute hand too, right next to him, swinging her legs. She flashed him a broad smile. His gaze lingered on her red hands, arms and cloak.

'Hi,' he said. 'Bloody Nora . . . I see the Mapmakers deserve their reputation.'

'We are trained from a very young age how to fight. It's true.'

'And you have no . . .' Alan searched for the word '. . . compunction?'

'We are trained not to,' Nora said. 'That too is true. Where we go, we are not usually required to fight humans, but no human life is more important than our work and so it is important to be able to kill people when they get in the way.'

'And torture?'

'Anybody with imagination can be a torturer,' she said. She smiled again. 'Anybody with imagination, and no . . . compunction.'

'And how does all of this fit into your work?'

'Have you ever met a Mapmaker before?'

He shook his head.

'Our work is the mapping of Gleam in its entirety. This means exploring constantly, and exploring quickly, given the rate of change. The factory is so big that—'

'The what?'

'The factory. Our current theory is that Gleam is one single factory.'

'Isn't it just a' – Alan waved his arms about – 'big jumble?'

'That is quite a popular theory, yes, though usually expressed via a variety of filters. For example, certain outlier tribes believe that Gleam is just a set of building blocks abandoned by a godly infant. Some believe that Gleam is the result of a single rogue building spell that has been running for millennia: just one little spell, building one part of Gleam and then flashing across to some other bit of it and adding another building there too, and on, and on, and on, never stopping.' She cocked her head. 'I find this theory quite charming, but I do not believe in that kind of magic.'

'Not that kind?'

'No.'

Alan waited for Nora to elaborate on this, but she didn't.

'A factory, hey?' Alan said. He looked back down between his feet at all the pools. 'Makes as much sense as anything else, I suppose. What was it for? What did they make?'

'We don't know yet.'

'And who were they?'

'We—'

'And where are they?'

'Wild Alan, I do not like being interrupted. Actually, nobody likes being interrupted.'

'Sorry.'

'We are talking about a significant timescale here. They became us, or rather, they begat us. Sometime after the factory stopped being a factory, and became Gleam, is what makes sense, and is what most Mapmakers believe. But what I was saying was this: coupled with the rate of change, the sheer size of Gleam means that mapping it fully is a never-ending task, one that generation after generation of Mapmakers must engage in. And the encroachment from the swamp means that the ground floors are unmappable. They were lost to the swamp generations ago. However' – and she held up a single finger – 'I believe I know of something that may aid us in our mapping. It's a place I wish to find: a place of records, of documents.'

'Of maps.'

'Precisely. Maps and plans made by the builders, those behind Gleam. The founders. Detailing the entire structure as it originally stood, thereby easing our mapping of the entire structure as it currently stands. And also providing an invaluable historical context to what we do.'

'But how does killing all those Arbitrators help you with that?'

'In two ways. Firstly, it puts you in my debt.'

'I'm not good at honouring debts.'

'You will honour this one. And secondly, it means that there are fewer Arbitrators to stand between me and those old maps.'

Alan sighed. 'They're in the Pyramid.'

'So I believe. My understanding is that the Pyramid was once the brain of the factory, the seat of its rulers, and that the secrets of Gleam can be found within.'

'I used to live in it, Nora. There're no secrets in there, just people performing the same actions, day in, day out. They're not manufacturing anything, just following patterns.'

'Not secrets, then. But perhaps records. Information.'

Alan shrugged. 'Perhaps.' He nodded at her bloody hands. 'But what about our friend down there? What did he tell you?'

'He has been overseeing this entire operation — your retrieval and your son's silencing — so he knew a lot.'

Knew. Alan didn't say anything.

'We can save your son. But the initial plan must remain the same: acquire the contraband, then you go to meet your contact amongst the Arbitrators. They will agree, whether they are more interested in the mushrooms or your head. Success is more likely if you have something to trade. Something of value, besides yourself.'

'One thing I don't understand,' Alan said. 'You're a Mapmaker – if you want to get into the Pyramid, why don't you just ask other Mapmakers? Don't you all have a common cause?'

Nora hesitated. 'Yes,' she said, 'we do.'

'Why don't you storm it?'

'The Mapmakers have excommunicated me,' Nora said. She smiled again, briefly, and then looked down towards the distant floor.

Alan shook his head. 'No,' he said. He refused to believe what he was hearing. *Not the Mapmakers too?*

'I'll show them,' Nora said suddenly, looking back up. Her face was set in a snarl. 'I'll show them how to do it.'

'The maps,' Alan said. 'It's just a rumour, isn't it? You just want to prove yourself. You don't know any more than any other Mapmaker.'

'I need to prove myself,' Nora said.

'What the fuck did you *do*?'

Nora rolled her eyes. 'Nothing,' she said. 'Desecration. It was nothing.'

'Is that . . . bad? Desecration? It sounds like it could be serious.'

'It was nothing. I just said that.'

'Nothing for us to fret about, then.'

'Well . . .' Nora pursed her lips. 'Punishable by death,' she said.

Alan stared at her.

'Don't worry,' she said. 'They have to catch me first.'

PART TWO

14

The Cup and Skull

'So we've got Daunt and her crew, the Pyramid, half of the House of a Thousand Hollows, maybe including Birdface. Bandits and general arseholes and now Mapmakers, too. Bleeding *Mapmakers*.' Eyes was counting them up on his fingers. 'Anybody else we gone and pissed off? Anyone else we want to, while we're at it? Why don't we just go and each lay a big fat turd in Old Green's mouth, eh? Just to make sure we're well and truly fucked.'

'Well, we're going to Dok,' murmured Spider. 'We could.'

'Don't be angry, Eyes,' Nora said. She sat cross-legged on top of the pipe next to Raspy's dead body, which was dripping blood into the red pool beneath, and cleaned her tools with a damp piece of cloth. She'd gone outside to wash herself in a half-barrel water butt she knew of while Alan filled the others in. Water sources were one of the many features Mapmakers were required to document.

'Don't be angry? Don't be bleedin' *angry*? Easy for you

to say, missy!' Eyes, beet-faced, pointed at Raspy's corpse. 'You clearly don't feel a damn thing.'

Alan watched Nora continue cleaning her kit. They needed her, he knew they did – more than that: they were utterly dependent on her. She knew the way and she could fight better than the rest of them put together. But she made him feel cold in his stomach. He couldn't deny that she was monstrous. Was she some kind of devil?

'My advice,' Nora said to Eyes, 'is to meditate every morning and every night. I can teach you. I have crystals and incense here in my pack. I know several highly effective mantras, and a sheaf of mandala designs that you could borrow if you so wish.'

'Meditate, she says!' Eyes shouted. He jabbed his finger at the corpse once again, looking as if he were about to explode, then turned sharply on his heels and marched away.

'You in particular would find it beneficial,' Nora called after him.

'What did you do?' Spider asked. 'What was your desecration?'

'It doesn't matter.'

'But what *is* desecration, to a Mapmaker?'

'The Mapmaker tribes are intensely ritualistic,' Nora said. 'My father always said that Mapmaking is not a religion, but it is. That's exactly what it is. We don't use the word "holy", but we have holy places, holy objects, and the force that gives our lives meaning is ... faith.

Understand, nobody is waiting for us to finish our maps. We will never finish. Our rituals revolve around the undertaking of some inherited, ancient, impossible task and not some intangible deity, but still . . .' She paused. 'Many actions are desecratory or blasphemous. Questioning the purpose of our work – that is blasphemous. Damaging or disrespecting a completed volume of maps, for example – that is desecration.'

'Do you consider such behaviour wrong?'

'No.'

'But you continue the Mapmakers' work.'

Nora leaned forward. 'I have my own reasons,' she said. 'Firstly, if I can find this cache, this trove, then they will let me back. My *sins*, such as they are, would be absolved. I don't need forgiveness or absolution, but I do not want to have to hide from my people for ever. I want them to see me.' She thought for a moment. 'I want them to thank me. I want them to be beholden. I want them to know that they were wrong.' Her voice hardened. 'I don't want them to forgive me. I want them to ask me my forgiveness. I want them to plead for it.'

Churr cleared her throat. 'We should think about our next move.' She looked at Alan. 'If they wanted you, they will still want you. They will know soon that their raid failed. They will come again. We should get moving.'

'Your instruments and provisions are over there.' Nora pointed towards the pile of material she'd gathered from the Cavern Tavern.

'Not my bloody drums,' Eyes growled.

'No, not your drums,' Nora said. 'Of course not.'

Alan was picking through the pile. 'I didn't actually have any money on me last night,' he said. 'Not after I bought the drinks. Anybody else?'

'A little,' replied Spider.

'Aye,' Eyes said, 'but only a little here, too.'

'And there's no food here,' Alan said. 'Only whisky. And cigarettes.'

'That's all you had,' Nora said.

'Well, what are we going to do?' Eyes asked.

'There's a lot to eat out here if you know how to hunt and forage,' Nora said, 'but you have your instruments – your livelihoods, unless I am mistaken? I propose you play for shelter and sustenance. Our passage will be easier and safer that way. And I do not want to have to try to keep you all alive on snails, moss and snake-meat.'

'I don't much want that either,' Alan said.

'There are communities, transient hubs, strongholds,' Nora said. 'If we can move from here and lie low for a few hours, then I can plan our route.'

'The Cup and Skull?' Churr asked.

'Yes,' Nora replied.

'Wait,' Eyes said, 'wait. Is that it? All decided, just like that?'

Nora slid from the top of the pipe and landed lightly, crouching. She stood up. 'That's where my materials are,' she said.

'So what? You're the boss now?' Eyes appealed to Alan: 'I thought this was your game. Who do we follow? We following her, or following you?'

'We're in the Discard proper now,' Alan said. 'This is Nora's country.'

'She's a sadist. She's a gorehound.'

'I'm *right here*.'

Alan closed his eyes. His shirt smelled bad and felt stiff against his skin. He found a crumpled cigarette in his shirt pocket, put it in his mouth, lit it, inhaled. He thought about Billy in a pale marble cell. 'Nora is our best hope,' he said. 'Nora knows the way.' Thick white smoke came out with his words. 'Nora is exactly what we need.'

She smiled at him. He could see that there was still dried blood beneath her green fingernails. He couldn't smile back.

The others set to gathering their belongings. Alan watched, the cigarette hanging limply from between his lips. He watched Spider shoulder his violin case, Eyes rifle through his sackcloth backpack, Churr don a thin leather jacket. He noticed a disturbance in the red pool and watched as a large flat toad hauled itself out of the sludge and onto the side. Its body was like a warty bag of sand. Oily red liquid ran between the pimply bumps of its skin. It blinked and puffed up its throat, croaked, and then lurched off across the expanse of floor, leaving a greasy crimson trail.

'That was a rustbelly flat,' Spider said. 'I think it's a wayspro rustbelly, to be specific. Very potent. I've heard them called Omentoads.'

'Good or bad?' Alan asked.

'Pretty much like anything else: depends on how much you take, and how you take it.' He licked his lips. 'I'm going to go and get it.'

'I *meant*, is it a good or bad omen?'

'Oh. Well, the details are in the visions they grant.'

'Spider, it just came out of that toxic crap. Don't tell me you're going to squeeze it.'

Spider looked at Alan. His beard made him difficult to read. 'Kill it, clean it, squeeze it,' he said. He drew a small knife from his belt, spun it, caught it by the handle. 'We'll be looking round Time's corners tonight, son.'

'Are we going to see anything good?'

Spider smiled. His eyes glimmered, deep, dark wells.

The Cup and Skull was low-down inside a labyrinthine concrete nightmare. From an open door green light spilled into a wide, dingy corridor that felt like the bottom of a ravine. They could hear the throaty chug of motorcycle engines as they approached the green light, and sure enough, when they got there, bikers were swarming around the place like bees around sunbladders. Concrete walls rose to darkness above. Nora told them the corridor was part of what the Mapmakers called the First Structure.

'We think that when the Builders created Gleam, they started with one vast building: one huge concrete shape, designed to house all of the different functions of the place. It didn't work, of course, so additions were thrown up all the time, but beneath it and through it all there seems to be this one primary structure. A Gleam-wide castle, almost, as if it were just turned upside down out of a mould. Then the various systems were put in: the pipes, the rivers, the machines. But you can traverse Gleam without leaving this one concrete . . . *thing*, if you want. A lot of it is too close to the swamp for most travellers, and much of it is dangerously enclosed – good for bandit ambushes. The bikers love it, though. The corridors are so flat and so wide.'

'I knew about the biker paths,' Spider said, 'but not the First Structure.' He raised his small, square glass. 'To Bloody Nora,' he said. 'To our education.'

Alan joined him, as did Churr. Eyes too, after a moment, but half-heartedly.

The Cup was serving great hunks of snail, grilled with lemon from the Archway Gardens. It was full of bikers and transients, all looking to get in on the feast. The small tavern was packed full of black leather and tattooed skin and the air smelled of oil.

'We should eat as much as we can,' Nora said, 'while we have the opportunity.'

'I'm not eating that snail,' Churr said. 'A snail that big will have been full of worms.'

'It's cooked, though,' Nora said. 'If we get it well-done, any parasites will be killed. Then they're as nutritious as the snail itself.'

'We haven't got no bugs,' Eyes said.

'Then play your music,' Nora said. 'For Green's sake, we've been through this.'

'Will they like us, do you reckon?'

'I don't know. Find out. I'm going up to my room to plan our route. Bring me some snail.' Nora stood up and pushed her way through the mass.

'Oh, I like that,' Eyes said. 'Just leaving us to it. And how's she paying for her room, anyway?'

'How do you think?' Churr asked. 'The normal way. Bugs.'

'Eyes,' Alan said, 'leave off Nora. I can't be doing with this constant sniping. Leave off Nora, or leave us.' He held his hands up, palms out. 'And *don't* start. I'm not going to fight with you again. Just . . . let her be. For the sake of this whole endeavour, let her speak without jumping down her throat. We've got enough to deal with without turning on each other.'

Eyes knocked his whisky back and frowned. 'Aye,' he said.

Pighead introduced them all to a couple of wiry, hard-eyed men. 'These're my Bastards,' he said. 'They'll clear some space for you.' The Bastards each had the sign of The Cup and Skull tattooed onto their cheeks. They didn't say anything to the band, just slid into the crowd and started shoving people aside. Pighead raised an eyebrow at Alan. 'You'll be good, right? Put on a good show?'

'Well, yeah,' Alan said.

'Our patrons are used to drinking uninterrupted. Better be worth their attention or they won't thank you.'

'We'll be good, all right?'

'You keep them in here boozing, even after we're all out of snail, and you get rooms. That's the deal.'

'Plate some up for us, eh?'

'You and me, laddie,' Pighead said, getting up close to Alan, 'we're not familiar enough for that kind of talk, okay?'

'Excuse me,' Alan said, 'your beard's tickling my nose. You're making me want to sneeze. Yes, that's – that's better. Thank you.' Alan pinched his nose for a moment, then said, 'Pighead. Pighead? Pighead, please plate us up some of that awful snail-meat. Is that better?'

'Ignore him, Pighead,' Churr said. 'He's a dick.'

'Too right,' Pighead said, and he moved on.

'Why do you do this, Alan?' Churr said. 'I've known you, like, three days and already I think you're a dick.'

'Three days? Is that all?'

'It's like you actively try to be a smartarse, actively try to piss everybody off. I think things would be easier for you if you tried *not* to be a smartarse.'

'I've got a reputation to maintain.'

'Not the reputation you think, maybe.'

Alan laughed. 'Maybe.'

'You're not in the House any more, Alan. You're not Wild Alan, the entertainer. You haven't got Maggie at your back. Things are different out here. We've got to be careful.'

'Yeah,' Alan said, 'sorry, Churr. I'm just . . . I don't know how to be.'

'I can see that. Hey . . .' She grabbed his shoulder. 'Looks like they're ready for you all to get set up.'

'Can you sing?'

'Not at all.'

'I'll see you afterwards, then.'

'I'll be watching.'

Eyes was wrestling the tarp from a drum-kit made of barrels and crocodile skin. 'Gonna sound like shite,' he said.

'It'll be fine,' Alan said. 'But you need to think of something to use in places where they don't have drums.'

'Bongos?' Eyes said.

'I don't know. I was thinking more of a set-up that means you can just use something that's already there. Like, if they have a generator, then you could just bang on any old crap and run it through a mic. And if they don't have a generator, then just hit harder.'

'Hit what, though?'

'I don't know. Rocks, logs . . . pots and pans.'

'Like a kid.'

'Yeah, like a kid. Like the big kid that you deep down

are. The big, deep, angry kid, that's you. Big angry kid with the shakes and hysterical episodes.'

'Yeah, yeah. I got a lot of respect for you too.'

'I know you do. Who doesn't?'

'Give me a hand, you. What are you? You're a turd with a hard-on, that's what you are.'

The Cup and Skull was small compared to the Cavern Tavern, so in theory they didn't need amplification. They did need everyone to stop shouting, though. Alan stood and looked into the press of bikers and transients and felt briefly that he and the band should not have been there: these people hadn't come to hear music, they'd come to eat and drink and they weren't interested, not in the slightest. But then Spider shut them up with a wildly dissonant shriek from his violin, and before anybody had time to protest he launched into a furiously fast melody that left Eyes and Alan struggling to catch up.

Within twenty minutes, Alan was standing on the audience's hands, howling lyrics down at upturned faces as he was passed from one to the next. The air was hot. The drums were loud and Eyes was doing something fast, syncopated; the rhythm had a juddery quality, as if it was on the verge of breaking down, but it never quite did. Alan looked down at bald heads, braided beards, hair dyed all colours and plaited into tight rows like seams across scalps. Somebody passed him a drink, which he necked, thinking it was water, but it wasn't. Somebody else passed him another one.

When he performed, Alan's mind split into two: the larger, unthinking part through which the music and the lyrics channelled themselves, and a small, quiet voice at the back of his head that watched and observed. And the small quiet voice was approving. Most of these people had never heard Alan or the others before. They were making new fans, new allies for what was coming.

At least when he was performing he felt like he was good at something.

'It tastes like mud,' Spider said, chewing thoughtfully, 'but perhaps it's a bit more bitter.'

'Needs a lot of chewing,' Eyes said, poking at the meat on his plate with a crooked-tined fork. 'It's like trying to chew noses.'

Alan gazed miserably down at his own meal. The aroma of lemon – and what else? Wild garlic, probably – was delicious, but the smell in no way made up for the off-putting appearance of the grey-brown lump of nod-uled flesh in front of him. They'd all asked for their snail to be grilled crispy, and it had been, but they might as well have asked for a jug of piss to be served ice-cold and expected it to be easy to drink. 'Come on,' Alan said. 'We've all eaten snail before. Raw, sometimes.' Though even to himself he could not deny that the hunk of giant snail was actually less appealing than a pile of small ones.

'No snail this big or this tough,' Spider said. 'The little ones are easier, but you've got to eat a lot to fill yourself up. And you shouldn't eat them raw, not really. Cooking them individually kills the lungworms.'

Alan remembered the weeks immediately following his exile from the Pyramid. He'd eaten a lot of raw snail then. He hadn't known about lungworms. He was starting to feel slightly queasy.

'Just stop whining and eat this while we've got it,' Churr said, between swallowing one mouthful and shovelling in the next. 'Big snail is good eating out here. And any bits of parasite you find are a treat, as long as they're dead. There are transients who'd kill for this feast. It's going to be rat and lichen from here on in. We're lucky to be getting a lot of ballast in us before we set off.'

The only other conscious customers left in the bar were a couple of bikers getting intimate behind the wreckage Eyes had made of the drum-kit and a table of transients playing strip poker beneath the green neon skull on the wall opposite the bar. A man with a long waxed moustache lay on his back on a table, snoring loudly and others had passed out on the floor. Pighead stood behind the bar, counting bugs.

'What did Bloody Nora say when you took her food up?' Alan asked Churr.

'Nothing. She was working. She had her papers out, and her crystals. Trust me – you don't want to break her concentration.'

'Is she still joining us for the Omentoad?' Spider said.

'Even I'm not joining you for that crap,' Eyes said.

'No,' Churr said, 'me neither.'

'You in?' Spider asked Alan.

'Not after this food,' Alan said. *And not after the last trip I embarked upon in this dive*. 'I feel sick enough already.'

'I'll wait for Nora,' Spider said. 'I'll wait half an hour.'

15

The Clawbaby

The slap shattered Alan's sleep. He brought his arms up to protect himself, confused and blinking.

'Get up!' somebody shouted.

'Who is it?' he said. His mouth was dry and tasted foul. His tongue moved only sluggishly. Somebody was standing over him but he couldn't see who it was. He could hear crashing and shouting. Whoever it was hit him again.

'Stop it!'

'Alan, get up. I can't believe the noise hasn't already woken your lazy arse.'

'Eyes?'

Eyes swayed above him, clearly not yet sober. His mouth hung open and there were bits of food in his red-grey beard. The ointment-soaked blindfold he wore to bed was skew-whiff across his forehead, still covering one eye. The other was wide and bloodshot.

'Haul yourself out of bed, lad,' Eyes said. 'We're under attack.'

Alan climbed out of bed, dragging the sheets with him. Disturbed bedbugs scattered, hopping erratically across the floor, and he staggered, grabbing hold of Eyes for support. 'My legs,' he said. 'They ache like hell.'

'You sleep in your trousers?'

'I don't know.' He looked down. 'Sometimes, I guess.' He found his shirt on the floor and slid his arms through the sleeves. 'The Arbitrators?'

'No. Something else.'

'Bandits? Daunt?'

'I just fucking said, didn't I? I said, *something else*. If I knew what it was I would have just bloody said what it was, wouldn't I?'

'Tell me what you do know, then.'

'I heard something smashing, then a . . . I don't know what. Some kind of voice. A roar. Churr woke up as well, like I did, like an ordinary human – I saw her on the landing. Then Spider and Bloody pegged it up the stairs. Come *on*, Alan! Get it together, will you?'

'Any of us got rooms with windows?'

'Aye, I've got a window. And a sense of honour.'

'Okay, okay . . .'

The Cup and Skull's rooms were spherical, like huge bubbles in the concrete superstructure. There weren't any storeys as such, but small clusters of rooms shared landings, connected to them by varying numbers of steps. There was one central spiral staircase from which all of the landings were accessible. Being a negative space, it wasn't really visible from any one point, but Alan visualised it as something like an absent bunch of grapes hanging suspended inside the concrete. If Eyes had a window it meant that his room, his bubble, grazed the side of the huge corridor that had led them to the place.

From the bar below came a crunch, a metal screech and a scream, and then a gurgle that rose into a slow, loud laugh. The sound crawled up Alan's spine. He stood at the archway between the landing and the spiral staircase, the others behind him, and shuddered.

'Go,' Churr said. 'Pighead's still down there.' Her face was pale. 'We've got to help him.'

More metal scraping, like somebody dragging chains across the stone floor, then heavy breathing, swelling into strange isolated laughs and low giggles. Footsteps. A clang. The footsteps stopped.

A voice like wet gravel, rising up the spiral staircase, bounced off the polished concrete walls. 'Are you up there, Alan? My friend Alan? Up these stairs here at the sign of The Cup and Skull? I'm going to come up, Alan, and peel you . . . smear you like a moth against these grey walls . . . take that voice of yours out of its box and wrap it around your throat, tighten it, tighten it . . .'

The voice trailed off into low incoherence, but the footsteps resumed, heavy on the steps.

'Okay,' Alan said, 'let's run. Pighead's dead. Eyes, you've got a window?' Churr grabbed Alan by the throat.

'Who is it, you cowardly fuck?' she hissed. 'Who is this now?'

Alan shook his head as best he could. 'I don't know,' he said. 'I really don't. Some new thug of Daunt's?'

'And you're prepared to just run? They've killed Pighead and anyone else who was down there, and you can just *run*?'

'What do you expect? At least if we get away then Pighead won't have died for nothing.'

'He died because of *you*!' With her free hand she slammed his head against the wall. There were tears in her eyes. 'Fuck you,' she said. 'You're nothing but fucking scum.'

'Stay here then,' Alan said. 'Do whatever you fucking want – I don't care. There's one thing in this world I care about, and it's not you, and it sure as fuck isn't Pighead. Is that not clear yet? Can I make it any clearer?' He pushed himself away from the wall, wrenched free of Churr's grip, grabbed her by the arm and her hair, then swung her out so that he was holding her over the dark stairwell. 'Do you need me to make it clearer, Churr?' he said, spitting as he spoke. 'Is that what you need? You want me to drop you? I will: I'll drop you into its path, whatever it is, and then you can die to help me get away too. Just say the word. I'm not fussy. Men, women, friends, lovers, I don't care. *I. Don't. Care.*'

Then there were hands around him, dragging him away, and Nora was holding Churr around her waist and pulling her back from the edge of the stairs. Everything was dark. His vision had scoped down to nothing but his fist wrapped in black hair. He wanted to rip it out.

Darkness was coming up the stairs. He could hear its feet, he could hear it breathing. Something was laughing – not someone but some*thing*, coming up the stairs, gurgling up around the spiral.

He saw it then, and he felt like he'd seen it before, but he didn't know when or where, or what it was. The darker shadow slowly rounded the central column of the stone stairwell. Green light spilled from its eyes: a sick glow that reflected off the long, sharp metal claws extending from its sleeves. They weren't neat blades but bundles of awful, rusty, mismatched shards, all different widths and lengths, but mostly long. Some were shining, some dull and all were vicious. That was all he could see: the green glow, the claws, the shadowed bulk.

'There you are,' it said, in its terrible voice. It was long-limbed and ink-skinned, a silhouette in a lit archway.

'Wild Alan. I've been looking for you, Alan. I've been following your voice. It led me like the scent of smoke. Such a voice, my friend. It will be a great shame to silence it for ever, but silence it I must.'

The two green lights held his gaze as he was dragged away, back into the middle of the landing and up the stairs, his heels bouncing on the steps. He'd seen those lights in the past, at a distance, looking at him from out of deep darkness, from beneath archways, from the blank windows of dead buildings, looking in from outside the House of a Thousand Hollows.

Nora slipped past him, towards the stairwell.

'No,' Alan said. 'Nora, no! You can't. Even you, you can't. Not this.'

She stood in the archway and looked down. Alan could see the green glow moving beyond her.

'Get out of the window,' Nora said. 'I'll follow.'

Alan tried to shake off the hands holding him fast, but they were long-fingered and felt like iron. Spider.

'Come on, son,' Spider said. 'We know Nora can fight.'

'But not that – please, don't let her, Spider.'

'I can't stop her.'

Nora drew a knife, and the thing on the stairs laughed again. 'A little mouse,' it said. 'A little pink-eyed mouse.'

Something flashed, and Nora reeled around to land face-first on the landing, her blood spraying against the walls. The knife flew from her hand and buried itself in the doorframe next to Alan. She was up again in an instant, long cuts striping her arms and face, and gesturing for the weapon. He worked it free. Inside Eyes' room, Churr was helping Eyes out of the window – Alan heard him yelp as he fell, but he didn't think they could be that high up. Outside was dark, but it was always dark in the chasms of the superstructure.

Alan threw the knife to Nora and she caught the tip between thumb and forefinger, immediately spun and threw it towards the archway, in front of which their attacker now stood. It was still obscured somehow, as if the shadows of the stairwell had come with it. It wore layer upon layer of tattered black cloth that swept the floor around its feet. Other than the green glow of its eyes – if they were even eyes – its face and head were impossible to see past. It was too tall to stand upright in this space, which meant it was too tall to be an ordinary person; far too tall.

The knife struck the thing right in the middle of the green glow, and stuck there. The lights wavered and dimmed and it fell to its knees and started rocking from side to side. Then it started crying, like a baby wailing. It was a sound Alan hadn't heard close up since Billy had been young, and it had the same visceral effect on him: sweat sprang from his pores in immediate response and his heart ached with something between sympathy and shared distress. He found his feet moving towards it, towards this *thing*, before he realised what he was doing.

It was clawing at the knife as it sobbed, its razor ribbons dancing. The sound it made as it pulled at the hilt was *clack-clack-clack* – metal on metal, as if beneath all those rags it was wearing one of the ancient rusty suits of armour the madder transients sometimes sported.

'Go,' Nora whispered. 'Come on, go.'

'It shouldn't have been that easy,' Alan said.

'I just buried a knife in its head and it's still alive. That's not easy. Now let's *go.*'

The thing tumbled backwards down the stairs, its wail becoming distorted by the echo.

Nora pushed him through Eyes' room to the window. He stuck his head out. It wasn't too far to fall. 'You first,' he said to Nora.

'Why the sudden chivalry?'

'Shut up. Do it.'

'No. I need my things.'

'Be quick.'

Nora disappeared into the stairwell and headed upwards. Alan turned around and, gripping the windowsill, lowered himself out, then dropped. Eyes, Churr and Spider were investigating the bikes. Two dead bodies were strewn across the main entrance, one with its intestines hanging out. Inside the bar the lights were still on, but nothing moved. The air smelled of lemon and garlic.

'Where's Nora?' Spider asked.

'Her room. She went back to her room for some stuff. But she got the thing, right between the eyes, with her knife. It fell back down the stairs.'

'Dead?'

'No.'

Nora fell amongst them like a kestrel to prey, swift and silent, her grey cloak billowing. A bag was strapped to her back, and a bundle of rolls of paper. Blood dripped onto the concrete around her.

'You're hurt,' Churr said.

'I do need to bind myself up,' Nora said, 'but first

we need to go. It's alive in there and it's going to come after us.'

Alan nearly let his bladder go as a deep, throaty roar came from the entrance to The Cup and Skull, but on turning, he saw Eyes sitting astride one of the motor-cycles. It had a low-slung brown leather seat, a deep red body, blackened twin exhausts pointing straight up behind the seat, long spring forks and workings that looked like a nest of chrome snakes. 'We could take these,' Eyes said. 'I did some electrics in the lab for old Loon. I can start them – I just need to bridge the coils.'

'Yes,' Nora said, 'yes, yes, yes. Good idea. We've got a long way to go and if we've got transport we can stick with the superstructure corridors.'

'Quick,' Alan said, 'the baby crying . . . I can hear it again.' The door to the bar was newly scratched and splintered, just hanging on its hinges. It was wedged open by one of the bodies. Green light spilled out around a pair of huge black boots. Alan peered through the gap. Something was moving at the back of the room, near the bottom of the stairs.

'It's coming,' he whispered. 'It's *crawling*.'

Eyes had hopped off the bike and was picking at the next with a knife. He kept stopping to rub at his eyes.

'Hurry up, man,' Alan said.

'It's my bloody eyes, lad,' he said. 'Come and give me a hand. You do the next one. See if that dead feller's got any steel on him. We can get two on each, so three'll do us.'

Alan chose a bike with matt-black bodywork and a seat built for two. A wolf's head snarled out from the handlebar boss. The crying was getting louder. He could still see through the doorway, just about. He could see the thing hauling itself hand over hand across the floor, weaving between the tipped-over tables and smashed chairs and leather-clad corpses.

By the time he was done, the thing was nearly at the door. Its green eyes were glowing again. Churr had climbed onto the first bike; Spider was sitting behind her. Eyes and Nora were on the second bike. Alan swung his leg over the third as whatever it was lurched shrieking through the doorway. Its cries increased in pitch, becoming hysterical, and it stood up as Alan gunned the bike. The machine shot forward, nearly leaving him behind, and he swerved, almost planted himself into one of the smooth concrete walls and then skidded away, barely managing to avoid the opposite wall.

He heard the other bikes coming up behind him, and once he had straightened up, he risked a brief glance backwards over his shoulder. Churr and Spider were at his left, Eyes and Nora at his right, and the thing, the green-eyed *thing*, it was *running*. He saw it reach up to its forehead and pull something free. Nora's knife clattered onto the concrete ahead as its baby-wail morphed into its inhuman laughing once again.

'Don't worry, Alan,' it shouted. 'I will catch up with you. Catch you. Catch you. Catch your friends, your lovers, your men, your women. Stick a knife in my head, stick in many knives. I'll just pull them out again.'

If it could run, then it too could ride. But really, Alan realised, it couldn't: it was too big to sit on one of these bikes. So what was it?

What was it? And who was it with?

A ribbon of sky was visible above them at the top of the canyon. This wasn't really a corridor so much as a cre-vasse. From the sky Alan could see it was still night; the ribbon was speckled with stars. The air rushing past was cold, and it felt good on his face, in his hair. The engines smelled of oil and heat. The greasy glass bulb on the front of the bike kept sputtering and dimming as the concrete sped past, grey and monotonous but for the cracks from which sprays of purple lavender grew and perfumed the night. He accelerated. He didn't know where he was going and for a moment he didn't care.

'I saw a warm place,' Spider said later, 'a magical place. A safe place full of orange light, and people with sated bellies. No. I didn't *see* it. I felt it. It was all very abstract.'

'Sounds like nothing,' Alan said. 'Sounds like it just gave you a fuzzy kind of buzz, not all that different from some of your leaf blends.'

'It was more than that.'

They had stopped at a corner in the superstructure corridor while Nora consulted a map. Alan didn't want to pause but she had insisted and he wasn't about to argue with her. There was no sound from behind but the wind, funnelled and intensified by the tunnels.

'Did it tell you anything useful?'

'An omen is an indicator of change,' Spider said. 'Warmth, safety, good food – that sounds like change to me.'

'Sounds like the House of a Thousand Hollows.'

'Well, then. That would be a good sign because as it stands, we're not welcome there. But I don't think it was. There was a sense of something *older* – an ancient presence, something integral to Gleam, to everything. I felt as if I was in the presence of magic.'

Alan grinned at his old friend. 'I don't think that was an omen,' he said. 'I think something in that sludge made your mind go funny.'

'Of course that's what you think,' Spider said, smiling back. 'But you are a filthy heathen. No gods, no faith. No reverence.'

16

Bridge

The bikes took them along the crevasse and out onto a wide boulevard that ran along a ravine in which a sluggish river oozed. The ravine was part of the same grey superstructure, and the river's perfect marble channel was adorned with titanic statues whose faces were almost unrecognisable. Their eyes and mouths had been widened by centuries of warm rain and the intimacies of small plants; they looked haunted, inhuman. Weeds hung from what had been ears, and their fists – raised up in triumph for who knew what – held nothing but long knots of slimy moss that trailed down all the way to the water. They stood along both sides of the river in various poses and, though far below, they were big enough for their warped features to be visible. They made Alan uneasy.

His distaste for the figures only increased when Eyes silently pointed out yet more, higher up on the other side of the ravine, crouching down and peering over the edge. An unwelcome thought crossed Alan's mind and, hesitantly, he looked up to see a great stone head directly above him, staring right back from unevenly sized eye-sockets.

The boulevard was a flat ledge halfway up the side of the colossal concrete cliff. As the sun rose it lit up and shone like a silver ribbon winding forwards. In the distance the ravine widened out, and beyond it could be seen a series of huge spheres, barely touching the ground, like bubbles that had just landed. They were still indistinct in the morning haze.

A long way off, over Nora's right shoulder, was a long arch bridging the canyon. The line of it cut across the even-more-distant distant orbs. Dragons blinked in the remains of the night.

The disfigured faces looking down at them passed by, one after another, on and on. Maybe they'd all looked the same when the Builders put them there, or maybe not. Either way, they all looked different now. Alan assigned them characters: this one was a thug, that one a drudge, the next a drunk, the next one lost. The sound of the bikes' engines became the new silence, but there was something rhythmic that chimed with the passing of the statues. The daylight came pink, tinged as it always was with Corval's colour.

Alan looked down at the river to the right. It was murky green, with algae, presumably. There were round holes in the smooth sides of the ravine from which the river had once been fed, judging by the green stains beneath them.

The air out there was fresh. They were on their way, and Billy was at the end of the road, safe and smiling. The route might be labyrinthine, it might be knotty, but it was the right road; the sunrise and the wind in Alan's hair and the clean scents of the canyon all conspired to convince him of that.

White birds hovered around and floated on the river like motes of dust, so far away that only their general movements were discernible. Perhaps their coarse voices were echoing up; Alan couldn't tell over the thrum of the motorcycles.

He let himself fall back to the rear of the group. On the bike in front, Churr was holding on to the pillion handles and looking down into the canyon with a faint frown. She had flattened her short hair with grease, so it didn't move much, even in the rushing backdraught. She glanced at Alan almost involuntarily as the motorcycles passed each other but did not make eye contact. Spider didn't even acknowledge Alan; his head was tipped back, his eyes half-closed, his smile wide, his expression almost blissful. Perhaps he wasn't yet done with his toad omens.

Further ahead, Nora's long blonde hair streamed out behind her, obscuring both her own and Eyes' faces.

Lizards darted from cracks in the stone, and then, at the sight of the travellers, darted straight back in. Most were no more than finger-big, but every now and again Alan caught sight of a fist-sized wedge of reptilian head vanishing.

The integrity of the stone was diminishing. There were more hairlines in the smooth cliff rising upwards on their left; there was more grit and detritus on the shining ribbon of the road.

The image of two green glowing eyes came unbidden into Alan's mind and he looked back over his shoulder, suddenly fearful of a living colossus on their tail, a giant claw-handed thing astride its own impossible vehicle, a black spiked bike huge enough to hold its unique rider, adorned with bones and trailing green fumes. But, of course, the road behind them was clear. Theirs were the only human souls around. They clung to their machines and the machines clung to the ground: a loud insectile convoy roaring through the dawn.

They came to the bridge, and the bridge was cracked – not catastrophically, and not decisively, but cracked enough for Eyes to spit and insist *no damn way*.

'That's the way we need to go,' Nora said, sliding down from her seat.

'That's not a way at all,' Eyes said.

'It's looked like this for longer than I've been alive.'

'Don't mean much,' Eyes muttered. 'That don't mean much of anything.'

The bridge, which projected out across the abyss, was maybe two feet wide and two feet deep. It had no walls, no rails, no barriers of any sort. It was made of pink-veined marble, and Alan wondered if it had originally been ornamental. The far end was blurred in the morning haze, but Alan could see no cliff-hugging path on the other side of the crevasse: the bridge became a road that cut straight through the mountainous concrete bulk, resulting in a deep sharp 'V' in the skyline opposite. So no, not ornamental. A bridge for crazy people, perhaps – but then, the Builders had been nothing if not inscrutable.

From up here he could see the globes were made out of beaten copper panels. They were gigantic, and there were five of them, arranged to form an 'X' shape. They stood in the centre of a vast concave dip in which shallow green water had pooled and stagnated. The orbs were reflected in the still water. They looked as if they were only barely attached to the ground, as if they could roll or float away at any given moment.

The statues beneath the bridge held metal things between them – grilles and filters and water wheels, all nearly destroyed by rust.

'What were they?' Spider asked Nora, pointing at the spheres.

'I don't know,' Nora said.

'Is anybody living in them?' Alan asked. 'We could play for some food that isn't fucking snail.'

Churr gave him a look. 'You can tell who grew up in the Pyramid,' she said. 'And anyway, soft lad, we didn't collect any snail. We were attacked and we ran away. Remember?'

'Oh, yes,' Alan said, 'of course. That's okay, then. No snail. Nothing.'

'We also have to start considering the consequences of our arrival for any hosts,' Spider said. 'Our hosts so far have not fared well. We have to accept that if we are going to stay with anybody else, then we have a duty of care towards them.'

'Alan here isn't going to honour a duty of care to anyone,' Churr said. 'He's made that very clear.'

Everybody looked at Alan. Maybe they were waiting for him to deny it. He scratched his chin and said nothing.

'What that means, then, is that we must hunt and forage,' Nora said. 'This is not ideal, and not the way I envisaged our journey, but if we are to move swiftly, unencumbered by responsibility for others, then it is the best way. I was not expecting to be targeted by such an indiscriminate enemy so soon.'

'I like that,' Eyes said, quietly. '*Unencumbered.*'

'Nora,' Alan said, 'do you know what that thing was, back at The Cup and Skull?'

Nora shook her head.

'Anybody else?'

Nobody said anything. Alan looked back over his shoulder again, but there was nothing moving along the path.

'Are we ready to cross the bridge?' Nora asked.

'I'm not crossing the fucker,' Eyes said. 'Can't we just go down past them big balls? Looks much more sensible to me.' Eyes had not yet taken off the blindfold; he rubbed his eyes underneath.

'Yes,' Nora said, 'let's just go wherever looks sensible to you. I'm sure that method will deliver us to our *very specific* destination in no time at all.'

'Didn't none of your tribe teach you to respect your elders?'

'They tried, but I respect those who behave respectably. Only those. And precious few of my elders met my criteria. Neither do you, for that matter. So you go ahead, Eyes. You "go down past them big balls", as you put it. I wouldn't advise it, because you would die, but in light of how little weight you put on my advice, I understand if you go ahead anyway. I wouldn't mourn you.'

'What down there would kill me?'

'Go and find out.'

Eyes ripped the bandage blindfold from his head, threw it on the ground and dug the heels of his hands into his sockets. 'Builders be damned,' he said through gritted teeth. 'I can't take much more of this infernal itching. It'll be the death of me.'

'Believe me,' Nora said, 'one as stupid and irritating as yourself has lots of deaths to choose from.'

'Eyes,' Alan said, picking the blindfold up, 'don't be so bloody foolish. This here rag is the only thing keeping you from going blind, and now it's all shitty and gritty. And it could have gone over the edge! You're a pig-headed dunce. Take it back.'

'You know when folks say they can't think straight?' Eyes said. 'When they're crazy with pain, or because of something so annoying it makes them wish they were dead?'

'The itching,' Alan said. 'Yes, yes. I know.'

'Not the itching, though the itching is infernal. *You*.' He thrust out a hand. 'But go on, then. Give me the damned thing back. I'll rinse it when we've got some water.'

Alan returned the blindfold, and Eyes stuffed it into his belt.

'So is it true?' Spider asked, inclining his head towards the orbs. 'Dangerous?'

'Yes.' Nora's shoulders slumped. 'Something there kills – it's something in the air, or in the water, or inside the spheres themselves. First your hair falls out, then your teeth, then comes a red rash that turns to lesions, then copious bleeding, then—'

'All right, all right, all right,' Eyes said, still bent over, still rubbing his eyes. 'The bridge it is. And I'm right sorry, but I can't barely see any more. Someone's going to have to take me by the hand.'

'Don't worry,' Alan said. 'I will.' He and Spider looked at each other.

'You haven't got your mister, have you?' Spider asked.

Eyes stood up, forearm across his face. 'Must've dropped out me pocket in the Cavern that night. I've got my ointment but it's running low. That's why I tried to keep the blindfold on. But without the mister it gets so itchy.' He frowned. 'It's a bloody mess, is what it is.'

'We can get water,' Alan said, 'and keep some in a bottle for you, or something.'

Nora and Churr both shook their heads. 'Not out here,' Churr said. 'Don't know where it's come from.'

'You must know some clean rivers or wells or springs, or something.'

'Not many,' Nora said, 'and things change. We have to keep testing those we do know because they can get contaminated – by swamp water, or when a gutter rusts through.'

'There is lots of life out here in the Discard, and lots of death,' Churr said. 'Poisonous plants. Venomous insects. Rotting bodies.'

'And from outside nature there are also threats,' Nora continued. 'Sickening metals. Brightly coloured sludges. Bandits spoiling well-known sources.'

'So if we're no longer playing for our keep, where do we go?' Alan asked.

'For the last time,' Nora said, 'we go over this bridge. If you're not going to trust me, you might as well turn back.'

She went first, in case of ambush. 'I can evade any missiles,' she said airily, 'and I will shout out loud, and then you will know that we are being watched.' She didn't wheel a bike, but crept out onto the span alone, exposed. Loose strands of her hair floated in the breeze. As she ascended the curve of the arch, her cloak started to flap about her legs. She looked very small and far away long before she reached the apex.

'Is the wind picking up?' Eyes said. 'It is, isn't it? Typical.'

'We spent too long talking,' Churr said. 'We shouldn't have stopped.' She looked sideways at Alan and then spoke to Eyes and Spider. 'I want one of you two – at least one of you – between Alan and me,' she said.

'I wasn't really going to drop you,' Alan said.

'I didn't know that. I still don't. Not sure you do either, in truth.'

Spider cleared his throat. 'These bikes are going to be a real joy to transfer,' he said.

'I'll go next then,' Alan said, 'and I'll take you, Eyes. Come on.'

'I'll follow them, Churr,' Spider said, 'if that would help put you at ease.'

'Puts me right at ease, Spider. Thank you.'

'Who's going to hold my hand?' Eyes asked. 'Will it be Daft Lad?'

'I suppose it will,' Alan said. 'Oh, the honour and the pleasure.'

'Just take my damn hand and stop flapping that mouth.' Eyes had his left forearm across his eyes still. He held out his right hand.

The humidity would increase as the sun rose, but this early in the day the air still retained an edge. In its high places, at the low hours, Gleam could be just about cool.

Alan tried not to look down as he walked. His body was twisted awkwardly so that he could hold Eyes' hand the whole way. He had to think about how he was moving, and walking was like breathing: as soon as you started thinking about it, it got trickier. His feet felt heavy and he was reluctant to lift them too far from the surface, or for too long, because he had this notion that it was in these brief periods of lesser stability that disaster might strike or that clumsiness might occur. So he shuffled, and was clumsy, and Eyes shuffled along behind him and was clumsy too. The surface of the bridge was rough and uneven, battered over time by the passage of hobnail boots. There were cracks in it, hairline cracks, but surely that was just what marble looked like, wasn't it? The bridge must be very, very old – it was part of what Nora called the original structure. Alan quailed as that meaning sank in. It wasn't as if he knew how old it really was, but it was *too* old. How was it even still standing? Its continued existence suddenly felt unlikely. Did Nora want them all killed? It was okay for her, she couldn't weigh more than a few stone, but for Alan and Eyes, together – and for the bikes, when they came to wheeling them over . . . His palms grew wet and keeping hold of Eyes became a challenge. It wasn't the height so much – heights didn't usually bother him – but the exposure. He was having a crisis of confidence in the ground beneath his feet. He started shuffling again. He felt as if the statues, so far down below, were looking up at him.

'What's it *for*, Eyes?' Alan asked. 'What's the bridge *for*?'

'Now's not the time for daft questions, lad.'

'The orbs. What are the orbs for?'

'What's got into you? They're not *for* anything, are they? They're just there.'

'But why did the Builders build them?'

'The Builders are just what we blame for all this chaos, Alan. "The Builders" is just a turn of phrase to make sense of all this nonsense by gathering it all up into one handy story. It's not real, you know that. Don't let that Nora get into your head with her talk of "original structures" and all that crap.'

'I've never made my mind up.'

Back in the Pyramid, Management said the Discard had arisen entirely from Pyramid waste: a twisted civilisation sprung from exiles, swollen over millennia. They'd said that the Pyramid used to exile many more people because Pyramid laws had been stricter then. It had been a harder place to live, with almost half of those born inside it eventually being thrown down the Discard Chutes for failing to meet all of the Utmost Vitals at their Annual Reviews. Management went easier on them now; the Pyramid had become soft and luxurious. That was the story, anyway.

But if that was true, why was the Discard not full? Why wasn't it thriving? Why wasn't it *all* shacks and shops and paths? Where was the degenerate empire? Where were their homes, their bars, their stores, their children? If they were all dead then why – and where were their bones? Sure, people lived in the Discard, but they were scattered. And they had *adopted* it. There was no sense that they had *built* it. It didn't really feel as if it had been built for people to live in at all. Or, at least, most of it hadn't, other than the odd bulbous concrete blob that felt like a honeycomb or a wasps' nest, places like the House of a Thousand Hollows.

So Nora's theories made more sense to Alan than what he'd been told in the Pyramid. And she was almost certainly unhinged, so what that said about the Pyramid . . . Well, it didn't say anything Alan didn't already know. The Pyramid was a knot of lies and rituals that referenced only each other and combined to mean less than nothing, and that the word of a remorseless killer shed more light on it just indicated the depths of the darkness the Pyramid operated in.

They were nearly at the highest point of the archway when Eyes slipped. His hand slid from Alan's hand, and he fell.

17

Daunt's Berserkers

McAlkie had been a barrel-chested man with a mane of brass-coloured hair, so shiny as to have been the metal itself. His skin was more or less the same colour from standing out all day, either butchering pigs in the yard or standing on his pallet, preaching. He did nothing but one or the other; friends of his, like Alan's parents, said he never slept. He didn't preach any of the religions, not Old Green's Way or Amphibiasm or the Builders' Intention, and especially not the Book of Satis or the Weight of Tradition, both apparently descended from Pyramid thinking, and both good for nothing but pissing on. But he was preaching all the same: he worked tirelessly to spread the word of the Anti-Pyramid League, which, back then, had really been something, according to him at least.

When Alan had been a child chasing chickens and kicking stones through the dirt of Modest Mills, McAlkie was part of the furniture. He was the closest thing the town had to a statue, standing proud in the square, towering over all those around him by virtue of his passion and the volume of his voice. He used to wear ragged trousers and a long brown leather waistcoat, the same one he used for his butchery, with nothing beneath. The sound of his speeches was the background noise of Alan's childhood, audible from whichever mossy ruin or muddy basin the kids were playing in, but more than that – McAlkie had a force that drew in those who passed him by, adults and children alike, which meant his words sank down deep and stayed there. He was respected in Modest Mills. Other Discard orators came and went back then, some insensible, some threatening, some powerful, but none had the power and reach of McAlkie. And it worked: word was spreading. Representatives came to Modest Mills from the House of a Thousand Hollows, from Wha House, from the Hinning House, from the Mapmakers, from the transients, even from various bandit tribes – those who did not self-identify as bandits. They came to forge alliances, to exchange news, to make plans, because McAlkie wasn't doing all that talking for nothing. He was building an army.

Alan did not always understand McAlkie's words, but he felt the fire in them. He could tell that the big red man was always angry at the Pyramid, but he couldn't necessarily tell why. Later on he came to understand, of course, but as a child all that mattered was that the words somehow promised a future different from the present; that things shouldn't be the way they were, and that they didn't have to be the way they were, that things could change for the better. Alan found the speeches inspiring – uplifting, almost . . .

'I get low, people. I get lower than the bright beetles, lower than a lizard's cock. I get so low when I look up at that high spire, that gleaming peak, the upper reaches of that dark Pyramid, the point of the pointed hexagon that spikes the sky beneath which we toil, Millers, the sky that they purport to share with us, but when they look out of their high windows, this is the question I want you to ask, and I want you to answer it too: when they look out of their high windows, do they see what we see? No, they do not. Now, this time I'm not even going to talk about the taxes, only the sky. Their night skies remain unspoiled by devilish shadows, by great blank shapes looming up over them like the house of a dead god. Their night skies are beautiful, and ours are spoiled by the same device that makes them so. And they might say, "Well, McAlkie, you are naught but a petty butcher. Is it right to incite anger over a mere disparity in circumstance? Stop being so jealous." And I do have it in me to be jealous, I will not deny it, because although I am jealous I strive to be honest, too. But it is not jealousy that drives me to this box each day to stand here and speak to you. It is justice. It is clear to me and to you, too – I know it – it is clear that what drives me is justice. I am not a wild man raving simply because I want something I do not have – something that somebody else has. I would be a pitiful creature indeed if my feelings towards other humans were cracked and riven as a consequence of their possessions. But I am an *angry* man. Because from where did the Pyramidders take the stone with which they elevate themselves so highly? Did it just rise from the ground beneath them, a divine reward for their inherent righteousness, their inborn superiority? Did they wake one morning up there in the great vault, surprised and relieved at having undergone some cosmic test and being found deserving? No, it did not; and no, they did not, people, no. No and no. Is there a good reason, a logical reason, a just reason, for them to be up there, where they are, keeping the stars from us? No. Because where did the stone come from? If it is not magic, then what is it? Let me tell you – last night I had a visitor. A small man with a great snail's shell on his back, and yes, you may have seen him, stumbling into our town, exhausted after his long journey. And he told me that he knew of a place – imagine such a thing, if you will – a great scar in the world, from which that fine black marble had been extracted. A quarry, its sheer cliffs dark and translucent, worked in ancient days by – by who? By people like you and me, that's who! Like the cotton that we turn into the robes they wear, like the pigs we farm for them, like the . . .'

His bare arms were muscled like twisted tree roots, and he'd wave them and clench his fists and point and gesture.

But he never seemed mad, not like some of the others. He never spoke too fast, and he never opened his eyes too wide, and he didn't spit, or at least not much. And he laughed, and sometimes he lowered his voice and spoke kindly to the children who sat cross-legged in front of him, the children whose parents were weaving robes in the long attics of the houses of Modest Mills. Alan often sat and watched him, on his own, with other children when they were tired of running around, and with his parents.

The last time Alan saw McAlkie like that – strong, and certain, and proud – he was being dragged through the dust between two Arbitrators. Alan was standing in the middle of the road and the houses all around him were in flames. The sky was full of red smoke that streamed from a hole in the side of the Pyramid. He was seven years old. Arbitrators were stalking through the fires, putting knives into those villagers who were still moving. He was looking at the bodies of his mum and dad. An Arbitrator was walking in his direction, blade out. He was so tall, and so *clean*. He wore a rounded helmet of dark leather. He wore armour – panels of beaten metal – between which folds of dark, loose, thick cloth were visible. This cloth was decorated with tiny crystals that shone as if they gave off their own light – and so was the skin of his face, Alan realised, astonished. Most Arbitrators wore masks, but not this one. A line of glimmering stones ran from the outside corner of each of this man's eyes, and he had beads beneath his eyebrows and cheekbones, which gave his face ridges. Later Alan learned these ridges signified rank, but at the time he had simply looked monstrous.

The man smiled. His long, pointed chin dimpled. He moved his knife languidly towards Alan's neck.

McAlkie's voice distracted him. 'Let the lad live, you fucking maggot!' he bellowed. 'You kill that boy, I'm going to try an' eat your mate here's sword and die meself, and then where'll you be, eh? You'll have no one to ask about the explosion.'

The Arbitrator frowned. He looked at Alan, then picked him up by the front of his shirt. He stared into Alan's eyes. The Arbitrator's eyes were green and bright. The jewel tears flickered orange. His face was thin – it looked thinner than it was because of the beads. The Arbitrator dropped Alan and he landed in a heap, his legs giving out beneath him. He felt the dust that clouded up stick to his cheeks, and he coughed.

'Troemius!' the Arbitrator said, not loudly, but precisely. An Arbitrator with its mask on stepped forward.

'Yes, sir?'

'We will take this boy with us into the Pyramid and raise him properly. You will be responsible for his passage back inside, and you will personally hand him over to the Teachers. Understood?'

'Yes, sir.'

The Arbitrator who had intended to kill Alan gave him a swift kick in the stomach and then moved on.

Alan curled up around the pain and shook with sobs. He could hear McAlkie yelling still, but was too far out of it to be able to interpret the words. He felt hands on his body, was thrown over somebody's shoulder. The bodies of his parents receded until they were obscured by smoke and flame. Somewhere behind him in the convoy of Pyramid troops, McAlkie was struggling with his captors, but Alan passed out then and didn't see McAlkie again until both of them were back on the outside of the Pyramid, and the great orator who'd saved his life had had his eyelids cut off and been tortured into the wizened, jittery drunk who could barely lift a cup to his lips without spilling everywhere, who couldn't cross a bridge without having a hand to hold, and maybe not even then.

Eyes' feet went out backwards and he waved his arms about in a panic as he fell forward and ended up landing heavily on his knee, right on the edge of the bridge. His legs and hips hung out over empty space for a moment and then swung down, dragging his whole body off into nothing. Alan saw him scrambling for purchase, his movements frantic, the look on his face so extreme as to be comical, and grabbed Eyes' right wrist with both hands – but Eyes was heavier than he looked and he pulled Alan off-balance. He didn't fall, but he wasn't strong enough and didn't have the purchase to lift Eyes back up. And his hands were sweaty . . . He dimly registered the blindfold, wrenched free of Eyes' belt by the edge of the bridge, tumbling in the empty space.

'Your other hand,' Alan shouted, 'get your other hand up here! You're a hell of a lot fatter than you look – grab hold of this bridge, come on, Eyes. *Come on, McAlkie*, do it . . . your other hand – come *on*.'

'Can't see,' Eyes said, staring up past Alan with his open eyes, 'I can't see for shit, lad. Just fucking drop me.'

'*Stop it*. Come on, lift that hand – just feel around. Pretend you're in the dark, that's all.'

Eyes groped in the air with his left hand, but kept stopping and wiping the tears from his face, just a reflex thing. He wasn't crying, but his eyes kept filling up and overflowing, and he couldn't leave them alone.

'Leave your damned eyes alone,' Alan said.

'Can't tell you how much they hurt, lad.'

'Maybe they do, but I can't hold you much longer. I'm trying to shuffle back here, but if I shift at all I'm going to fall.' He shook his head, tried to laugh. 'Your eyes are hurting, my back is hurting . . .'

'I've a dense and solid body,' Eyes said, 'I will not deny it. Where is that Spider friend of ours?'

'Doubtless he is on his way,' Alan said. 'It's a long bridge, far longer than I knew.' He looked up, and whatever hope he'd had of help drained away.

'Spider is fighting,' he said. 'Spider and Churr are

fighting with somebody at the end of the bridge. How thoughtless of them.' He could see somebody else rappelling down the cliff above the road on a rope.

'What about that Nora girl?' Eyes said. 'Where is she, our great hope?'

'She is over the crest,' Alan said, 'but I don't rightly know where she is. Nor will she know of our predicament, not unless she comes back. Though perhaps she too has been assailed.'

'So it all depends on you,' Eyes said, 'a drunk and a layabout with a passable voice and not much else.'

'It's more than passable. And in truth, no, it doesn't depend on me: it depends on that left hand of yours. Come on, Eyes. If you can talk so much, you can find this massive bit of rock. It's not like your arm isn't working.'

Eyes did find the edge of the bridge, and took some of his own weight. He tried to pull himself up and then yelped. 'Slippy,' he gasped. 'It's so damned slippy, this marble.'

'Wait,' Alan said. He was able to move now, so he pushed himself backwards, stabilised himself and swiftly transferred his right hand from Eyes' right wrist to his left. 'Now,' he said, 'you pull, and I'll pull.'

This time it worked, and between them they got Eyes back up on the bridge.

'Old Green be damned, I'm sorry,' Eyes said. 'By Green, by the Toad, by the Builders, I'm sorry. Leave me here, lad. What just nearly happened will keep nearly happening until it does happen, and each and every time it'll slow you down.'

'I'm not leaving you out here with no food, no water and no good eyes. You're with us now for the duration and I won't have this nonsense polluting the air between us again. For all that, stay here: just lie here and don't move. I'm going to go back. Spider and Churr can't defend the bikes all by themselves, and we can't afford to lose them. I don't want to lose them.'

'Who *are* the bastards?'

'I don't know yet.'

'I want to help.'

'Keep going, if you can. Crawl. Try to get to the other side and send Nora back.'

Eyes nodded and rose onto all fours. 'Look at this,' he said. 'Look at me: a blind old beast with a ruined knee.'

'I'm going now,' Alan said.

Once free of his charge he found he could move quickly. He stayed low and drew his long knives from his boots as he moved.

Spider and Churr were retreating along the bridge, their backs to Alan as he approached them. They were fighting a gang of berserkers: shaven-headed men with thick arms, foam around their mouths, and Daunt's mushroom symbol tattooed onto their foreheads. The air between the berserkers and Alan's companions was a blur of flashing metal. Spider and Churr were quick and strong, but Daunt's fools were no doubt fighting for the promise of their queen's body and her gracious satisfaction of their various addictions. They wore dead lizards around their necks and had long yellow teeth pushed through their ears. Their faces were misshapen from past brawls – noses bent, cheekbones uneven, ears so swollen and puffy they were only recognisable by their location on these dented heads.

There were three on the bridge, two in front and one, still chewing his mushrooms, waiting behind to replace one if he dropped.

Too eager, Alan thought. Any moment now the frenzy would descend and drive the meathead right on through. This was no planned, co-ordinated attack; no way would Daunt send these foamers out on an actual kidnap mission. Probably the encounter was pure chance; they were most likely one of several gangs out gathering supplies for her.

A blade flew out from the combat, spinning wildly into the void, and Churr's berserker turned his head to watch it go, his empty hand still moving as if nothing had happened. Churr sank her own steel into the man's neck and then used her foot to push him off the knife and off the bridge before stepping around and stabbing Spider's opponent in the side. He screamed, and then he too was falling headlong towards the distant river. The third berserker was already sprinting away, his frenzy lending him an unnatural speed. Alan nearly went to throw his knives, but stopped himself. He'd only miss. The man ran and ran until he reached the concrete cliff, and then he started pulling himself hand over hand up the rope.

'Back to Daunt, no doubt,' Spider said, panting.

'Let him go,' Churr said. 'He doesn't know anything.'

'He knows where we are,' Alan said, 'and that we killed two of her men.'

'Will he know *who* we are?'

'What route does Daunt take to Dok?' Alan asked. 'Are we on it?'

'I don't think so. I don't think Daunt has a *route*, as such. It's more of a relay, a chain of buyers and sellers. She uses local communities where she can, and bikers, transients, you name it. Her people do the bit at the dangerous end – in Dok itself – and safeguard the rest of the trade.'

'And it just works? Nobody messes her around?'

'No.' Churr ran her tongue around her teeth, still staring at the man climbing the rope in the distance. 'Well, not until now.'

18

The Oversight

Once over the bridge they roared across a concrete plain, the roof of something, blank but for cracks and weeds. Alan always thought he'd been comfortable with the scale of their habitat, but he felt monstrously exposed beneath Satis and Corval and the stars here, when they came out. He had known Gleam was big, but had never realised it was big enough to accommodate such expanses of nothing. Nora called this place the 'Oversight'. They all came to smell of engine fumes, but he thought it was preferable to the scent of stale sweat. That night they built a fire of uprooted sunwort and redgrass, though it burned dismally, and Alan picked at Snapper and sang a song about the golem army that some believed built Gleam. He made some notes in his lyric book about there being magic in the stone itself, but nowhere else.

Eyes lay on his back and moaned softly as the night sky turned. Spider worked on new tattoo designs. Nora had unrolled several scrolls and sat with her back to the others, her work illuminated not by the firelight but by an uneven chunk of white stone that worked in the same way as the reservoir globes they used in the Pyramid. 'This particular light has certain qualities I require for my maps,' she explained. 'Firelight is good for some Map-makers, but not for me. We all work differently.' Alan didn't know if she was making a map or reading one, but he presumed the latter as from behind she was motion-less. But later, when he saw her hands, they were black with ink, or something like it.

After Nora was done working each evening she would lie down behind Churr, who was often restless, and wrap her arms around Churr's waist, and then Churr would quieten and sleep like a dead croc – apart from one night, when Nora and Churr whispered long into the small hours. Churr's voice was louder, and she was crying. Alan thought that they thought he was asleep.

'I don't want to be that way any more,' she was saying. 'I don't want to live in the dirt, eating nothing much and what there is is either stolen or bought with stolen bugs.'

Nora was murmuring assent or platitudes, or maybe no words at all, just soothing sounds.

'I don't want to steal from the rich any more,' Churr continued, 'I want to *be* the rich. I don't want the crumbs, I want the loaf. I'm not like my people any more. I'm like you, Nora. I'm like you.'

And when Alan did sleep, he slept badly. He woke repeatedly, the sound of a baby crying in his ears.

In the morning it was Churr who found the detachable metal cans built into the body of the bike she shared with Spider, and in between them, hidden deep inside the body of the bike, weapons. Upon investigation, the other bikes were also found to hold such a cache. The cans were empty for now, but still ... The weapons included chains with handles, knuckledusters of gruesome design, gnarled cudgels sprouting razor blades, slingshots, and – inside Alan's bike – a small crossbow.

'Who'd be best with this?' he asked. 'There's only one quiver of bolts. We shouldn't waste them.'

'I have never used one,' Nora said, 'and Eyes is blind.'

'Aye, lass,' Eyes said. 'Thanks for that.'

'I'll take it,' Churr said. 'I had one of those once. Lost it at cards. Give it to me.'

'I think Churr is probably a better shot than me,' Spider said. 'What about yourself, Alan?'

Alan felt disinclined to give the weapon to Churr but he could not justify keeping it himself, so he handed it over. Churr strapped it to her back, climbed onto the bike and motioned for Spider to sit behind her. She kicked the rest up, coaxed the machine into life and sped away.

Clouds of dust came up behind their bikes on their second Oversight day and the engines sounded sick. Nora assured them that she would get them to fuel before the fumes were gone. The bikes had bulky tanks designed for deep Discard foraging, she said, and they would be okay.

It wasn't only the bikes that were running on empty, though. Already the companions were down to chewing plants, though Nora was scornful when Eyes complained. 'I have lived half my life like this,' she said.

'You keep talking about your life as a length of time,' Eyes said between grimaces, his leg bloody and his eyes raw, 'but even when I could see, I couldn't see that your life has been as long as all that.'

'I am thirty-two years old,' Nora said.

'Aye, but by whose calendar?'

'I believe the Mapmaker calendar is not significantly different from that which you used in the House, which itself is not dissimilar to the Pyramid Year Clock,' Nora said. 'Built on sun cycles, all.'

'You never have thirty-two of our years,' Eyes said.

'People have thought me a child all my adult life,' Nora said, 'and it grows more wearisome with time, not less. Now, Eyes, I will put this gently on account of your various conditions: shut your fucking pipehole.'

Spider laughed uproariously at that, which put Eyes in a right sulk. Spider had the highest spirits of all of them, but then, he had survived on little more than whisky, smoke and hallucinogenics for as long as Alan had known him – ever since Spider had put that first tattoo on Alan's shoulder: the Black Pyramid set against a broken skull that rose like a great bad moon. Alan thought it doubtful that Spider had much of a functioning stomach behind all that hair, inside that knot of dried-up organs and leathery sinew. His insides probably looked like a rack of meat hung up for curing.

Alan could not stop thinking about food.

Nora pointed out the petrol tank as the sun neared the horizon. It was a black cube shimmering against the reddening sky. 'It will be manned,' she said, 'but they might help us out for a song or two.'

'Will they survive it?'

'We approach the tank, or we give up the motorcycles.'

'It's not like they've got nothing to barter.'

'You think our green-eyed friend is interested in petrol?'

'I don't know. I don't know how it's tracking us, or if it's tracking us. I don't know what it is.'

Alan did not admit that he had seen it in his head during the brief snatches of sleep he'd achieved the previous night. He did not say that he'd heard its infant voice carrying across the plain, or that its nature was somehow familiar to him.

'We can't give up the bikes,' he said firmly. 'Not with Eyes the way he is.'

'To the tank, then.'

What Alan had thought was the whole tank turned out to be just one end of it protruding from the stone. A black metal cube with edges of about twenty feet, a riot of green, yellow and purple grasses growing thickly from the small gap between it and the ground. Alan was actually excited to notice a few decent-sized snails sheltering amongst the foliage.

There was a ladder on the side of the tank.

'Hello?' Alan shouted up.

'Back away,' croaked a voice. 'Back away.'

Alan looked up to see a hunchback, wearing goggles, crouching on the top of the cube. She looked more like a giant toad than anything, dressed as she was in a shapeless green waxed cotton coat, the kind of attire you didn't often see out in the open, given the heat. She was pointing an old blunderbuss down at him.

'Back away,' the woman said again.

'We mean no harm,' Alan said, holding his hands up.

'Nobody ever does, do they? Nobody goes around all, like, I'm gonna *harm* you.'

'How does this work? Do you barter? Do you serve only the biker clans?'

'What you got for me? What you got for me, eh? Let's see what you got.'

'Bartering, then?'

'Show me what you fuckin' got!' She jabbed the blunderbuss in Alan's direction. 'No more talk!'

'We can play you a song,' Alan said.

'What good's a fuckin' song gonna do me? That a joke?' A sudden shriek of laughter. 'That a joke? I'm gonna eat a song, am I? Gonna drink your lovely voice?'

'We've got drink,' Alan said. 'Eyes – give the good lady your flask.'

Eyes looked towards Alan, his gaze unfocused. 'No,' he said.

'Eyes, come on.'

'I'm going to die soon, Alan,' Eyes said. 'Let me finish my whisky.'

'You're not going to die.'

'I am.'

'You are not.' Alan dismounted, strode over to Eyes and wrenched the flask from his pocket. 'Here,' he said, turning and holding the flask up to the woman. 'This flask for us to refuel completely.'

'What's in it, eh?'

'Whisky.'

'But what whisky, *what* whisky? Is it good whisky? Is it the good stuff? Or is it nasty bathtub shine, eh?'

'It's good stuff,' Alan lied.

'And is it full?'

'No. But it is made of silver. And it's heavy.'

The woman was silent for a moment. 'Throw it up then, quick – come on, throw it up here for old Mother Margo to have a look.'

Alan was about to throw it, then he changed his mind. 'I'll bring it up,' he said. 'The cap's loose.'

'Wait, wait, wait – what else?'

'We've got some bugs,' Alan said. 'Not many, mind.'

'I'll have 'em,' said Mother Margo. 'All of 'em.'

'Do you need anything else?'

'Handsome fella over there – you got gold hidden in all that beard?'

'I've got two chains around my neck,' Spider said. 'But we need some fuel before we agree on anything else.'

'Gather the bugs, songbird, and come on up. Just you on your lonesome, like. We'll talk terms. And take them damned knives from yer boots. I'm ugly but I'm not a fool.' Mother Margo disappeared from the edge of the tank.

Alan nodded. 'Bugs,' he whispered to the others. 'Hand them over. I know everybody's got some.'

Spider took a small pouch from behind his beard and shook out a handful. Churr withdrew a couple from a pocket sewn to the inside of her black vest top. Eyes shook his head. He was shining with sweat and as white as some of Nora's parchment.

'I don't have any,' Nora said. 'Mapmakers don't use them.'

'Come on,' Alan said.

'I don't have any. Take this.' Nora handed him a small pink crystal. 'Not very valuable but conducive to rest.'

Alan threw his last five bugs into the small collection, dropped his knives onto the ground, then climbed the ladder.

There was a small wooden hut on top of the tank, bleached grey. Mother Margo settled herself into a chair by its door and took off her hat. Her white hair was short and curly. Her goggles were home-made from bottle bottoms and some kind of gut. Her mouth rested open, not closed, displaying what teeth she had left. They were pointed, but not filed; it was as if she had nothing but canines, all pointing in different directions. She waved a hand at the metal tank on which her home was built. 'Put it all down, then,' she said. 'Spread it all out like.'

Alan did as she demanded and stepped back.

'Not enough for all the tanks,' she said after a moment. She plucked a snail from out of a fold in her coat and examined it. It retracted its horns and retreated into its shell as she brought it close to her goggles. 'I want that hairy lad's chains an' all, and then you can fill all the bikes right up.'

Alan nodded. 'Thank you. I'll go and tell the others.'

'Wait.' Mother Margo levelled the blunderbuss at Alan and then threw the snail into her mouth. The shell crunched as she bit it and juice spurted from between her lips. Alan looked away as he waited for her to finish her snack. When he looked back she was wiping brown fragments from her chin. 'Maybe I'll have a song or two after all. Gets awful lonely up here, it does. Traders come and go but they don't hang around any longer'n they have to, and they don't offer nothin' but food.'

'Food's important, though.'

'Yeah, but . . .' Mother Margo raised her gun. 'Just sing a fucking song, all right?' She spat more shell as she spoke.

'All right,' Alan said, raising his hands once more. 'All right.' He swung Snapper around. 'He's not at his best,' he explained. 'The heat, the conditions—'

'Tell me about it.'

'Can I shout to the others?'

'Yeah, go on then.'

Alan shouted down, 'Spider, throw me your chains. I'm going to play a song or two up here. And start filling the tanks up.' He turned back to Mother Margo. 'I need a moment to tune him,' he said, indicating Snapper.

'Them's down there'll need this t'release the valve.' Mother Margo pulled an unusually shaped spanner from her pocket, and threw it over the side of the tank. There was a clatter and a curse from below. Then she started undoing her voluminous coat. 'You know any baby songs?' she asked.

'What, like lullabies?'

'Yeah, like lullabies.' Mother Margo withdrew a small wooden box from inside her coat and took the lid off. She held up the box so that he could see its contents more clearly.

He tried not to recoil.

Inside the box were little bones, and a little human skull. The skeleton was surrounded by dried flowers and scraps of bright cloth. 'My daughter,' Mother Margo said. 'Birthed her alone up here, tried to feed her, but I didn't have much milk, did I? Not here, not on my diet. Didn't have much water. Didn't see any traders for a long time. I woulda taken her elsewhere but for havin' her did for my back good and proper – couldn't barely walk. She didn't starve but I couldn't keep her strong, not strong enough to fight off whatever got her. I dunno what it was. A sickness, some dirt, I dunno.' She rocked the box. 'Couldn't do much for her but talk and sing. She liked the singing, she did. Still sing to her sometimes, but my voice ain't what it used to be. Too much weepin' and wailin'!' She cackled. 'We'd like a song from you, though, singer, if yer could.'

Alan stared in horror at the skeleton. From out of the reaches of Gleam drifted the faint cries of a baby.

'Yeah, I could,' he said. He ran his fingers over Snapper's strings, unable to look away from the box. Mother Margo had Nora's crystal in her hand. She placed it in a small hollow beneath the skeleton's lower jawbone.

Alan swallowed. 'So,' he said, 'what song would you like?'

'I don't know their names,' Mother Margo said, shaking her head. 'I remember some tunes, you know.' She hummed tunelessly. 'I remember some tunes like that from my own ma, but I don't know the names.'

'I know them from my mother, too,' Alan said. 'My mum and dad, they were in a band. They'd get them all round to practise in the house. I used to live in Modest Mills. They'd come round in the afternoon for just a couple of hours, but then they'd stay and play all night, and I'd sit in the corner and watch. They asked me if I wanted to play something. I always said no. I said . . . I said to them . . . you're too loud. I won't be able to sleep.'

'What did they play, eh?'

'Mum played the fiddle,' Alan said, 'and Dad played the accordion. I never learned to play anything until they were dead. Then I . . .' He stopped. He remembered those early days in the Pyramid, the grief and the rage that never went away. 'I wasn't allowed, for a while. I wanted to learn the fiddle like my mum but they didn't have instruments in the Pyramid. My friend, Eyes, he's down there now, he smuggled a guitar to me. This one here: Snapper. I played it in secret. I found that I could remember some of their songs.' He shook himself. 'Sorry. Okay. Do you know "Baby Beetle"? I'll do "Baby Beetle".' He picked the melody slowly and gently, and played for a long time before starting to sing. The sounds of his companions refuelling floated upwards, but they weren't speaking. The sun was nearly down now and the stars were out and Corval and Satis were bright in the darkening sky. Mother Margo nodded slowly along to the music. The red of the sunset was visible between the planks of her hut. When he started singing, Mother Margo started crooning herself. He couldn't tell for sure but he thought that behind her goggles her eyes were closed. By the time he'd finished, she was asleep. He went over to her, thinking he'd wake her up, but he saw that her cheeks were wet and he decided to leave her be.

He took a deep breath, put the lid back on the coffin and climbed quietly down the ladder.

19

Going Down

The Oversight was abutted by a hillside of large, perfectly spherical cobbles, furry with thick bright moss, down which a wide road zigzagged. The stones were piled up in banks on either side of the road. With the morning came a warm fog that smelled of rust. Every now and again these weathers could descend, like a god dropping a cloying grey cloth over Gleam. Nora scraped a boulder clean of its green coat and squeezed the damp matter into the bottom of the dented metal flask that hung from her belt. The flask clinked against what she referred to as her 'skinning knife', the sound dead in the mist as she climbed back onto her bike. Periodically she would dismount and repeat the process. The sky had become something that pressed at their skins and at the ground beneath their spinning wheels. The sun was invisible, yet this was the hottest day of the journey yet. Hot and sticky. After two hours easing down the decline, Spider grew impatient and accelerated and the wheels went out from beneath them. Spider's trousers tore wide open and one side of his right leg was stripped of skin. He gazed in horror at the wound. 'Three days' work at least,' he said, 'taken in a moment.'

Churr was wearing leather and her tattoos survived intact. 'Though,' she said, 'I'm as sweaty as a night in the Sleepless Pavilion.'

By the time they made camp, Alan was shaking with hunger, but he didn't want to ask the others how they felt. Part of his sickness was guilt at dragging them all out here, but he was also beginning to feel burgeoning lust: he wanted to feel Churr's sweat patter against his chest once more. He wanted to smell her. He badly wanted to fuck and to be fucked. This hunger was not as urgent as the hunger of his stomach, but it was as real.

He sat first watch at the base of a solid round tower of stones and tried not to imagine Churr naked. His hands moved restlessly across Snapper's strings, drawing from the instrument a soft sequence that never repeated.

The tower, like the boulders, was mossy, and knobbly orange metal stubs protruded from it, presumably the remains of a ladder.

If this place was supposed to be a factory, then the designers must have been very stupid people, Alan thought. *What were these damned balls for? What kind of factory has the space or the room for a mountain of giant marbles?*

Once he was done he woke Spider to replace him and lay down in the lee of a tarp stretched from bike to ground. The bag beneath his head felt lumpier than usual and he spent a good while shuffling around, trying to make at least a semi-decent pillow out of it.

'Damn it,' he whispered. 'Damn it, fuck it all to hell, this is fucking shitty and I hate it.'

The fog was still masking the stars and the other worlds.

In the morning Alan ate a bitter stew Nora had made out of moss, moss water, toad bones and a handful of fat pink slugs she'd found inside an ancient broken goat skull, and he started to feel a little bit better.

The road forked and Nora led them to the left. The new road became a spiral tunnel, burrowing on down into the superstructure. The bike lamps lit up each vehicle, but did little to illuminate what lay ahead. The travellers were strung out, islands of light and gleaming metal growling through the darkness. Though the descending spiral felt endless, it had to end somewhere, and nobody wanted to encounter that end at speed, so they moved slowly, the motorcycles muttering instead of roaring, the cavernous tube rumbled with echoes. Every now and again one would leapfrog another. When he was at the rear, Alan hung back and watched first Nora and Eyes, then Churr and Spider disappear around a long curve, leaving him alone in the ocean of darkness. The sound of his own vehicle was all he could hear, and before long it had become, to him, the sound of the dark itself: its breath, or the rushing of blood through its veins. It was shot through with something else, though: something thin and desolate. Something like the crying of a baby.

He sped up again.

At one point he veered to the right and came upon the side of the wide passage. His lamp revealed a row of uniform doorways alternating with windows. There were the remains of wooden doors in the doorways. Gleaming yellow in the glow of the headlights, the bits of wood looked like rotten teeth at the tops and bottoms of stretched black mouths. The windows had similarly worm-eaten shutters, some with glass reflecting the light.

Alan shuddered and swerved away, immediately besieged by visions of people – *people?* – watching him from within those pitch-black rooms, drawn to their ruined windows by the sound. Almost as disturbing was the realisation that even if these strange compartments were empty of life – which they probably were – they had once been lived in. They reminded him of Pyramid quarters. The thought that these subterranean boxes had once been homes caused something like panic to blossom in him. Who could live in a place like this? Had they had a choice? Though back then – *when?* – it would surely have been lit. But still. *But still* . . . Underground, light can never truly banish the dark.

And then, revealed from around the curve like a ribbon extending horizontally, there was a long, thin rectangle of orange. At first he couldn't work out what he was looking at, then he saw that the rectangle was an opening out into space. Across that space was a red brick wall, glowing.

At the window they turned off their engines and looked up into the sky. The sky was on the other side of a red glass dome. From the window where they were standing they could see a jumble of red-brick shapes and blue-slate roofs. The buildings were similar to each other in only one respect: their size. Together, they formed a gargantuan, three-dimensional labyrinth of towers, blocks, teetering high-rises, bridges, archways, ramps, tiers, courtyards and turrets. Metal pipes shining orange in the tinted light ran crazily across and between everything, emerging from windows, wrapping around buildings, leaping bottomless gaps and plunging directly into the brickwork of another structure. Wooden walkways spiralled around, branching off from spindly black metal ladders and staircases.

Spider pointed wordlessly to a nearby rooftop, on which a bent old man shuffled about in some straw. On his back was a cage at least four times his size, full of tiny white birds. The man found something in the straw and held it up to his face. He examined it using a small brass magnifying glass: an egg. The man grinned, satisfied, and placed it into a wooden box strapped to his front. As he turned around he stared at Alan and company, but he ignored them and continued his search. The birds in the cage hopped between perches but remained eerily quiet. The man was perhaps twenty feet away from them.

'This is Glasstown,' Nora said. 'Some Mapmakers

think that the red light affects people's brains. I don't know about that. But from here is the easiest way down. This is where we begin our descent.'

'Eh?' Eyes said, after a moment. 'I – I – you're all looking at something, I can tell that. Whatever it is, though, I can't see it, not a damn thing. I can see red light, like, but that's it.' The skin around his eyes was crusty with pus and blood. The whites of his eyes were clearly shot through with nasty thick streaks of something. 'Can't see a damn thing,' he repeated.

In Glasstown the people apparently ate a lot of lichen. They just scrabbled at the brick and then sucked the spoils from beneath their long fingernails. They all wore dirty pale robes, and they shared their ruined brick palaces with flocks of the tiny white birds. Many of the walls had fallen away. At Nora's insistence, Alan and the others stripped the bikes for all they could carry, ditched the vehicles on a rooftop, and dropped through a skylight into a dusty room with a black-and-white chequered floor. An ornate fireplace sat squat and cold in the middle of one wall. The other three walls were missing, except for some supporting columns at the corners. The light turned the white tiles red. At the edges of the floor, some had just fallen away into space. Above the fireplace were three large framed paintings, though the colours had long since faded and the subjects were impossible to discern.

Alan and Spider held Eyes between them as they

descended endless stairs. Glasstowners lurked in the shadows. One walked up the stairs towards them as they came down and stood directly in front of Nora, blocking her way. She put a filthy hand to her chest. 'There is another world, in which people live in small houses,' she said. 'When those people die, they come here, and all of the rooms they ever lived in are here, connected, all of the rooms connected to each other, their childhood bedroom and the room where they first made love and the room they died in, and all of the kitchens, all of their houses combined into a big house, a memory house. Old spaces in a new configuration. This is that afterlife, sister. We are their shades.'

She turned and stared into Alan's eyes. Her skin was smooth, her teeth yellow, her long hair lank. 'We're the dead, seeking for the places where we used to live. Some of us know it and some of us don't.'

Nora shook her head in panic and rushed on down the steps.

Alan hadn't thought that anything could shake Nora like that, least of all something as innocuous and nonsensical as the Glasstowner's comments.

The Glasstowner slowly turned and watched Nora disappear around a corner.

The stairs went on and on, and every now and again, Nora would dart through a doorway and lead the group through a series of rooms, before plunging down yet another staircase. Some were grand, some were not; some were narrow and dark, some were precarious and exposed. Some were wooden, some metal, some stone.

Nobody spoke. At one arched window a great glass raven peered in, its detail shining red. Everything that was not under darkness was red. At the next window Alan saw that there were a great many great glass ravens adorning the nearby buildings. Some had their wings folded; others were poised as if to strike.

The deeper they got, the more the stonework wept. Lichen gave way to slimy mould. Vines with fat green leaves crawled through windows. Slugs oozed along beneath mantelpieces. Water dripped from dark, damp patches in the ceilings of rooms they cut through. Toads bathed in puddles. Eyes was pale and shaking, and he smelled bad. Alan could feel the swamp getting closer. 'Down is out,' he muttered. 'Down is out.'

Nora looked at him askance. 'Stop saying that,' she said.

'That's the first time I've said it.'

'No, it isn't. You keep saying it, over and over. It's like I've got a parrot at my shoulder. A stupid parrot.'

'My voice is not that of a parrot. And I don't keep saying it.'

'You have been saying it since the chequered floor – the first chequered floor.'

Alan shook his head, then he realised his lips were moving and he put his hand over his mouth. He caught Nora looking at him again, but this time she quickly looked away and didn't say anything.

Head-sized snails with whorled pearlescent shells left trails so wet and viscous they dribbled down the walls and sagged from the ceilings. They webbed dark rooms like the spinnings of spiders. And there were spiders, too: pale, round ones with long sharp legs that reached out in front of the globular bodies. The spiders clustered together where the shadows met the light.

Faintly glowing slime coated the insides of old pots. These places were not just empty or sparsely populated: they were abandoned and decaying – abandoned by people, that is. There was lots of life. Pale lizards sloped away behind old bookcases.

'You're talking again,' Nora said.

'No, I'm not.'

When they came to a window, the light shining in was red. In all directions they could see endless sheer vertical surfaces, all invisible behind coats of moss and leaves and tiny stunted trees. Everything was discoloured by the light. Snakes, curled around branches, gazed back at Alan and he saw himself through their eyes: a pale face at a window in an infinite wall, a small pale oval here for a moment and then gone. These windows weren't really windows; they were just more holes.

Several storeys later, Nora opened a door and on the other side was a spotlessly clean bathroom. A white bath stood on four reptilian feet. The walls were white tiles. The floor was black tiles and the ceiling was decorated with swirls of black and white. There was a white sink, with a tall silver tap. Nora turned the tap and clean water spilled out.

Alan stared. Churr stared. Spider stared. Nora washed her hands. 'Drink,' she said. 'Eyes first, then everybody else. Then we clean Eyes' wounds. Then we clean ourselves.'

'Wait—' Alan said.

'We know places,' Nora said. 'Places to go.'

'But the pipework – the source – everything. Where does it come from?'

'There are maintenance teams,' Nora said. 'They travel in caravans.' When that did not alleviate the bemusement, she threw her hands into the air. 'Certain features are maintained!' she said. 'You think it all just hangs together?'

Once they were clean and refreshed, Alan washed Eyes a clean bandage and tied it around his head.

They came to a long room full of long belts made out of wooden slats. The belts were wrapped around cylinders designed to roll, though everything was gummed up and the metal cogs were rusty. But Spider managed to get one working – he turned a heavy handle and the belt groaned along, before something snapped and the handle spun loosely round, smacking him in the knees and putting him down. There were chunks of painted metal on the belts, which appeared to be some kind of assembly mechanism; at the side were baskets containing more bits of metal, which had evidently been attached to the chunkier items as the belt moved along. Churr picked up one of the things, which fell to pieces in her hand as she examined it. 'They're crocodile toys,' she said. 'They were green once.'

'And not just any old crocodile,' Nora said. 'Three eyes and six legs.'

'They were making Old Greens?' Spider said from the floor. 'For the churches?'

'Or for children.'

'Why would the Builders have created a place for people to make little metal Greens?' Alan wondered.

'The Builders probably got just as much wrong as you do, Alan,' Churr said. 'Maybe they didn't account for everything people needed, or wanted. We're not in the concrete at the moment, remember: we're in brick. This came later.'

'But we're lower down. We were in the superstructure, and then we spiralled down, remember, and then we came out under the glass . . . but . . . everything was brick. We came out lower down, and everything was brick.' He screwed up his eyes. 'Am I making sense? My brain feels bad. Nora, are we close to water? How long since we ditched the bikes? How many days?'

'The Oversight was once the top of a tower,' Nora said. 'Now the rest of Gleam has risen to its level. Yes, we came down, but we have moved sideways out of the superstructure into architecture that came later. Probably Old Green was not even a story when the Builders were placing Gleam's foundations, let alone a god.'

'Growth,' Churr said. 'Look, on the wall there. That's

what it says, I bet.' She pointed at one of the two long walls. The large letters 'TH' were visible from where they stood, but when Alan moved his bike lamp along the wall, they all saw the 'W' emerge from the gloom. The rest of the wall was coated with a fur of tiny black mushrooms.

Alan started sweeping them away and they turned to mush beneath his sleeve, splattering his face with bitter, foul-smelling droplets. But Churr was right. The word 'GROWTH' had been painted on the wall, and after further exploration, the long wall opposite revealed the word 'GLEAM', and both short walls bore the word 'FOR'.

'It says: "GROWTH FOR GLEAM FOR GROWTH FOR GLEAM FOR GROWTH", repeated,' Alan told Eyes.

Eyes nodded, grimaced, said nothing.

Later they found a large glass bottle full of a pale yellow liquid inside the once-locked drawer of a wooden desk now slowly turning to mush.

Alan picked the cork out with a penknife, getting increasingly agitated as it resisted. 'Let it be whisky,' he muttered, 'not piss. Whisky, not piss.' When he finally broke through the plug, the odour spilled out and he rolled over onto his back. 'Oh, thank fuck,' he said. 'Thank fuck, thank fuck, thank fuck.' He sat back up and put the bottle to his lips.

Then he pulled it away again without tasting it. 'Eyes,' he said, 'whisky.' He went over to the old man and put the bottle in his hands.

Eyes sipped it gratefully, and winced, and sipped it again. 'Thanks, lad,' he said. His voice was hoarse.

Then Alan had a drink, the liquid burning his mouth and turning into hot mist inside him. He felt as if it were evaporating through his brain and clearing it out. He closed his eyes and shuddered with pleasure.

'Everybody,' he said, 'fill your flasks.'

'They're full of water now,' Spider replied.

'Seal the bottle with a candle,' Churr said. 'Nora's got candles.'

'Here,' said the Mapmaker, handing over a red one.

After drinking a little more, Eyes grabbed hold of Alan's arm. 'Lad,' he said, 'I don't want to go down into that swamp.'

'I know,' Alan said. 'I'm trying not to think about it.'

'Aye,' Eyes said. 'You're good at that, all right.'

20

Swamp Life

'We're here,' Nora said. 'The swamp.'

The party stood in a room that looked like Maggie's kitchen, though it was dark and damp. *Oh, how I want to be back in Maggie's kitchen*, Alan thought, *with a pot of chilli bubbling away on the stove!* The glass had fallen from a long window, and a row of plant pots crowded the window-sill, from which had grown a thick mat of some kind of lemony herb. The thin wiry branches had wound around a pair of heavy, sagging shutters that kept the room mostly dark. However, cold light peeped in around the edges and through little holes everywhere, dappling everything with patches of silver. *Not red*, Alan thought. A long rotten table occupied the centre of the room, and the walls were lined with wooden cupboards, the tops covered with rusting pots and pans of all sizes. A huge black wood-burning stove sat dormant in a wide alcove. The door glass was cracked and ash had spilled out across the flagstone floor. The kitchen was far too big to have been purely domestic: this must have been a tavern of some sort.

'Doesn't look much like a swamp.'

'Look at you,' Nora said. 'You've got whisky back in you, and now you're full of fight again. Shut yourself up and open that.' She pointed at a door that looked much like the one they'd come through.

Alan did as she'd said and immediately recoiled at the stench. There was a ten-foot drop on the other side down to a smooth and featureless surface of thick green sludge. There was nothing else: no red brick, no glass ravens, no concrete superstructure, no hills or walls of cobble, not even any vegetation. Just the sludge, a blank and shiny green floor stretching off into the mist. Alan stared.

He turned back to his companions. 'What the fuck is this?' he said, pointing over his shoulder with his thumb. 'Where's everything gone?'

Spider and Churr ventured over to the doorway and looked out. From the middle of the room the doorway was just an opening into nothing; a void of white and green roiling together. Spider and Churr were silhouetted against it.

'I feel like we're at a high window, about to jump out,' Alan said. 'Like we're high up – it doesn't make sense.'

'A lot of buildings in Gleam have grown together at their higher levels,' Nora said. 'They have slowly leant against each other, or people have stuck extra bits onto their sides. They all end up looking like mushrooms, with other little buildings on top of their caps. Am I explaining it well?'

Alan nodded.

'So the deeper you get, the more space there is.'

'How does it all stay up?'

Nora smiled. 'That is one of the mysteries of Gleam.'

Alan looked back out of the door. 'How do we move through it?'

Nora's voice came from behind him. 'There is a Boat-man coming.'

The words made Alan's bones cold. 'There are people down here?'

'There are people everywhere.'

'But they always said the swamp is hell.'

'People adapt. And besides' – Nora appeared at his side – 'they say that about the Discard too, don't they?'

At that moment, the sludge was disturbed. Some-thing brushed the surface of it from beneath and slow ripples spread outwards. Small bubbles rose up and burst. Alan twisted the candle from the bottle of whisky and took a swig. He brushed flakes of wax from his hand. They floated down and settled onto the green and just lay there.

'How are these regions illuminated?' Spider asked.

'The swamp itself gives light. See how there are no real shadows here? The light is too soft. But look at each other, look at the light on each other's faces, see how it lands on the skin.'

Alan gazed at his companions. 'It makes us look ill and ugly,' he said.

'Iller and uglier,' Churr said.

'There is something in it that glows,' Nora said, 'but we don't know what it is.'

Perhaps half an hour later, a stronger light showed through the mist; a quiet sucking sound accompanied the light. An indistinct figure appeared. The Boatman was approaching.

'How did you get a message down here, Nora?'

'I didn't,' she said. 'The Boatman listens for visitors.'

'Have you been here before?'

'Yes. But I have never been further. I have never taken the boat.'

'You know the way?'

'I will find the way. So far I have been merely your guide, pointing this way, that way, that rooftop, this door. Now I will be working.' She looked up at him. 'I will change, now. My nightly meditations are preparation, like a creature in a cocoon, rearranging itself on the inside.'

'And the outside,' Alan said.

'Yes, but I have mostly just changed my insides.'

The Boatman was more distinct now. He was very tall, and his bare arms and bald head were marble-white. The rest of him was cloaked in something rough and brown, like the potato sacks that had always ended up piled in the alleys of Market Top. He was punting a long, wide

raft – to call it a boat, Alan decided, was a little bit generous. It looked more like a big crate. His progress was slow.

Alan tried to quash a growing panic: the man's flesh *was*
glowing. His eyes were big and round and his gaze did not
waver from Alan's own. His face was gaunt, his fingers
long and his ears were oddly sized, large and pointed. And
he had a large wound in the side of his neck.

The raft bumped against the wall and the Boatman
picked up a hooked ladder from the bottom of the craft
and raised it so that it was hanging from the bottom of the
doorway. Then he stood back and waited. Alan turned to
descend, then whispered to Nora, 'Can we trust him?'

'You can trust me,' said the Boatman. His voice was
deep and somehow off: the sound of a broken bell.

'Dammit,' Alan said, and dropped down the ladder
and sat down in the raft. The Boatman smiled at him, but
it was an empty smile and Alan couldn't return it. Then
he realised that the wound in the Boatman's neck was
smiling as well. It was not a wound; it was a second
mouth, with thin ragged lips and little teeth. The end of
the dark wooden staff he used for punting was carved
into the shape of a woman's torso and, as Alan watched,
he stroked the model's disproportionately large breasts.

The others joined them on the raft. Nora came down
last and unhooked the ladder.

'Where?' asked the Boatman. The word came from
both mouths, saliva strung between all four lips. 'Where?'
he asked again.

'Dok,' Alan said. 'We want to go to Dok.'

The Boatman's mouths both curled into something like sneers. 'Dok?' he said. He made the *k* sound long. 'You are fools, then.'

'No.'

The Boatman held up a hand. 'I have no need to prove my assertion. I will take you as close as I can, and the consequences will be yours to face.' He used the stick to push the raft away from the wall.

They passed strange trees that were nothing but knots of root, and then went through a huge, intricate mechanism that was battered and bent and dented and rusted into a single lump. 'This fell from above,' the Boatman said as they slid between cogs. They passed along a channel that wound between mounds of junk: furniture, tools, toys, swollen books, unidentifiable objects, general rotting matter, bones. And something passed by them; the same sinuous movement that had disturbed the sludge back at the doorway. Even after just a few hours, that kitchen felt like a world away.

'What is it that lives in the swamp?' he asked Nora.

'What is it that lives in the swamp?' she repeated. Her eyes were glassy. 'Scales and teeth and tongues live in the swamp. Mouths with legs and molten birds live in the swamp. Dead things live in the swamp. Shells and slime and croaks and eyes and eggs and insects and slick fur and bloodied snouts and stones with ears and glass diseases and creatures with no brains and mistakes and failures and discarded children live in the swamp. Old Green lives in the swamp. Broken objects live in the swamp. Algae and fungi and lichens and moulds live in the swamp.' She dug her fingers into Alan's wrist. '*We* live in the swamp. We live in the swamp.' She fell silent, let go and sat back.

From out in the mist came a sound like that of a kettle coming to the boil.

Nora's skin was clammy. Beads of sweat ran down her forehead and cheeks. Alan wiped her face with his sleeve, then he turned to Eyes and did the same. After wiping Eyes' face his dirty sleeve was pink. He looked back at Nora. 'The pink,' he said. 'The pink around your eyes? I thought it was some kind of powder, a dye . . .'

'Needlestick,' Nora said. 'Needlestick, needlestick, lie still, don't kick. Pinned down in the birthing wagon, my father with his needlestick, outside the wolves, crystals clicking, Corval and Satis wheeling, me kicking, screaming, the tip of the stick pink with ink from the abdomen of the needlestick beetles, the don't-kick beetles, the click-click beetles, wind chimes singing the ghost song, knees on arms, a stranger's palm on my brow, the needlestick changing my face, blood dribbling down, blood in my eyes and mouth, the taste of it going deep, deep, new to me, then, it was new to me and it was strong, the taste of it like a visitation, its spread throughout me like possession, the pain in my face making everything white, the needlestick moving across me, pricking and sticking, poking and piercing, setting fire . . .' She drew up her legs and rested her cheek on the tops of her knees, and lowered her voice. 'Setting fire,' she said again. 'Setting fire to me.'

Spider was standing over Nora too, now. 'A tattoo,' he murmured. He bent down. 'Quite splendid work. The graduation is remarkable. That intense colouring below the eyes, fading away to nothing lower down the cheek, with no discernible banding. And the colour has held remarkably well, considering the shade, the vividity. So vivid. It doesn't look like a tattoo. It looks like mere paint.' He stroked his beard. 'Magnificent.'

'Does nothing bother you?' Alan asked. 'Like, not the swamp, not Nora's distress? Not anything?'

Spider put a hand on Alan's shoulder. 'I have a small, well-swaddled soul,' he said. He patted Alan. 'I could panic and quiver and gnaw at my fingernails if you prefer. But it would not help much, and it would be dishonest.'

'You're like her,' Alan said, gesturing at Nora.

'Maybe.' Spider frowned. 'Though I feel as if we do not know *what* Nora is like, not truly.'

Nora was talking still, but her words were too quiet and mumbled for her companions to make them out. She drew three crystals from her pack and clutched them tightly.

'I don't know the way,' Alan said at last. 'I don't know where we're going or how to get there. Nora is the one who knows everything.'

The mist was thicker now, and the raft moved through

the sludge smoothly and silently, except for the faint squelching sounds of the Boatman's pole. The bottom of the craft scraped against something.

A frozen moment.

'What was that?' Eyes said. He turned his head one way then another, the bow of his bandage flopping against his neck.

'Knives out,' said the Boatman, his voice guttural, the words tolling.

All the drawn metal sounded sharp, but looked dull in the fog. The Boatman drew his pole up, revealing a vicious crosshead iron spike at the opposite end to the naked woman. The raft rocked gently from side to side and slid ever so slowly forward.

Nora was oblivious.

The something came again; a knocking, almost, from below. The sound was loud. A dark shape broke the surface, but sank again so quickly Alan couldn't make out any detail. Slow ripples spread out.

'A crocodile,' whispered the Boatman. 'A spike-backed beast.'

They waited for it to reappear. From a distance impossible to ascertain, a bird — Alan thought it was a bird — shrieked. The disturbance in the swamp had released a bad smell, of rotting vegetatation. Where the crocodile had been, the smooth green liquid was broken by brown swirls.

They waited a little longer.

'We will continue,' the Boatman said, 'but keep your weapons to hand.' He sank the pole into the sludge once more and pushed off.

The crocodile rose up out the murk almost silently, its great long head facing the front of the craft. Its head was as long as Alan was tall. He stared in horror. It looked as if it was smiling. Its skin was mostly dark green, but its snout, eyes and bumps were pale yellow, as if the creature was actually made out of bone and the green was just paint that was wearing off. Its eyes were bulbous, lime-green with vertical slits. Its crooked teeth were long and white and crossed over each other. Two black nostrils flared, and from them came that boiling-kettle hiss. The great mouth opened, revealing a smooth, soft-looking white interior, and suddenly Alan could hear the motor-bikes again, the guttural roar of an engine, but it wasn't that, it was the crocodile. The growl shook the ragged flaps of skin at the back of its throat and its foul breath rolled over the raft. It subsided back to a hiss and then rose in volume again. Then the crocodile launched itself forwards, leaping out of the water like something spring-loaded. Its thick forelegs landed on the front of the raft and the whole thing upended, tumbling its passengers forward towards those snapping jaws. All was noise. The Boatman's pole looked very small and thin now. The beast's mouth snapped shut as Alan fell towards it, but it was somebody else who screamed, not him, and instead of him landing between its teeth its snout caught him in the stomach and knocked the wind from him; pain shot through him as he fell over the crocodile's head and landed on its back. The long hard spikes raked his spine as he rolled off, and then he was in the sludge and the sludge was in him, in his mouth, and he felt something probing around his teeth, and it tasted like Bittewood's fingers. And the cold. *The cold!* The cold was a vicious spirit moving through him.

He tried to swim, but the swamp was not water and forward motion was difficult. He wriggled and writhed, and things moved beneath his feet and pressed at his eyes. He did not know which way was up. The swamp was a living thing trying to force its way down his throat. Claws tore down his chest. Then pale scales were before him: a wall of crocodile flesh, flexing and pulsing. He grabbed it and pulled himself up into a maelstrom of foam, thunder, teeth and blades. Green slime poured from his mouth and the beast's spikes pierced his stomach as it bucked. There were threads of blood in the whipped-up froth and bloody drool hanging from the crocodile's mouth, leaving bloody smears in the boat. Alan found crevices in the reptile's ancient skin and dug his fingers in. The thing bellowed and thrashed, its jaws repeatedly closing with a baleful snap, but on whom exactly, Alan couldn't see. There was roaring coming not only from the crocodile but also from his companions. He still had his knife in his hand and the crocodile was still half on the raft, and Nora, Churr, Spider and the Boatman had all fallen on their arses and were slashing and spearing whilst trying to shuffle backwards. Eyes wasn't there.

Alan embraced the crocodile as best he could. It was far too thick for him to get an arm all the way around it, but he reached beneath and clutched a fold of skin at its throat. He ignored the pain as he lay down on its spiny back and held on for his life as it reared up and tried to twist around. Those teeth closed just inches from his side. The icy chill of the green mud was working its way into his core. He moved slowly, inching his right hand forward. He wanted to move it more quickly, but he couldn't. His fingers felt numb; if he rushed, the knife would just fall from his loose, clawed grip. Maybe his arm had been injured: maybe the tendons on the far side had been sliced and the wound was open and inviting to the putrid matter and the demonic cold of the swamp. Perhaps the crocodile had swung its tail and smashed his elbow when he was submerged. Whatever the cause, his arm wasn't working properly.

The Boatman got in a good jab with his pole and the crocodile recoiled, grunting. Alan slid down its side. That damned bird out there in the murk shrieked again. Was Eyes drowning? Already dead? Eyes had paid the price for Alan's foolishness once more.

Eyes – Eyes! Don't get distracted.

Alan heaved himself back up onto the beast's back, pain incising itself across his face. With a howl he dug his heels in and propelled himself forwards, almost overbalancing as he fell forward over the crocodile's head into the danger zone, but just in time he rocked back and raised his hands up, and then brought them down and plunged his thumbs into the crocodile's beautiful eyes. He felt the gelatinous orbs squeak and saw them pop out of the protruding sockets. The crocodile screamed and whistled and he wrapped his hands around the eyes and squeezed. His left hand was more responsive still than the right, but still they both burst and jelly splattered out between his fingers. He pulled and felt the cords tighten and then snap, and the crocodile spasmed and dived into the sludge, but then it rose straight back up again, roaring.

The animal was terrified and confused, making sounds like nothing Alan had ever heard, and he let himself fall while the crying blind monster rampaged away into the swamp, and a chorus of shrieking birds rose unseen into the air.

21

Swamp Madness

Alan opened his eyes to a grey-white nothing, and a sense of doom stitched all the way through him. It took him a moment to remember where he was: on the raft. On his back, on the raft. He sat up.

Eyes was there, lying on his back as Alan had been, still unconscious. He was wrapped up in something rough and brown: the Boatman's cloak. The Boatman himself was gone and Churr was poling the raft through the green sludge. Spider was watching the swamp, poised, hand on hilt. Nora was sitting upright, eyes closed, and breathing deeply. She seemed to have calmed down.

'Where's the Boatman?' Alan asked.

'Croc got him,' Churr said.

'No,' Alan said. 'No, it didn't. He was here when I . . .' Words failed him. He felt sick. He made a gesture with his thumbs. 'He was still fighting.'

'He was bitten.'

It was possible – probable, even. 'Shit,' Alan said. 'Shit,

shit, shit. Where's that whisky? Give me some of that whisky, Spider.'

He concentrated on drinking for a short while. The raft moved slowly.

'You took the boatman's cloak and wrapped Eyes in it,' Alan said.

'Yes,' Spider replied. 'It was Eyes or you. We thought Eyes had the greater need.'

Alan nodded. 'What was the Boatman like?' he asked. 'Y'know. Underneath?'

Spider shook his head. 'Different,' he said.

Alan did some more drinking.

'How do you know which way to go, Churr?'

'Nora pointed. She came up out of her babble and pointed this way. Then she went quiet.'

'Is she meditating again?'

'Something like that.'

From out of the mist came a distant crocodilian roar, which rose and broke. Churr and Spider both tensed, Alan jumped, but Nora did not so much as open her eyes. Alan thought he could hear pain in the sound. He knew it was the same animal they'd fought off. The surface of the swamp was not so smooth any more, but there was nothing else to be seen – no ridged backs breaking it, no bubbles.

Alan put his hand on Eyes' forehead. His friend was still breathing, but he looked so cold and pale. He looked dead.

'I'm sorry,' Alan said quietly. 'Sorry, Eyes.'

'What are we looking for?' asked Churr, after a few minutes more. 'A building? An island of junk?'

'I don't really know,' Alan said. 'Some kind of shoreline.'

'I didn't think we'd reach the swamp,' Churr said. 'I thought Dok was above the swamp. Close, but above. What if the swamp has taken it?'

'We will ascend again,' Nora said calmly. She still didn't open her eyes. 'I know the way now.'

'What? How? And where?'

Nora didn't answer.

'Nora,' Alan said, trying not to sound too desperate, 'Eyes needs help. Can you help him? Will there be anyone down here to help us?'

Nora still didn't answer.

Time passed. There was nothing solid for her to push on now, so Churr laid the pole down in the boat and lifted up a paddle. After a while, Spider took over, and then Alan, who felt the paddle hit something solid and looked down to see a slimy skull looking back up at him. Then the swamp was full of bones and rags, all bobbing silently.

'How many dead has the swamp released from their resting places?' Spider asked nobody in particular. Nobody answered. He reached into the luminous liquid and withdrew another skull. 'I'm going to do some drawing,' he said.

Alan thought about saying something, but didn't. He turned away.

Birds shrieked. Forms loomed through the mist, and then, when Alan was expecting to encounter a rotten structure or an island of waste, there was nothing there. Sometimes he heard something splashing around, or saw movement in the swamp. On more than one occasion he caught himself waking up and realised that he'd been dozing. Once he was awakened by the sound of a baby crying. He dreamed about Mother Margo and her little coffin, that she was floating through the sludge on a black metal cube. He woke up again, and saw more white and green.

'Oh, for fuck's *sake!*' he shouted.

Churr and Spider kept swapping around, switching positions, just to mess with him, he was sure of it. He knew it. He heard them whispering to each other and laughing. Once he heard Eyes speak and spun around, only to find him lying back down again. He knelt and slapped Eyes across the face. 'I know you're awake,' he hissed. Spider and Churr didn't say anything. Spider was still drawing that stupid skull – though when Alan looked, the drawing was a mess, just a great tangle, and there was nothing like a skull discernible in it – and Churr was vomiting over the side of the raft.

The swamp grew busier with creatures and with movement. Large dragonflies alighted, black-winged, and then they rose again. Their buzzing hummed through the mist. Pale, gnarled trees with crooked trunks began to appear, with roots that looked like intestines piled up. Thick reeds rustled as if they themselves were turning to watch the raft pass. Alan had the sense of space closing in. He took up the pole, and found that he could feel something solid with it. Soon there were walls on either side: dark, slimy, endless, occupied by a rash of large slugs and snails. He lit the paraffin lamps at the corners of their raft. Trees clustered thickly at the sides of the channel, many growing from the walls themselves, as if they were climbing up out of the swamp. He tried to pick a strange red flower from one of the closer specimens, only to find that they weren't flowers but long centipede-type insects curled up into balls. In brushing the tree, he disturbed a load of them and they fell into the raft, wriggling furiously. He stamped on those he could see and spent the next few hours shuddering, imagining that he could feel them crawling beneath his clothes.

Of course, it was probably Eyes' clothes that they would have found their way into, as he was just lying there unmoving.

Now the substance of the swamp was less strange – it was thicker, muddier and full of dead leaves and twigs – but it smelled worse. The smell of decay burst up out of it, disturbed by the raft. It had a rainbow sheen, and in places puddles of oil rested on the top. Small things moved in it, and through the trees; probably just insects, or rodents. That bird shrieked again.

Alan used Snapper to knock snails from the wall and into the boat. He aimed for good-sized ones, about the size of his head. 'Sorry, Snapper,' he murmured, 'but needs must.' He could try to cook a snail himself – that might impress the others. Though why he should try to impress them, he didn't know. It was as if Spider and Churr weren't even there; they weren't even present in their own heads.

He stabbed at the swamp with the pole and shouted. *This is too slow. My son is in danger and we are stuck on this stupid fucking raft, bloody punting along in the dark, knowing nothing.* He shouted again, and screamed, echoing up the chasm. There was the fluttering of wings above as the noise disturbed things that he couldn't see. He fell to his knees and cried, though the sounds he was making sounded strange to him, distorted by the space he was in. He rolled over and lay on his side. He wanted to see his parents. He wanted to be a boy again. He wanted to relive all of those moments when his mother had got home from work and given him a hug. He convulsed with sobs as he remembered his father, that smell of dye and whisky. All those hours his parents had spent making cloth for the Pyramid robes, and for its wall hangings, for its flags and its rituals: time spent away from him and away from each other. He thought about Marion, going to her Stationing every shift, and him, too. All those hours at the Station, reading the discs and punching the cards accordingly. All of the Bleeding. They should have spent that time together, talking, playing with Billy, watching the dragons, watching the moons, making love.

In the Pyramid, Stationing was a moral obligation. The enthusiasm and commitment with which you went to your Station was one of the factors in determining exactly what your Station was, and what kind of quarters you were allocated. If you did well – if you rhapsodised about your Stationing, if you went willingly, if you didn't express any interest in doing anything else – you'd get noticed, and promoted to another Station, on the floor above. You could work your way up, in theory becoming an Astronomer or an Alchemist, if you didn't make the cut at School, or even Management. But most people were born into Admin or Manufacturing and stayed there all their life, perhaps ascending by several storeys, and then they were shunted off into the Gardens when they were incapable of performing their Stationing any longer, and in the Gardens they died.

Maybe better the Gardens than this dank, stinking hell-hole, though. Alan looked around him. He looked at Eyes lying sick on the damp raft; at Churr and Spider acting like mad people. That was the trade-off: perform your Stationing, and you can stay warm and dry and well fed. Oh, and bled. Don't forget the Bleeding. But for all that, you get . . . No. Alan shook his head. He remembered the seeping welt on Billy's palm. He remembered his parents. They'd been kind to him. There was kindness and safety in the Discard. Well, there had been, before the Pyramidders razed Modest Mills.

Alan's Stationing had usually consisted of standing at a long desk full of slots, each numbered with a ten-digit number. There was a large clipping device attached to the desk that reminded him of a long set of jaws with sharp teeth. Baskets hung from the wall next to him, full of cards, and from the ceiling extended tubes from which, every minute, small stone discs fell. The discs were patterned with symbols that matched various symbols on the cards in the baskets. Alan had to take a card from the basket corresponding with the tube from which the disc had fallen, and then he clipped it in accordance with the symbols on the disc. Then he put the card in the slot on the desk indicated by the pattern on the disc. Then he dropped the disc into a kind of bucket-on-rails that he'd kick down the room once it was full. The bucket passed through a flap in the wall and disappeared. Alan had once stuck his head through the flap to see where they went, but all he saw was a long tunnel with shining rails disappearing down a slope and round a corner. That had earned him an extra Bleed. Presumably the discs were collected from wherever they went and then somehow passed back up to the storey above to be reused the following day. That would be the purpose of somebody else's Stationing. The Stationings were supposed to be performed reverently; they were rituals. They were to be performed in the right robes, in the right manner, with the right words being spoken. The Stations were lit in a particular way and certain scents emanated from censers and candles. At Alan's usual Station, the air was full of a fresh smell, something organic and green – something that he had not yet encountered in the Discard. It was a nice smell; that had been the best thing about it. But the dullness had been deathly, and the frustration of being told repeatedly that there were no consequences to his Stationing had come close to driving him mad.

'The Stationing is a ritual that will develop your mind,' he'd been told by one of the more patient Assistant Administrative Managers. 'That is its purpose. Your time and date of birth determine your personality and your own particular defects, which in turn determine the Stations you will be assigned to throughout your life. The Stations are chosen in order to correct you. The timing of your Stations is dictated by the positioning of Satis, Corval and the stars. The Astronomers pass on shift and Station changes down to us here in Administration, and we obey. So you never know, Wild Alan' – the Assistant Administrative Manager smiled – 'perhaps some cosmic realignment is on its way and you'll be re-assigned to the Manufacturing Sector. Some of their work is a little more intricate.' The smile vanished. 'But you have to be achieving your Vitals here first, of course. Otherwise you'll miss out on this re-assignment and have to wait until the next one. If there is a next one.'

Alan had his doubts about the Astronomers. Their methods and rulings were complex and arcane – impossible for anybody not of their order to understand – and he suspected that they merely promoted and re-assigned the most obedient – or, no, probably up there in their Observatories they just set all of the brass machines spinning and got drunk out of their skulls and ordered the rest of the Pyramidders' lives at random. You only had to look at some of the Management to know that there was no moral dimension to the way it worked. The idea that the Stations shaped your mind and somehow prepared you for more challenging Stations or for responsibility for those below you, was demonstrably false . . . unless part of the whole Pyramid design depended on some of those higher up in the hierarchy actually being cruel and unpleasant; unless some Pyramidders were assigned Stations that actively *shaped* them that way . . .

Alan sat up in the raft. Something was scraping against the side. He slowly turned to look. At first, he couldn't see anything, but then there it was: a rock. They must be near the shore. But the rock was gently moving. Alan reached down and lifted it up. It was as heavy as it looked. He poked at the swamp with the punting pole, and there was a good three feet between the surface and the bottom. And yet the rock had been floating. He threw it back into the swamp and it sank, and then it bobbed back up.

Alan lay back down.

Nora came back to her body at some point. 'I've been looking ahead,' she said, by way of explanation. 'I've been projecting. My people have a way of leaving their bodies behind and journeying onwards.'

Alan wondered who she was talking to. Neither Churr nor Spider appeared to be listening, and he wasn't either, really. Eyes was not dead, but he was as good as dead. Maybe they should have left him behind after all. Nora tutted when she saw him lying there in the Boatman's cloak, and she used her skinning knife to dribble a little of her moss juice – now fermenting, to judge by the smell – between his lips.

'Has nobody been caring for poor Eyes?' she asked.

Nobody answered.

Spider was still scribbling away. His drawings looked incredible: some of the most intricate and powerful geometries he had ever created, with here and there sketchy records of some of the swamp flora. He was not eating, not even drinking, though sometimes he still stopped to build a roll-up with his trembling fingers. There were green fibres in his beard that looked like a kind of lichen.

Churr was delirious, muttering a low stream of words to herself that Alan couldn't make out. And Alan, for his part, was trying to stay low so that the Clawbaby didn't see him. The Clawbaby was what he had taken to calling the big thing with glowing green eyes that had attacked them at The Cup and Skull, because of its metal claws and its baby cries. It was down here with them, he knew it. The glow of its eyes was the same as the glow of the sludge that had greeted them when they opened that door. Perhaps the Clawbaby had beaten them here and was just keeping itself submerged, slowly following them by walking along the bottom of the swamp. Though not them: *him*. Alan knew that it wanted him, and him only. He wondered how he knew what he knew about it. He wondered if they were connected.

'So where is the Boatman, then?' Nora asked.

'Crocodile got him,' Alan said.

'There are no tooth holes in his cloak,' Nora replied.

Alan shrugged. He realised that contradicted what he knew, but his mind was sluggish and he couldn't get past the contradiction to think about it. 'There's a fog in my head,' he said. 'I can't help you.'

'Hunger, exhaustion and the proximity to Dok,' Nora said. 'Dok reaches out and gets into you. It corrupts over time. It has twisted many. Some are more susceptible than others. Many find themselves drawn to it, and without knowing why – without even knowing that Dok is the source of their problems – they wander on down here. Dok has claimed many souls.'

Alan could not construct a meaningful response. He fell back on habit and scrabbled around in his bag for the bottle of whisky they'd found in the old desk. There was not much left. *There never was.*

'Soon we will find the Pilgrims,' Nora said. 'Then we will be able to clear your head.'

22

Mushroom Gatherers

The channel narrowed. The sound of dripping water was constant, and too loud. It echoed. It felt invasive. Soon the raft really did encounter a shoreline, of sorts: stinking mud humping up from out of the thick liquid. The mud was full of rubbish – bones and sharp metal wire. Churr and Spider kept falling over, which they found hilarious. Watching them, Alan struggled with a monstrous anger. How could their spirits be so light? But the journey meant so little to them, of course; for them it was just an *adventure*. Nora tied Eyes to Alan's back and he followed her carefully through the filth. He listened to Churr and Spider giggling behind him.

The channel ended at a gateway in a wall as huge as those at either side. The heavy, ornate gate was lying in the iridescent mud, slowly corroding. Nora led the party through the gap. There were cobbles protruding from the mud. Eyes was heavy on Alan's back, and the breath that escaped his mouth as his head lolled from side to side smelled intensely bad.

They travelled at a painfully slow speed, following the shoreline until they found themselves on a causeway crossing an expanse of oily sludge. Then those intestinal trees closed in again and Nora led them through a squat forest, bidding them to stand only on the roots. Between the roots was the oily sludge, and here it stank, reminding Alan of the drains in the House of a Thousand Hollows' after a monsoon.

Alan had to stop frequently to put Eyes down. Sometimes his old friend would cough and splutter and speak unintelligible words, but he would at least swallow fluids – a bitter sap that Nora bled from the trees, then boiled and cooled – and he would eat, if someone pushed tiny morsels of food between his lips. They ate snail, mostly, or if they were lucky, Nora snared them a snake. And Spider was good at identifying the myriad varieties of mushrooms that sprouted from the damp tree trunks around them.

Alan knew night from day only by Nora's new routine. Every evening she took herself away from the group to perform a sequence of movements that she called her 'carto'. She started standing straight, feet together, palms towards the sky, and then she stretched as if pushing away something hanging over her. She moved through stances and poses, sometimes fast and sometimes slowly, incorporating wide, sweeping movements and tiny, more intricate motions that Alan couldn't quite make out. She finished by placing her hands over her ears and raising one leg so that she was standing on one foot, lowering herself into a one-legged crouch, and then gently starting to spin. It was not obvious what started the spin, or how she did it, but the spinning speeded up and up, until she was nothing but a blur, and then suddenly she stopped.

She was never dizzy afterwards.

After watching her perform the carto back and forth along a wide, low branch, Alan asked her about it.

'I have to be receptive to the spirit of Gleam,' she said, rummaging in her satchel for a glowing crystal. 'The spinning is how I draw it into myself. I draw the spirit in, and it tells me a little about Gleam. Then, when I sleep, I dream through what the spirit has told me, and when I wake, in the morning, I have worked it out a little. The carto is how I learn the way. And it is also how I record my findings. See this?' she said, and took hold of a small green gemstone dangling from a twisted branch on a leather thong. 'I hang one of these before performing the carto. The stone remembers that I was here. When a Mapmaker performs their carto – they are all different – all of the hung stones sing out to them. They are like beacons, radiating the spirit. They tell Mapmakers where others have been, and they give a little more detail than if there were no green gems in that place. Next time a Mapmaker comes near here and they carto, they will receive

visions of this particular place, and they will know that
one of us has been this way before them.'

Alan stretched. He was lying across a knot of fat roots,
and it was not comfortable, but it was still a blessed relief
for his aching back. The swamp forest was alive with
sound and movement: unfamiliar birdcalls, the occasional insect chirrup, and fireflies. Eyes lay on his side on
top of another bunch of roots, Spider was collecting fungus and Churr was hunting for large cricket-like bugs
that she liked to toast.

'But if there was no stone hanging here?' he asked.

'They would still receive the spirit. But the spirit is
more abstract. It is a voice that you have to decipher. And
you have to dream to decipher it.'

'So you're only doing this now because nobody has
been this way before? No Mapmakers?'

'Yes. Before we took the boat, all of that has been
mapped. And I had been to that doorway before too, so I
did not need to perform the carto, and nor did I need to
record my journey for the others. Whereas now . . . now,
the stones I leave behind will tell the Mapmaker tribes
what is here – what I have found.'

Alan leaned forward, and whispered. 'I actually thought
you lot had been down this way before.'

Nora frowned. 'No,' she said. 'Why would you think
that?'

'I thought you'd been everywhere.'

Nora shook her head. 'No,' she said, 'but we are better

at navigating than anyone else, even if we haven't been to a place before.'

'So,' Alan said, 'Daunt doesn't employ any Mapmakers.'

'We are not *employed* by anybody.'

'No, but . . . you know what I mean.'

'Well. She may have secured the services of a renegade.'

'Like you.'

'Like me, but one who does not adhere to the principle of the carto.'

'Won't your carto and your . . . What do you call them? Green gems?'

'Yes, green gems.'

'Not very imaginative.'

'We rarely need to speak of them.'

'Won't it all give away where you are?'

'The process does not reveal the identity of the Mapmaker.'

Alan paused, then asked, 'And what's the spirit of Gleam, anyway?'

'It's . . .' Nora opened and closed her hands as she tried to put it into words. 'So many questions, Alan. Gleam is not alive, but there is a force in it. We do not know where it comes from. It is not a soul . . . it is a feeling. A nature. A spirit. "Spirit" is simply the best word for it. There is a spirit in all of the structure. Structures – structures both old and new, but it is stronger in the old. The super-structure has the strongest spirit of all.'

'And what is the spirit telling you about where we are now?'

Nora sighed. 'It is difficult to know,' she said. 'The spirit here is sick, warped. We are nearing a great corruption.'

'Before I went into the Pyramid,' Alan said, 'my parents used to tell me stories. I remember books, but I haven't seen any books since Modest Mills was destroyed.' He picked absent-mindedly at Snapper, lying across his stomach. 'Some of the stories were adventure stories, and there'd be dangerous moments in the stories, scary bits, all of that. *Threats*. But there'd be nice moments too, happy parts where everybody was just kind of able to relax.'

'What are you trying to tell me?'

'I'm tired of feeling threatened. Of feeling scared.'

'I thought that that was the primary appeal of the Pyramid? If you live in the Pyramid then you don't have to worry all of the time.'

Alan frowned.

'What I find interesting,' Nora continued, 'is that there are no books in the Pyramid.'

A firefly drifted blurrily through Alan's field of vision, leaving a bright trail across the criss-cross network of branches above him. 'No books,' he said. 'I've told you: there's nothing in the Pyramid but Stationing and Bleeding.' He thought of Billy and Marion. 'There are people, of course there are, but you never see the ones you love because your Stations are scheduled that way deliberately. One gets in from their Station as the other is going out to theirs. It's so that you're not tempted to make love out of cycle, see.'

'You have scheduled love-making?'

'Of course. The Astronomers dictate when you can make love. It depends on your birth skies, how the moons and stars and dragons burned when you were born. They look at yours and your partner's and that determines the optimum birth sky for your child. The conception has to occur nine months before the optimum birth sky so they schedule the Stationing accordingly.'

Nora laughed. 'I do not believe that can work. Some things cannot be managed in such a way.'

'They try.'

'So no child is ever born beneath the wrong sky?'

Alan felt the darkness pressing in. He looked around for another firefly. He could not speak until he found one. He sat up and watched the little creature dance. 'They cannot completely control the love-making,' he said slowly, 'that is true. But to answer your question – no. No child – no living child – is ever born beneath the wrong sky.' He watched Nora as the weight of his words sank in. 'It's one reason that they named the Discard the Discard.'

Nora looked as sick as he felt. 'What is their reason for this?' she asked eventually.

'They want citizens perfectly suited to the Stations,' Alan said. 'Like I said – there's nothing else. There's nothing else they care about.'

'But what are the Stations for?'

Alan shrugged. 'I don't know,' he said. 'Nobody else does either. It all just keeps going. That's what it's all about: keeping going. Perpetuity. It's a giant machine that mustn't ever stop. But nobody in there sees it that way. They see the Stationing as intensely personal, something that they have to do for themselves, to make themselves better people. The Stations are all rituals. Oh, that's right – there *are* books. Books for each Station – they contain all of the recitals, the details, the precise instructions. They're bound in ancient metal and chained to the walls. But they're not like the books when I was a child.' He paused. 'Maybe I'm the one who's wrong, though,' he said. 'Maybe if I'd done the Stationing with all my heart, and the rituals, then I wouldn't be in this mess, and my family wouldn't be in this mess. Maybe approaching them as personal rituals is exactly what we should be doing. Maybe that's what they're for: making your life work.'

'But the babies,' Nora whispered.

Alan looked at her. 'I know,' he said. 'The babies.'

'Everyone else in there, they're okay with that?'

'It's not that they're okay with it. It's that they don't think there's another way.'

'You do, though.'

Alan snorted. 'Must have been born beneath the wrong sky,' he said.

'There are no skies down here.'

'No,' Alan said. 'No, there aren't.'

The next night, they saw a distant fire flickering through the trees.

'Daunt's people?' Churr ventured. 'We're bound to run into some eventually.'

'Most likely,' Nora said. 'I'll go and find out.' She had performed her carto and spent some time meditating. Spider had been collecting firewood – generally bits and pieces of old furniture from the abandoned brick towers of Glasstown – but his backpack was now empty, so they were not lighting their own fire that night. All they had for light were a few small starstones, which Churr had wrapped up as soon as she'd spotted the other fire. Nora melted soundlessly into the darkness between the trees. Her silence was quite unnerving and Alan was reminded of the unease she had originally stirred in him; he had forgotten it during their conversations, which were, generally, far longer and far easier than those he had with any other member of the party. Eyes was incoherent when he did speak, which was less and less now, Churr was still distant, and Spider had never been talkative.

They held their breath as they watched the faraway flame and listened. The swamp was very faintly luminescent here in the forest – the gutwood, as Alan thought of it – but not enough to shed any light upwards. Sometimes he could make out somebody or something moving against it – a brief and incomplete silhouette – but he didn't know if that was Nora making her way towards the fire or not. Though he knew that Nora was more capable of defending herself than the rest of them put together, worry rose in him. What if they were Daunt's people, and there were lots of them? What if Nora was surrounded?

Or what if the fire was a decoy?

A hand on his shoulder. He spun round.

Nora was standing behind him, a finger across her lips. 'They are far away enough for us to speak quietly,' she whispered. 'But no screaming, please.'

'By the Builders!' Alan breathed. 'You scare me, Nora!'

'There are two of them,' Nora said. 'Daunt's people: two men, bearing the symbol.'

'You didn't kill them?'

'No.' Nora looked puzzled. 'Did you want me to?'

'No.' Alan glanced around. 'No, I don't think so.'

'I thought it was better that they don't know we're here. Let them return to Daunt and so let us avoid arousing further suspicion.'

'Which way were they going?' Churr asked. 'Were they on their way back up? Were they carrying much stock?'

'Yes, I think so. They had full backpacks, at any rate, and we have not noticed them travelling alongside us, have we?'

'We need that stock,' Churr hissed. 'That's how we begin. The bug value of all those mushrooms – we could buy a gang or two with that. We can buy bandits.'

'Let's just get to Dok and get back again,' Alan said.

'That wasn't the arrangement.'

'Yeah, but—'

'Daunt still doesn't know it's you she's looking for, does she?'

'No, but—'

Churr put two fingers in her mouth and whistled. 'Hey!' she yelled. 'Hey! Your lady, she looking for a thief? We've got him over here!'

Alan froze.

Churr's shouts were followed by what felt like a deathly silence. Then, raised voices from the distance.

'Thanks, Churr,' Alan said. 'Thanks a lot.'

'Now we've *got* to kill them,' Churr said.

'I know that. That's why I'm pissed off.'

'We're not all here for the same reasons,' Churr said, drawing her knives. 'Remember that.'

Movement and noise, the flapping of unseen wings and ragged croaks that could have come from birds or toads. There were splashes as swamp creatures slipped beneath the surface. Silhouettes obscured the orange flames as they moved through the trees towards their target.

Alan drew his own blade, resentful that he might have to use it. Spider wielded the Boatman's pole. And there was Nora, of course. Four against two, so in theory this would be an easy win. But Alan had never been able to fight in the dark, so it was more like three against two. And even if they won, well, it didn't mean that nobody would get hurt. And the *killing* . . . Even if they won, there would probably be *killing*. Well, definitely: they couldn't let these people get back to Daunt and bring down all of her might on him. His stomach was in his boots. Maybe he could just hide behind a tree, or jump into the swamp and wait until it was all over.

But he didn't, and Daunt's mushroom-gatherers broke into their camp right next to him, so he was first in line. He heard a swish and a yell right in front of him and stumbled backwards, feeling something cold stinging the end of his nose. He fell onto his arse with a bump, rolled over and crawled across a tangle of roots, then clambered to his feet again once he was reasonably sure that he wasn't standing up into the path of a swinging sword.

He stood up and saw that any swords that had been swinging were now still. The fight appeared to be over. 'What?' Alan said, to nobody in particular. 'What? Have they gone?'

'Nora got them,' Spider said. 'See. They're here on the ground.'

'We didn't even get a look-in,' Churr said. 'She's a demon, that one.'

'I did not get to twirl the staff,' Spider murmured. 'Most disappointing.'

'There were only two of them,' Nora said.

'I take it that this is why Mapmakers generally don't get involved,' Spider said.

'Yes,' Nora replied. 'We are too powerful. There is no question.'

'And modest with it,' Alan said.

Churr unwrapped the starstones again, and their pale light glimmered over the scene.

Daunt's men were thin and bearded, and both sported topknots. They had the mushroom symbol on their foreheads and more elaborate fungal designs tattooed on their naked chests. Their loose trousers were tied up around their knees and their bare feet were caked with hardened mud. Strangely, both of them had eyes exactly the same colour: a very, very pale green, so pale as to be almost white, like the Boatman's. And their skin was luminously pale, too, their black tattoos standing out sharply in contrast. Their pale green eyes were wide open, their faces shocked. What was left of their faces, at any rate.

'Why?' Alan asked, looking away. 'Why, Nora, do you always go for their faces? Is it a Mapmaker thing?'

Nora waggled her head. 'Yes, in that it is a practical thing, and Mapmakers are practical. If you are fighting with your bare hands, which is what we usually do so as to avoid carrying extra weight, then it makes sense to target soft and vulnerable – yet important – parts of the body. Like you did with the crocodile, if you remember. Faces and genitals are most effective.' She surveyed her handiwork. 'Also, of course, there's the psychological aspect. People don't like seeing excessive damage done to another's face. They don't want it to happen to them. Seeing a friend or ally – or indeed, even a stranger – hurt like that can be a much greater deterrent to attack than, say, seeing a friend or ally being knocked out with a stick.'

'A crocodile isn't a person, though,' Alan said.

Nora looked confused. 'Oh,' she said, after a moment. 'Well, no. But an enemy is an enemy. And the difference in intelligence between you and a crocodile may not be so much greater than the difference between a Mapmaker and a normal human being.'

Her words were met with a long silence.

'Right then,' Alan said, clapping his hands together. 'Okay. Shall we raid their camp? I mean, morally, now, it's small potatoes, really. As far as I can see.' He glanced down at the dead bodies and then looked away again.

'I need to wash my hands,' Nora said, holding her hands up. It looked as if she was wearing long red gloves.

'Is there any point?' Alan asked.

'Drying blood feels unpleasant,' Nora said, plunging her arms into the swamp and sluicing the dirty water over them.

'Somebody should stay with Eyes,' Churr said.

'I will,' Spider said shortly. 'I am very excited to see what kind of fungus these two unfortunates may have been carrying, but Alan here has been quite literally shouldering the burden of care for my old friend and so I will remain by his side.' He stroked his beard. 'Then tomorrow I will take my turn at carrying the poor fellow. All I ask is that I can spend some time drawing any unusual specimens before they are ingested.'

'We're not going to ingest anything,' Churr said. She was almost dancing with excitement. 'Not unless Alan has one of his emotional episodes and feels like a binge. But' —and here she addressed Alan directly – 'he'd better fucking not. Now come on, people.'

As the group hopped from root cluster to root cluster, Alan thought about the gatherers that Nora had killed. They had lit a fire, but they had not been reticent about fighting in the dark. He remembered what Daunt had once said to him, about taking mushrooms in order to open her eyes. He had thought she was speaking metaphorically – and maybe she was, in part – but perhaps there were mushrooms that could actually help a person to *see*.

Spider would know.

There was nothing much at the mushroom gatherers' camp apart from the fire, now burning low, and a couple of large, bulging backpacks. Churr fell upon the backpacks with delight, but stopped herself opening them. 'We'll open them back at our own camp,' she said. 'It'll be more exciting.'

Alan looked longingly at the fire. 'We could make this our camp,' he said.

'Yeah, sure, if you want to be the one to drag Eyes over.'

Alan didn't say anything. His back and shoulders were on fire.

'Yeah,' Churr said. 'Thought you might have had enough of that by now.'

Why had Alan even invited Eyes along? He couldn't remember. It had been a bad idea and he was angry with himself for it, but almost immediately the anger was subsumed by guilt. Eyes was not a burden; he was a *friend*. Alan got angry with himself for feeling angry. 'Oh, come on,' he growled. 'Let's fuck off.'

'Tomorrow,' Nora said from behind him, as he led the way back to their own camp, 'we will come back here and I will track the gatherers directly to Dok. Our journey will be quickened. This encounter has been a stroke of luck.'

'For us it has,' Alan muttered.

23

The Bottom of the World

'So sometimes the swamp is deep, and sometimes it isn't. Why is that? Are there more buildings beneath us? Are there chasms in between them? Deep trenches full of sludge?'

'Yes. Obviously we don't really know what is sunken, what is lost.' Nora raised an eyebrow. 'Not yet, at least. I will find out.'

'But sometimes it is shallow and marshy and it feels like *ground*. Like the hill the Pyramid is built on.'

'Well, of course: the swamp is not just water, Alan. We do not fully understand its provenance, but wherever the water is coming from, it is bringing with it earth, mud, silt. And whatever you think about magic, about the structure of Gleam being imbued with something that keeps it standing, there is no doubt that buildings are crumbling into the swamp and becoming part of it. Perhaps the stone lasts longer than it should, or at least longer than you would expect a new construction to last, but it does not last forever. Not all of it, anyway. So perhaps some of the ground you feel – perhaps some of the mud that supports this forest – was once brick. Perhaps towers have risen and fallen time and time again before the Gleam that we know came to be.'

Alan was silent for a time as they walked through the gutwood. There were signs of other human life now: treehouses with candles in the windows, snailshells bearing the remains of cooking fires, a paraffin lamp screwed into a trunk. 'Are there any plans to, y'know' – Alan waved an arm – 'save it? Stop it? Save Gleam, and stop the swamp? Find out all about it and reverse it?'

'Quite possibly. There was much about our work that I was never told. I wanted to know, but . . .' Nora sighed. 'They didn't talk to their young ones – well, not to their young *girls*.' She held up a hand and stopped the party. 'Shuddersnake,' she whispered, pointing with the other hand at a thin, pale yellow serpent lounging somehow insolently atop a wide branch. It gave them a lazy hiss as they gave its tree a wide berth.

'Nora, when we first came to the swamp, you said you would change. And you seemed to undergo some kind of . . . episode.'

'I was opening up to the spirit, letting it change me before performing the carto.'

'You talked a lot about a needlestick.'

Now Nora fell silent. Eventually she said quietly, 'I wish I hadn't.'

Alan didn't press it.

When Alan was not pestering Nora with his questions, Nora would converse quietly with Churr in a language of murmurs and half-smiles and subtle tactility. But Churr would not remain at Nora's side when Alan was there. She would look coldly at him and then slip away. Alan wondered at Nora's tolerance of him, given the way he'd treated Churr, but that was only one of the many things about Nora that he did not understand. As for Churr herself . . . He knew that he had been cruel to her back at The Cup and Skull, and knew that he ought to apologise. He ran through conversations in his head. When he'd worked out how to phrase it properly, and when the atmosphere between them was not so bitter as to make anything positive he might say sound insincere, he would say sorry properly.

Nora was on the trail of the mushroom gatherers, looking not for signs of their recent passage, but evidence of an established route. And indeed, there were mushroom symbols carved into the bark of some of the trees.

'It seems a trifle thoughtless,' Spider opined, upon their discovery of the first. Surely they would not *literally* signpost the way to the source of their power and wealth?'

'There must be more to it than merely knowing the way,' Churr said. 'It must all be protected.'

'By what?'

'I don't know.'

'In truth, I thought we would have had more trouble

by now,' Spider said. 'I would have expected Daunt to be more of a presence. And where are the murderers? Where are the monsters?'

'Maybe Nora's scared them off,' Churr said, laughing.

We've got the monster with us, Alan thought. *The greatest monster of them all.*

'Yes,' Spider said, 'a formidable ally indeed.'

'Nora has already saved our lives more than once,' Churr said, seriously now. 'It's hardly been a relaxing trip. If it wasn't for her, then we would have had more than enough trouble.'

'Though some of us have had more trouble than others,' Spider said. 'I'd say Eyes was on his last legs, but he is beyond even that point.'

'We're not leaving him,' Alan said.

'Well, no,' Spider replied, appraising Alan. 'Of course not.'

They saw figures watching them from the trees and Alan thought about the Boatman with his second mouth. Sometimes they heard cackling, and sometimes songs, though nothing Alan knew, and not ones that he liked. The voices were eerie and the songs were tuneless and meandering. They saw distant fires, but even Churr resisted the urge to investigate. Sometimes the swamp was bright, sometimes it was not. 'I have heard stories about the lights in the swamp,' Churr said one evening, as they watched Nora perform the carto. 'Some say it is like lightning, but deep, deep down. The flashes last a long time in the thick slime. They start slow and fade slow. Some say there is a great war going on, far beneath us, where the drowned dead are battling each other with fire and magic.'

'The deeper we get the more and more we talk about magic,' Alan pointed out.

'It is not about heading deeper,' Churr said. Now that there was plenty of wood around, she was using it to make some basic crossbow bolts. 'Those of us who don't enjoy the security of a House talk about magic all the time. It's about *exposure*. It is about being out in the Discard wilds, away from the business of employment and bugs and rent. It becomes more important to those of us on the outside.'

'Do transients travel much through the swamp?'

'No.' Churr shook her head. 'It might not feel too bad really, but if Nora wasn't with us, things would be very different – much harder. And it's so bloody wet and dark and miserable.'

They saw people watching them: bald, pale people with sharp teeth and crooked smiles who stood in the mud and stared. Their clothes were ragged with swamp-rot, and rashes and sores covered their flesh. The odd figure was sitting cross-legged on platforms amongst the tree. Some had extra mouths or eyes. They saw one woman leaning out of a treehouse window who vomited a shower of tiny frogs into their path. 'Sorry,' she called down, her voice broken. 'Too many in – in here.' After they passed they heard her vomit again, and the frogs chittering as they plopped into the swamp. One night they heard splashing from behind them and turned to see a wild-haired man running in their direction; his arms terminated not in hands but in misshapen glass lumps. His wrists were semi-transparent, something between glass and flesh: you could see bones and blood in them. The man starting laughing hysterically once they'd turned to him, and waved his arms in the air.

'See?' Churr said. 'Magic.'

'The corruption?' Alan asked.

Nora nodded. 'I think so,' she said.

'Will it corrupt us?'

Alan had wondered at Spider and Churr's strange behaviour during the journey on the raft; perhaps that had been the corruption at work. Neither of them had acknowledged it, so it was difficult to talk about. Maybe they were unaware of it. Maybe he too had been behaving strangely, and was equally unaware. He remembered Nora telling him to stop muttering . . .

They saw no snails as big as the one that had crested the rooftop the night Alan met Churr, but they saw colossal empty shells, some of which had been turned into homes. The trees were bigger now too, and they did see a slug the size of a motorcycle, wearing an empty saddle. They found half-submerged cages that looked empty until you got too close, and then a crocodile would burst from the swamp, growling and snapping against the metal bars. Thick vines hung from the branches around them. Sometimes they could hear hissing, and at night the insect sounds were loud and sleeping was difficult. They took turns to watch for attackers, human or otherwise.

Churr started to find plenty of targets for her crossbow: bright birds and fat little rat-things that jumped from tree to tree. She kept the colourful feathers to fletch the new bolts that filled the quiver. And Nora found chubby purple grubs – you couldn't just pull them from the tree because they'd stick fast, but if you tickled their backs they'd just fall right off. Nora and Churr ate them alive, juices running down their chins, the grubs' bodies wriggling from between their lips, but Alan couldn't bring himself to. Nora squeezed the grubs over Eyes' mouth. 'These are rich,' she said, 'sustaining. They're good for him – good for all of us.'

Once Nora shot at a flash of white darting in between the trees and came back with a large white long-haired cat. It didn't have any mud or dirt on it at all. Everybody looked at it mutely.

'I don't think we should eat this,' Spider said eventually, and the others all agreed.

Soon they realised that they were not the only ones travelling in that direction. The man with glass hands was one of them, and there were others, shaking so badly that they could only walk very slowly. Their limbs shuddered and their features twitched and they kept falling over.

Others had less strange problems: lesions, body wounds, stomach problems. They came across dead bodies, slowly being claimed by the flora and fauna of the swamp.

One morning they met a girl with thin tendrils growing from her scalp, entwined with her hair. Her skin was dyed dark green, and she had the subdermal facial implants of a worshipper at the Dome of the Toad. 'What is your ailment?' she asked them, in a high, clear voice.

'None,' Alan replied. 'Our friend here is injured, but otherwise we suffer no ailments.'

The girl's eyes brightened. 'Then where are you going? Do you know why we're here?'

'We're looking for Dok,' Alan said. 'What do you mean, do we know why we're here?'

'Many of us do not know,' the girl said, and indicated the forest at large, through which many travellers could now be seen. 'We are drawn, but we do not know where. We wake up in the morning and something in us compels us to travel. It looks like those of us who suffer are compelled to travel to the same place.'

'Those of you who suffer . . . ailments?'

'Yes.' The girl ran a hand through her hair. The tendrils writhed and she flinched. 'Not usual ailments.'

The gutwood was increasingly busy with the ailing. There were people from communities that Alan recognised, like the girl from the Dome of the Toad, and hermits with their shell homes on their backs. There were perhaps more Glasstowners than any other type.

There were bikers who'd obviously long since abandoned their vehicles; they plodded along, shades pushed up onto their foreheads, tripping over their beards and struggling to carry their own weight, and even the occasional resident from Wha House, recognisable by the distinctive hairstyle they were obliged to adopt if they wanted to stay there. Not all of them displayed a visible affliction, but their eyes were all feverishly bright and burning.

'The source of the corruption is close now,' Nora said, after two more days. The gutwood was almost as crowded as Market Top and the swamp, which had always smelled bad, was now thick with the dead and the dying, the bones and bodily fluids, and the air was increasingly difficult to breathe. But the trees were thinning out, and through them could be seen an expanse of space, and even some light – not just luminescence, but actual light, coming down from above.

And sure enough, soon they were free of the forest. The open expanse turned out to be marsh: black water, rotting wood and tufty grass. A network of wooden boards laid across it was jammed with people making their way towards something large, dark and bulbous. A thin mist cloaked everything.

Alan looked at Nora, and she nodded. 'It's in there,' she said. She looked unwell. 'A great sickness in the spirit is in there.'

They joined the queue and shuffled along the boards.

Even here there were bodies: people who'd slipped or fallen or been pushed into the marsh, just left there. Some were fresh, some were just bones, many displaying signs of illness: skulls with more eye-sockets than usual, skulls with horns, hands with thick, bristling clusters of finger bones; skeletons of unusual size and arrangement.

'This is it,' Churr whispered. 'This is where everybody comes when they've fallen through – when they've fallen right down, all the way through all of the levels, all the way down through Gleam, right to the very bottom. The bottom of the world.'

'I suppose there might be others like us,' Alan said, 'people who chose to come here.'

'Do we know that we chose?' Spider said.

Nobody answered him.

'There,' Alan said, later, after the party had progressed a little. 'Daunt's people. See? Over there, not on the next path, but the one beyond that? Wearing the mushroom?' They were dressed like the mushroom gatherers that Nora had killed. 'The mushrooms must be inside, then,' he said. 'We haven't missed them.'

'Of course we haven't bloody missed them,' Churr snapped. 'Some of us have been keeping our eyes open.'

The looming shape resolved itself into a building or, at least, the top of a building. It was a great dome, the rest of which had been swallowed by the swamp, and the boards all converged into a wooden walkway that ran around its circumference. From the walkway, steps had been carved into the dome, leading to a large hole. Alan suspected it hadn't been part of the original building's design; it was too jagged and ugly – not that the dome itself was pretty, because it wasn't. It was made of something smooth, grey and featureless.

'The original structure,' Nora said.

'You think there's something in there other than sick people?' Alan asked.

'There's something in there. Definitely.'

'Not anything that's particularly houseproud,' Spider said. 'Nothing that fancies cleaning up this mess.' He prodded at a corpse lying in the sucking mud with his foot.

Alan spun around at the sound of a baby crying, but there were lots of babies and children being carried along the boards by harried parents, and when he listened more closely, there was a whole tapestry of baby cries winding through the general hubbub. The noise had accreted at such a slow pace that he hadn't really noticed, but now he could hear babies crying, children wailing, the murmur of hundreds of low conversations and individuals talking to themselves, the occasional shout or scream as somebody's pain became too great for them to contain. These were people in sorry states indeed, but they weren't ill with diseases that Alan had encountered before. All of these people were suffering from wild, weird afflictions that appeared to have only one thing in common: they had compelled their sufferers *here*, to Dok.

Some had little to no control over their bodies or bodily functions. Others had bits visibly missing, or clutched at their bodies like they were missing something internally. Sometimes there were wounds, sometimes there were smooth, bloodless holes – one woman had a perfect circle cut out of her middle so that you could see through her, and yet she was staggering along, still alive. There was a little boy with a forest of long, sharp spines growing from his back, wincing as if every footstep hurt. A whole family couldn't stop blue fluid pouring from their noses. An enormous man had a tiny version of himself sitting on his shoulder, and then Alan noticed an even smaller copy tucked into his shirt pocket.

Some of these were not afflictions; 'conditions' might be a better description, or – and the word came to Alan unbidden – *effects*. But the effects of *what*?

Eventually it was their turn to climb the ladder. Nora went first, and then Alan, who carried Eyes on his back. Eyes was still breathing, but shallowly now, and his face was emaciated. He was much easier to carry than he had been, so much weight had he lost. Spider followed Alan, and Churr came last.

Alan had no idea what to expect when he crested the broken edge, but even so, he was momentarily stunned.

The first thing was the smell. It was not the swamp stink that had permeated everything for days on end now, but something earthy, pungent and rich. It made him hungry. Then the sight: he was looking down into something as busy and intricate as an ants' nest, except that the tiny grey things hurrying around beneath him were not insects, but people: bald men and women wearing uniform dark robes, their hems sweeping along walkways made of wood or platforms that were . . . they were mushrooms, Alan saw: large, flat mushrooms growing from the interior walls of the structure. The walls were liberally scattered with torches that burned and shed good light, and much of the stone and wood itself was luminous with what he presumed were some other kinds of fungus.

There was no swamp in here, though the building was tall – or, rather, deep – and obviously extended far below the level of the swamp surface, so the swamp must be pressing in all around. All those tons of sludge: the very thought of it made Alan cold. There was fluid running down the walls, and long green streaks of slimy lichen. The wooden walkways spiralled down round the interior, spanning the gaps between the giant mushrooms, all the way down to the distant bottom, where – Alan squinted to see properly – it looked as if a massive white tent gently inhaled and exhaled. He knew that didn't really make sense, but that was the impression that he had. And then he realised that he could *hear* it. As the white thing expanded and collapsed, there was a sound like breathing, except . . . except it was almost musical, like the sound of air passing through a squeezebox. He could see people going in and out of the white thing, and judged that it was about the size of a large house. He suddenly felt vertiginous.

'What the fuck is this?' he said, but Nora shook her head and no one else said a word.

They clambered down a ladder and dropped down onto a wooden platform that mirrored the one on the outside. Spider and Churr were behind them. From here, they could go down to the left, or one that led to the right. Alan was so busy trying to absorb it all that he missed the figure standing right in front of him.

'Greetings,' said a smiling woman wearing a clean grey robe, 'my name is Ippil. Welcome to Dok.'

'Thank you,' Alan said uncertainly.

'What are your symptoms?'

'I'm sorry?'

'With what are you suffering?'

'I'm not – I'm not ill.'

'Your friend, the one on your back. You came with him? What are his symptoms?'

'Um – his eyes are gone. He's blind. But recently he got an infection and it's bad, it's got into him deep. He won't wake up.'

'Well then, you brought him to the right place. We will take him from you and do what we can.' Ippil gestured to another woman standing next to a trolley, who came and helped Alan lift Eyes onto it. She wrapped a blanket round him and went to take him away.

'Wait,' Alan said, 'where's she taking him?'

'The Sanctuary,' Ippil replied, waving the woman with the trolley away. 'The creature below.'

'What?'

'The Pale Goddess. The Sanctuary. The Giving Beast.' Ippil pointed. 'The big mushroom at the bottom.'

Other travellers were constantly arriving on the platform and being dispatched to the left or the right by people in robes. Mostly, like Eyes, they were being directed leftwards.

Alan looked down at the Sanctuary. 'Who are you?' he asked.

'We are the Pilgrims,' Ippil said. She opened her arms wide. 'This is where we're led, and this is where we stay. Now, if you came in order to bring your friend and you yourselves are not ill, then you take the right hand path. But first, hold out your arms.'

Alan looked at Nora, who nodded, and the four of them held their arms out straight in front of them.

Ippil walked along the row, carefully studying their hands. 'Okay,' she said. 'You're okay.' She smiled again. 'You can go now.'

Alan set off before Ippil could change her mind, though he wanted to know why she had checked their hands. She made him uneasy.

'We're not safe here,' Nora whispered, as they followed the spiral down. 'I can feel it. It's down there.' She pointed down towards the Sanctuary. 'The corruption.'

'That's it? The Giving Beast?'

'No. It is deeper than that. But not much.' She looked around for Churr, and then took her hand and the two of them walked on together.

'The corruption,' Alan said. 'Are you starting to get the feeling that that's what we came for?'

PART THREE

PART THREE

24

The Giving Beast

On their way down they noticed Pilgrims dangling from ropes, gently plucking outlandish-looking mushrooms from the walls. They placed their spoils gently into muslin bags that they then dropped over their shoulders into open backpacks. They worked with practised ease, quickly and confidently, never dropping a thing. Churr and Nora exchanged glances, and Alan thought he knew why. The backpacks were the same as the ones Daunt's mushroom gatherers had been carrying. *Maybe Daunt's gatherers are not truly gatherers*, he thought. *Maybe 'thieves' was a better word for them.*

The deeper they went, the more the fungi, Alan noted, but the wall within reach of the walkway was completely harvested – presumably so that visitors or patients could not help themselves. Obviously the Pilgrims knew they were potent, or valuable. Maybe Daunt's gatherers were not even thieves – perhaps they had just come here and *bought* them. Alan's lip curled. *So much for the brave explorers!*

But he was jumping ahead. He didn't know how it worked yet, and more importantly, he still hadn't spotted any of the pale green caps that he'd come for, though he'd seen every other colour under the sun, and a fair few that he suspected could only be found down here, far, far away from the sun: bright reds, ill greens, rich purples, stinging yellows, glowing whites, shiny blacks, strange pointed things and low, flat ones. There were big, bulbous, powdery puffballs that were mostly coloured orange-brown; masses of tiny bats swarmed around them, flicking out long tongues to gather the powder. Alan didn't know much about mushrooms, other than their effects when ingested, but that struck him as unusual.

Churr was almost salivating. 'There!' she whispered, just about resisting the urge to point. 'Look: old Green's teeth! And there, spirit wings! Tunnellers! Dream-meat! Toadhats!'

'Stop it,' Alan hissed. 'They'll think we've come thieving!'

'Any idea how many bugs all this could fetch? A fucking mountain! Why doesn't Daunt just march on down here and take it? That's what I'd do. That's what I *will* do.'

'I don't care what you do as long as you don't do it until *after* I've got what I want.'

'I'm not sure that was the deal, was it?'

'Just . . .' Alan fell silent.

'I really do bring out the cock in you, don't I?'

'Doesn't take much, to be fair,' Alan muttered. 'It's pretty close to the surface.'

Nobody spoke.

'Might want to rephrase that,' Spider suggested.

'Shut up,' Alan said as Nora giggled. 'All of you, shut up.'

They descended the rest of the way in silence.

They were met at the bottom of the walkway by an older Pilgrim who'd done a bad job of shaving his head and had a couple of missing teeth. He introduced himself as Weddle as he gave them a thorough look up and down.

'So, you're here with a sick friend, yes?'

'Oh,' Alan said, 'yes. Yes, that's right.'

'Yes, yes. Very well. Yes, then, if you'd like to follow me, I will show you to your rooms.' He gave a little bow and hurried off. He was small, but he moved quickly.

'Our rooms?' Alan said, following. 'But we don't have any bugs—'

'Yes, no, well, we don't use bugs here,' Weddle said.

'Then how do you know how long we can stay?'

Weddle turned, looking confused. 'You will stay until your friend is better, yes?'

'Well – yes, but—'

'Very well,' Weddle said, and he was off again.

Alan guessed the Pilgrims could afford to house everyone because the rooms they offered were cells, really. Compared to the accommodation at the Safe Houses, or in the Pyramid, they were tiny and rank, not exactly desirable. You had to bend over in order to fit in, and the original-structure concrete walls were stained green. The ancient mattresses were lumpy and damp. Instead of proper doors, they had lockable gates.

And even so, Alan felt his heart lift when Weddle gestured at one with another slight bow. His own cell! A bed! An actual, proper bed! And a lock! After Green knew how many nights spent out in the swamp, or in Glasstown, or on the Oversight, this was luxury.

He locked the gate, threw himself onto the bed and kicked off his boots, wincing at the smell. Spider took the room opposite him, and his actions mirrored Alan's almost exactly. Nora was next door, and he thought that Churr was opposite her, though he couldn't tell without leaving his room and looking. 'I might go to sleep,' he shouted, then, 'That's it! I'm going to go to sleep!'

'I'm sure we'll manage,' Churr replied.

Nora didn't say anything, and Spider was already snoring.

But he couldn't sleep. He could almost feel the swamp pressing in whenever he closed his eyes. Instead of darkness, he saw Marion's bruised face, and he saw Billy. he kept imagining his son being kept in a cell like this. The Pyramid had its own dungeons – Eyes had told him about them, though he hadn't gone into detail and Alan hadn't pushed the man; it was obvious that the memories were too painful for him to fully recount.

He couldn't keep Eyes' visage from his mind either. That ravaged face, all the pain he'd suffered – and so much of it recently, on this half-cocked quest to come and collect a bag of bloody mushrooms. Eyes was the one who'd taken the fall, time and time again. And maybe he wouldn't even come back. The Pilgrims sounded confident in their abilities, but . . . Alan had fully expected Eyes to die before they'd reached Dok, and he still wasn't sure.

He sat up when he realised that, and hit his head hard on the stone ceiling. 'Fuck,' he said, and touched his scalp gingerly. No blood. He slipped off the bed and sat on the floor with his back against the wall. He *had* been expecting Eyes to die, and yet he hadn't acknowledged that until now, not even to himself. Marion had always said he was good at compartmentalising, but he hadn't realised just *how* good.

He wanted a drink, and he wanted a body to hold close. The urge for physical intimacy roared in furiously whenever he had a moment's peace; it was as sudden and profound as drunkenness. He wanted some of those damn mushrooms, too.

Maybe the Pilgrims could help him out on that front. It might take his mind off all the other stuff, anyway.

He unlocked and opened his gate as quietly as he could, and then set off down the long corridor back to the central hall.

The Sanctuary was a soft, white globe that expanded and collapsed almost as if it were breathing. Air rushed in and then out via a series of gills along its side, creating the squeezebox sound that Alan had heard from the top of Dok. It looked like a mushroom itself – a gigantic puffball – but Alan had eaten puffball back at the House of a Thousand Hollows and knew that they were generally solid. And they didn't breathe. But then, this was Dok, and things seemed different here.

Close up, he could appreciate the true size of the thing. Pilgrims hurried in and out, pushing trolleys and carrying baskets through its frilly, fringed base as if they were merely passing through bead curtains. Seeing them next to it like that, Alan estimated it was big enough to contain four good-sized storeys, and plenty of people. The trolleys the Pilgrims were pushing in and out bore people, usually moaning in pain or gibbering softly to themselves, though a few of the trolleys coming out were empty, and occasionally stained. Many Pilgrims were wearing the mushroom-collecting backpacks.

'Curious?' came a voice from behind him; a familiar voice.

'Yes,' Alan said, turning. 'Ippil, right?'

'That is correct.' Ippil smiled.

'I *am* curious,' Alan said. 'I'm tired, too. I'm a lot of things right now. I'm in danger of being overwhelmed – or maybe I was overwhelmed already and now I'm just . . . I'm just going through the motions.' He waved a hand. 'I'm walking and talking like a real person, but in

truth something crashed through me recently and I think
it took all of the important parts away.'

'When was this?'

'I can't pinpoint the exact moment. Maybe it wasn't
even that recently. Maybe it happened some time ago.'

'You do look exhausted,' she said. 'And emaciated.
You and your companions need to eat, and perhaps then
you will feel a little more human.'

'What do you eat down here? Mushrooms?'

Ippil shook her head, and laughed. 'No – well, not any
that grow here. Nothing that grows – or lives – here can
be eaten for sustenance. Our crops are for medicinal purposes only.'

'Your crops? You're . . . fungus farmers?'

'That is correct,' Ippil said again. 'The swamp imbues
these walls with properties that are perfect for our needs.
Of course, the swamp is also the cause of many of the
afflictions we try to treat, but' – she sighed – 'such is the
nature of things.'

'So what do you eat?'

'The mushroom people trade with us. They supply us
with food from the – what do they call them? The Archway Gardens? Food, and other essentials.'

'The mushroom people – the guys covered with the
mushroom tattoos?'

'Yes,' Ippil said, and then, after a moment, 'That is
correct.'

Alan pursed his lips. 'I've got a lot of questions,' he said. 'I'm just trying to work out where to start.'

'People often find it difficult to gather their thoughts when first exposed to the Giving Beast,' Ippil said. 'It's partly because of its physical strangeness, but mostly because it fills the air with spores that affect the mind. It encourages honesty, and peace. So some people – people who, for example, try to focus on one thing at a time, or mask certain aspects of themselves in order to present one particular facet, or achieve one particular goal – suddenly find themselves unable to function in the manner to which they are accustomed. Everything they repress comes to the surface and they find themselves telling the truth, even to perfect strangers – and even if doing so is detrimental to their aims.'

Alan opened his mouth to speak, and then closed it again.

'In addition,' Ippil continued, acknowledging Alan's reticence with a brief smile, 'it aids us with our healing. It calms down our patients, many of whom are distressed, and it provides an environment conducive to recuperation. It does not necessarily heal people, but it seems to slow the progress of various conditions and diseases.'

'So it is a mushroom?' Alan asked. 'It is a big giant mushroom?'

'It's a fungus,' Ippil replied, 'but it is much more than that.'

'And it just happened to grow in the exact right spot? Right in the middle of this sunken tower where you can grow all these other mushrooms that heal people?'

'It *is* one of the mushrooms that heals people.'

'And they're all just mysteriously drawn to it?'

'No, they're not drawn to the Sanctuary; they're drawn to what rests *beneath* the Sanctuary.'

'And what's that?'

'The Sump,' Ippil said, frowning. She moved her hand in front of her face in a gesture like a cross, or maybe a mushroom. Either way, it was clearly a gesture of warding. 'It's where the Pyramid's produce ends up. The fruits of its folly, and of its labours.'

'I used to live in the Pyramid,' Alan said. 'The Pyramid doesn't produce anything.'

Ippil gazed seriously into his eyes. 'I know you're telling the truth,' she said, 'but you're wrong.'

'The afflicted, then,' Alan said. 'They're drawn to what the Pyramid puts out.'

'Yes.'

'And what's that?'

'We don't know, exactly. For the past few decades we have kept the Seal closed – ever since Idle Hands.'

'Okay,' Alan said. 'I want to know what Idle Hands is, but this is all too much. Earlier you mentioned food. Maybe we could continue this conversation over a meal?'

'Later,' Ippil said. 'Go and get yourself something to eat. I have to attend within the Sanctuary, but I will meet you back here in four hours. For the kitchens, head around to the other side of the Sanctuary and beneath the wide archway.'

'Can I go in? To the Sanctuary? I want to see my friend.'

'You can, but you won't be able to see him yet. Tomorrow, maybe. It depends on his recovery ... if he recovers.'

'Okay. Thank you, Ippil.'

Ippil smiled and left, and Alan watched her slip through the fringes of the Sanctuary and disappear from view.

The kitchens were long, with a low ceiling. Communal tables ran the length of the room. Even here the grey stone walls were slightly damp, though no mushrooms grew on them. Pilgrims and patients sat side by side, eating from tin plates that they'd filled themselves from a row of big bowls at the far end. Behind the bowls, yet more Pilgrims, dressed here for the heat, were sweating over fires and ovens. The room was redolent with the smell of fried onions and something that Alan hadn't smelled in a long time: roasting meat. And proper meat, too – dog or cat or goat or something, not snail or snake or slug. It was clear Daunt was keeping the Pilgrims well supplied; this wasn't just swapping a sack of potatoes for a bag of mushrooms. There must be caravans supplying the Sanctuary every day. How was she doing it?

And how could Churr ever compete? They'd been under the impression that Daunt's people were fighters and explorers who braved killer hornets and starvation and ten-headed swamp monsters in order to pluck the mushrooms from between the teeth of giant crocodiles, but that clearly wasn't the case. She *traded* for them, and that was worse, much worse. It was almost cheating. Churr couldn't offer anything like that – she didn't have the resources or the infrastructure. Being brave, clever and handy with a knife wasn't going to be enough.

So what would Churr do now? And what would she expect *him* to do to help her? She'd fixed him up with Nora, and without her he would never have got here, so he did owe her, there was no doubt. And he owed her for being such a pig. But then, if Churr and Nora were together now, which they did appear to be, did Churr even need him at all?

Was he now surplus to requirements?

He shook himself, collected a plate and went to fill it up. Using a pair of wooden tongs he picked up some little round dog steaks, a heaping spoonful of oily potatoes, some roasted onions and a couple of tiny fried birds that he guessed you ate whole. They were delicious. Once he'd started eating, he couldn't stop. It was a long time since he'd had food this good. He tried to work it out. The last time was probably . . . it was at Daunt's, when he'd played at her feast; when he'd stolen the mushrooms. And he still hadn't found a supply of them. He mustn't forget why he was here. While he ate, he tried to work out how long he had left. Two weeks, he thought, and the journey down here had taken about a week and a half, so he didn't have time to waste. If he didn't get back to that fucker Tromo in two weeks, with the damned mushrooms, then Billy would pay the price, whatever the price was.

The food was rapidly turning to ash in his mouth, but his body was demanding that he eat it anyway, and though his mood did not lift, as he filled his stomach, he felt his mind and body immediately growing stronger. He had not realised how hungry he'd been.

Alan ducked beneath the curtained base of the Giving Beast, looked up and drew his breath. There was a strong floral scent with earthy, musty notes. The interior was humming with a low, repetitive chant: the Pilgrims were singing. It sounded like it was coming from up above. There was a fat central stalk with a wooden door in it, he noted, and wooden steps spiralling up and around that reached up and split into branches that supported the cap — although 'cap' probably wasn't the right word. *Canopy*, maybe. The underside of the canopy was orange, and ribbed with thick white horizontal ridges like shelves, almost. They reminded him of the wooden walkways spiralling around the inside of the tower they were in. They were busy with Pilgrims, who at first glance appeared to be doing something to the sponge-like gills of the canopy. Then Alan realised that there were bodies tucked into the gills: the patients, packed like larvae in a honeycomb, with their heads sticking out. They were out on gurneys of some sort, and the Pilgrims were able to slide them out and back in again. The air was thick with motes of dust that— No, they were spores, dancing in the light. The light came from glass jars that hung on ropes; they were filled with some brightly glowing sludge, fermenting mushrooms, Alan decided, upon closer inspection. They were as bright as paraffin lamps.

Then the Giving Beast 'inhaled', the canopy expanded and everything receded. There must have been some elasticity in it. The Pilgrims on the ridges didn't react at all – they just carried on with their work – but Alan wobbled on his feet and nearly fell over. He reached out a hand to the ground to steady himself, and then everything came closer again. The effect was disorientating, especially when coupled with the spores. It was like he'd actually taken something: lemonsnake extract, or some of Spider's pipeweed.

But none of that was as strange as what he then noticed: high up, at the very top of the canopy, a great glass globe was nestled in amongst the branches of the stalk. It looked like the Sanctuary had grown around it; it was entirely a part of the structure, and surrounding it were Pilgrims, kneeling on branches and small wooden platforms attached to the branches. It was they who were chanting. They faced the globe and one by one would get to their feet, approach the glass and press their foreheads to it.

There was just one thing he could see in the globe: points of pale green, stark against something dark. They were as bright and alluring to Alan as the stars of the night sky.

He'd found them.

25

Idle Hands

Alan went to the bottom of the staircase that wound around the Sanctuary's central pillar. It was a stalk, a stem, a pillar, or maybe even a leg, but he wasn't sure if this was a mushroom, an animal or a building. Most likely it was all three. Before ascending, he reached out to the handle of the thick wooden door.

'Can I help you?'

Alan turned to see Weddle standing there, smiling toothily, his arms folded, hands buried in the opposite sleeves of his grey cloak. He hadn't even realised that Weddle had been nearby.

'I was just wondering what was inside?'

'Yes, yes, of course – that's our storage room, but it is off-limits to visitors, yes? For our medicines, that kind of thing. Very valuable. Very dangerous, in the wrong hands.'

'Sounds like exactly the kind of door I don't want to open,' he said. 'I'll stay well clear.'

'Yes, yes,' Weddle nodded. Then, loudly, 'Better had!' He threw his head back and laughed uproariously.

Alan hovered, one foot on the ground, one foot on the bottom step. After listening to Weddle laugh for a moment too long, he pointed upwards. 'What about going upstairs?' he asked. 'Can I do that?'

'Yes, yes, of course – why wouldn't you be able to?'

'Thank you,' Alan said, but Weddle was already trundling off, laughing quietly to himself.

Alan really didn't want to open the door. He didn't want to cause any trouble, not here. *It must be the spores*, he thought, *affecting my mind. Changing my behaviour*, but it still left some deep part of him unaffected, able to reflect on himself, as if he'd been split into an actor and an observer. *Will they affect Churr in the same way if she discovers what's inside the trunk?*

He spiralled up and around, passing Pilgrims on their way down and being overtaken by others racing past him on the way up. The chanting grew louder. There were Pilgrims with small vials of dried mushrooms, others with blood on their robes bearing trays loaded with salves and compresses and cutting tools. He could hear the occasional scream and, as he watched, a group of Pilgrims used a pulley to raise a trolley up to one of the shelves and then lifted the occupant – a person with crocodile arms? – into a vacant gill. Alan was pretty sure that 'gill' wasn't the correct term for one of the small, irregularly shaped compartments that the canopy afforded, but that's what he would call them.

A door he hadn't noticed suddenly opened next to him, and a Pilgrim popped out of the central trunk, wheeling a trolley on which stood a steaming kettle and some mismatched cups, mugs and teapots. Before the Pilgrim closed the door after himself, Alan caught a brief glimpse of a dumbwaiter-type contraption with deep shelves packed with jars, bottles, vials, bags, and various instruments that he could not identify. He continued upwards as the tea-Pilgrim bustled off along a branch and started handing out the drinks.

And then he reached his destination. The chanting was loud and powerful up here, and the sound was somehow circular; and he realised that the Pilgrims were performing it in the round. He was ascending into the middle of their company and he could feel their eyes on him from amongst the branches. But he wasn't here to cause trouble. He just wanted to have a look.

There were no visible openings or stoppers in the glass globe; it appeared to be completely hermetic. And it was full of life: thick, glossy leaves pressed against the glass, and pale pink flowers with rich red veins unfurled further in, and right in the middle was a lump of stone, or maybe a large wooden log, from which all of the plants grew. Vibrant green mosses spilled from this central object in cascades that looked like waterfalls. Lichens covered unknown objects and ferns pushed through everything else. Condensation misted the glass at the top; at the bottom was clear brown water.

And here and there on the central object were small, unassuming, pale green mushrooms. They looked dull and inconspicuous, but they burned brightly in Alan's eyes.

'What is this?' he breathed. He hadn't meant to say it out loud.

'The Terrarium,' a Pilgrim replied. This individual was not as friendly as Ippil or Weddle; she was big, and strong-looking, with a neck like a toad's and eyebrows like masses of spider legs.

Alan thought the Pilgrim would elaborate, but she didn't.

'Is it . . . important?' he asked eventually.

'It is everything to us,' the Pilgrim replied. 'It is the heart and soul of the Pale Goddess, and the Pale Goddess is at the root of everything. She is buried deep in our core, as we are in hers. The Terrarium is where we come to thank her, and where we come to pay our obeisance.'

'So it's part of her? I mean, part of the Goddess? The Sanctuary?'

'What is it you want, man?' the Pilgrim asked. 'I'm trying to worship.'

'I wanted the mushrooms,' Alan said, pointing. He realised what he'd said as soon as he'd said it and clapped a hand over his mouth.

The Pilgrim looked at him angrily.

'I didn't mean to say that,' Alan said. 'Bloody *hell*.'

'We do *not* curse in the presence of the Goddess,' the Pilgrim said. 'This is a sacred place. And we do *not* reach into her soul so that we can pilfer it for our own gain. Now,' she said, and she prodded Alan's chest with a finger, 'you will be gone from here and you will not come back. You profane us.'

Alan cast a brief glance back at the Terrarium and hurried away, back down the trunk.

He tried to process what he'd seen in that last look. The object suspended in the middle of the Terrarium was not a stone block or a tree stump; it was a huge, leather-bound book, sodden and rotting, and from it grew all of the vines, the ferns, the flowers, the lichens and the mosses. And the mushrooms.

'Idle Hands was a parasitic fungus,' Ippil said. 'It came before my time. It devastated much of the Low Discard. The outbreak came from an exploratory mission into the Sump, and the Pilgrims were best placed to deal with it because of our location, and because of our experience in healing. It has not been reported since, though the Discard is a big place.'

'And what was it?' Alan asked.

Ippil, Churr, Nora and Spider followed suit, then Ippil continued, 'The first symptom took weeks to manifest, but when it did it was moving hands: a sufferer's fingers would bend and wiggle, and they wouldn't be able to control them. Then their hands would start shaking. That was partly how it got its name.' She looked around. 'It was a very unpleasant disease. I don't know if I should elaborate while you're eating.'

'Please,' Spider said, through a mouthful of little birds. Crumbs flecked his beard. 'Do continue.'

'All right. This was a fungus that thrived inside the human body, and in order to replicate itself, it made its way into the sufferer's mind and prompted them to pass it on. The second symptom was usually paranoia, which would develop into full-blown murderousness – this indicated that the fungus was well and truly embedded in the host's brain, physically growing in there. Eventually, it would take over the brain, and the host would be little more than an ambulatory unit, carrying the fungus around until it was ready to spill from the host's eyes, ears and mouth. Most strikingly, it would soften the top of the skull and erupt from there in the form of two long, curved horns. And that's the second part of how it got its name.'

Alan looked confused.

'Idle Hands,' Nora said. 'Idle hands make the devil's work.'

'That's a sentiment I can't quite get behind.'

'It's something you can joke about now,' Ippil said, 'but the outbreak was brutal: people turning on each other; families ripped apart. There was a lot of bloodshed. And the elders say that it was incredibly difficult to treat. If the fungus takes hold, then it controls *all* the body parts, even bits that have been amputated.'

'So how was it treated?'

'Well, I told you that the various powers and potencies of the mushrooms are a consequence of where we are. We believe that what the Pyramid dumps into the Sump is magical, and that as a consequence of the rising swamp, that magic is leaching out. It is our belief that this magic is causing these various afflictions throughout the Low Discard; making people ill, making them mad, making them . . . different. And that's why they're drawn here: they're drawn to the source of their condition.'

'Why would they be drawn to the source?'

'It's a theory,' Ippil said, 'that's all. Once we suppose the presence of magic, though, it's difficult to rule anything out.'

'The corruption – *I* can feel it,' Nora said. 'It is a corruption of Gleam's spirit. If Gleam itself is somehow magical, and if these people are indeed touched by magic, then it is possible that they can feel the corruption too.'

'Why would they head towards anything that feels like a corruption, though?'

'It's not them, it's the magic – the magic is compelling them.'

'Hang on,' Alan said. 'Idle Hands – let's go back to that.'

'We use our experience and what understanding we do have to manage the growth of various fungi. Back then, the Pilgrims were experimenting with growing a fungal antidote, but they were working in the dark. Many of the effects of these mushrooms – again, this is just our belief, but it is based on decades of experience – are magical, so they thought they'd try to manipulate the magic in the mushrooms. They were good with the fungus, but they knew little to nothing about magic and it took them a long time, while all around them, the world was falling apart.'

'But they succeeded.'

'That is correct: they did. They hit upon a new strain; not a fungus like Idle Hands, but a mushroom that could be cut up, dried and ingested. It could not undo any damage done by Idle Hands to the host's brain, but it could halt it, and it did negate the aggressive urges.'

'It stopped the spread.'

'That is correct.'

'So that's why you don't open the Seal.'

'That is correct.'

'And that's why we can't know what the Pyramid is making.'

Ippil nodded silently.

'But,' Nora said, 'we know that Idle Hands is something they made.'

Ippil nodded again.

'Good point,' Alan said. 'But . . . if you've got an antidote, why the fear of Idle Hands?'

'There are dangerous side effects, but mostly, the

reason is that the antidote is very hard to grow. There is only one culture in which we can keep it alive, and it does not support a large crop.'

'The Terrarium,' Alan said. 'The little pale green mushrooms.'

'That is correct,' Ippil said.

Alan ran a hand through his hair. 'For fuck's *sake*,' he said.

Ippil pointed a finger at Alan. 'We do *not* curse in relation to the Terrarium,' she said, her face transformed in anger. 'You need to learn to hold your tongue, Alan.'

The others murmured their agreement. 'Why does the nature of Green's Benediction upset you so?'

'That's what it's called, is it?'

'It is.'

'Well,' Alan said. He paused. 'The truth is . . .' he said, trying again, but he didn't get much further. He could see Churr slowly shaking her head at him while Ippil wasn't looking, mouthing the word 'no'.

'Look,' he said, 'Ippil, it's what I came for.'

Ippil's expression froze, and she said nothing.

'Don't look at me like that. It can't be unusual. You must get people coming down here for them all the time.'

'We certainly do not. Why would we? Idle Hands is not a threat any more. We have the only specimen left.'

'I *know* that the Mushroom Queen had some of these, so one of your Pilgrims must have supplied them. Somebody here must be trading them.'

'Well, yes: the Mushroom Queen *could* have some. Dried, they last indefinitely. And Daunt is our only trading partner with regard to Green's Benedictions, so she might have some from previous giftings. But the issue is that they are not for us to harvest. We cannot simply open the Terrarium and take them. The Giving Beast releases them in accordance with its own cycles. So, no matter how desperately you want them, you cannot have them. No matter how far you have come, they are not yours to take. Another possibility, of course, is that the Benedictions you encountered were fake. Some Tunnellers perhaps, dyed green with the juice of refinery beetles.'

'They were *not* fake,' Alan said, angry with himself for not considering that. Though if they *had* been fake, it was a good job he'd lost them, instead of giving them to Tromo in good faith.

'How do you know?'

Alan cast about for an answer. 'She *really* wanted them back,' he said. 'She was going to great lengths for them if they were not genuine.'

'Regardless,' Ippil said, her voice even, yet steely, 'coming here to secure some for yourself was a mistake. We cannot sanction a breach of the Terrarium, and besides, we are, first and foremost, *healers*, not one of your topside gangs, looking to make a profit by peddling poisons to the desperate. Nor are we here to supply such parasites. We trade with Daunt, but only out of necessity. Our preference would be to offer something else in return for goods, but, unfortunately, we have nothing else to offer.'

She stood up. 'I thought you were here because you had brought your friend, but your motives are far from altruistic. I am going to have to ask you to leave.' She frowned. 'All of you.'

'But—' Churr started.

'No.' Ippil had turned white with rage. 'You have come to steal from us. You are not worthy of our hospitality. You are not worthy of the Giving Beast. And you are not welcome.'

'What about Eyes?' Spider asked.

Ippil thought for a moment. 'You can go to see him, but then you must leave. You can wait for him out in the swamp. You have half an hour before I send Pilgrims to enforce your banishment. Remember: you are now being watched.'

She turned and swept away, head down, almost vibrating with fury.

'So,' Alan said.

'Nice one,' Churr said. 'Good work, dickhead.'

'I'm not a good liar.'

'You're not good at anything.'

'He's quite good at singing,' Spider said.

Churr rolled her eyes.

Alan turned to Spider. '*Quite?*' he said.

Spider shrugged.

'You can't lie, you can't kill, you can't—'

'I can fight a bit.'

'What good is that if you're not going to kill?'

'I'm pretty sure I could kill, actually,' Alan said, quietly. 'It just hasn't been absolutely necessary yet.'

'My understanding,' Spider said, 'is that Alan chose his companions with his own limitations in mind. He is not generally comfortable with killing, so he asked me along, for example. Not to mention Bloody Nora.'

'*I* secured Bloody Nora,' Churr said, 'and don't you idiots forget it.'

'Lest anybody forget,' Nora said, 'I'm here for my own reasons.'

Churr glared at Nora, then slammed her hands onto the table, stood up and strode off.

Alan took a deep breath. 'Right,' he said. 'Coming to see Eyes?'

'This is the place,' Spider said to Alan as they entered the Sanctuary. 'The place the Omentoad showed me. It feels the same. I knew it augured something good. This is where we succeed.'

'You are too optimistic,' Alan said. 'We may have found our Benedictions, but we have not yet succeeded in anything.'

'I felt the magic,' Spider said. 'I felt it coming up from underneath. I don't feel it now, but I did then – that must be what the afflicted feel. That must be what you feel, Nora.'

Nora nodded briefly, but her face did not betray anything like the wonder that was in Spider's words.

Alan, Nora and Spider stood around Eyes, lying on his wooden gurney. Once Nora and Spider had taken in the nature of the Sanctuary, the Goddess and the Giving Beast, they relayed the recent developments. The flesh of the Giving Beast smelled much stronger this close to its interior 'wall', and the surface of the gills was soft-looking, inviting.

Alan had to resist the urge to climb inside one of the gills and lie down himself. 'I wish I'd made better use of my bed,' he murmured during the silence that followed their story.

'Aye,' Eyes said, 'if you'd just stayed in bed, you'd likely not be getting the boot.'

The old man was much, much better – in fact, his recovery was almost eerie. Alan was shocked when they first saw him. Although Eyes was still blind – he'd lost his sight permanently, it appeared – the skin of his face had healed and the infection had diminished almost totally. Apart from being far too thin, he actually looked better than he ever had before.

The Giving Beast. Alan couldn't shake his unease. It was giving, yes; it was giving very much. But was it taking anything in return?

'It all comes down to the Pyramid, then, eh?' Eyes said. He chuckled softly to himself. 'Sending all their shite out here for the likes of us to deal with the consequences.' He laughed again. 'Ah, well. It should be no surprise to me any more.' He shook his head. 'No surprise at all.'

Alan waited for the onset of the trembles, for the agitation, for the explosion of anger and entreaties for action that usually accompanied Eyes' musings on the Pyramid.

But they didn't come. He just lay there, calm and sanguine, a clean cloth wrapped around the top of his head, laughing quietly. It must have been the effects of the spores.

Then Alan cocked his head. 'Can you hear that?' he asked.

'What, exactly?' Spider replied. 'I can hear lots of groaning, talking, children shouting.'

'Babies crying,' Nora said, standing.

'Yes,' Spider said, 'babies crying, too. The breath of our great host here, the squeaking of these pulley systems . . .' He trailed off.

'The babies,' he said.

Alan stood up and simultaneously a cacophony of screams erupted outside the Giving Beast. Wound through it all was the high wail of a crying baby.

26

Green's Benediction

As they ran from beneath the fungal curtain, warm blood spattered across their skin. Screams echoed throughout Dok and bodies rained down from the hole at the top of the tower, splattering onto the stone ground and bouncing from the Giving Beast's canopy, fluids spraying wildly from tears and ruptures.

'By the Builders!' Spider said. 'Holy hell!'

The baby cries became that awful gurgling laughter and then warped back again, all the time growing ever louder. Alan couldn't see much up at the top of Dok – he could just about make out the large aperture through which they'd all entered – but there was no bright sky beyond to illuminate anything, not when they were this deep. There was just a paleness, and the impression of movement. And, of course, people falling: Pilgrims and the afflicted alike. Some Pilgrims were running down the walkway and some were running up, armed with staffs, swords and crossbows.

'We're up, Nora,' Spider said, but Nora was already on her way, moving fluidly through the chaos, slipping between the Pilgrims and flowing up the spiral like something betraying the laws of physics.

Spider put a hand on Alan's shoulder. 'Now's your chance, Alan,' he said. He gestured back at the Giving Beast. 'We'll handle the Clawbaby. You get in there and secure those Benedictions.'

'I should fight it,' Alan said. 'It's here for me.'

'We don't know that.'

'I do – I can't explain it, but I know. It used to wait for me outside the House of a Thousand Hollows, I'm sure of it now. I used to think there was something out there, watching me. It's been there ever since I was young. Even when I lived in the Pyramid. Sometimes when I was out on the terraces I felt it, watching.'

'Alan, we don't have time for this. Go and get what we came for; you take the Benedictions and you take Eyes and you go. Just go. Because once this is over, there will be no mercy for you. The Pilgrims are dangerous: you know it and I know it. You will have to run. We will all have to run.'

'Where's Churr?'

'I don't know. Now go.'

'I—'

Spider shoved him back towards the Giving Beast and then set off at a run, shouldering his way across the increasingly congested ground floor. Alan heard a wet yell from directly above and instinctively side-stepped; a woman with her head twisted right around smashed into the ground right where he'd been standing. The sound of her bones breaking made Alan want to cry. He looked at her and realised that her neck wasn't twisted; she just had faces on both sides of her head.

When he looked up again, Spider was gone.

Alan ran back to the Giving Beast, to find that inside was no less chaotic. There were obviously different denominations within the Pilgrims' order, and some of those were trained to fight, and many of those were on their way up to do battle. But those who were not fighters were gathering here and Alan's heart sank when he looked up and saw how crowded the branches of the Sanctuary were: a bountiful crop of pious greycloaks clutching their cuffs and chanting at the Terrarium. *Praying.* Yet more Pilgrims were climbing the trunk, and many were simply kneeling on the floor, facing the centre of the great dome. Though most of them would not pose much of a threat individually, he had no doubt that together they could easily overpower him. And there were a few more threatening people pacing around the inside: lithe, bare-chested, wearing loose trousers instead of cloaks and twirling staffs in their hands.

There weren't any attempts to move the patients out – maybe there was nowhere else for them to go. And perhaps they believed the spores in here would slow down or even stop any attackers, overwhelming them with a pacifist spirit. Maybe that would work on normal human beings, but Alan was pretty sure that the Clawbaby would not be dissuaded from its grisly work, whatever that work was.

Eyes wasn't in his gill. His gurney lay empty. He must have made his own way out, but he couldn't see, so maybe somebody was helping him – Churr, Alan hoped.

Something heavy landed on top of the Sanctuary and it released a thick cloud of the mind-altering dust. Choking on the stuff, he made his way back towards the trunk, wondering as he stepped between the praying Pilgrims where Ippil was, and Weddle. He wondered if he should just get down on his knees and pray himself – maybe that would be the best thing, to pray for himself, and for Billy, and Marion. Perhaps he should give up his own pathetic quest to save his son, and put his faith in . . . *something else*. It couldn't be any more ineffectual than he was, even if it didn't work at all. Besides, this wasn't some abstract god; this wasn't Old Green, or the Holy Toad. This was a real, living entity, with real, tangible powers.

No. *No.* He felt his knees bending and forced himself to straighten up again. He was nearly at the trunk now. He joined the queue, the devout all about him: a sea of bowed heads. And all around them was that awful noise: the screaming and crying; the inordinately loud wailing of a baby that was not a baby. Something was pattering onto the canopy above them.

The Clawbaby was the only opponent that Nora had

not simply neutralised, as far as Alan was aware. He didn't want it to hurt her. And Spider; really, he didn't stand a chance. He was almost overwhelmed with guilt. But the Clawbaby's crying turned into Billy's crying and he saw his son's tear-stained face, and Marion's bruises and he pushed his way through. He could see Tromo in his mind's eye, sneering at him. He remembered Tromo's face from the Modest Mills massacre – he remembered all of their faces, leering in the flickering light of the fires. There was something in his way and he struggled past it. He could hear shouting close by and he speeded up. When he paid attention he realised he was pushing Pilgrims off the narrow spiral staircase, though they weren't falling far, and they were getting a soft landing – unlike the poor sods being pushed from the much larger wooden walkway by the Clawbaby.

Something inside him smiled at the echoes in action, but the smile did not reach his face. He could feel those hands clawing at his back as Pilgrims raced up behind him and he spun around, pulling his long knives from his boots as he did so. The Pilgrims behind him pulled back when he waved one knife at them. He held the other out the other way, pointing up the steps, and the Pilgrims in front of him moved faster now, trying to put as much space as possible between the steel and their bodies. Alan followed them, his weapons still drawn, keeping at a distance those who would grab him and throw him down.

He was getting there, but he'd soon be into the

branches, with Pilgrims coming at him from all directions – those who were not busy with their worshipping, that is. He had to get the mushrooms and get out before the Clawbaby got here, for it would.

And then it did. There was a hush, somehow; a not-quite-total silence falling. The screaming stopped, and the crying, until the only sound was the chanting, clean and pure, and Alan wanted very badly to fall down and join in. In that moment he believed in its power.

But the moment did not last long enough, and with a great ripping noise, the Clawbaby tore through the side of the Sanctuary and stepped in, its green eyes glowing, its black rags billowing, its bulk bringing with it its own darkness. Alan drew his breath and the Clawbaby's green eyes found his. Nora and Spider were dead, then.

The thing started laughing. 'Wild Alan,' it said, its voice a whisper, yet loud enough to fill the Sanctuary. Its voice was a pollutant, and the Pilgrims all turned and the screaming began again. 'It is a shame for you that those metal steeds cannot carry you up and down all of the stairs in the Discard.' Its voice carried above all of the other noise – unless only he, Wild Alan, could hear it.

Wild Alan.

The Clawbaby spoke like a Pyramidder.

Alan threw himself up the stairs, forcing his way past the Pilgrims who were blocking his path. Many of them were now on their way down, trying to join the headlong rush out of the Sanctuary, and he tried not to knock them over the edge, but in fact they were throwing each other off in their rush to save themselves. Evidently not even the Giving Beast's influence could negate the natural instinct for self-preservation.

The Pilgrims whose role it was to guard the Sanctuary were rushing the Clawbaby, but their staffs were bouncing harmlessly off it. One started making his way to the bottom of the steps, having spotted Alan's knives, but there were a lot of greycloaks between them and soon the stick-spinner was caught in a tide pulling him in the wrong direction.

Alan jumped from the staircase onto a wide branch and from there pulled himself up onto the next one, escaping the stampede on the walkway. He was nearly there. He could hear the Clawbaby laughing, and when he took a moment to look briefly over his shoulder he saw that the beast was spearing its attackers on one of the staffs, one after the other, like one of the Cavern Tavern's cat kebabs.

'Where are you going, friend Alan? Are you still hoping to escape me?'

'What do you *want*?' Alan raced up the trunk, clambering from branch to branch.

'I want to take your life from you, as you took mine.'

'What? You're here, aren't you? You are obviously not dead.'

'Who do you hate, Alan?'

Alan froze.

'You remember those words, don't you?' The Clawbaby was fighting as it spoke, and yet there was no trace of exertion in its voice. 'How pathetic of you to pretend that you do not kill, when you have killed so many.'

Alan found that his cheeks were wet, but he forced himself to continue the climb. He was level with the Terrarium now, but there were still Pilgrims chanting in the branches around him: the most devout. They would not be happy with him. The Green Benedictions stood out, shone out, called out to him. He moved towards the glass.

A figure dropped down from a higher branch. 'Halt.'

'Ippil.'

Ippil was dressed differently; she was wearing trousers and her chest was bound. She held a wickedly curved blade in her left hand. She dropped into a fighter's stance. 'You are the lowliest,' she said, 'the most unworthy. You have brought horror with you and you would let it rip us limb from limb while you pillage our Sanctuary.'

'I'm not arguing.'

'You do not wish to defend yourself?'

'You don't know half of what I've done. You think I'm bad, but I'm even worse than you think. As for my intentions, you are absolutely right: I've come for the Benediction and I will not leave without it. I did not mean for that thing below to follow me, but I did not try to stop it. But I did not know you were here, Ippil – you Pilgrims, I mean – at our destination. I did not expect to find a safe haven and good people at the end of our journey. If

I had, I would have taken steps to throw the beast from our trail. And since arriving, I have been so fixated on the completion of my quest that I did not consider what would happen when it finally caught up with us.'

'But it's here now – and that doesn't change your plans?'

Alan bit his lip and shook his head. 'I'm sorry, Ippil. If I had to choose between saving hundreds of Pilgrims and my family, I would choose my family. As it is, I don't think I can save you anyway.'

'You're using us to enable your actions and your escape.'

'Yes.'

Ippil swung at him and he parried with his long knife, then stepped backwards. Her face was full of hate, and she was trained, strong and careful. She moved slowly, purposefully.

More Pilgrims were running along the branches to the sides of the Sanctuary. She was forcing him to move backwards, away from the Terrarium, and further from the staircase and the Clawbaby too. If it came up now – he risked a glance, and yes, there it was, at the bottom of the steps, though it was moving slowly – then Ippil would be between it and him. But it would be between him and the Terrarium.

He didn't want to fight. He was tired and weak. Then Ippil struck again, and he blocked her blade with one knife and tried to strike with the other. But he felt the block fail, and Ippil's sword sent his weapon spinning through the air as her blade bit into his knuckles. He jerked, shouting, and missed his target, instead nicking her shaven skull – not deeply, but enough to send her darting backwards. She clamped one hand to her head.

'Ippil,' he said urgently, '*behind you!*'

But his warning came too late; by the time he'd seen Churr appear on one of the ledges and spoken, she had pulled the trigger of the crossbow – the crossbow Alan had given her – and a bolt was erupting from the Pilgrim's neck.

Ippil gargled and clutched vainly at her throat.

'Fucking hell,' Alan said. He watched Ippil's blood flow and felt as if his own spirit was leaving him. The Pilgrim fell still and Alan was utterly emptied.

He found Churr's eyes. 'I wish you hadn't.'

'I didn't do it for you.' Churr grinned wildly, pointing the weapon at Alan. Her eyes were alive. 'Dok is *mine* now. Don't you see? This is how it begins! Daunt's major supplier is gone and in their place is *me*. And I'm not going to fulfil that function.'

'You killed the Boatman.'

'That's right: a major link in Daunt's chain. I gave him a third mouth and spilled him into the swamp. Everyone else was too busy with the croc to notice.'

'Somebody else will take his place.'

'Eventually, I'm sure. But right now, the more disruption, the better.'

'Alan!'

Alan didn't want to turn his back on Churr so he moved backwards a bit more and looked down. He felt a kind of strength return: that was Spider's voice – Nora and Spider had come back. *They were alive*. They were coming up the staircase – they were running. Alan didn't know where they'd been and right then he didn't care. They came up behind the Clawbaby, which whipped around, its bundled claws hissing through the air, all metal death, and battered them both from their feet.

'Churr,' Alan said, 'how are you going to hold it? Against Daunt?'

'The afflicted will support me in return for their treatment.'

'But how will you treat them? You don't have the knowledge or the expertise.'

'I know more than you think.'

'Well, then, this is where we part ways. All the best, Churr. Thank you for your help.'

'You go and get your mushrooms. But we're not done yet. You still owe me for getting you down here. I'm sure I'll find a use for you in future.' Churr lowered the crossbow. 'We'll meet again.'

'I don't doubt it.'

She stepped to one side and threw Ippil's body to the ground below.

Alan approached the Terrarium. The Pilgrims who had remained were gone. He looked down. Nora was moving around the Clawbaby with her customary speed and grace, slicing and punching, reaching deep into it with her hands. It was not welcoming her attentions. The Pilgrims must have hurt it a little because it was moving more slowly than it had been at The Cup and Skull. Spider was jabbing at it when he could. The two of them looked like flies on a frog.

Alan placed one hand on the cold glass. The Giving Beast was still inhaling and exhaling, and the branches and the Terrarium still rose and fell in sync. Alan could see his reflection staring back at him. It did not look like him. It was too skinny and hollow-eyed. Beyond the reflection, green chaos thrived and the Green Benedictions beckoned. Alan took a deep breath, brought one knee up to his chest, and drove his boot right into the Giving Beast's heart.

The glass shattered, hung in the air for a moment, and then fell like a sheet of white water, raining down onto the staircase below with a sound like bells. A complex fragrance escaped: something fresh and green but mingled with rot. Everything shook, and the Giving Beast inhaled, the sound of the air rushing in like a discordant accordion, like a scream, and it didn't stop inhaling; it swelled right up, and up, and up, and up, and the branches flew upwards, and the trunk stretched out, and the canopy thinned. All of the gills widened and patients slid from their alcoves on the wooden gurneys, some of them falling all the way down to the floor. A howl of rage came from beneath and Alan saw that the Clawbaby had slid and fallen too, but Nora and Spider had been able to cling on.

He plunged a hand into the mass of plants before him and anchored himself, then went about plucking the Green Benedictions from the sodden remains of the book with his other hand. He cursed himself for having nothing better to put them in than his pocket, but it probably didn't matter if they were crushed, he hoped.

Their value was not in their life.

27

A Speedy Getaway

The Clawbaby's fall had given Nora and Spider the chance to join Alan at the top of the giant fungus trunk and they arrived as he grabbed the last of the Benedictions. The three of them glanced briefly at each other as the Sanctuary reached the peak of its expansion. Everything fell still for an instant, then the collapse began. Alan didn't know whether it was the Sanctuary was screaming or him and his companions, but they held on tightly as the trunk snapped back, their hair and clothes whipping around in the rushing air.

They lost their grip and were thrown onto a branch – Spider lost his footing and slipped over the edge, but caught hold of the branch and hung there.

Beneath them, the Clawbaby was slowly climbing up.

'We'll split up,' Nora said breathlessly. 'We'll attack it from different branches, from different angles. It cannot win.'

'It can,' Alan said. 'Remember the knife in its head?

It's not human – it's not like us. It will defeat us. At best we can escape it, but only temporarily.'

'Alan,' the Clawbaby said, its voice that terrible rough gurgle, 'Alan, my friend. Let your fellow travellers go. Disband the remnants of your little party. It's you I'm here for. Only you. Only ever you.'

Spider wasn't able to pull himself up without dropping his knife. He tried, failed, and remained dangling.

'Let them go, Alan. Anybody who remains by your side will die there.'

Alan grabbed Spider's arms and pulled him up. 'Go,' he said, 'you go – Nora, you go too. The thing's right. This is all my doing.'

'How?' Spider said, rolling onto his back. 'How is it? This is a trick. This is the Pyramid, or Daunt, somebody trying to stop you, Alan.'

'Spider is right,' Nora said. 'And besides, together, we can beat it.'

'No,' Alan said, 'it *is* my doing. It said something to me – it said, "Who do you hate?" I know what it's talking about.'

'We cannot discuss this now,' Nora said. 'It is nearly upon us. It is time to fight.'

'Your girlfriend ran,' Spider said. 'You go too. Be with her.'

'There are lots of things we don't know,' Nora said, 'but one thing we do know is that if I go, you will both most certainly die.' She leaped to a nearby branch. 'I don't want that to happen.'

'Please go,' Alan said.

'It's not your choice,' Nora said.

Spider clambered to his feet. The Clawbaby was laughing now.

Alan moved to another branch, and then walked along it and positioned himself above the wooden walkway so that the Clawbaby would have to pass beneath him. It stopped before it did so and looked up.

'Remember, Alan?' it said.

The Sanctuary had stopped breathing. There were muffled sounds of Pilgrims and the afflicted, but they were distant; Alan pictured an exodus.

The Clawbaby's words were loud and clear. 'Do you remember that day in Modest Mills? Do you remember what you did?'

'I remember,' Alan said.

'Did you think there were no consequences?'

'I know fine well how terrible the consequences were.'

'For Modest Mills, yes, but for those of us inside the Pyramid?'

Alan didn't say anything.

'For those whom you hate, Alan?'

'I'm sorry,' he said. 'I am. I am truly sorry.'

'I was a *baby*, Alan,' the Clawbaby said. 'I was not much younger than you yourself.' It looked as if it was shrugging its shoulders. The black mass of its body was shifting and splitting and a squall of baby wails spilled out of it, then as quickly faded away. 'I am still a baby,' it said, and briefly they saw the shape of an infant revealed within its cloud of what looked like dust or smoke – not rags, as Alan had originally thought, but a shroud of black dust. The baby was in its chest, below the point from which its green eyes glowed. 'My life, as one might understand such a thing, ended on that dreadful day. My life ended and something else began. You are my killer and my midwife, Alan.'

'I didn't mean to.'

'You don't *mean* to do anything. You just move from one incident to the next, playing on.' The Clawbaby gathered its dust once more and closed itself up. 'Until now. Now it ends. And then I can rest.'

'You want me to die,' Alan said, 'and that's fine. I can understand that. Maybe I should. But let me save my son first.'

A stomach-churning cackle rose from the creature on the stairs. 'You want to *atone*?' It shuddered with laughter. 'I think not, friend Alan.' Then it darted forward with unexpected speed and Alan found himself jumping down and landing on its back. He sank into it, finding himself coated with ash and dust, the taste of smoke filling his mouth. With one arm round its neck he pummelled its head, but his fist did nothing; it felt like punching mud.

Then he stabbed it in its crown – not the baby's crown, but whatever housed those green orbs – and the knife went in right up to the hilt, and it howled, and cried and its glow dimmed and it stumbled on the steps. Alan didn't let go, but it spun around and slammed its back, and Alan, into the trunk, and Alan's spine cracked and he screamed and slid from the Clawbaby onto his arse and white light shone inside his skull. He opened his eyes to see the thing drawing back its horrid metal hands of a million blades, readying itself to punch him through the stomach, and behind it was the warm orange blur of the Sanctuary, its spores doing nothing whatsoever to calm down the Clawbaby, and a soul-rending pain tore through him at the thought of dying here, so far from Billy and Marion, so far from home. Though he didn't know where home was, exactly, he knew it wasn't here, deep in the bowels of Gleam; ruined by his own foolishness.

He rolled to one side, and something was holding the Clawbaby back and its blow landed too late. Alan saw that it had been Spider clinging on to the beast's bladed arm, and he saw the Clawbaby turn to face its new opponent and bring its right arm around and plunge its rusty bunched knives right through Spider's middle, lifting Spider from his feet and holding him up in the air as blood ran from him and down into the metal claws, a steady flow, a tide of blood, running into the Clawbaby like – *like a Bleeding*.

Spider's mouth was open wide, but no noise was

coming from it. His eyes were perfect circles. Blood soaked through his red shirt, making it even darker.

Alan knew the Clawbaby was laughing or crying or both at the same time, but he couldn't really hear it; all he was conscious of was Spider's face: his old friend, dying to save his life.

There was a flash of silver at the Clawbaby's neck and Nora was at work, sawing with something serrated. Alan jumped up and grabbed hold of the back of its head, pulling it backwards, opening up the wound that Nora was creating. It couldn't get at either of them, couldn't reach back far enough with its spare arm. It flung Spider away and his body fell and landed amongst the others on the ground below.

Then it stabbed upwards, at where Nora was, but Nora was too quick for it; she leaped directly upwards and the blow pierced only the air beneath her feet. Then she landed in the same place and resumed her work, and with Alan's help, the Clawbaby's head was soon hanging off. Then it was torn free and she held it aloft triumphantly.

The Clawbaby fell to all fours and cried and Alan jumped away from it. It looked defeated, but then its crying turned to laughter.

'You can take my head,' it said, its voice coming from the ashy bundle Nora held, 'but I'll keep on coming.' It crawled around, clearly sightless, laughing. It looked like a gigantic demonic dog, with ropes of dark dust trailing from it instead of long fur. 'You can cut me limb from limb,' it said, 'but you killed me long ago and you cannot kill me again. I'll find you, friend Alan, and I'll keep finding you.'

'We must kill the baby,' Nora said as the two of them hurried down to Spider's body. 'The baby inside it.'

'No,' Alan said, 'I can't. No.'

'Then I will.'

'No.'

'Alan,' Nora said, looking around, 'the Pilgrims are regrouping out there. Spider and I, we could not reach this beast for them. They have not gone, and *we* are their enemy, not that laughing thing. We have destroyed everything they held dear. You must take the Benedictions and go. I will remain, and I will finish the Clawbaby.'

'*No*. No more killing.'

'It is not a real living thing.'

'I said no.'

'I want to persuade you,' Nora said, 'but I see that we do not have time for that. You must understand, though: I'm not requesting your permission. I am informing you of my immediate actions. Now you *go*.'

'I don't need *your* permission to stay. I want to stay and – and – Spider—'

Nora placed one of her many knives at Alan's throat. 'You do need my permission,' she hissed. 'I am more powerful than you. Green damn it, Alan! You are usually so good at running. Now, you'd better run. There will be no mercy here.' She withdrew her blade and pushed him.

'What about Spider?' came a voice, and Eyes emerged from the doorway in the trunk. 'What about Spider, lad, eh?'

The door was no longer there; the drastic movements of the Sanctuary must have destroyed it. Eyes was walking with a stick. Behind him, the liftshaft, or pantry, or whatever it was, was jammed full of broken jars and shattered wood.

'Eyes,' Alan said, 'Eyes, thank fuck! How did you get in there?'

'Churr,' Eyes said. 'Churr got me out of my gill when it all started going wrong. She got me this' – he waved his stick – 'and packed me away in that cupboard. She's a good lass, that one.'

'Eyes,' Alan said again, then he stopped. He thought about how to break the news. 'Spider is dead,' he said. 'The Clawbaby got him.'

Eyes walked over towards where Alan and Nora stood and Alan took his hand and helped him kneel. They knelt together, and Alan guided Eyes' hands to Spider's face. Tears ran from beneath the blindfold.

'A damned shame,' the older man muttered. 'A damned shame.'

'You two need to go,' Nora said. 'Let us meet at Market Top.'

'Market Top it is,' Alan said.

'I'm too slow,' Eyes said. 'I'll make me own way back.'

'The Discard is not kind to the disadvantaged,' Alan

said. 'We all know that. You're coming with me. But don't worry. I've got a plan.'

Alan closed Spider's eyes and kissed him softly on the forehead. Then he stood, smiled wryly at Nora, and led Eyes from that place.

They picked up a pair of grey cloaks on the way and put them on over their clothes, drawing up the hoods and making their way slowly to the Giving Beast's curtain. They found a rip that they could slip through without disturbing it too much – they didn't want to cause any ripples that might draw attention. Once outside of the Sanctuary, they found groups of Pilgrims bustling around still, but most of them were focused on finding and helping the afflicted. There were gangs of guardians assembling, ready to head back into the Sanctuary, pre-sumably to attack both him and the Clawbaby. There were many dead.

Alan resisted the urge to move quickly; anybody who was looking for him specifically would be watching for somebody who appeared to be running.

The damaged and dying were being treated in the kit-chen. The wounded were laid out on the long tables and Pilgrims were busy cutting and cleaning and stitching. Still holding Eyes by the arm, Alan slipped all the way through the room, winding his way between tables, mak-ing their way right through to the back and behind the row of huge heated food bowls, now being used to boil water. Alan took the opportunity to fill up their wine-skins, like other Pilgrims, then they carried on through an archway into the storerooms.

This was where Daunt's caravans deposited supplies. Shelves groaned beneath the weight of potatoes and turnips and carrots. Joints of smoked and cured pig and cat and dog overflowed from woven baskets. There were jars of salted crickets and bird tongues. Spicy red sausages hung from hooks in the wall, along with ropes of garlic and bunches of dried herbs. It all smelled divine, but they kept going. The storerooms extended quite a way back and Alan started to think that this had been a bad idea, or that he'd led them the wrong way, but then he spotted a black archway with a dumbwaiter system inside it. He looked up the shaft. There was light at the top –not bright light, not the kind of natural daylight that he was really craving, but swamplight. It was a way to the outside.

'Get in here,' he said, guiding Eyes through. 'We're going up.'

He found the rope and started pulling. The platform was sturdy; it had to be, to transport the volume it did, but it was heavy, too, and progress was slow.

At the top, a small archway opened out onto a large courtyard. He took a deep breath, and Eyes did the same. The air smelled foul, but it was a change from the mushroomy scent inside. A wispy-bearded man with a topknot and a mushroom symbol on his forehead stepped forward from the wall next to the door, where he'd been leaning beneath a lit paraffin torch.

'Business?' he said.

'Do you know what's been going on in there?' Alan asked.

'No.' He was chewing on some kind of leaf.

Alan grabbed him and smacked his head into the wall before he'd a chance to react. He toppled sideways, out cold.

'Where are we, lad?' Eyes asked.

'We're at the caravan unloading station,' Alan said. 'This is where Daunt's caravans drop off their loads, and where the caravans . . . feed.'

'Feed? What are they?'

'Snails,' Alan said. 'Great big snails.'

He surveyed the animals before him. They were nearly as big as the one that had appeared on the rooftop so many nights ago. Their shells were dull and scratched, but white mushrooms had been painted on them. They had lots of satchels and boxes screwed into them, and saddles, too, with straps and harnesses to keep the rider secured when the snails were on the vertical.

'We're going to ride snails back up?'

'In a manner of speaking,' Alan replied.

Eyes snorted. 'They're not the quickest of rides, lad, and we'll be sitting ducks up on them shells.'

'They're slow, but steady, and the main thing is that

they can go straight up. there'll be no messing about with stairs – or even having to *find* the stairs. And we won't be up on the shells. We'll be inside them. Nobody's going to see us – or look for us – there.'

'I— What?'

'It's not going to be a very pleasant journey,' he admitted.

'You're not fucking kidding.' Eyes pinched the bridge of his nose and then let out a huge sob. 'Green damn it,' he said, 'Green *damn* it all. Poor Spider.'

Alan didn't know what to say. He pulled Eyes into a hug. After a moment he said, 'We have to go. The Pilgrims will want retribution.'

Eyes wiped his cheeks. 'Are you crying, lad? I can't hear any tears.'

'No, not yet. But I will, Eyes. You can trust me on that.' He walked over to a snail and patted its shell. Its horns retracted. 'We'll have to grab the reins and pull them up inside with us.'

'I'm not listening any more.'

'We crawl inside the shell from behind. That way they can't bite us.'

'There's room in there, is there?'

'I don't know for sure. I imagine it'll be a bit of a squash.'

'What are we going to eat?'

'What do you think?'

'I think if we're going to spend the next few days

together inside a snail shell I'm going to go and have a quick dump. And I suggest you do, too.'

'Very well,' Alan said. 'You go over there, and I'll go this way. But look—' Alan pulled a much smaller snail from the wall in order to examine it. 'You *can* lift the back up,' he said, 'but not the front. It looks like – oh.' The shell broke beneath his thumb with a crunch. 'Whoops.' He picked pieces of shell away from the snail's flesh. 'It looks like under the shell is where they keep their organs and stuff.' He flicked the remains away and wiped his fingers on his robe. 'But you never know. There might be a nice comfy air pocket or something in the big ones.'

But as they found after emptying their bowels, there wasn't.

The next three days were, Alan was certain, the most physically uncomfortable and disgusting of their lives. They'd chosen the largest snail and found themselves stuck between the ridged shell that was pressing into their backs and a soft, wet, slimy bag of guts pressing into their faces. It smelled bad, and if they weren't careful, it leaked into their mouths. They were in pitch black darkness. They had to urinate where they lay, but thankfully fear helped both to suppress bowel movements. There was no space to move their heads, no space to recoil, even. It took them hours to work their hands – and wineskins – up into a position they could sip from, and once they'd done so, they kept them there, even though the resulting cramps were like nothing Alan had ever known. He knew Eyes had experienced far worse, but perhaps that meant that all of this was even more painful for him. Occasionally one or other couldn't hold in a whimper.

Their presence on the snail's back had been enough to galvanise it into movement. Alan's plan had been to use the reins to guide the snail onto the vertical axis and then keep it there – he thought they'd be able to tell when they were heading directly upwards, and he was right. But that was when their ride got really bad, when gravity pulled the snail's insides down on top of them and they suffered a curious and thoroughly unpleasant combination of intense claustrophobia and dizzying exposure, because there wasn't much between them and the ground below, which was getting further and further away.

Alan occupied himself by trying to work out where on the topside they'd emerge – ideally he wanted to be able to scoot around the Oversight, not traverse the top of it, which would be an unnecessarily long journey, given their current mode of transport.

But before that they'd have to pass through Glasstown, and that would be very difficult to navigate. He'd made small holes in the shell before they'd forced themselves inside, not just for ventilation, but so he could see a bit. Every now and again he tilted his head backwards and stuck it through the hole to get an idea of where they were and which way they were going. The hole was masked by a flap of leather that had rested between the shell and the saddle, but he'd removed the saddle so that it didn't block his view, just leaving the leather pad buckled on. He'd also strapped Snapper on to the side, amongst the baskets and boxes .

They got hungry, but never hungry enough to start taking bites out of the raw snail offal that was all that was available. They eked out their water and wine. They didn't speak. Sometimes they heard noises from outside the shell: running water, the cries of strange birds, animal sounds – grunting, snuffling, yelping – and the distant howling of scavengers. Once, they heard music that sounded like it was coming from an amplifier, but there was no other indication of human presence and Alan didn't dare stick his head out to look. The greatest threat to them both was somebody attacking the snail for food, but this was one of Daunt's, covered with her symbols, and he didn't think anybody would dare.

Generally, nobody in the Discard was stupid enough to anger the Mushroom Queen.

Alan closed his eyes. But he couldn't sleep.

28

The Exchange

The light coming from outside was orange and softened by a cloud of dust hanging in the sky. The sun was at the skyline, burning crimson. Satis and Corval were just two hazy glowing discs. The vast Discard architecture was red-lit and looked like the bloody ruins of some gigantic broken creature.

'You bring Billy out,' Alan said, 'and my man over there will come up with the goods.'

Tromo's head turned to face the shadows to which Alan had gestured. This was in the direction of Archway Gardens: the huge, rusting metal frames webbed with vines and beans, with orchards planted along the top. Archway Gardens had once kept Modest Mills fed and watered; it had been farmed by Modest Millers and protected by the community. Since the massacre, control of the strings, nets and topside beds had passed to a gang who were good at growing, but kept putting the prices up. No wonder, if they were Daunt's people. Maggie sometimes spoke about moving in to take control, but she hadn't yet, as far as Alan knew. It was a good job, too: a running war between the Safe Houses and the Mushroom Queen would not be good for anybody.

He'd have to get a message to Maggie.

So the road between what had once been Modest Mills and Archway Gardens was now a grey and desolate affair: a long, flat avenue descending down the blasted hillside into shadow, smothered in sticky ash. Grand white columns lined either side, for this had not just been the road to Modest Mills, but the road to the Pyramid's now defunct main entrance, where Alan and Tromo now stood. The columns rose from the darkness into the red light. They were all broken and jagged at the top.

Tromo looked down the road into the shadows between the columns, where Eyes, standing with a stick, his blindfold on, was just visible.

Then he looked back at Alan. 'Why haven't you come alone?'

'Because then you could just kill me.'

'We could just kill both of you anyway.'

'There are more than two of us. Anything goes wrong, our companions will take the mushrooms from my blind friend over there and disappear back into the Discard.'

'The goods, then,' Tromo said, flatly. 'You mean the mushrooms, I presume, and not an arrow in the neck.'

'Look at him,' Alan said. 'He's wearing a blindfold. That's why he's the one carrying. He's not a threat. He's not going to shoot you.'

Tromo inhaled, held his breath, sighed.

'Take off that mask,' Alan said. 'Let me see your face. If this is going to be the beginning of a new professional relationship, we may as well try to trust each other.' He lit a cigarette. 'No, not trust each other – that's too much. But you wearing a mask and me not, well, it's not fair.'

Tromo undid the strap beneath his chin and removed his helmet. The metal of his armour was tarnished and the fine chain of the mask was missing a few links. His expression was as blank as the mask had been.

'So,' Alan said, breathing out smoke, 'come on then. Where is he? Where's Billy? Show me that he's safe.' He was tapping his foot and kept running a hand along Snapper's strap, as if to reassure himself that the guitar was still there. Above the Discard flocks of birds turned and wheeled in the bloody sky. The Pyramid loomed above, so close and big that Alan could not see all of it. It was the night made solid. 'Show me that he's safe and you can have your damn mushrooms and I can get the fuck out of here.'

'You're not thinking of abducting him, are you?' Tromo asked with a smirk. 'Because, obviously, if you took him with you, you wouldn't have to worry about keeping the supply going. It must be quite an appealing course of action.'

'Well, *obviously*,' Alan said with a roll of his eyes, 'but I know you're not stupid, and I know you would have prepared for that eventuality, and besides,' – he smiled – 'now we've got a supply route set up, you are not our only customer. So this operation could become quite a nice little earner for me out here in the Discard, if I keep it going. Delivering to you each month will not be a problem.'

The lies came easily now. Ever since Alan had slipped greasily from inside that snail's shell, not far from Market Top, he'd felt like a new man, reborn from a snail mother. The touch of sunlight and moonlight worked like medicine: he'd slimed from out of hell into a fresh, light heaven. He just wished that Spider had had the opportunity to return to the sight of the sky as well.

Tromo nodded. 'What if I up my demands again?'

Alan took the cigarette from his mouth and jabbed it straight into Tromo's throat. There was a sizzle, a scream, a smell of burning, and then Alan had his hands around Tromo's neck, his thumbs pushing into the hollow beneath his Adam's apple. He could feel his lips drawn right back around his bared teeth. He could feel his heart shaking his ribs. 'Listen to me, you fucking creep,' he spat. 'I want to kill you. My friends advised me to kill you. I could kill you, right here, right now. I'm desperate enough, and angry enough. Yeah, there'd be consequences, but even if I didn't survive, you'd take no pleasure in it, because you'd be dead, and so you wouldn't know. Just don't fucking push me.'

A rain of crossbow bolts thudded into the ground all around them, raising clouds of ash. Alan barely even noticed, so intent was he on Tromo's hated face. 'You didn't come alone, then?' he sneered.

Tromo didn't answer the question. 'Even if you did survive, Billy wouldn't and neither would Marion.' Tromo's voice was cracked and wavering, and tears of pain rolled down his cheeks.

Alan maintained the pressure on Tromo's neck for a moment, and then threw him to the ground and spun away, cursing. 'Fuck this,' he said. 'Fuck you. Bring my boy out here right now.'

Tromo crawled back towards the Pyramid, his red cloak twisted and filthy, and then got to his feet. 'Hold fire,' he shouted, holding one arm up. 'Hold fire.' He stumbled into the Pyramid's cavernous antechamber.

'Nice big porch to keep yer muddy boots in! Or is it just for hostages? Come on, Tromo! Let's get this over with!'

No response. Alan's stomach spasmed and a cold sweat sprang from his skin. Was he gone? He couldn't have gone. He couldn't have gone. Gone to kill his son, his wife . . .

Tromo returned, holding a chain in one hand. On the other end of it was a small figure in a brown cloak, hood up, wrists cuffed.

'Here,' Tromo said. He pulled down the hood. 'Your son.'

'Billy,' Alan said, his voice catching. His son stood

there in the dusk, cheeks wet and red. His lower lip was out and trembling. 'Billy,' he said again. He ran towards his son and threw his arms around him. He could feel Billy trying to pull away but he didn't let go. 'Billy, I'm so sorry,' he said. 'I'm sorry. Are you okay? I'm sorry. Is your mum okay? Have they hurt you?' He was crying too. His son's hair still smelled the same as it used to: fresh bread, warm milk. He remembered his own childhood. He remembered feeling safe. 'I want you to feel safe,' he said, into Billy's ear.

Billy was sobbing, struggling, trying to get away. 'What have you *done*, Dad?' he said. 'What did you do?'

'They're using us,' Alan said. 'It's what they've always done, it's what they'll always do.'

'No!' Billy said, 'It's *you*! *You* did this!'

Alan gazed into his son's furious little face. There was no doubt in him. His eyes were hard: those eyes that once had lit up at his presence, that had been full of such love.

Alan couldn't think of anything to say. He was falling through the bottom of the world.

He wanted a drink. He imagined whisky shimmering in the bottom of a glazed clay cup. He closed his eyes. He was shaking.

'Very well then,' Tromo said suddenly. Alan was almost grateful. 'Enough.' He yanked on the chain and Billy fell onto his knees, and then his front. Tromo pulled him through the ash, away from Alan. 'You've seen him. You know he's alive. I've delivered. Now it's your turn.'

'Can I spend some time with him?

Tromo considered for a moment. 'After the exchange.'

Alan needed to get Billy and Marion out of the Pyramid. Tromo had been right about that. But this wasn't the time or place. If they killed Tromo now, they could take Billy, but not Marion . . . But no, they couldn't, because Tromo had backup with him and they would all be dead within seconds. And Billy maybe wouldn't even want to come. Given freedom from his captor, he might just run back into the Pyramid. *His little face* . . . Alan felt like he had a knife in his gut. They'd give Tromo the mushrooms. He didn't want to provoke the bastard any further. They'd give him the mushrooms and buy themselves another month. With another month they could plan a rescue mission. They wouldn't have to trek all the way to Dok this time; this time they could devote themselves to preparing properly for the exchange. They wouldn't be all beat-up and pathetic. Well, not beat-up, anyway. Although . . . although there was still the Daunt problem to solve.

Maybe they would be just as beat-up next month after all. And what would happen to Billy if Alan got killed?

Alan turned to face Archway Gardens, standing solid and black against the darkening red night. 'Come on, Eyes,' he shouted. 'Billy's here. He's alive. It's time.'

A faint reply: 'Aye, right.'

Alan's mind was racing, but it was going nowhere. It couldn't settle on anything, spinning like the wheels on the motorcycle after Spider had tipped it over. Get Billy and Marion out. Don't let Tromo take Billy back inside. Give Tromo the mushrooms. Don't give Tromo the mushrooms. Demand Billy in exchange. But then what about Marion? And Tromo wouldn't agree anyway. Don't get shot. Don't get everybody killed. Don't fuck up again. Billy's eyes. Billy's angry, hate-filled eyes. A motorcycle on its side, wheels spinning. Green darkness. Red light. The scent of whisky. The burn of it.

Tromo watched approvingly as Eyes made his slow way through the wastes of Modest Mills, sweeping in front of him with his stick, changing direction when he encountered the low walls of a ruin. His balance had improved a lot since the Pilgrims had healed him at Dok, but his movements were still uncertain.

They'd give Tromo the Benedictions, and they'd keep giving Tromo the Benedictions, and Alan would see Billy as often as possible, and he'd try to make things better between them. He couldn't take Billy from the Pyramid against his will. He couldn't separate the boy from his mother. Not when Billy loved his mother and hated his father. Tromo wouldn't hurt Billy, not if he wanted his mushrooms – and he *did* want them. In fact, when Alan thought about it, he wasn't the only desperate one here. An Arbitrator wouldn't go to such lengths – risking expulsion from the Pyramid – just for the kind of spirit journey the mushrooms enabled. No, Tromo was far more likely to hurt Billy and Marion if Alan tried anything stupid, or tried to trick him. Considering how co-operative the swine was being even after Alan had attacked him, he obviously wasn't confident that he was holding all the cards. Even if Alan wasn't holding many cards himself.

Alan tried to catch Billy's eyes, but the boy had raised his hood again. Tromo had positioned himself between Alan and Billy and had the chain wrapped around his fist. The Arbitrator's throat was blotched red from Alan's throttling and the cigarette burn.

'Where are you?' Eyes said. 'Speak up.'

'Here,' Alan said. 'We're here.'

Eyes shuffled forwards, his stick arcing across in front of him. A large leather pouch hung from his belt. He had one hand on it. 'Pyramid boy,' Eyes said, unable to keep the contempt from his voice. 'Let me give this to you. Then we're done, yes?'

'For now,' Tromo said. 'For this month.'

Eyes unhooked the pouch from his belt and held it out. 'Take it from me,' he said, 'damn you. Take it – I can't see where your hands are at. Just take it.' He leaned on the stick. His hands were trembling badly.

Tromo reached out and took the pouch. 'I'm sure you understand if I'm a little cautious,' he said. Then he raised his voice. 'Arbitrators! Aim!'

Eyes spat into the ash.

'Should anything untoward happen as a consequence of me opening this bag, both of you and the boy here will immediately receive several bolts through the head. Do you understand?'

Alan looked at Billy, who was kneeling, utterly motionless, his face hidden by the deep hood. Then he looked at Eyes. 'It's clean,' he said. 'It's safe. We're not that foolish.'

Alan had checked the bag himself, and double-checked it, in case any venomous insects had crept in, or any toxic worms had emerged from the fungus. He didn't want to get the blame for any of the natural dangers that the Discard could manifest.

Tromo looked at Alan.

'It's fucking fine, all right?'

'Very well,' Tromo said. He tugged open the pouch and reached inside. He withdrew a small parcel wrapped in waxed parchment and bound with string. He cut the string with his dagger and unfolded the paper. His face split into a broad smile as he surveyed its contents.

The mushrooms had retained their green colour even though they were now completely dry. They looked like peas with long white shoots growing out of them. They were densely packed, and they fragmented as the little parcel loosened. 'Yes,' Tromo said, 'oh, yes. Very good. Very good indeed. You did well, Alan. I've heard rumours, though . . . Is it true that the Mushroom Queen herself is on your tail?'

Alan said nothing.

'You're in *trouble* – I hope my supply is secure? Regardless of whether you yourself survive or not?'

Alan couldn't speak. Tromo was right: it was something to consider. He'd have to arrange something.

Tromo refastened the package and felt around inside the bag.

'Just one of these parcels?'

'Yes. That's the same as the vial I originally promised you.' They'd apportioned all of the Benedictions that they'd collected; this wasn't all of them, not by a long shot.

'Very good,' Tromo said again. 'Very good.'

Suddenly Alan could breathe more easily. Some of the dreadful tension was lifting. He knelt down next to Billy and gave him a hug. Eyes made his way over to them and put a hand on Billy's head. 'Malcolm's son's son,' he said. 'It's an honour to meet you, lad. I know your father's a little touched but he's a good man. Don't hold his principles against him. It's good to have principles, even if living by them does make things tough from time to time.'

Billy drew back his hood and looked at his father. His big eyes were red-rimmed and wet. He looked up at Eyes.

Eyes shook his arm and a knife fell from his sleeve and into his hand. With unerring precision, Eyes pressed the knife through the sole of one of Billy's sandals into his foot. Billy jolted with pain and screamed.

The knife was gone so quickly Alan wasn't even sure he'd seen it, but Billy was crying again. Alan held the boy against his chest. 'What did you do, Eyes?' he yelled. 'What did you do, you big fucking bastard?'

'What's going on?' Tromo said, distracted from his haul. 'What's happened?'

'By Green,' Eyes said, 'Alan, I'm so sorry – I'm sorry, Billy. These damned eyes . . . I just got the lad here with me walking stick. Where did I get him? It wasn't deep, was it? Is he okay?'

Alan stared at Eyes. He didn't understand the lie.

'I want to go,' Billy said, through his tears. 'I want to go home.'

Tromo helped the boy up. 'Very well.' He turned to Alan. 'See you next month, Wild Alan.'

'Wait,' Alan said.

'What?'

Alan didn't know what to say. Would telling the truth endanger Billy? He didn't even know what Eyes had done.

'What?' Tromo asked again.

Alan was frozen.

'We're done,' Tromo said. 'Come on, boy.' He pulled on the chain and Billy hobbled after the Arbitrator, back to the Pyramid entranceway. Alan heard movement from the slope above the structure as Tromo's backup lowered their weapons.

'Wait!' Alan shouted, but neither Tromo nor Billy responded. 'Wait!'

29

WHO DO YOU HATE?

Alan watched his son and the Arbitrator vanish into the Pyramid. His head was full of roaring. He blinked and blinked again. He slowly brought himself to face Eyes.

'What did you do?' he whispered.

Eyes let his stick fall to the floor and then untied his blindfold. His eyes were still crusty and sore-looking, but the black veins that had run through the whites had retreated and his vision looked clear.

'You can see,' Alan whispered.

'Aye. Them Pilgrims really sorted me out good and proper. I couldn't see straight away, like, but it came back to me after a few days.'

'So what did you *do*?'

'I stuck to my principles, lad. I'm sorry, I truly am, but after everything – after everything they've done to us, after all those days being carried around by you lot, feeling the rot spread from the wounds they gave me, learning what they're doing down in Dok, releasing all that crap out into the Discard – I couldn't let this opportunity pass.' Eyes grimaced. 'Those mushrooms weren't all we brought back from Dok. I picked up something else.' He shook the concealed dagger back down into his hand and held it up. 'See this? The black ichor on the blade is Idle Hands.' He nodded towards the Pyramid. 'It'll devour those fuckers like you get through Dog Moon.'

Alan said nothing.

'You're not the only one with grievances, lad. Not the only one on a quest. This isn't all about you and your family. There's history to consider here. There's justice. Righteousness.'

'Billy? Marion?'

'And you don't act like you care all that much about them anyway, with your drinking and your bed-hopping. You didn't appreciate them when you were in there, did you? You didn't ever try to make it work! Besides – how many Billys and Marions did they kill in Modest Mills? How many are they still killing and twisting out here, with their . . . corruption?'

'So it's worth it, then? It's worth the lives of my son and my wife to get your revenge?' Alan spat. 'To get your own back?'

Eyes pursed his lips. 'These scumbags,' he growled, advancing with the diseased knife in his hand, 'they dragged me through the burning streets and into their halls, through their corridors, through their tunnels of black stone, and they tied me to a wet wall, and they kicked me, they cut me, they squeezed me, they broke me. They put creatures in my ears. They stamped on my dick. They carved their names into my chest. They fed me poisons that set fire to my insides and gave me night-mares the like of which I cannot describe. They tore off my eyelids and pissed in my face. You know, my torturing – that was a – a – what do they call it? A Sta-tion? It's a job they have people doing *all the time*. What other poor bastards have they got in there, eh? They had torturers on fucking shifts, coming in and speaking all this nonsense, like prayer, it was, and they'd be dressed in a particular way, and they'd be consulting all these huge old books, and then they'd lay into me.'

'It doesn't mean—'

'And we know why, don't we?' Eyes yelled, pushing his face right into Alan's. 'You and me, we know why! Or have you forgotten, eh? Is it just one of those things you don't think about?'

'I haven't forgotten, Eyes. Not ever.'

'It was right here, wasn't it? We were right here when they took me! And they were going to kill you, but I stopped them. I saved your life back then and they took me, but it was you they should have taken, wasn't it? *It was you.*'

The morning of the Modest Mills massacre, Malcolm had sent Alan down to the market with some bugs to buy lemons to go with the chicken he was preparing for

Violet's birthday meal. Violet – Alan's mother – was working in one of the mills in the middle of the village and so he took a roundabout route to the fruit stalls, circling the village, rather than going through it. It was a sunny day and there was a pleasant breeze. Back then Modest Mills had been surrounded by trees and the slope down into the rest of the Discard had been heavily wooded. In the woods lurked weird statues and old ruins, if you went looking – but you weren't supposed to go looking. Alan's parents always told him not to go looking, but he still went.

Further out, the slope dropped away steeply and the trees gave way to densely packed buildings with tumble-down walls, rickety bridges and scary black windows. Very few of the Modest Mills children ever went beyond that point; it was a lonely wilderness, in which odd-looking people could sometimes be seen, staring back at you. And they all knew the stories about the children who went out to explore the Discard and never came home.

So Alan ran through the trees, walking along fallen trunks, swinging from low branches and clambering across mossy rocks. The buildings of Modest Mills were visible on his right, and he could hear the sounds of the market – the loud voices of traders, the shouting of other children, the lowing and clucking of livestock and poultry, the strains of the bard. He kept checking that the bugs were still in his pocket.

His mother loved lemon chicken, but lemons were

expensive. The meal would be a surprise treat, and he was excited to be a part of something that would make her happy. She had not been very happy recently. Neither had his father. When Alan asked them what the matter was, they had alluded, vaguely, to money trouble. 'Damn Pyramidders,' his dad had muttered, 'putting the squeeze on.'

Alan hadn't really understood.

He was about to cut back into the village streets when he heard a voice.

'Child.'

He froze. He became aware of a figure standing amongst the trees of the slope. She hadn't been immediately obvious because of her pale outfit and the way it blended with the sun-dappled woodland. She was tall, wearing what looked like a white sheet that covered her whole body – all but her little round head, from which tufty white hair grew. Her skin was badly sunburned, and she had big blue rings around her eyes. She wore a large cage on her back, which was full of small boxes and bundles and bags. It looked too heavy for her. Small white birds fluttered around her.

'Child,' the figure said again, 'I have come from Glasstown. Do you know of it?'

Alan shook his head, mute.

'It is a place far from here, deep in the Discard. I have been sent as an emissary to speak with the one they call McAlkie. I have come to pledge the support of

Glasstown to McAlkie and the Anti-Pyramid League. We believe that all souls should have the right to move freely throughout Gleam, in order to find the rooms that were theirs in life. Those who live in the Pyramid prevent this. Can you show me the way?'

'To McAlkie?' That the woman wanted to see McAlkie was about the only thing that Alan had fully understood.

'Yes. To this McAlkie.'

Alan nodded. 'Follow me,' he said. Then, after a moment of picking their way slowly through the woods, he said, 'Would you like me to carry some of your things?'

The woman smiled gratefully. 'Oh yes,' she said. 'That would be most welcome. Thank you.' She undid the buckles and belts that secured the cage to her back and let it slide to the ground.

Alan undid the latch on the cage door and took what he could. He shoved small parcels and pouches into his pockets and placed the straps of larger bags over his shoulders, and then gathered up boxes in his arms. After setting off, he realised that he had perhaps been over-ambitious, but he didn't want to admit as much so he struggled onwards. He kept dropping bits and pieces and stopping to pick them up, and every time he tried to pick them up he'd drop other items.

The woman laughed at him, but not unkindly. 'I'm sorry to have so much with me,' she said. 'My people accumulate strange things – trinkets, ornaments, relics. We don't mean to, but we do. They arrive in our homes, in our buildings. I gathered so much for my journey so that I would have material with which to barter and make exchanges. However' – and a frown passed over her face – 'the Discard was quieter than I expected. It has been many, many years since I left Glasstown, and I have never travelled so far. Perhaps the Discard has always been this quiet. As a consequence of the quietness, though, I have not had much opportunity to shed weight. Nor have I adequately sustained myself, or found good shelter from the heat and the sun.'

'You stayed high,' Alan said. He didn't know a lot about the Discard, but he knew that it was a good idea to stay high, if possible.

'Yes. I kept to the rooftops and the high places, and so I burned.' The woman smiled again.

Eventually the two of them reached one end of the street where McAlkie preached, and Alan pointed the visitor in the right direction. 'I can't go down there myself,' he said seriously, 'because Mum might see me, and then she will know that I'm buying lemons for her birthday.'

The woman laughed again, and crouched down to give Alan a brief hug. 'Thank you, little man,' she said. 'Your mother will be delighted, I am sure.' She struggled to get back up again.

Alan waved goodbye to the Glasstowner, and then turned his mind to the business of buying lemons.

On his way back, the lemons safe in his pockets, he saw something gleaming in the moss of the woodland floor.

He rushed over and found a greasy cloth that was partially unwrapped, and recognised it as something he'd carried for the Glasstowner – he must have dropped it. Inside the cloth was a piece of metal shaped like a dented egg. It was dark and heavy. It looked as if it was made to split into two parts. He would have to give it back to the lady. She was nice, and she wanted to help McAlkie, so he would help her. But he could have a look inside it first. He could have a quick look and then just put it back together. He wanted to see what kind of treasure could be found out there in the Discard. He peered around himself, to make sure there was nobody around, but he was alone.

He hit the egg against a rock on the ground, but that did nothing, then he got his fingernails into the crack that ran around its middle and tried to prise the two halves apart, but that didn't work either. With every failed attempt, he grew more desperate. He couldn't give it back without seeing what was inside, and yet he had to get home with the lemons so that his father had time to cook his mother's tea. He'd already been out too long.

Finally he gripped one end of the egg in each hand and tried to unscrew it. It gave a little and his heart lifted. He twisted some more, and the egg slowly began to undo. He spun the top half round and round and it rose from its base until it became loose and he could take it out.

Inside the egg was a small glass cylinder, secured by an intricate metal framework that flexed and bent and shifted so the cylinder was safely suspended away from the sides. Despite the battered exterior, the workings all looked clean and well-oiled, yet when Alan touched them, no grease or anything stuck to his fingers.

Inside the cylinder was a flickering white light. Alan withdrew it from its place. It was rounded at both ends and completely sealed, with the light trapped inside. It wasn't a bulb; Alan had seen those before. There was nothing else inside the cylinder but the light. It was weird, and it was beautiful. It lit up Alan's face, and the trees around him. It was *magic*. Alan had never believed in magic before, although some of the wilder preachers had spoken of it, how it was in the stone, how it preserved Gleam, kept it standing, but everybody said they were crazy and that there was no magic. But this *was* magic. Alan had it – he'd found it. All thoughts of Glasstowners and lemons and parents receded. There was a tiny metal plaque on the side of the cylinder, with words engraved on it. Alan brought it close to his eyes so that he could read it. The words read:

WHO DO YOU HATE?

Alan laughed slightly to himself. What a strange thing. 'I hate the damn Pyramidders,' he whispered, 'putting the squeeze on.'

The light brightened and the glass suddenly burned his fingers. He let go, but it stayed where it was, in the air, then it rose and floated up, and up, and up, and then it tore through the air in the direction of Modest Mills and . . . the Pyramid.

'No,' Alan said, suddenly realising what might happen, 'no, no, *no*—'

But he couldn't do anything about it. He heard the explosion and the screaming before he'd even taken a step, and long before he got home, he could see the plume of smoke billowing from a great jagged hole in the black stone of the Black Pyramid.

The reprisals came later that day, and they came hard. They came wearing battered metal and wielding crossbows and curved swords. They came with fire and with beads beneath their skin. They came, and they killed Alan's mother, and his father. They took McAlkie alive, because they thought he was responsible, and because they wanted McAlkie alive, McAlkie could negotiate for Alan's life. So they let Alan live, too.

'I think about it,' Alan said. 'I think about it all the time. I try not to, but I do. I told you about it – I told you when I got out of the Pyramid. I found you and I confessed, and—'

'Aye, right. But now you can't barely think a thought. You're always too pissed or high or . . . busy, with some easy lay. You don't think about anything, and you sure as shite weren't thinking about how to solve the Pyramid problem.'

'No,' Alan said, quietly, 'I was too worried about my family.'

The sun was down now, and the stars were out. The moons glowed, their colours not reaching the world on which Alan and Eyes stood. Theirs was a black and confused architecture, a riot of twisted fingers reaching up into the cool, clean sky, grasping for space and for blessing. For forgiveness, Alan thought. The Pyramid was a vast blot, the shadow of which they could not escape, and their boots were swollen into mutant hoofs with the sticky dust of their old home town. Out there in the Discard, fires were being lit. The sound of distant motorcycle engines and occasional drunken cackling drifted over the ruins – ruins, that was what they were – and sometimes the harsh shriek of a raven could be heard. Alan thought for a moment that he glimpsed a couple of tiny green pinpricks of light out there, high up on some tower, but then they were gone.

He didn't much care about the Clawbaby right now. It had come slowly, but the rage had come. He was thinking about Billy – not as the six-year-old child he had just seen, or the two-year-old he'd left behind when he left the Pyramid, but as the whole human being: Billy at every age, all at once, all of the things he had been, all of the different moods, all of the different haircuts, crying and laughing at the same time, two years old and six years old at the same time, and all ages in between, and all ages before, and all the ages that he would yet live to be. *Should* yet live to be: Billy as a teenager, as a young man, as an old man, all of the different people that he could yet become – *should* yet become. Would yet become. *Would*. Alan could not tally the love he felt; he could not total it. It was a bottle that once uncorked would overflow and never stop, and he could not cork it again, and it would fill him up, it would rise up and flood his lungs, and it would drown him.

Alan stepped forward and fastened his hands around his old friend's neck. It was how he'd attacked Tromo, but this time his anger was greater and his body and head were full of red mist and his vision had blackened and narrowed and his opponent was more feeble. Eyes had dropped his knife – Alan's thumbs had straight away pierced the papery skin of his throat and he'd spasmed and dropped his knife – and now he was trying to pull Alan's wrists apart. He fell to his knees, and Alan knelt too, and increased the pressure. His strength was infinite: he could just direct energy to his hands and his grip would tighten. It was a simple, effortless thing to do, and there was no end to it.

Eyes choked and struggled, and then he stopped, and then he died.

30

Resolution

The night blurred quickly. Alan hurried back into the Discard, smoking, the smoke flowing from his nose and mouth and drying his eyes. He stopped at a bucket fire and drank moonshine with some transients, which they let him share for a song. Then, his nausea and shakes quietened for a time, he rushed on to Market Top, where he played some more and drank some more, all the time thinking. People were burning bunches of dried lavender in the tavern fires at Market Top, scenting the night air. Alan paced the square, thinking, thinking, thinking. He could hear laughter and talking and other singers singing, but he did not want to spend time with other people. He felt nothing but an incredible rage, which, despite being also love, somehow, meant that he was not good company, and he knew it. He paced the small network of narrow streets and thought and smoked a roll-up, and he looked up at the sky and listened to the noise of people and the backdrop of the Discard, the whispering, the creaking, the distant howls, the venting of steam, the occasional metal-on-metal shriek that signalled some forgotten machine springing back into life, if only briefly, as was usually the case.

He finished his roll-up and flicked the stub to the ground.

He thought about Spider and Nora and Eyes, and even through his terrible anger he felt a sickening guilt. Eyes had been right, ultimately: the Pyramid's time had come. But he had to get Billy and Marion out first, and for that, he had to find Nora. Then no more acquiescing, no more negotiating, no more wasting time trying to do it right. They would break into the Pyramid and save his family – not through the main entrance: that way, they wouldn't stand a chance. They would go in through the Sump.

Alan looked at the Pyramid. His eyes were drawn to the framework of brass and glass and strange machines that rotated slowly around its peak, reading the skies and harvesting light. They gleamed red and pink by the light of the moons.

Alan stared a moment longer, then stumbled through the glowing doorway of a tavern, trying to blink his eyes clear.

Acknowledgements

Thanks to Beth and to Jake, for – amongst too many other things to mention – love, motivation, kindness and inspiration. Thanks also to the members of the Northern Lines writing group: Jenn Ashworth, Emma Jane Unsworth, Richard V Hirst, Claire Dean, Nicola Mostyn and Michelle C Green for their insight, support and company. Thanks to my parents, and all of my ever-growing family. Thank you Nicholas Royle, as ever, for your life-changing mentorship. Huge thanks to the enthusiastic and wise Euan Thorneycroft at A.M. Heath and to everybody at the great Jo Fletcher Books – especially, of course, Jo herself, Nicola Budd, and Andy Turner, for all their advice, hard work and patience. And thank you to Mervyn Peake, Grimes, Lewis Carroll, Hayao Miyazaki, Robin Hobb, Jim Henson and Timber Timbre, for the things you've made.

Turn over for your bonus content!

Reading Group Notes

What do you feel is the central theme of this book?

How did you feel Alan changed over the course of the novel?

A lot of the main characters are inherently selfish creatures. Do you think a sympathetic protagonist is a prerequisite for a successful novel?

How does Tom Fletcher explore group dynamics and relationships?

Pyramid, or Discard?

During the course of the novel it becomes clear that this is not a straightforward fantasy world. Do you think the author is successful in blending genres?

An Interview with
Tom Fletcher

At the beginning of the novel Alan walks away from his family without much argument. However, almost everything he does outside of the Pyramid – including going on the quest – is for his son, Billy. Was it important to you that this contrast was established?

At the beginning, he walks away for his family's sake. He doesn't want to, but he recognises that his presence there, with them, has put them in danger. This is one of the key narrative conflicts of the novel. Alan knows that the system in which his family lives and participates is corrupt, and he fears that ultimately it will devour them – yet to act on that knowledge and fear alienates him from them. He chooses to act on it anyway, taking the risk that it will all pay off in the end – for those he loves, at least – but the consequences of that decision force a change of heart. He cannot reconcile his politics with putting his family at risk. It was very important to me that this conflict was established at the beginning of the novel.

The relationship between Alan and Eyes is the longest running relationship in the novel, and this gives us the sense that Eyes is an important part of Alan's past. Do you feel that his death in some way marks the moment Alan lets go of his past?

Eyes is a lot of things to Alan; friend of the family, then saviour, then father figure, friend, mentor, bandmate . . . but their relationship is increasingly uneasy. Eyes has a history with the Pyramid that's radicalised him, to an extent, and he wants Alan and their companions to cleave to the one goal of undermining the Pyramid; that, as discussed above, is in conflict with Alan's primary goal, which is to save his son. Eyes is almost an externalisation of Alan's anger towards the Pyramid; Alan's anger incarnate. So Eyes' death marks the moment that Alan realises his past is not the only narrative. Or, rather, the story that Eyes has always told him is not the only reading available. On the other hand, it's Alan's first deliberate kill; he's a slightly atypical fantasy hero in that he tries to avoid fighting and killing at all costs. So it's a huge moment in Alan's life for a variety of reasons.

Do you think the bond between Alan and his son offers an inherently selfish character some form of redemption?

This is an interesting one! I suppose the answer is yes in some ways — without his love for Billy, Alan's demons would get the better of him pretty quickly. He would be almost totally selfish, and very probably dead as a result of his various appetites. But I didn't deliberately give Alan an important familial relationship in order to balance out his flaws. For one thing, people aren't necessarily balanced in that way, and for another thing, I resist completely the idea that a sympathetic protagonist is a prerequisite for a functional novel. It's perhaps more important to read about people you don't like than people you do like.

If Alan's relationship with Billy saves him from true villainy in the eyes of some readers, then that's all well and good, but really the relationship is only there because that's how I imagine Alan would feel about his son.

Which character was your favourite to write?

My favourite to write was definitely Bloody Nora. She's not as big or as loud or as domineering as the others, but she knows more than them, and she knows how to take them all down a peg or two. And she's the closest thing that the series has to a spellcaster, so she's fun to write in that way too. I want to write a trilogy with her as protagonist, after this one's finished. (Hint hint, JFB!)

The settings in your novels are all described very vividly, and they are all very different. Is there a setting you enjoyed writing/imagining the most?

I liked imagining Glasstown. In fact, that was how I first imagined Gleam; just a neverending labyrinth of weird, non-functional redbrick architecture and black-and-white tiled floors extending up, down and in all directions. Staircases hanging in space and buildings with various walls missing. Everything lit strangely.

But if I were to visit, I'd stick to the rooftops. The top of The House of a Thousand Hollows, or the expanse on which Eyes has built his hut. I'd like the different colours of the stone in the sun – red, slate blue, and white – and the heat, and the variety of flora, and the night skies. The surface of Gleam – that is, the rooftops – is analogous to a rural fantasy landscape: taverns, villages, thoroughfares, travellers, vegetation, wild animals – they're all there, they're just a bit different, and instead of being situated amongst farmer's fields and rolling hills, they're sprouting from an ancient roofscape.

Or maybe I'd go to the Gutwood. Swampy, magical, lots of fireflies . . . if I had a Mapmaker with me, anyway.

What gave you the idea for *Gleam*?

I really can't pinpoint the origins. I've always read and watched fantasy, and it was always what I wanted to write. But I never felt the urge to write in that semi-historical epic style that characterised so much of what I read. My instincts drove me more towards the fantasy films of my childhood; *Labyrinth*, by the Jim Henson company, *The NeverEnding Story*, *Return to Oz*, that kind of thing. I think those utterly bizarre and impossible worlds, and the stories – which were usually quests – were deeply influential. I wanted to read books in that vein, I suppose, and couldn't find any (that's not to say that there aren't any, of course) so thought I'd have a go at writing one. It didn't end up exactly like that, but then novels never end up as they're intended!

Another major influence was Mervyn Peake's *Gormenghast*. I never shook the sense of scale he created with just one building. Again, *Gleam* didn't end up as just one building, exactly, but *Gormenghast* was definitely a factor.

An author I've loved for a long time is the late Iain Banks, with or without the M. I think his science fiction novels are pretty perfect adventure stories, and there's always a quest that hops from one incredibly vivid location to another – I'm sure his books had something to do with *Gleam*.

The contrast between the Discard and Pyramid is stark, but where the Pyramid offers luxury of a sort, the Discard offers freedom – and the Discarders seem happier. Do you think that is an accurate assessment? And if so, was this theme used purposefully in your writing?

I think that's definitely an accurate assessment of the first book. But then, most of the first book is set in the Discard – in the second book, we'll see a bit more of the Pyramid, and find out how the other half truly live.

What does become clear is that the Discard is not a good place to fall ill, or grow old, or to have children. If you're reasonably fit and strong and can live by your wits, then the Discard will do you just fine. It could even be fun. The Pyramid, on the other hand, will look after you for your whole life, if you don't step out of line. But it's intolerant, and it demands all of your time and your energy.

Gleam is not an allegory, or an analogy, or satire – but the Pyramid vs. Discard question is analogous to how we choose to live our lives. The Pyramid is a stable job with good pay and a good pension, and it's yours if you want it – but, as with most well-paid, stable jobs in our modern world, you're plugging into a system that is intertwined with, and dependent on, all sorts of other systems that you'd probably rather not know about. It alienates you from the fruits of your labour, and it alienates you from the consequences of your consumption. The system is destructive, but the destruction is wreaked far away, on other people (by bombs bought with taxes, climate change, third-world sweatshops, corporate lobbying, whatever), and it looks after you, so you stick with it – because the thought of growing old without a pension is pretty scary. And emotionally, morally, physically – it drains you, completely.

The Discard, on the other hand, is life outside the system. And it does offer freedom, but I don't want to be naïve or romantic about it. There's no freedom in not having enough money to eat. Poverty drains you too. Insecurity gnaws away at you, until there's very little left. The Discard is dangerous, and it attracts not just the idealistic, but the predatory, the reactionary, and those confident enough in their own strength and power to be able to just take what they want, when they want it, from those weaker than themselves.

Finally, Discard or Pyramid?

I'd like to say the Discard. But I've lived that way before, and I know now that I'd choose the Pyramid – because I choose it every day.

You too can join in the debate. Let us know @Jofletcherbooks with the hashtag #DiscardvsPyramid. Don't forget to follow Alan's story in *Idle Hands*, The Factory Trilogy Book 2, coming September 2016.

Tom Fletcher has published a number of his short stories in various publications, as well as three standalone novels with Quercus and Jo Fletcher Books, *The Leaping*, *The Thing on the Shore* and *The Ravenglass Eye*. The Factory Trilogy is his first Fantasy series. He lives in Manchester with his wife and son. You can catch up with him on www.writertomfletcher.com and also on Twitter @T_A_Fletcher.

Author photo © Nicholas Royle

COMING SOON

IDLE HANDS
Tom Fletcher

Desperate to cure his son Billy of the disease Idle Hands, Wild Alan must find a way back into the Pyramid from which he was exiled. But, trapped in the barren wasteland that is the Discard – the area surrounding the Pyramid – there isn't much he can do alone.

Bloody Nora, the mapmaker, has her own reasons for wanting to get into the Pyramid; she believes that the secrets of Gleam's history can be found in the Pyramid's vaults. And she has worked with Wild Alan before.

There are more secrets there than either imagined: those vaults hold the key to destroying the Pyramid's tyranny, but saving Billy and uniting the Discard against the Pyramidders is going to be far from straightforward.

PUBLISHED SEPTEMBER 2015

Jo Fletcher
BOOKS

www.jofletcherbooks.com

ALSO AVAILABLE

THE LEAPING
Tom Fletcher

When the sky is blood-red, when the rivers freeze and snow lies upon the fells, it's time for the wolves to cross – time for the Leaping.

Jack and Francis work in a call-centre in Manchester, where they are endlessly tormented by irate customers and sinister bosses.

When Jack's girlfriend Jennifer buys Fell House, a mysterious ruin out in the remote mountains, a move to the country seems like the answer to all their problems.

But an ancient evil is waiting in the valleys – and Fell House has another owner.

Time to lock the doors. Time to bar the windows.
Time for the Leaping . . .

Jo Fletcher
BOOKS

www.jofletcherbooks.co.uk

THE THING ON THE SHORE
Tom Fletcher

Arthur was twelve when he watched his mother jump from the cliff into the sea.

Wasted by grief, he and his father stayed at the family home in Whitehaven, as life became dull and meaningless. Years later, Arthur works in a call centre and dreams of something extraordinary to change it all.

Arthur's right. Something is coming and nothing will ever be the same again . . .

Jo Fletcher
BOOKS

www.jofletcherbooks.co.uk

THE RAVENGLASS EYE
Tom Fletcher

Edie is a barmaid at The Tup in the small town of Ravenglass. So far, so normal. But when she is caught in a freak earthquake she subsequently develops 'The Eye' – a power that allows her glimpses of other worlds and strange events.

At first Edie passes her visions off as nightmares, but when a corpse is found, murdered, she realises that she has seen this death before, and that her visions are not imaginary, but real.

Mankind had better hope that Edie finds a solution to the murders soon, because it's more than just the influence of 'The Eye' that has entered the world. A power far more malevolent has been released, and that power is hungry for death.

Jo Fletcher
BOOKS

www.jofletcherbooks.co.uk